ABOUT THE AUTHOR

Syd Moore lives in Essex where the Rosie Strange novels are set. Prior to writing, she was a lecturer and a presenter on *Pulp*, the Channel 4 books programme. She is the author of the mystery novels *The Drowning Pool*, *Witch Hunt* and the Essex Witch Museum Mysteries, *Strange Magic* and *Strange Sight*.

STRANGE
FASCINATION

SYD MOORE

A Point Blank Book

First published in North America, Great Britain & Australia by
Point Blank, an imprint of Oneworld Publications, 2018

ISBN 978-1-78607-257-3
ISBN 978-1-78607-258-0 (eBook)

Typeset by Fakenham Prepress Solutions, Fakenham, Norfolk NR21 8NN
Printed and bound in Great Britain by Clays Ltd, St Ives plc

Oneworld Publications
10 Bloomsbury Street
London WC1B 3SR
England

Stay up to date with the latest books,
special offers, and exclusive content from
Oneworld with our newsletter

Sign up on our website
oneworld-publications.com

MIX
Paper from
responsible sources
FSC
www.fsc.org
FSC® C018072

[definition] Strange /streɪn(d)ʒ/

Adjective: strange
1. Unusual or surprising; difficult to understand or explain.

Comparative adjective: stranger; *superlative adjective:* strangest

Synonyms: Odd, curious, peculiar, funny, bizarre, weird, uncanny, queer, unexpected, unfamiliar, abnormal, atypical, anomalous, different, out of the ordinary, out of the way, extraordinary, remarkable, puzzling, mystifying, mysterious, perplexing, baffling, unaccountable, inexplicable, incongruous, uncommon, irregular, singular, deviant, aberrant, freak, freakish, surreal, alien.

PROLOGUE

It was too late.

Even with her quick legs and knowledge of the land.

For in her terror she had forgotten the traps hereabouts.

Struck dumb by what she had just witnessed, full of fear and scented with death, she made off with the speed of a hare darting through roots, skipping over rocks and stumps, ducking under branches gaining good ground until, with a clink and a snap, she was finally snared. The rusted iron teeth cut just above her ankle.

It was her strangled yelp of agony that finally gave her away.

'Oh God,' she thought. 'Please save us.'

She had met him so briefly. It was not fair.

Her lungs let go the beginnings of a moan, as the rustle of leaves betrayed their nearness.

Within moments they were upon her.

Despite the fullness of the moon, the light did not make it beneath the trees. She could see only their outlines, but that was enough to discern who they were.

The three of them were approaching. Two at the front,

panting hard, one, stouter and further back, leaning his hands on his knees.

The tallest wasted no time and marched over the bracken towards her. A low hollow laugh penetrated the trees. In it, she heard his intent.

Her heart was beating so quickly it made her vision pulse. Panic pulled in a deep breath. 'Please no, I saw nothing,' she sent her plea whispering through the air to them.

Though she had.

And they knew it.

The question was what they would do about it now.

The short fat man caught up, huffing and puffing, cursing in the darkness. Aled, from the stables. As he turned she made out his greasy profile. A jovial man, full in the cheek and throat and gut. But greedy. His flaw to all who knew him. Easy swayed and easy paid.

'Black Anne,' he said, his voice heavy, as if he were passing judgement. 'He'd have you conjure demons then? Is that it? To fetch familiars, send for the fairies to find the mound? For the treasure. To keep to yourself? We brought him back to work for us. What he finds is ours. He should have said so.'

Her eyes darted between the three. Too many.

'He told us that, you see,' he said again. 'That you are helping, plotting against us. To keep it.'

A midnight breeze fluttered through the uppermost branches of the trees, parting them briefly so that the moonlight pierced the tiny clearing. In that moment she saw the glint of the blade in the tall man's hand.

'No. He would not say that,' she said fiercely and scrambled back, away from them, ignoring the pain at her leg, the warm wetness creeping down her foot. Into the mossy earth, her fingers clawed and burrowed, trying for purchase on a root or branch to lever herself back. Away. But all she met were leaves and soil, and the heavy smell of the damp night.

She tried again, bolder this time, ''Tis not true.' But her face did not convey such faith. Fear was contorting her features, mounting her eyes up high on her head.

A small delicate sob came out of her and suddenly she appeared to the others fragile and weak. The man with the scabbard paused and cast his eyes at his friend, the thinnest of the three, whose face was still in shadow.

But Anne glimpsed the high cheeks and beaked nose, and knew the gentleman there. Immediately she understood it was only he of the three who might show mercy.

'Sir,' she said. 'Please. Let me help you.' And she tried to frame her trembling lips into a fair smile.

But the thin one shook his head slowly. 'Do not try,' he said at last. 'Like your mother before. That foul creature glammered my father.' And he unsheathed his weapon and eyed the forest as if the mention of her mother made him uncertain, hesitant, though she was nowhere near. 'Four month he ails at his bed,' he said over his shoulder in Aled's direction. 'For some slight, years since passed. Sickens fast.' His lips hardened into a line. 'But you, oh Anne, will cease those witch ways now. You, Black Anne, will not glammer me.'

He took a step forward. A decision had been made. They all knew it.

The lord's sure resolve was making ripples in the air.

In the distance a fox shrieked, a slow strangling noise.

It is an omen, thought Anne. And she was right. Desperate and full of hot fear she tried once more to pull away, but the trap kept her near, biting through skin and tissue to the bone.

'So strange,' said the thin man, the lord, 'though there be darkness only, I still see the whites of her eyes. Shows she is an unnatural beast caught in a snare.' The thought of her an animal, made him rattle out a laugh. The noise further thrilled him. Bolstered him.

He made for her.

The fat one, Aled, gasped when he understood his employer's intention. 'Enough, surely, my lord?' he said, to stay him.

But the Lord of the Manor didn't care. His blood was pulsing.

He stepped up so she would be able to see the smile on his face.

Then he put the sword through.

CHAPTER ONE

'Portrait of a beauty queen.' The music was thumping and Sam was following Madonna's instructions with fervour, clearly quite the superstar.

'Yes, that's who you are,' I mouthed as he did a spin then pirouetted off the dance floor to throw some shapes at a rather hot-looking Audrey, our resident protestor. And when I say 'hot' I do not mean sexy hot. More cardiac-arrest hot. In fact, Audrey wasn't really allowed to be on the premises at all. We'd only overlooked the current injunction as it was a very special occasion – the launch of our spankingly brilliant new website, complete with matching social media, and the newly updated Ursula Cadence wing of the amazing Essex Witch Museum. Well, that's how I had bigged it up on the DIY promotional literature I'd disseminated around the village. Lots of adjectives and hyperbole.

I bet Audrey was spitting feathers.

Usually Sam gave the old girl a wide berth, but the booze had uninhibited him tonight in a rather spectacular manner. His tie was off and wrapped around his head like a bandana, and he'd let the buttons on his shirt fall open way past the nipples, though I wasn't sure if he was totally conscious of that. A lunatic grin had been plastered over his face since he'd hit the dance floor at 8 o'clock when the one and only Adder's Fork mobile disco – 'The Royles' – named after its duo of DJs Roy and Les, had kicked off the festivities. I'd honestly never seen him in such high spirits. Which was a shame because he was undoubtedly about to get a right mouthful off of Audrey. The relaunch pretty much stood for everything she hated.

Oh well.

I managed to get halfway across the dance floor, thought better of it and instead craned my neck to see what kind of reaction Sam was getting. On closer inspection however, Audrey looked all right. Clearly, she'd been enjoying the free prosecco. Her red nose had deepened in shade and the rest of her face had taken on a hectic flush. The old girl had even relaxed her brows and let her mouth fall into a neutral line. It was the closest I'd ever seen her come to smiling.

Audrey wasn't the only one enjoying the free prosecco. The whole marquee was full of loud, shouty, sweating locals who had become extremely benevolent, one might even go so far as to use the term 'enthusiastic', about the relaunch of our little museum.

It was funny – the place was full of sigils, spells, grimoires and enchanted talismans, yet none exerted such magical powers of attraction as the two little words I'd added to the invitation: 'free bar'.

The only person who hadn't had a single sip yet was me.

It was blimmin' unheard of.

I'd held off until I'd got the welcome/opening speeches over and done with. Now that they were well and truly in the bag I thought it about time I got myself stuck in. Drawing a determined breath down into my stomach I headed out of the throng, passing old Bob Acton from the farm next door, vogueing with serious intent (there but for the grace of God etc.). I'd noted his pitchfork leaning against the marquee earlier. It was nothing to worry about. Our neighbour was an old-style farmer: pitchforks were to Bob Acton what buckets were to Bronson, and this season's turquoise sandals were to my good lady self. Molly, Bob's daughter, told me it was like his security blanket. Bless him.

I popped out of the dance-floor scrum and hit a queue of Adder's Forkers chatting at the aforesaid free bar. It was brilliant – there were absolutely loads of them here tonight. All full of bonhomie and happy to slap us on the back, shake hands or offer us drinks (knowingly pointless). Which was a turn-up for the books and very different to the reception my grandfather Septimus had got when he opened the place over sixty years back. Though, I thought, he'd be delighted if he could see the numbers here tonight: both inside the marquee and out in the museum grounds. A sizable portion of villagers, well-wishers and nosy parkers were taking the opportunity to stroll around the place in the warm evening air. Even more had actually gone *inside* the Essex Witch Museum to have a gander. Tonight's admission fee had also been waived. I had been on my best behaviour and shown God-knows-how many visitors around explaining the exhibits and roughly outlining our mission statement and aims in an attempt to *foster community bonds and engender outreach* which according to Sam was vital for a 'sustainable future'. Personally, I thought the alcohol policy would be working the miracles in that department tonight, and as the numbers in the marquee attested, it didn't look like I was wrong.

This was costing me a bloody fortune.

Still, I was sure it would reap benefits.

I waved at Vanessa, one of the local girls who worked some days at the museum and who I'd hired to help out with tonight's bar. She nodded and handed over a couple of glasses of prosecco. Briefly, I considered grabbing another flute for Sam, but one glance told me he was now the Adder's Fork 'Dancing Queen', young and sweet, only thirty-two or there-abouts. What the boy lacked in precision he was certainly making up for in enthusiasm and as such was surrounded by a gang of seventeen-year-olds, who were finding his unique Abba moves exceedingly amusing. When I say 'gang' I might add that I use that word in an Adder's Fork context, which has more to do with Gang Shows and 'riding along on the crest of a wave' than inner city deprivation and grime, or dub-step or whatever their Leytonstone equivalents were getting down to these days. I mean, there were two girls here in Girl Guide uniforms and they didn't even care. When they walked in, out of my mouth popped the word 'strippergrams' but Sam pointed out they were barely in their teens and I was pretty sure that was a bridge too far. Even in Essex.

It occurred to me that maybe I should attempt to salvage the swaying curator's dignity but, I thought he looked happy and probably wouldn't remember too much detail and anyway, it was rammed and becoming so unpleasantly hot inside the marquee that my mascara was melting. A girl has priorities, you know.

I left Sam to it and went outside for some fresh air taking the extra prosecco for Bronson, our stalwart caretaker.

We weren't too far off mid-summer and though it was nine, the sun was only just dipping behind Puck Hill in the west. The grounds of the Witch Museum were looking very festive in the gloaming, even if I did say so myself. We'd spent hours getting ready, stringing pretty Chinese lanterns and fairy lights over everything. Vanessa and I had blown up at least a hundred balloons each, which we'd attached to the climbing frame and swings in the new 'children's area'. Beyond them were the beginnings of a Garden of Remembrance for those who lost their lives to the witch hunts. It was early days yet, though Bronson and I had managed to clear the space and dig some flower beds. I'd ordered seven large stones which I was thinking of getting engraved with the names of the lost, although there were so many in Essex, it was going to take a very long time and a hell of a lot of money. And a lot more stones. If indeed we could ever find out all the names. Sam said only the court prosecutions were recorded. Those that didn't survive the tests simply slipped from history.

I needed to find a stone mason at some point.

Till that was sorted, we were going to have those little plaques on the benches in the garden, like you see in parks. Between the seats we'd shoved in solar path lights, which having soaked up all the energy they needed, now illuminated the lavender bushes and double bloom peonies in whites, reds and pinks. I'd also planted lilac catmint and roses – different varieties for different reasons. Some for their smell – tea, honey, peach. Some for their colour and shape. In the middle of all of this was the beautiful but rather cumbersomely named Ethel-Rose Rose, or as most of the locals called it – the Ethel Rose. For it was a very special hybrid, more luscious and creamy than all the other flowers, created for and named after my very own grandmother. How nice is that?

Entwined with the sexy evening scent of jasmine, the fragrant damask of the roses carried all the way over to the new picnic area, where a rosy glow from the setting sun was perfectly complementing another dozen Chinese lanterns. You'd never guess they'd been a job lot from the Pound Shop. The whole area was full of people chatting and laughing amongst the trestle tables. Fairy lights hung low over them, twinkling like a tiny galaxy of constellations. It all looked magical. As did the centrepiece of the grounds, the star of the night as it were, my very own small and imperfectly formed museum. We'd had it whitewashed so tonight it gleamed above us inspecting the proceedings like a wise owl. Often, I found it brought to mind a skull, but we had strung bunting over its façade for the launch and this gave the impression of lightly fluttering pink and blue feathers. The large arched windows on the first floor looked just like eyes. As I weaved between the candlelit tables I knew the giant bird was watching me. At least if *felt* that way. Had done since it came into my possession. Or I had come into its. Hard to tell which sometimes.

Bronson's craggy face flickered in the candlelight. He'd removed the yellow sou'wester that was perpetually glued to his head. I'd never seen him without it till tonight. Underneath where it used to sit was a thick thatch of healthy white hairs each making its own decision about which way it wanted to point. Boris Johnson, eat your heart out. Never really a man of many words, it pleased me to see him chatting to another couple with great animation.

He broke off when I reached the table's edge, raised his fingers in a vague salute and sent me his big shaggy moustached smile. There was a strong possibility he was enjoying the evening.

I lifted the glass. 'Prosecco, Bronson?'

He declined with a shake of his head and held up a silver tankard. 'You won't be offended that I brought my own.' It was a statement. Considering we'd only gotten to know each other over the last five or six months, the man knew me quite well.

'More for me,' I said and let my gaze cross the table to the old people sitting opposite.

The bloke, in creamy linen trousers I recognised, as Edward de Vere. Everyone knew him – the owner of Howlet Manor, a stately home to the north of the village. He saw me and began struggling to his feet.

'No, no,' I said. 'Please. We don't stand on ceremony here.' I slipped my bum along the bench next to Bronson's.

'Quite,' mumbled de Vere, relieved, I think, also to be able to sit down again. He was very wrinkly with fragile papery skin that needed a damn strong moisturiser. However, there existed still a decisive accent to all his movements, probably wrought from military training. When he was settled he stuck out his chest, crossed his arms over it. His natty sports blazer contained an almost-portly form. It had a satin handkerchief in its breast pocket, a matching tie. Atop Mr de Vere's head was an elegant Panama hat that I suspected had probably been imported from Ecuador. It was battered, but looked very high quality. Underneath it the hair was tamer than Bronson's but the same colour, and slicked into a more conventional short back and sides.

'You haven't met Mr de Vere,' said Bronson, nodding in his direction. 'This is Rosie,' he told the old guy. 'She's the proud owner of the museum. Septimus's granddaughter.'

I wasn't proud. Not really. Tonight was the closest I'd come to it so far, but in essence the whole thing was really just about trying to make a silk purse out of a pig's ear. When I'd inherited the museum earlier in the year, my first instinct had been to take the money and run, but with one thing and another I just hadn't managed it yet. If I didn't know better I would say the museum itself had somehow managed to chuck a number of obstacles in my way – several rambunctious escapades, a couple of tasty mysteries, a little bit of a windfall and the curator, Sam, who I loved or loathed depending on how friendly, sexy or irritating he was being at the time. Recently I'd come to the decision that, as house prices in the South East were going bonkers, it was probably worth my while sitting on the property for a bit. While I waited for the optimum selling point I had decided to invest lightly but strategically so that in the meantime the place might generate some profit. Hence the children's playground, picnic area, relaunch et al.

'Ah, yes. Of course,' said Mr de Vere, retraining his eyes on my face. 'You know you do look so very much like your grandmother.' I was surprised by the tone of his voice, I think all of us were – it sounded almost wistful.

Bronson smiled and nodded in agreement. The woman next to Mr de Vere fidgeted.

'Thank you,' I said. 'I've seen the portrait you painted of the family. It's in the upstairs living room. Takes pride of place over the fire. You convey Ethel-Rose very vividly and with some skill, so I'll take that as a compliment.' I was sure he was being oily but I took the flattery where I could get it these days. Plus, Ethel-Rose had been a beauty indeed. Long dark hair, Liz-Taylor black, beautiful shining eyes, with long lashes, possibly falsies. Not false boobs though. I don't think they had them back then in 1952. That was when the picture had been painted. She'd disappeared the year after. It was another mystery I intended to crack at some point. And I also envisioned having a chat with Mr de Vere about it some time so this introduction was timely. Couldn't be tonight though. There was too much else going on.

'Yes, she was ravishing,' he said with a sigh. Was I hearing right or was that wistful back again? 'And do call me Edward.'

'Thanks, I shall.' The statement came out sounding unintentionally posh. I let my hand fall from his clasp. It was picked up at once in an altogether more clammy embrace. Strong, long fingers closed hard over my knuckles.

'Araminta,' declared its owner, shaking my arm up and down roughly. The woman sitting next to Edward was about the same height as he though broad. Not broader. But wide and stodgy. Despite the warmth of the evening she still had a cotton anorak done up to her cheeks. 'I'm his daughter.' She rolled her eyes at Edward as if he'd done something stupid.

'Nice to meet you, Araminta. What a lovely name.' And what massive hands you've got, I thought but didn't say. Definitely the outdoors type.

'His blasted fault,' she cocked her head in her father's direction. 'All airs and graces.'

'Oh come now, Minty,' Edward motioned for her to leave my hand alone, which pleased me as all the yanking was hurting my arm socket. The woman was a couple of decades older than me but clearly strong as an ox. 'It's an elegant name. Protection and prayer, I believe.'

Araminta snorted. Not like a horse. It was a sound that I could imagine coming out of a rutting boar – all sinusitis and raw tonsils, with a baseline of rage. I think it surprised her too because she said, ''Scuse me,' and fluttered her big hand to her throat. 'Had one too many sherries.' Then she recovered herself and slapped her dad on the back, possibly a little too hard. 'Well, come along then Padre, time we got you off to bed.'

Edward's mouth twitched like he was about to protest, but he quickly dropped his eyes to the table and nodded. 'Well, yes, I suppose it is getting on and we can have a nightcap back at the house, can't we Mints?' Despite his commanding presence, I felt a bit sorry for him. 'Come and have a cup of tea sometime, Rosie.'

Ooh an invitation to the Manor House. Perfect. 'Rather,' I said, realising it sounded either like Penelope Keith or like I was taking the mickey. 'I mean, tops. Yes, I will.'

'Splendid,' said Edward and gave me a wrinkly smile. 'Any excuse for a jammy dodger. And doughnuts too. Do you like doughnuts?'

'Fresh cream cakes are my favourite, to be honest. But I'll always go for a doughnut if it's on offer.'

'In that case I'll get Collins to order some in.'

'Collins?'

Araminta broke in. 'We manage our affairs perfectly well between the two of us,' she said with her chin high. 'But we have a housekeeper, Collins, who comes up and helps out during the week.'

'And a cleaner and agency gardeners. But they're part-time,' said Edward. 'Not really staff as such.'

Blimey, I thought. They had more than us and we were a commercial property.

'What about éclairs?' said Edward. 'I'm very fond of éclairs.'

'Yes, happy to do éclairs too,' I said.

'Wonderful.' Edward's eyes twinkled. 'Now, the old place is just up by the Seven Stars inn. Our road's directly opposite the car park. You can't miss it. Anytime you fancy . . .'

Edward's daughter did the snorty-sounding noise again. 'Really, you old goat. Stop flirting with the ladies,' she said and made a big thing of grimacing at us all. 'At his age!'

I was guessing Araminta was rather headstrong: she had a silver-grey Farrah Fawcett haircut that was Camilla Parker-Bowles in length. It didn't suit her face which was not long and horsey, but fat and squat. The effect of the mini-Farrah amplified the broadness of her features. I absolutely understood she would have to have a mighty strong will to resist the efforts of the hairdressing fraternity over the decades – undoubtedly, they'd be desperate to update that look. But, fair play, Araminta had succeeded. She was stubborn for sure.

'Well, it was nice to see you tonight, Miss Minty. Edward,' Bronson said and shook the old man's hand. 'Don't leave it so long.'

'I shan't Bronson, indeed. You must come up for tea or dinner sometime too. You know, Araminta is a fine cook. Does everything. You should try her Beef Wellington. Cuts the joints herself. Grows the herbs. Everything. Fine woman I produced there, what ho!' he said and winked.

Araminta made a sort of gurning face at Bronson, who managed to repress a squirm and cast his eyes at the ground and said, 'Oh indeed.'

Goodness, was Edward trying to set him up? I hoped not. I imagined being pursued by Araminta might be something akin to being chased by a double wardrobe on legs.

'Well,' said Edward, oblivious to my friend's discomfort. 'Might potter down and take a look at that Remembrance Garden sometime. See if I've got some cuttings you might like.'

'That would be a treat.' Bronson nodded, easier now.

Araminta was standing up, hoisting her skirts and

straddling the bench. I copped an eyeful of large navy-blue knickers, and averted my gaze while she stooped behind her father, stuck her hands under his armpits and, with another boar-like grunt, lifted him into a standing position. Edward gave a little groan as he landed on his feet again, then put his hand on Araminta's sturdy shoulder so he too could raise his feet over the bench.

I made to get up and help, but Bronson stayed me: shaking his head minutely – stay put. Then he hopped round to help the old bloke himself. Edward de Vere was a proud man, then. Possibly sexist. Certainly old-fashioned. Which meant sexist anyway.

The three of them had just about managed to extract themselves from the trestle and bench when they were intercepted by a middle-aged woman with long red hair piled high in an updo and gold hoops in her ears.

Araminta sucked her lips into a tense little hole, but Edward was pleased to see the newcomer. 'Hello Carmen,' he said with warmth and kissed her on the cheek.

Whilst Araminta's style had come out of what must have been her seventies heyday, this Carmen's was inspired by fashions a good 150 years earlier. Evidently, she was a graduate from the Pre-Raphaelite school of fashion. Several wraps were draped over a dark silk dress: she was festooned with necklaces and bangles that made little tinkling sounds as she moved and prompted me to think about visiting the loo.

'You look well, Edward,' she said and laughed flirtatiously. 'Save the last dance for me?'

Edward enjoyed the idea for a moment then said, with regret, 'Oh, I'm afraid you're too late my dear. We're just leaving. Minty needs to get back, don't you dearest?'

'Sorry Carmen,' his daughter told the woman, her face now more jubilant than remorseful. 'It's nothing personal. Padre has to get home. It's way past his bedtime.'

But Carmen had just spotted me. Her eyes ignited with interest. 'Of course,' she said, with great sincerity, patting Minty's hand. 'Completely understandable. I'll see you at our next critique, Edward.' Then she stepped aside to let them pass.

Bronson went to see them off the premises, leaving the stranger alone with me.

'Rosie Strange, I believe,' she said and parked her ample behind on the bench opposite. I felt my half of the trestle table rise out of the ground and leant back a little to even out the weight distribution. It'd be a PR disaster if I ended up catapulting over the heads of the gathered revellers. 'So nice to meet you at last.' Carmen extended long manicured nails.

Her voice was rich and trilled like she was singing. She was very pale, but not unhealthy-looking. Probably a natural redhead. Delicate. Though when I felt the skin around her hands it was hard and calloused. An odd combination.

'Nice to meet you too,' I said, doing a cracking job of impersonating the hostess-with-the-mostess. 'Carmen is it?'

'It is.' Her eyes glittered in the candlelight. She'd done well with the brown eyeliner and dotted some green sparkling dust over the lids. 'Carmen Constable.'

'Oh,' I said, 'as in . . .?'

'Yes,' she replied. 'Appropriate really as since we've moved here, not a stone's throw from Constable Country as it were, I've been stirred to take up my oils once again. Watercolours sometimes too. Such an inspirational landscape, don't you think?'

I was glad she'd interrupted before I mentioned The Fuzz, and regarded the landscape in front of me – the museum and the line of pines that bordered it, now happily decked with Chinese lanterns and lights and people. 'Er, I suppose so.'

Carmen leant forwards and lowered her voice. 'I've not been here long.' She sent me a conspiratorial wink. 'I understand we're both relative newcomers. Takes a while for the village to accept you, I hear.'

I sent a micro-glance at the gathered crowd. Seemed all right to me. Although we'd had that break-in a few months back. However, the burglars hadn't taken anything. In fact they'd left a whole lot of flowers instead.

'Only eight months,' Carmen was saying. 'Though Edward de Vere has been very friendly. And the Patels. He's taken over the surgery in Snakehouse Rise. Dilpreet Patel and I regularly go up to Howlet Manor for drawing sessions.' She twirled the beads around her neck and stared. At me.

'Oh, right,' I said, gathering from her waiting gaze that I needed to say something more. 'My family have lived here for a long time. Since the First World War, I think. On my dad's side,' I added.

'Yes, I know, but *you*'ve not been here long have you? You, Rosie Strange.'

I wasn't sure what she was getting at? Was she after some rookie camaraderie or something?

The Carmen woman took a moment to appraise me then smiled with purpose. 'I mean, you're not an Essex Girl?'

Something fizzed in my head. 'Yes, I am actually. Moved to Leytonstone when I was fourteen, I'm still very proud of the county? Aren't you?'

There must have been a note of defiance in my voice because Carmen's smile slid off her cheeks. 'I just meant, that you seem . . .'

'Seem what?' I clenched my fists in anticipation of the onslaught of stereotypical 'joshing'. Which plastic attribute was she going to throw at me now? Promiscuous? Thick? Perhaps common? She sounded quite posh after all.

'There's something more, I don't know, metropolitan about you,' she finished. 'You don't seem very . . . country.'

'I'm not thick,' I said before I could stop myself. 'We come in all different shapes and sizes.'

'Yes,' she said vaguely, gave me the once-over and continued. 'I was talking to Sam back in January. He didn't mention you.'

Mm. Was she now? He hadn't told me about that. 'I've been popping down at weekends and for bits and bobs whenever I've had time off, but I've just taken a sabbatical from work, so I can get to grips with the place.' And maybe do some tinkering on its charming curator.

'Oh really,' said Carmen eager to find out more. 'What's work?'

'Benefit Fraud,' I told her.

Plucked eyebrows rose sharply. 'Oh,' she said and floundered. I waited for her to talk, as she seemed quite good at it, and spool out something predictable about my job choice. But she didn't and when I didn't say anything either her hand reached into a little beaded bag and pulled out a tin of ready-rolled cigarettes. She lit one and laughed at nothing. 'Right. I imagine you're used to that being a bit of a conversation stopper.'

'No?' I said. 'Why?'

'Oh.' She waved the cigarette around. 'You know.' Then she blew out a plume of smoke. 'Well, you must be relieved to have some time off from work.'

'Not relieved as such.' I shook my head. 'I like my job.'

She laughed, but her eyes were nervy. 'It's ironic though, isn't it? Considering . . .'

'Considering what?' I was suitably perplexed by her stream-of-consciousness gabbling.

'Considering this,' she said and gestured about the garden, finally poking her hand at the museum.

I scrunched my face. My expression must have demon-strated my confusion because she clarified with a smile. 'Benefit Fraud. You're a modern-day witchfinder.'

That stopped me. 'What?' I said. 'No. It's different. I don't make the rules. I enforce them.'

'Yes,' Carmen said, unconvinced, though a cloud of uncer-tainty had begun to pass over her. 'I just meant that, you know bullies . . .' she petered out and coughed. 'Anyway, the Witch Museum. It looks good.'

I was still rather shocked by the ridiculous comparison, but I was a good host and was prepared to rise above it, so moved on quickly and said, 'Thank you, but yes, there's a lot to get sorted out. I wanted to make a start on the garden.' I bowed my head in the direction of the circle of benches and the Ethel Rose.

Witchfinder indeed!

'Oh yes,' she said. 'Lovely idea. I hear you're looking for a stone mason?'

'That's right,' I told her, guessing she'd got that from Sam.

'Well,' she said and laid a calloused hand on her chest. 'I do the odd bit of sculpture.'

'Really?' I said, thinking *that* was more likely to be a conversation stopper if you asked me. I hoped her hands were a hell of a lot more subtle than her mouth.

Witchfinder indeed!

Not that I cared. What nonsense. Such a stupid observation. Completely, almost completely, well nearly totally without foundation. Nearly. Almost. Mostly.

'Yes, I'm an artist,' Carmen went on. 'It was a hobby of mine for a long time, though I did do a Fine Art degree.' Nothing short of a locomotive engine ploughing into the party could stop Carmen's conversation, I thought. 'But since I sold the house in Clapham and moved to Adder's Fork I've been able to go mortgage-free and give up the day job. Art teacher,' she added. 'So much bureaucracy . . .'

My nostrils flared unintentionally as I repressed some left-over anger that had reduced into a yawn. The woman was boring as well as rude. And idiotic. I mean – a witchfinder. What a load of rubbish, I thought and finally pushed it to the back of my mind.

'Most people,' Carmen was saying, 'think it's a dream, but the paperwork is a full-time job in itself. Kills inspiration. Encourages homogeneity . . .'

Perhaps Sam needed that rescue operation now.

'Yes,' Carmen went on, doubling her chin as she sucked in the smoke. She wasn't very overweight, but probably exceeded her BMI. She was fighting a battle though, you could tell. As my mum would say, 'Fat wanted her'.

'I never realised how much the old place was worth.' She blew smoke out of the side of her mouth, which made her look a little bit Mae West and quite perky. 'It wasn't anything to look at, as such. Detached though and in London, well, the prices are preposterous now . . .'

I nodded and finished my prosecco while Carmen expunged her guilt about making a mint, buying some place in the village for peanuts and going mad on the renovation/demolition. Over her shoulder I could see a few people swirling glasses and having a good time. I recognised Steve and his partner Nicky, from the local shop-cum-newsagents-cum-dry-cleaners-cum-post-office talking with Karen, the local rev. Just behind them Bob Acton's middle-aged recently divorced daughter, Molly, was conducting some kind of jig with Terry Bridgewater, part of an old Adder's Fork family who lived by the church in the village. Molly was forty-five, only twelve years older than me, but had fully embraced middle age. Her hair was cropped short and grey and she had dangly earrings and a peasanty-style smock top on. Scary. Terry's twenty-something son, Tony, or Tone, as he preferred to be known as, was standing next to the pair of them, looking away and simultaneously mortified. There was no one in the near vicinity who would understand eye-blinking Morse code – S.O.S. Where was my friend Cerise when I needed her? I was wondering if I should text Sam and see if he could rescue me when I heard Carmen say, 'I thought you might like to look at it. After all, it probably belonged to your grandparents. Or your great-aunt.'

That got my attention. 'What?'

'The cottage. On Hollypot Lane. Sam said it used to belong to your family. I believe your grandparents lived there with your great-aunt Rozalie. At least I found her name on some of the old deeds. And before that it was your grandmother's parents – Fred and Anne Romanov. Romantic name.'

'Really?' I tried to remind myself of the family tree: at the top were Frederick and Anne Romanov. They were the dad and mum of George and Ethel-Rose. Rozalie Romanov was Fred's older sister, wasn't she? I asked myself and answered with a nod. 'Yes,' I said out loud.

'Great,' said Carmen, taking my affirmation as an acceptance of her invitation. 'Because there's something I'd like you to see. How about lunch on Sunday? My boyfriend, Florian, will be down too so you'll get to meet him. Bring Sam.'

'Er, yes, I think we're free . . .' it depended if Vanessa or her mum, Trace, could sit on the till.

'Great. It's a date.'

'Um,' I said. Lunch would be at least two hours. And there was going to be a man called Florian there too. My stomach began to sink. On the other hand, I'd get to see the house where Septimus, my benefactor and barely known grandfather, husband of Ethel-Rose, had lived. That might contribute to a greater understanding of what was now my new, potentially life-long, study of the family. I didn't know much about them to be honest, though the little I'd learnt had started to exert a strange fascination over me.

My dad was the complete opposite though. He'd never been big on our ancestral history. Plus, he had grave reservations about me getting involved with the family business which he'd spent most of his adult life distancing himself from. He'd even made up some excuse not to come to the relaunch. Mum had sided with him too, which was unusual, but there you go. Parents are weird – we all know that.

At least they'd sent a card. A big A4 cardboard effort with a cartoon of a boy in a mortarboard and graduation gown. It said 'Wishing You Every Success' on the front. It was the thought that counted. Though talk about mixed messages.

'Oooohhhhh there you are, babe!' a shrill and utterly penetrating cackle cut through my thoughts and stopped Carmen's manicured monologue mid-sentence.

I didn't need to turn to find out who it was. I'd recognise that voice anywhere.

Sure enough, at the end of the table was a woman dressed in what might have been mistaken for a collection of colourful rags, but was in fact a designer evening dress, full of feathers and beads that hung in strands off some kind of body stocking/boob tube affair. A Victorian Mahogany tan had been dabbed on for the occasion and a smattering of blonde extensions enhanced the loose beehive that perched on her head.

Auntie Babs unloaded a very fuzzy but happy-looking Sam onto the bench I was sitting on.

'Go awn,' she said to Sam, 'shove up to Rosie.' Then she sent me a very very theatrical wink.

Part of me cringed. Another part thought 'oh goodie' as I felt Sam's thigh line up against mine. The curator of the Essex Witch Museum was a very attractive man, to my mind. Though if I'd met him in a club I wouldn't have gone for him at all. Not at first. However, he was quite fit, with a good set of muscles, had all his own teeth and amazing eyes – brown with hints of amber. Yes really. But there was also something borderline posh about him and he was wedded to his work, a PhD he was writing here, using the resources of the Witch Museum. Also, on first impressions I had thought that he was a bit sheltered. Ironic really, as he knew a heck of a lot about some really hardcore nasty stuff that made me queasy. Anyway, he wasn't posh either. Just well-spoken and academic. A bit nerdy. Quite sweet. A little on the sexy side. Good bum. And since the weather had got warmer I'd noticed some adorable freckles across the bridge of his nose. When he smiled his mouth pulled slightly to the left. Sometimes it made me catch my breath.

So why hadn't I gone for him? Well, it was complicated. There had been a fair bit of dancing around at one time, but nothing had happened. So I'd accepted a date with a policeman, Jason, who we'd met on an investigation in London. It hadn't worked out and he'd gone back to his ex-fiancée. Since then Sam had been most comforting and supportive. So much so that I'd decided to do the sabbatical thing and come down here to sort out the museum.

It was difficult. We really liked each other but now we were practically living with each other we'd entered into some kind of stalemate. I mean, what if something did happen to move the relationship on? That would change things massively. And what if things didn't work out? What if we ended up hating each other? What if he ended up leaving?

That would be too much to bear.

I couldn't chance it.

It was mega-frustrating.

However, there was nothing wrong with a little bit of a flirt now and then. Just to keep your oar in, so to speak.

And let a bit of steam out of the pressure cooker.

I necked the dregs of my prosecco. 'Oh look – I'm empty,' I said and glanced meaningfully at Carmen.

'Oh, I'll get another. I'm a bit parched too.' She stubbed out her cigarette in the ashtray and made to get up.

Auntie Babs, always quick on the uptake, clocked the disproportionate weight balance and immediately went and plonked herself next to Carmen to avoid the bench upending.

Oblivious to all this Carmen picked up my glass and said, 'I'll get four.' Then disappeared into the crowd. Maybe she was all right after all.

'Fancy a voddy, while you're waiting, love?' Auntie Babs hoisted a bottle out of her bag and cracked open a can of diet coke. 'Wasn't sure if it was a free bar. You can never tell with some people.'

'Have you met me?' I said as she filled her glass.

She nodded. 'Heavy on the spirit, light on the mixer. Just how you like it. Your mum's the same.'

'Where's mine?' Sam whined and hicced at the same time. His hair was all mussed up. Sweat had wetted his forehead which had, in turn, wetted his hair and made it flop down at the front like some member of an indie boy band. I quite liked it.

'I think you've had enough don't you, young man?' Babs warned. But her voice lacked conviction.

'Am I hearing this right?' Sam was outraged. 'The Gin Queen of High Wigchuff and her niece are preaching *to me* about drinking? Come on.'

'It's not gin, it's vodka,' said Babs firmly. 'All right then,' and she winked at me. 'Heavy on the mixer, lighter on the clean.'

'Too right.' Sam nodded his head in an exaggerated fashion. 'That's great,' he said and hicced again, then nudged me. 'Makes me almost feel like one of the family.' He sank a cheesy smile. Before his eyes crossed, I noticed, despite the droopy lids he looked kind of slinky. That, I suspected, was probably more to do with the effect of four pints of prosecco and a vodka chaser than thoughts of amour.

'Ooh,' said Babs surveying us both. 'Have you two . . .?'

'What?' Sam and I both said at the same time.

Oh no, I thought. She's going to be really unsubtle.

'Watched *When Harry Met Sally*?'

'Not yet,' I cut in.

Auntie Babs assessed us, then cocked her head to one side and squinted at me. 'Before you do, Rosie love, come over to the salon, and I'll do you a vajazzle.'

'What's a vajazzle?' said Sam.

'A dance,' I quickly misinformed him.

'Oh yeah,' he said and grinned. 'I'm in the mood for that. Show me how to now.' Then he picked up my hand and pulled me to my feet.

I glanced at Auntie Babs to see if she minded me leaving her on her own. Though I knew she'd be off chatting up the Forkers before long.

'Go on,' she said. 'Go and give him a spin. Maybe it'll end up in a test drive.'

I rolled my eyes. 'As a brick, Auntie Babs.' But she didn't hear.

'Yes, come on.' Sam yanked my hand about.

By the time we reached the dance floor the DJ had decided to 'slow things down a little'.

Roy, or was it Les, was instructing the 'gents' to 'find the one you've got your eye on and get them on the floor'. My irritation at the sexism was only softened by the fact they'd chosen one of my all-time favourites.

As Al Green professed his love, Les dimmed the lights and Sam fell into me. I felt his hands slip down to my waist and I put mine up around his neck and leaned into him. 'Let's Stay Together' was so fitting for our curious coupling. For I wanted to stay together with Sam more than I wanted to be with him. How odd was that?

Tonight was just a fun flirtation. Things needed to stay like that for the time being, so we could make the museum work. But then after that, who knew.

'I love this one,' I murmured.

'Rosie,' Sam whispered in my ear. I could feel his hips just above mine, syncing into the rhythm.

Despite my firm resolve, a sudden unbidden feeling of optimism filled my abdomen, giving rise to several 'maybes'.

Every time I repressed my feelings, all he had to do was touch me and everything puffed up again. Pathetic.

'Yes, Sam?' I buried my head deeper into his chest and tightened my grip.

'I think I . . .' His breath was hot against my neck.

'Go on,' I urged. 'What do you think?' Then I held my breath.

His hands gripped my waist. I heard him swallow. Then he said, 'I really like vajazzling.'

I was working out what to make of that when the music abruptly ended, and the marquee was filled with the discordant sound of a needle skidding across the record.

A commotion had started up to my right. In fact all the dancers had stopped and turned towards the entrance.

Sam and I followed suit and saw, in the shadows just outside the tent, the silhouetted form of Farmer Acton. His chest was heaving and he had his pitchfork back.

As he stepped into the whirling lights of the disco it was evident there was something gravely wrong. His mouth was open and his eyes so wide that even from this distance you could see the whites.

Sam's hand wavered on the small of my back and then dropped. I was in half a mind to grab his clammy paw and plonk it back on my hip but I too was keen to know what was going on with old Bob Acton.

A certain stillness had infected the tent.

All eyes were fixed upon the farmer.

Acton took another step forward then raised his pitchfork in the air. 'Quick!' he yelled with urgency. 'They're trying to roll the Blackly Be.'

Around me there was a collective in-take of breath so synchronised I thought for a second all oxygen might get sucked from the tent. I needn't have worried – a millisecond later I was shoved out the way as a horde of Adder's Forkers stampeded from the room.

CHAPTER TWO

By the time I had caught up with the mob they had settled in the car-park-cum-beer garden of the Seven Stars, one of the two Adder's Fork pubs.

The main part of the village was formed by the joining of two Y-shapes. The bottom Y was inverted, its left 'leg' forming Hobleythick Lane. That was the road which led, eventually to the Witch Museum and then on to the Actons' farm. The right was formed by Elmwood Avenue, which pottered out of the village in a curling south-westerly direction alongside fields and past a narrow byroad, Savage Lane, where a long-abandoned building stood, or tried to. The local kids referred to it as 'The Cannibal House'. I had yet to find out why. Where both Y trunks met was the High Road, the main artery of the village, home to the old post office now newsagents/village shop/dry cleaners/grocers/offy and coffee shop.

A couple of large cottages were dotted about on either side and a children's play area to the east which backed onto the lower of two large woodlands – Mab and then Silva Wood. Opposite the play area, handily for parents, was the other

Adder's Fork pub, the Highwayman, named, as legend had it, after Jack Good, who was rumoured to drink there on his way back from stick-ups and came to a bad end when he got his head shot off. Allegedly.

At the top of the High Road the two upper legs of the Y comprised Rectory Road on the right, which funnily enough on one side passed the church, rectory and village school, now a residential house that belonged to some commuters. The north-westerly prong formed the border of the de Vere family estate. This was called Mentorn Road, although it was commonly referred to as Hangman's Hill. About a quarter of the way up you could find the private drive through which you accessed Howlet Manor. Almost opposite the drive, where the village gallows once stood, was the Seven Stars public house and it was here, in the car park that I finally caught up with my launch party guests.

They were gathered in a loose circle, all facing the same direction and gurning at something or other. It was difficult to see from the back of the crowd.

My heel had been broken in the crush out of the marquee and although Sam had said he'd follow the herd and report back, as he could not even manage to walk in a straight line I decided to take a bullet for the team and had consequently speed-hobbled my way here as fast as my beleaguered strappy sandals would take me.

Whatever was going on was generating a lot of argy bargy. Reluctant as always to settle for second-best viewing position when there was potential gossip to be had, I elbowed my way down to the front where a workman was sitting on the gravelled floor rubbing his head. He had come to rest beside the large boulder that has stood in the entrance to the Seven Stars for as long as I'd been in Adder's Fork and probably quite a few centuries more.

Oh yes, I thought, remembering what Sam had once informed/lectured me about it – this was the so-called 'Blackly Be' boulder. I couldn't recall exactly what the story was but I think it had something to do with a witch. After all – this was Adder's Fork, home of the Witch Museum, in Essex, formerly known as Witch County. You couldn't swing a black cat without hitting some old witch legend or other.

Another man, skinnier than his floored co-worker, wearing a similarly emblazoned high vis vest and helmet, was holding his phone in front of him as if it might have been a shield. I wasn't sure if he was threatening to use it or hoping to frighten people, which was a bit odd really. Adder's Fork might be a slightly cut off rural community, but we were no Amazonian tribe paralysed by the sight of the 'strange new gods in their tiny talking boxes'.

The whole scene was well confusing, truth to be told.

Beyond the boulder a regular open-top truck still had its engine going. It was the kind of vehicle you see carrying around bits of large equipment – cement mixers, traffic cones, signs – that sort of thing. A rope had been strung from it and fastened around the Blackly Be. There was evidence that digging had taken place at the base – namely mounds of earth and another guy holding a spade. No flies on me. A number of angry villagers were shouting and jabbing the spade bloke in the chest. He was doing a good impression of looking reasonable in the face of a (literally) pitchfork-waving mob.

An old man sitting at a nearby table who I hadn't noticed before, began shouting and waving an aluminium crutch around. Half the crowd swivelled their eyes over.

'That's Granddad,' said a voice beside me that I immediately recognised as Vanessa's, the bar staff for the night and hired help at the museum.Fresh as a daisy at nineteen, she was pretty-ish. Tall with long straight blonde hair and a great figure that ended in weirdly sturdy ankles. She had gapped front teeth which I found quite endearing.

'Your granddad?' I asked.

Vanessa shook her head and let several strands of hair unloose themselves to fall over her shoulders. 'No. Everyone in the village calls him Granddad. I don't know why. He's a hundred or something.' She nodded.

'Oh, right.' I snapped my head back at her. 'Hang on – you're meant to be on the bar.'

She smiled revealing the cheeky gap. 'Oh, your Auntie Babs said she'd hold the fort.'

'Oh my God,' I said and blanched.

Vanessa nodded at the truck. 'Yep, it's a bad move.'

I was going to ask her why she'd let Babs have the keys to the kingdom, so to speak, but she tutted loudly, 'Granddad remembers the last time they tried to move it, you see.' And she put a serious face on.

'Moved what?'

'The Blackly Be,' she said with an expression that suggested

I was being a total plank. 'That's why we're here, Rosie. To stop all hell breaking loose again.'

'Again?' I said. 'What happened last time?'

Vanessa was looking over my shoulder at the boulder. I turned round and saw that the Granddad bloke had managed to haul himself over and was now using his crutch as a makeshift baseball bat, swinging for the guy in the high vis with the phone.

A group of drinkers by the pub entrance were encouraging him on.

The barmaid bit her lip. 'Go on, Granddad,' she called. 'It's not right. Bob said the brewery that owns The Stars has sold half the car park. Developers want to build new homes on it.'

It didn't look big enough to house more than maybe four semis, which was surely not enough for all this fuss. When I expressed that to Vanessa she grimaced. 'Rumours are that the council have sold them some of the common land.' She pointed over the fence that separated the pub boundary from the shadowy pasture. 'That'll be a chunk out of Silva Wood I expect,' she said. 'They won't like that.'

'Why are the builders starting work now?' I asked. 'It's the evening.'

Vanessa shrugged. 'I dunno. Maybe they thought they'd do the deed at night when there was no one around.'

'But it's in the car park of a pub!' I said.

She sighed. 'Don't ask me. Maybe they're just thick.'

'Mmm,' I agreed, and was going to ask about relationships with the council's planning committee when I spotted a villager with bleach-blonde hair in a rather striking red kimono dress. She had separated from our mob, and with a battle cry suddenly launched herself onto the boulder, arms and legs spread-eagled.

There was a general muttering. Some of the front line took a step forwards, starting to envelop the boulder and its assailants on either side. A bunch of the young lads, who had come out from The Stars to see what all the commotion was, began grumbling all at once. One by one they downed their drinks and rolled their sleeves up.

Oh dear, I thought, as someone at the back of our mob shouted 'fight!'

I felt a pressure behind my back as the pack started to stir and it was at that very point that the wail of a police siren cut through the night air.

Instead of continuing the pincer movement forwards, collectively the mob (including me) said 'Oooh' and faltered.

On sight of the approaching panda car the boys from the pub executed a swift u-turn, collected their pints from the table and legged it inside. Only Granddad continued bashing his crutch, possibly too deaf to heed the blues and twos.

The car bibbed as it swung into the car park and we obedi-ently parted to make way for the agents of law and order, or at least to avoid being run over by them. When he finally registered the cops, Granddad made a big thing of clutching his heart and threw himself, gently, onto the floor with a few groans about his 'ticker', which in my expert opinion clearly lacked conviction and did not present legitimate evidence of any pre-diagnosed medical condition.

One of the policemen made straight for the boulder. The other headed towards us, his arms already sweeping back and forth in a 'shooing' gesture.

'Nothing to see here,' he said, though there blatantly was. 'Please disperse.'

There was more localised mumbling, then the group began to scatter.

Me and Vanessa gave each other a silent nod and seized the opportunity to slip off into the night.

I left Vanessa at the bottom of the High Road. She lived on a new(ish) road that came off Hollypot Lane. It was a housing development that had been built after the war. Optimistically named 'Gay Bowers', I was puzzled as to why this didn't raise a chuckle in the locality. It must have been too familiar. I imagined the address might be a bit of a sore point for school kids having their friends over to tea. If any children lived there. It wasn't a big road.

I took a right into Hobleythick Lane. The museum was about halfway down, but it was a nice mild evening. Okay for a walk.

I was about fifteen minutes in when I had to take my sandals off. There was one big blister on my left foot and another two on the right where the leather had been rubbing against my flesh. They were really killing me. So much so, I realised there was nothing for it but to sit down and rub a dock leaf on the red bits.

To be honest, the rest was very welcome: I'd been on my feet since about 7 a.m. and hadn't sat down for more than ten minutes at a time. The grass under my feet felt refreshingly cool, vaguely moist but prickly like a mild exfoliating scrub. It was such a relief to have the sandals off that I took a second under the big summer moon to enjoy the feeling and nab a quick lie down.

Up above you could see stars. A lot of them. More than you could ever imagine seeing on a clear night up town. Because the moon was out too I got a good view of the road, the trees and hedgerow. There was no one about. I repeat – no one. The lane was completely deserted. It was weird. But not creepy. Which was also weird. I mean I wouldn't lie down on the side of the road back home. Well, not usually. There were instances of course when it had occurred – hen parties, divorce parties, some heavy nights out with the girls. But anyway this wasn't one of them. It was completely different.

The irony that I was back in Essex at the Witch Museum was not lost on me as I sat there on the grassy verge beneath the branches of a spreading elm. When I had first set eyes on the museum that Granddad Septimus had left me, I had not been impressed at all. The whole place had been broken down and dust-filled – a lost cause. I never thought that months later I'd be living in it. You couldn't make it up.

At work we did a test once. My personality type came in as an 'actualiser' which meant if I wanted something I'd go and get it or do it or eat it or buy it or wear it or catch it or, infrequently, snog it. Which was making me wonder if actually, maybe, possibly I *did* want to be here after all. Or, at least, a large part of me, maybe a subconscious section, did.

The idea was semi-surprising, but then again, this whole year had been about discovering things that I had never known existed. And some family secrets too.

The moon was almost directly above me as I listened in on the crickets doing their squeaky chirpy thing in the field behind.

It was so quiet.

Vastly different to the roaring London with its 24-hour policing, diverse tongues, constant traffic, etc. I wondered how my great grandparents, Frederick and Anne Romanov, had felt when they relocated to the village.

Bronson had told me they'd also come from the East End where Frederick made a living as a bookbinder. Anne had worked in the office of his family business, a cigar factory. According to the caretaker, Fred didn't have much to do with it on account of his weak lungs so it was run by his father and elder brother Mischa, or Mickey as he preferred to be called. The factory however did provide my great Granddad with dividends which meant he and Anne could be relatively comfortable. Nonetheless it was indeed relative. Living conditions in the East End a hundred years ago left a lot to be desired. The couple got by okay until they had their first son, who developed Fred's lung condition, probably asthma but then undiagnosed. Originally intended to be Georg, the registrar added an extra 'e' anglicising the Romanov's son, much to Anne's relief. Though he was a solid, happy little boy, his health took a turn for the worse after the first Zeppelin bombing of the war. So Fred made the decision to take his family away from the Smoke and try his luck in the country.

With a little help from his parents and with the encouragement of Mickey, Frederick Romanov was then able to pursue that well-trodden path of many an East Ender and bid cheerio to the city to seek out Essex's pastures new.

It must have been a culture shock. I wasn't sure how much Adder's Fork had changed since 1916 as there were still loads of old cottages dotted about the place. Some had an air of abandonment. You could tell which ones were occupied by the competitive gardening going on. Vivid flora adorned the walls and front gardens and burst from the window boxes. It was all to do with some 'Blooming' competition or other. The Romanovs probably loved that. Fred had later opened a nursery and Anne's front lawn was, apparently, the talk of the Adder's Fork WI.

I contemplated whether or not their daughter Ethel-Rose had got on with the place and its inhabitants. She'd been born here, in the twenties, so country living would probably have come more naturally. Though she didn't look rustic in any of the pictures back at the museum. Quite the opposite. Her hair, often depicted coiled and of a lush glossy black, reminded me of the type of sultry woman so beloved of the kitsch sixties artist J H Lynch. Ethel-Rose had his models' big eyes and curves, that were possibly too voluptuous or 'gaudy' for serious artists to capture. Yet Ethel-Rose's clothes spoke of a sophistication that couldn't have come just from the village shop. Or maybe I was being snobby here.

And then again, as I often did, I found myself distracted by questions – where had she gone on that fateful night all those years ago? Why she had charged out of the village hall never to be seen again. She left everything behind her, abandoned her kids and her husband and her clothes. I supposed some women did do that. For all sorts of reasons. But never to have contacted the family again . . .? Well, that was, as I said, a bit odd. A mystery.

I sucked in a breath and followed the belt of the hunter, Orion, out on his perpetual celestial hunt, and found the North Star twinkling somewhere over the car park of the pub. That you could see the actual stars here was another bonus. Not that I was a stargazer as such, but I did find them pretty, and Sam had begun to teach me some of the constellations. Though I already knew the Plough and the North Star as my dad had shown me those when I was little. Excellent navigational tools should you ever find yourself lost at sea. Well, you never knew what kind of situations you might find yourself in, did you? Not really. Personally, I never thought I'd be chased by mad alchemists, conduct a séance or relaunch a museum. And one for witches too. But there you go. Stranger things allegedly happened at sea, where, if you did happen to find yourself caught up in them, confused and disorientated, then you could at least work out roughly where your disaster was occurring if you fixed your eyes upon the North or Pole star, in the constellation of Ursa Minor, or the Little Bear as it is known to anyone who didn't go to private school. You just had to find the Plough or the Saucepan or the Big Dipper and then track up from the stars that formed the furthest part of the pan or the blade of the plough. 'Second star on the right and straight on till Polaris,' said my dad, adapting the Peter Pan quote. Bless him. The

North Star was another constant in the churning changing universe. Wasn't even that bright. The star, not my dad. Its constancy was its unique quality. Something to fix on. An anchor of sorts. And there it was now, twinkling here over the north of Adder's Fork, showing me where the Blackly Be was.

As I continued to inspect it, however, it was momentarily and super ironically blacked out. Which was odd. As if something dark was flying across its surface. Though I could hear nothing mechanical in the nearby air, only sounds of nature. Maybe it was a witch, I thought, and smiled at the absurdity of the notion. On a broomstick. With a cat, like Hecate, sitting on the end. These kinds of fancies were becoming more common, I noted. Must be an occupational hazard for anyone connected with the museum. And I giggled again. Out loud this time.

There must have been a lot of fragrant flowers in the hedgerow, maybe dog roses, cowslip, honeysuckle. For as I inhaled once more my nose started to prickle. The merest of breezes floated a delicious laced scent to me. Up above the leaves of the elm rustled. I must have been having a narcissistic moment because as I listened to them I thought I could almost hear them calling: 'Rossssssssssiiiiiiieeeeee.'

It was a moment of sensual pleasure during which I became aware keenly of the earth beneath my back, solid and calm, the blades of grass under my shoulders growing, the plants breathing in the hedgerow, the tree moving its arms, the clarity of the navy sky, the stars above blinking in the heavens. And, of course, it was then that it happened, in that moment of full sensory awareness.

If I was a *Star Wars* fan I would describe it as feeling a tremor in the force. Like something huge and full of power had just shuddered and sent an invisible wave undulating through the atmosphere about Adder's Fork. A stream of air, or draft or fast-flowing current. It was a motion that was fluid. Though I didn't see it I felt it pass over me and for a second I thought I heard in its wake, the very faintest tinkling of tiny silver bells.

Startled out of my comfort zone, I reflexively gripped the grass and prepared for both possibilities of flight or fight.

The sudden honk of a car horn pierced the silence and the interlude abruptly ended.

Normality returned. The air around me seemed to relax.

The magicky pregnant moment had gone as if it had never happened at all.

I shot upright and peered into the gloom, alert now to a very real threat: people. Farmers even.

'Rosie! Is that you?'

A Land Rover was idling on the opposite side of the lane.

I spied a familiar wooden handle poking out of the rear window and a middle-aged woman's bonce protruding from the front: Molly Acton, old Bob's daughter.

Phew.

'You all right love?' Molly yelled. 'I'd be careful about camping out. We lost some cows hereabouts and if they see you they might well fancy a nibble on your nice straw bag.'

'It's not straw, it's raffia,' I said. 'Matches the frill on my sandals.' I waved them at her.

Molly blinked and then squinted. 'Oh, that's nice dear.'

'Just having a rest. Broken heel,' I added.

'Oh right,' she said and eyed me. 'You want a lift back or you going to stay here all night?'

It seemed like too good an offer to refuse, plus I was getting quite tired now. Perhaps I had dropped off as I'd lain down amongst the grass, I thought. And all memories of the fleeting strangeness disappeared, replaced by the fresh desire to return home.

'Can't 'ave it like last time,' Bob piped up as soon as I'd settled in the passenger seat which smelled strongly of animals and eau de manure.

Molly twisted the long gearstick, accelerated the car down the road and tutted. 'Here we go,' she whispered.

It seemed Bob had surprisingly good hearing for his age because he answered her at once. 'You might well roll your eyes, Molly,' he protested from the back. 'But you weren't there back before, were you? You don't remember what happened then. Not like me and Woody do.'

I glanced sideways at Molly, who visibly cringed. 'Woody?'

She made her voice quiet again. 'He's named the pitchfork.'

'Oh,' I said and felt sad for her and Bob.

My face must have given me away because Molly shrugged as she steered round the curve of the road and said, 'I think he's just doing it to irritate me.'

I nodded and made an empathetic murmuring sound. In the backseat Bob let out a whistle. 'Clock struck thirteen on the church tower last time they tried to move it.'

'He's still on about the Blackly Be boulder,' Molly told me in a low breath, then raised her voice for the backseat. 'You can't remember it, Dad. It was 1944, wasn't it? You'd have been three.'

'Remember the tales though,' he said and then went on, 'Oh, them tales.'

I twisted round and put my arm over the seat and said, 'It seems like a lot of bother about a rock. What happened to it back then?'

'It was in the war,' he said, pleased he had an audience and hamming it up for my benefit. 'Oh, it was a very strange time all round, you know. See, the Americans were posted here. They was trying to get their trucks into the Seven Stars car park for some operation or other, but the Blackly Be was in the way. They tried tying ropes round about it, just like them jokers been trying tonight. My father and a few of the villagers told them they needed to leave it be. That it marked the grave of Black Anne, the old witch. And she weren't to be disturbed. You must know about her?' he said, and jogged my arm.

I didn't. There was lots of stuff in the museum I hadn't discovered yet. It was large and sprawling, a warren of rooms and secrets. But I nodded to Bob anyway – it would be easy for me to find out. All I had to do was stick her name in our very own museum witchipedia (Sam) and the results would instantly tumble out. I'd do that tomorrow.

'As it happened, they got nowhere with the boulder so gave up for the day. But that night, like I said, at midnight the clock struck thirteen. It was an omen of ill-doom, for the very next day when my dad got up all his haystacks had been pushed over.'

Out the corner of my eye I saw Molly's mouth purse into a straight line. Her head shook slightly. Though she kept her silence this time I could tell she either didn't approve or didn't believe.

'Not just that,' said Bob, as if he had picked up on his daughter's displeasure telepathically. 'Cows in calf gave birth prematurely. Chickens escaped from all the hen-houses. And then some of them were found drowned in water butts. Not nice at all.'

'Oh,' I said again. It had seemed, at first, like he was going to hit us with a proper Hammer Horror-type story, what with the clock and everything. But dead chickens seemed a bit 'so what?' to me. 'And that was the end of it?' I asked.

'Oh no,' said Bob. 'The mayhem continued. Sheep strayed out of pastures with no holes in the hedges. Like our cows.' He paused. I guessed he was wondering if their stray cattle were anything to do with the recent meddling around the Blackly Be. 'Hens stopped laying. Geese disappeared from the pub's back garden. And in one of the rooms at the Seven Stars a nasty dark stain began to spread.'

'Damp course needed?' I suggested helpfully, but Bob ignored me.

'A London journalist came down from the *Mirror* to report on it. He stayed the night and when he woke up every single piece of furniture, every picture, every stick of wood in his room had been turned upside down.'

Okay, I thought, he'd slept in a pub. Someone had got pissed and played a joke on him.

'Soon things started disappearing from folk's homes,' Bob went on, eyes wide. 'A pair of horses dropped dead in their stables. Nearly everyone in the village had a story to tell about belongings going missing – pens, keys, knives, money, jewellery. You name it, someone had lost it. People were uneasy, troubled, you see. A heavy malaise,' he said, lingering on the vowels of the word like a practiced story-teller, 'descended over the village.'

It seemed quite a list of trivial misfortunes, as often presaged the initiation of a witch hunt and accusations of witchcraft. Or at least as it used to happen in the sixteenth and seventeenth centuries. I had got to know a bit about some of them. 'And?'

'And then,' he said, lowering his voice, 'the village children started talking about a woman in black, or sometimes in white like mist, wandering around the place. Strange lights appeared over the graveyard. That psychic investigator bloke, Harry Price, the one who did all that business with Borley Rectory. Most Haunted House in England. Him – he come down too and looked into it. He told the Americans that they might have triggered poltergeist activity after they interfered with the stone.'

I could see that going down a treat with our War Allies. 'S'pose they laughed him out of town, did they?'

'Oh no,' Bob shook his head from side to side. 'After he spoke to them, the Yanks stopped even thinking about moving the Blackly Be. They could see what was going on. The soldiers tore down the fence on the other side of the stone. They knew they'd been warned and they decided to leave well alone. Sensible buggers.'

'And the, er.' I paused to select the right word. 'The "activity" stopped, did it?'

Bob nodded his head long and slow and gripped hold of Woody. 'Those fools up there don't know what they're getting into. You don't mess with the Blackly Be. Not if you value your sanity.'

In the driving seat Molly sighed audibly. But I didn't.

I had noted an irrational prickle of energy shivering down my spine.

When I finally got back to the museum I promptly forgot about the Blackly Be, for the party, which I had been kind of expecting to be winding down, had ended, been cleared up and packed away. The gardens were clean and restored and overall litter-free. In fact, it was great. The museum itself had a look of contentment, albeit a slightly wonky one: the only thing that I had neglected to fix, in my haste to get ready for the opening, was the sign in the middle of the museum's 'face': an outline of a witch on a broomstick which had shaken free of one of its hinges and looked like the museum's broken nose. But still its air was happy.

I meandered round the gardens, turning off the handful of Chinese lanterns that had been left on, I supposed, to illuminate the way for me.

In the office, on the long wooden table that was frequently laid for tea for three people, I found a note from Babs telling me that she had tucked Sam in bed and would see me in the morning. Someone had thoughtfully left out a couple of biscuits and a cup with a sachet of Ovaltine in it.

I never knew who did this. Though logic suggested it might be Bronson, in less rational moments I wondered if it was the museum itself somehow. But I was too tired anyway to bother with a hot drink. Instead I locked the front door and then toddled upstairs in the forlorn but temptingly naughty hope that my aunt might have accidentally rolled Sam into my comfy four-poster.

Chance would be a fine thing.

CHAPTER THREE

'Are you saying it's the loincloth that you object to?' Sam asked. His face was tense, edged with frown lines of concern.

I reached over and fingered the fabric. It was ancient. In fact, I was surprised that it didn't crumble under my touch.

'It's not just the loincloth,' I told him. 'It's the chains, the dungeon and all that. I just think it's a bit of a turn-off.'

'But I thought that's what people liked. What they came for?'

'I've got to say, Sam, I'm sorry, but it does nothing for me.'

His face sagged so I stroked his arm and said, 'We can do better,' and he perked up a bit.

We were standing in the lobby of the Witch Museum looking at the exhibit that had been there ever since Septimus opened the place. It was the first thing you saw as you came into the museum and I didn't want to keep it. Gave out too many mixed messages, in my view. And it was naff: behind a sheet of glass, three waxworks were depicted against a roughly painted dungeon backdrop. A lopsided sign fastened over the glass read 'The Inquisition'. Underneath it, hanging from the wall in chains, was a waxwork of a prisoner. The expression on his face appeared to suggest he was mildly irritated by his predicament. Before him stood a menacing dark-robed figure. This guy had his back to the prisoner and smiled at the viewer with malevolence. His hand gripped a wooden lever, which, when the power was on, he jerked back and forth. The motion activated a blunt crescent blade that swung low over a second prisoner chained to a bench, threatening to slice him in two. Unfortunately, this dude looked like he'd just come out of a fetish club all-nighter. He used to wear shorts, but they'd fallen away about a month ago, exposing his Action-Man-like genital-free groin. Sam had covered up his modesty with the loincloth he'd borrowed from a redundant exhibit. Where it had come from or what scene it had been used in I didn't care to know.

As the blade went up, tortured loincloth raver pushed up his moth-eaten head. As the blade returned, down it wobbled again. Unfortunately, as well as losing his lower lip over the ages, his glass eyes had also slipped and crossed. Now his face gave the impression that, far from excruciating terror and pain, Mr Loincloth was trying to keep a lid on the giggles.

It really was time for a change.

'The thing is,' Sam said, folding his arms, 'I have a distinct memory of you trying to add blood to the Ursula Cadence exhibit in the past. "To sensationalise" I think was your rationale.'

'Yes, and you objected if I remember rightly.' I said it with as much gentleness as I could muster. Sam had worked with my granddad for seven years and I think regarded him as a bit of a father figure. This museum piece had his name all over it. 'Look, I know you were fond of Septimus but I think we should move with the times. This is neither scary nor informative.'

Sam knew it, and deep down he did agree with me. He was just having a hard time letting go of this link to the past, to his beloved mentor. It was ironic really that it was I, Septimus's granddaughter, who was more keen to bin my grandfather's work.

'Listen,' I urged. 'I've been really taken by some of those statistics you drop in whenever you do your talks to kids and that.' The Talks Area at the back of the museum could seat up to a hundred bored children who would rather play with their phones and often did.

He frowned. 'Which ones? What statistics are you referring to? There are so many I am apt to pepper in.'

'You know,' I said and waved my hand. 'That between 1560 and 1680 in Hereford, Surrey and Sussex there were 200 indictments for witchcraft or something . . .'

'185,' he corrected and brushed back his mop of hair. It was auburn with golden threads that were natural but would cost a bomb in a decent salon.

'Yeah that,' I said, dragging my eyes away from his hair and wondering if he'd let me style it. I dismissed the thought and tried to concentrate on the matter at hand. Statistics. Not my favourite subject. 'Yes, in those three places there were 185 indictments for witchcraft, but for the same period of time in Essex, on its own, there were, like, millions.'

His mouth puckered. '503. Or thereabouts. As far as we know. At this moment in time.'

I nodded with vigour. 'Yeah that. I mean this is the ESSEX Witch Museum. People want to know why it's here, specifically. So.' I took a breath down. 'We could take out this exhibit and put in panels with some of these stats on them.'

'Hmm.' He crossed his arms and cupped his chin with his hand as he viewed the space. 'Is it enough though? Panels?'

I checked the Inquisition exhibit. Even statistics would be better than this. 'Yeah it's enough. It's shocking right? People come in, they read that while they're waiting to get their tickets then they go in and the horror behind the statistics hits them.' I waited for a response. 'It brings it home.'

He was still considering the proposal. Clearly, it was not enough.

'Okay,' I pushed on. 'And we can have another panel that mentions your theory about the stereotype of the Essex Girl coming out of the witch persecutions blah blah blah. You know – that Essex was called Evil County or something . . .'

'Witch County,' he revised.

'Right, that's what I said. That it was known as "Witch County". And that loads of the witches had the same characteristics as the Essex Girl – low social class, "loose", dumb . . .'

He nodded and smiled at me. Goddamn it, that smile when it was genuine and did the eye-crease thing, I just couldn't help wanting to give in to a wild impulse and grab him. But that wasn't going to happen. Not right now.

'And that the tide hasn't washed that stain away,' he said, still grinning, oblivious to the effect it had on me. Or maybe not oblivious, maybe . . . Nope. I coughed to still my thoughts and refocus. Not going there.

'Tides of time,' he repeated. 'That was your phrase. Do you remember? You came up with it on the day we first met.'

'I do remember,' I said and chucked him a smile of my own. 'You said you were going to use it in your thesis or book or whatever it is – *Everything You Always Wanted to Know About Witchcraft in Essex But Were Too Afraid to Ask.*'

He threw his head back and chuckled. 'Yes, I might shorten that title.'

I allowed myself a further ten seconds to linger on his shoulders, today encased in a khaki T-shirt, which set off that flaming bonce so nicely. 'So, did you?' I asked.

'What?' he rotated his shoulders to face me.

'Did you put it in? To your thesis?'

He relaxed a little and leant against the wall. 'Not yet. I've had quite a lot to do around the museum lately. We've inherited a new lady owner who's made a few changes about the place and keeps demanding more.'

'Oh yeah?' I leaned towards him slightly, so I could smell the tang of manly shower gel. Wasn't that great: eucalyptus and something like pine, which put me in mind of toilet cleaner. Still, never one pass to up on a bit of flirt-action if it came my way, I made my eyes big, 'So what's this new lady owner like?'

'Not bad,' he said and swallowed.

I held his gaze. The swirling flicks of lava in his eyes had ignited. It was intense.

Manifestly too intense, for he withdrew and looked back to the exhibit. 'Quite touchy about Essex Girls though.'

Then he coughed again and ran a finger around the neck of his T-shirt.

'Ha! Cheeky.' I slapped his arm playfully. 'Not that you can blame me. But, good point.' Flirting intermission now evidently over, I too swivelled back towards the goons in the dungeon. 'So, about these panels then – you can write about how in the eighties and nineties when the Essex Girl stereotype first appeared she was taken up so quickly and firmly. How everyone thought they'd heard about those women before. And how they kind of had. But how "those women" were witches. Put all of that on the panels and you'll get people reading them. It's clever, Sam.'

'One tries,' he said, but I could tell he was bloody loving the flattery.

'Pictures perhaps might be a good way of illustrating the points made.' He gestured at the wall to which the mildly irritated torture victim was shackled. 'Break it up a bit. No one likes to read big chunks of text. Unless it's in an essay or a book or the like.'

On that I agreed. 'Well there are lots of contemporary woodcuts of the witch trials.'

'Mmm,' said Sam. 'But they're more illustrations of what the accused were alleged to have done.'

'Maybe we can create our own photographic panels. My mate Curly Dan could do it. We could mock up some photos of the accused women, then do some pictures of Essex Girls looking glamorous. My friend, Cerise, would be perfect for that.'

Sam swung his head to me. 'Cerise? But isn't she . . .?'

'What?' I answered, not missing a beat.

He swallowed again but it was a different kind of prickly energy that was coming off him now. 'I'm just guessing but – isn't she black?'

I reared myself up on my cowboy boots. 'And your point is?'

'Well, with Essex Girls – the stereotype – you always think white stilettos, short skirts, blonde . . .?'

I crossed my arms. 'Yes, that's the point. It's a stereotype, Sam. A projection, just like the one the women condemned as witches had projected onto them. It's a warped and oppressive generalisation designed to keep the recipient down. And it's completely inaccurate and reductive, just like theirs was too. Essex Girls can be black, white, Asian, Muslim, Afro-Caribbean and more. Essex Girls in fact might have started life as Essex Boys. This isn't the bloody fifties, Sam. Or the eighties any more for that matter.'

He shook his head, but it was more at himself. 'You're right, of course. It's insidious. We just don't realise, do we? Anyway, yes, let's use a picture of Cerise. Is she glamorous?'

'Does the pope wear a funny hat? She's my friend. Of course, she's glamorous.'

'Good, good, then we can point out that connection to the glamour. Make people realise that it was originally a spell. A type of fairy magic used to convey illusion. Remember MT?'

I most certainly did. On our last case we had encountered Marta Thompson, MT for short, who had touched Sam in a rather surprising way that had involved breathy admiration and stirrings deep down in his mojo. I think.

He could also have been faking it to wind me up. Anyway, I knew that he had thought her incredibly glamorous whilst I'd thought her simply average-looking, though a master with the contouring brush and clearly streets ahead of her competitors in terms of debt-inducing cosmetic enhancements. Her beauty, I thought, was an illusion and said so. Sam had then made the connection between the idea of twenty-first-century concepts of glamour and the origins of the term as a magical spell.

'I've been reading a book about glamour as a matter of fact,' I said.

'The Essex Girl can read?' said Sam and threw his hands up in mock shock.

My hands twitched. They wanted to fist up. I restrained myself. 'Oh, shut it.'

'I'm taking the mickey out of taking the mickey out of the stereotype,' he said a little plaintively.

'As I was saying, it's funny you should say that because glamour actually might be linked to the word "glammer", which may have its etymological root in "reading" . . .'

Sam started and held up his hand to quiet me. 'Phone.'

I closed my mouth and bristled. I hated it when he turned into a bossy patriarchal git. Why I fancied him at all was anyone's guess. In fact, when he acted like this, the 'grab' instinct transformed into something a little more aggressive.

I was also galled because I thought he would enjoy the point I was going to make. The term 'etymological', which I found out related to the origins of words, sounded incredibly Sam-like indeed. Very academic. But maybe that was the very reason why he didn't like me using it. Maybe he was threatened! Hah!

'It's a text from Carmen,' he announced, still looking at his mobile.

'Oh yeah?' I'd forgotten we were due at her place in a couple of hours to meet her and the bloke with the weird name. I wasn't looking forward to it. Although I was interested in nosing about her house.

'She says her oven's "on the blink", so can we meet at the Seven Stars instead?'

Oh no. 'But I wanted to see the cottage!' There was a big dose of teenage pout in my voice.

'She says she'll buy. Maybe she'll invite us back afterwards? I can suggest it?'

I sniffed.

'Go on,' Sam cooed. 'It's a free lunch?'

'Is there really such a thing?'

'Shall we see?'

'I suppose so,' I said.

I'd been to the Seven Stars several times, but never on a Sunday. On the outside it was fairly bland, painted a kind of creamy yellow, just two storeys high. Inside however, it was old and traditional, with low wattle ceilings and beams everywhere. Horse brasses adorned the large inglenook fireplace, which was fully functional and apparently kept lit throughout the winter months. Though the eighties inspiral carpets had been ripped out to uncover good solid wooden floorboards, elements of the interior still clung to that era's interior decorating style. The tables were laid out with bistro-style pepper pots and placemats with paintings of flowers and fruit printed on. The clientele was usually villagers but at weekends you tended to get a few tourists and what the locals called 'Townies'. Both categories were used broadly to describe anyone they didn't know.

I got a couple of quizzical looks from some customers in these brackets, when I entered the lounge. Ridiculous really, you'd have thought they'd never seen a girl in gold cowboy boots and shorts before.

Anyway, the pub was renowned locally for its legendary roasts with all the trimmings so each of us ordered one, apart from Florian, Carmen's boyfriend, who turned out to be vegetarian.

Florian was a freelance journalist with an interest in eco issues and some other complicated green-related matters that I zoned out of as he explained. He was all right. Focused and driven but he smelled of patchouli essential oil, which put me off a bit. I found the perfume often indicated dabblings in aromatherapy and/or homeopathy, which could at times manifest in an evangelism. Depended how passionate the person was. I couldn't tell with Florian yet. Dark blond with similarly coloured lashes he had a bit of hair at the back of his neck that had been left long and was plaited with a tiny leather bow. I kept looking at it and wondering how Carmen had resisted cutting it off. It went perfectly with the woven waistcoat produced in India. From one ear dangled two earrings: a stud and one that I thought first of all might have been a pentacle, but was actually just a gold star. Thank God he had leather sandals on and wasn't one of those vegan types who wouldn't wear anything to do with animals and sported plastic shoes. It was hot today and stinky feet were one of my pet hates. Especially prior to the cheese course.

They were clearly besotted, although Florian kept referring to Carmen as Caroline, which happened to be her real name. This prompted her to make a big thing about telling us that her parents had originally intended her to be named after the romantic Spanish gypsy but diverted to 'Caroline' when an old aunt of that name, with a large fortune, became terminally ill.

I had a mind to delve deeper into that one but a kick under the table from Sam silenced me. So I shut up and let them chatter on while I admired the rare horse brasses over the fireplace.

Inevitably as the meals arrived the talk turned to the Blackly Be furore that had prematurely ended our museum relaunch. We could see the boulder in the car park from our window table. Someone had erected a perimeter around it, fashioned out of iron rods that were hung with white-and-red tape. Florian was naturally curious to find out the tale.

'I expect you're well versed in this kind of thing,' he said to Sam.

Florian, I noted, was well spoken. Both he and my colleague had quite similar voices. 'Witch myths are your field of expertise, aren't they?' he added.

'Indeed,' said Sam finishing a particularly long chow on a section of stuffing, which I had discovered was dry and tasteless, and clearly not as fabled as the rest of the roast.

I watched him dab the corners of his mouth with a napkin.

'The Blackly Be is a very old story,' he said. 'I'm not sure how much of it is true. I haven't researched it thoroughly.'

Blimey. That was a turn-up for the books. 'Why not?' I asked, genuinely intrigued, but aware that my tone and phrasing lent the question an air of provocation. I hadn't meant it to. Sometimes my voice sounded a bit more shouty than I intended. A trait I reckoned I'd inherited from my mum.

'Just haven't got round to it,' said Sam and began to blush.

He hated having his credentials questioned so I said, 'Fair enough. It's on your doorstep.'

His eyes flicked up, as did his chin, and he met me with what I supposed he thought was a suitable response to my challenge. 'What's that meant to mean?'

Blimmin' heck – he was so prickly sometimes.

'You know,' I began, trying to sound conciliatory. I tilted my head to one side and reached over to pat his arm. 'Sometimes you, I mean "one", doesn't investigate things that are right before your eyes. They're too familiar. Too ordinary. Like your own family, for instance. And then something happens, and things change. You decide to pay them more attention.' I turned to Carmen meaningfully, hoping that she'd pick up the reference to my ancestral seat, which I still wanted to see. Unfortunately she was too busy shoving a Yorkshire pudding in her gob.

So I returned my eyes to Sam. 'Tell us what you do you know about it. I don't believe for one minute that you are completely unaware of the Blackly Be legend.' I looked at Florian and Carmen and jerked my head at Sam.

'He's like a walking encyclopaedia on all Essex witchery. Honestly, the things he could tell you about witch-prickers. Mind-blowing.'

Suitably inflated, my colleague stretched his neck up and nodded. Ego-damage thus averted, he leant his elbows on the table. The left one was very close to a gravy spot but he didn't notice and I wasn't going to distract him.

'Yes, well,' he said puffing out his chest. 'I do know that the Blackly Be boulder is said to mark the spot where "Black Anne" was buried. It's also there, allegedly, to keep her in the ground. She was, according to legend, a very evil witch.'

'Weren't they all?' I said and rolled my eyes. Carmen smiled at me.

Sam bent his head and pushed his plate away. 'She presumably went to trial, was found guilty, hanged and buried out there. Then the stone was rolled over the top of her grave to stop her springing back to life.'

'How marvellous!' Carmen shrieked and clapped her hands together in delight. Her bangles rattled down her arms. A couple on the next table stopped talking and looked at us.

She adjusted her voice and said, 'I mean, it's an interesting story. Did it happen then?'

The three of us frowned at the question, but Florian said what we were thinking. 'It's a legend, Carmen. Not historical fact.'

Sam saved her, 'But you're right to think that legends usually have a grain of truth somewhere within them. I'm not sure where it is in this one.'

Florian considered this explanation and crossed his knife and fork together over the remains of his veggie Toad in the Hole. 'So why don't these guys want the boulder moved?' He laughed, then, when neither Sam nor I joined him, screwed up his face in an expression of contempt. 'Surely they can't still believe the witch will resurrect?'

That annoyed me a bit. How typical that some bloke from London should come down and act as if we were all like something out of *The Wicker Man*. Personally I thought you couldn't blame the villagers for getting arsey about strangers rolling in to their home patch and changing the place around without any consultation or warning. Especially when there was common land involved, as Vanessa had alleged. I was sure that there were stringent procedures in place for situations like this. Although I had nothing to do directly with my local Town Planning, the Leytonstone department was sited on the ground floor of Margaret Thatcher House, where I worked. As such I was aware they had to jump through a lot of hoops and pile through numerous public consultations to move forward with any ambitious plans or sales. They were always moaning about it at lunchtime. That and the canteen pizzas. So, if somehow, all of the relevant consultations regarding the new development in the car park here and on to Silva Wood, well if all of them had slipped through the cracks then someone on the council this way had either been negligent or greedy. By my reckoning the Forkers had a right to be peeved. Didn't make them yokels.

Plus there was all this local legend that came with the boulder. Old Bob Acton's recollection of what occurred back in 1944 had taken place in living memory. Whether you believed there was anything supernatural going on there or not, there were certain local sensitivities which should have been considered by the authorities a long time before anyone finally got around to moving it. I thought their anger fair enough.

'Someone tried to move it back in the forties,' I told the vegetarian.

Sam arched an eyebrow at me. 'How do you know about that?'

'You're not the only one who researches around the subject you know,' I said and switched to Florian and Carmen, who was eyeing her boyfriend's limp vegetarian chipolata, and that was no euphemism. 'The night they first tried to move it, at midnight the church bell struck thirteen.'

'Ooh,' said Carmen. 'That's given me goosebumps. How marvellously spooky.'

'There was more,' I told them, beginning to enjoy the attention. 'Chickens in the bathtub. Or something.'

Florian made a squeaking noise then started to giggle.

'Drowned,' I said, lingering on the 'o' and just managing to resist adding 'drowned, I tell you'.

'Yes,' I went on. 'In fact, some specialist called Harry was brought down to investigate.'

'Harry who?' asked Sam and took a sip of his ale. His eyebrow, I noted, remained hoisted onto his forehead.

I couldn't remember what Bob had said the investigator's surname was so tried evasion, 'I understand he was the primary ghost hunter in the Borley Rectory haunting.'

At which Sam spluttered and sent a mouthful of beer over the table. Carmen offered him her napkin. Florian inched his pint protectively into the crook of his arm.

'Harry Price?' he asked when he'd recovered.

That rang a bell so I wagged a finger at him and pretended like it had been a test all along. 'You got it, Sam. As always – totally on the ball. Yes, it was Harry Price, the very one.'

'My,' said Sam. 'I had no idea.'

Carmen leant over the table and said, 'Who's Harry Price? Sounds familiar. I think I saw something on the telly about him. Christmas.'

'We have a collection of his works at the museum, of course,' said Sam as quick as a flash. 'He was a twentieth-century psychic researcher. Well known originally for his investigations into certain areas of supernatural phenomena. He also claimed to expose fake spiritualists. He was a writer. In fact, I'm sure if he was involved in an incident with the Blackly Be it will be recorded somewhere in one of his books.'

'So he investigated Adder's Fork, did he?' Florian withdrew his pint and took a long glug then said, 'What did he think was going on?'

I glanced at Sam, who shrugged, so went on with old Bob's tale. 'He determined the attempt at moving the boulder had unloosed poltergeist activity. He told this to the Americans and, guess what?'

Everyone shook their heads, though the answer was obvious and sitting in the Seven Stars car park. 'They decided not to move it after all and everything went back to normal.

No one's laid a finger on it since,' I paused, and then added, 'till this Friday night when the developers rolled in. The whole village went up in arms. I was there, I saw them.'

'Me too,' said Carmen eager to join the conversation. 'They were most upset. Neighbour Val from down the road, literally threw herself onto the boulder to prevent them moving it.'

Florian made another smug face. Sam nodded with approval at Neighbour Val's protest.

I recalled the incident and turned to Carmen. 'Kimono dress? I thought it might be silk.'

'It was,' said Carmen. 'eBay apparently. She's got an eye for a bargain has Val.'

I sighed. 'Can never find the right size on there. They list it as "large" but then it turns up and it can't be more than a ten. A twelve at a push.'

'Oh, I feel your pain,' said Carmen. 'I bought a pair of shoes the other day. Sevens they claimed. Turned up and they were kids'. Honestly, the pictures are very deceiving.'

I was going to launch into an incident I'd had with some thigh-high boots when Florian interrupted us. 'What exactly do you two . . .' he pointed at Sam then myself. '. . . What do you two think would happen if they moved it? This Blackly Be?'

I looked at Sam and shrugged. 'The developers want some of the common land too. Silva Wood. The Forkers would go mental. Justifiably so.'

'The what?' Florian said.

'The villagers.'

'And,' Sam piped up, 'who knows what ghastly phenomenon might be unleashed.'

'For real?' said Florian then muttered to himself, 'Now there's a thought – I wonder if they even studied the environmental impact?'

Sam gave a shrug of his own. 'To be honest, Florian, I've no idea what will happen. But you can bet your bottom dollar if anything out of the ordinary does then it'll be blamed on Black Anne.'

'Always is,' I said, then clarified. 'Blamed on witches, I mean. All sorts of weird stuff was. Is.'

'And where do you stand on all of this?' Florian fixed his pale blue eyes on me.

'On what?' A vision of Neighbour Val protesting atop the boulder flashed across my mental screen.

'Are you both believers?' he asked, his eyes flicking between the curator and me.

'Mmm,' I demurred. I wasn't sure if I wanted to have a big discussion about this now. Not after a large roast dinner. I batted the answer to Sam with a look.

The boy did good and stepped up to the task. 'We have a healthy scepticism and open minds. Rosie tending more to the former and myself perhaps more representative of the latter.'

Carmen nodded. 'Sounds reasonable.'

Florian however was not so convinced. 'But have you witnessed, you know,' he leaned over the table and whispered, 'supernatural phenomenon?'

The curator of the Witch Museum let it hang there in the air for a moment without answering. He leant forwards and his fringe flopped over his eyes. I couldn't tell what he was thinking.

In fact he didn't answer straight away, so I took up the baton of conversation and said, 'Hard sometimes to distinguish between natural and supernatural.' Three pairs of eyes turned to me with curiosity.

'Some of the stuff we've seen which was made to look like it was supernatural was created by people. Living ones. With their own nasty agenda. Albeit a hidden one, I might add.'

Sam came in too. 'Though.' He snuck a glance at me. There was a dimple beginning in his left cheek, which meant he wanted to smile. 'Some things Rosie has experienced herself are ambiguous, not entirely explainable . . .'

I wasn't sure if he was teasing me about the séance we had orchestrated recently.

'We are always keen to record evidence,' I said to Florian. 'Whenever possible. But sometimes we are let down by technology.' I nodded at Sam. He knew what I was talking about. Although that performance had worked well and to our purpose, when Sam reviewed the videos he was disappointed: the cameras had picked up the loud hum of the air-conditioning. This had muffled the dialogue we were expecting to hear. Flickering candlelight also meant the cameras kept zooming in and out of focus, blurring and obscuring the scene, so it was impossible to ascertain any potential supernatural activity.

Personally, with that particular incident, I wasn't really sure if there had been any. We had worked with some members of the Met, who I suspected weren't averse to the odd prank or two. Though none of them were currently owning up to any jiggery pokery. Anyway, summing all of that up I said, 'We carry on doing what we're doing. Like he said – open minds and all that.'

Florian wasn't going to let it rest though. He crossed his arms and asked, 'So you sound like you want to believe in magic, then? You're on the lookout for it?' His eyes glinted. I wondered if he was gearing up for a bit of a hypothetical argument.

Didn't bother me. My own cynicism has been challenged over the past few months since the museum had passed into my hands. Though, as Sam had implied earlier, I still erred towards the pragmatic.

In one of our recent cases I had a brief interaction with a young girl. She just happened to have not been visible on any of the video-tape evidence that had been reviewed. Sam suggested this might have been an apparition. I considered this. In fact I talked it over with a shrink. We concluded that the most obvious answer was that I must have misjudged the space between us and that she had been standing too far away, beyond the camera's field of vision. And then hot-footed it out of there when we heard the window smash behind us. Which was a fair enough reaction in my books.

Although a couple of days after that, one of our exhibition pieces, a clairvoyant automaton called Madam Zelda, had come to life during a thunderstorm. Sam hadn't yet espoused his theories on that particularly odd episode, but he'd had his 'concerned and thoughtful' face on for a while afterwards. I had told him that I thought Madam Zelda had probably somehow channelled the charged electric particles in the air. He'd made agreeing noises, but I think the jury was still out as far as he was concerned.

Anyway, I was getting behind the idea that absolute scepticism was just as blinding as absolute faith. There was a possibility that truth lay somewhere in between. As my grandfather was allegedly fond of saying, 'perspective is a shifting sand'.

So, I summed up my thoughts on the matter like this: 'If you open your eyes fully to the world, you start to realise that not every question has an answer, like they said it did at school. There are loads of aspects of life that are equivocal and mysterious. And it's quite likely that a lot of them will remain unknowable too. Now and in the future.'

For a moment at the table there was silence as the others digested my pronouncement. It had sounded more articulate than I expected it to, which pleased me mightily.

Then Sam said, 'Wow Rosie! The muse is upon you. You should write that down.'

'No need,' I told him frankly. 'I am my own muse.' Then I tapped my head. 'It's all up here. But you can have it for your book if you want.'

Florian cut in before Sam could reply and said, 'That sounds like a cop-out to me. I thought I might get a yes or a no.'

I narrowed my eyes and decided he was attempting a wind-up so simply smiled back. I was beginning to feel like

I knew what I was talking about. 'The world is uncertain,' I went on. 'It always will be. And that's okay. I think it's cool to have mysteries.'

Sam grinned at me and nodded, like I was a student who'd just come up with the right answer. Despite myself, I squirmed with pleasure.

'Talking of which,' said Carmen. 'Mysteries – that reminds me. I've something I want to show you. Do you two fancy an après-lunch liqueur at my place?'

CHAPTER FOUR

Carmen's cottage was bigger than I had expected. That said, I hadn't been inside many other Forkers' homes. I'd been for coffee at the Actons', which was large and sprawling with a conservatory stuck on at the back. The kind of place that neatly ticks all the boxes you think of when you hear the term 'farmhouse': big fireplaces, muddy wellies in the porch, that sort of country stuff. And I'd only got as far as Vanessa's hall, which was as nondescript as most of the places that Auntie Babs had lived in.

Carmen's place had a lot of charm though. Outside it was white, and weatherboarded, with a lovely neat garden and a path that led up to the cottage through a rose-covered arbor. Around it, honeysuckled hedges had firmly established themselves over the years. The fragrance was delicious as ever and rather calming in the afternoon sunshine. Carmen unlocked the front door and pointed to a horseshoe that had been nailed above it. 'Original,' she said and beckoned us in.

Once inside, Florian took charge and led us through a large lounge/diner, which he said Carmen had knocked through. There were folding glass doors, which he pushed back soundlessly. We hopped through them and down onto the deck. It smelled of fresh varnish. Florian motioned for us to take a seat at a spanking new garden dining set. At least I was pretty sure it had to be new – I noted no red wine stains or ash marks. This was its first season in use. Sam and Florian seated themselves around a raffia table with glass on the top, but I decided to find Carmen on the pretence of giving 'stereotypical womanly' domestic help, but really to have a good nose around.

I went back through the folding doors and took a right into a kitchen, where Carmen was staring into an open fridge.

'This is nice,' I said looking at the gleaming new jet-black units, which privately I thought were far too dark.

'Thank you,' she said. 'Chose them myself. The kitchen was an extension which was added on to the original building in the thirties.'

I told her that was interesting.

'Yes, apparently by your Great-Aunt Rozalie,' she said. 'I believe she was Frederick Romanov's older sister. Your great-granddad. She'd been living in the East End too but there was anti-Jewish feeling growing, and because of the family surname, the factory was attacked. On one occasion Rozalie was present and was scared half witless.' Then she simpered, obviously embarrassed. 'Sorry, shouldn't pry. I have just found the history of the place fascinating.'

I told her that was okay and that I was keen to find out more about my family history.

'Well,' she continued, 'the Romanov family money built the extension. In fact it was paid for by Mischa Romanov, the older brother.'

'How do you know this?' I asked, frowning.

'Oh, Edward. Mr de Vere. His family goes back centuries. Age-old connections to this part of the world. He can tell you a lot about the history of the village. If you're interested you should go and have a chat with him. I'm sure he'd love to talk to you. He remembers Rozalie well.'

'I plan to,' I told her and made a mental note to try and get up to see him this week.

Carmen reached up to a shelf and picked four glasses from it. 'This part of the kitchen was a separate sitting room originally, but the last owners changed the ground floor round a bit.' She put the glasses on a tray and walked over to a rear wall. 'In here,' she said and opened a door that looked like a gate, 'was a bathroom. I've kept it as a shower room.' Then she nipped into the hallway and gestured at another door that was half open. 'Not sure what that would have been, but we use it as a winter snug.' It was smaller than the other rooms, with a sofa, a telly and a log burner. I told her it was very cosy and she smiled, gratified, and asked if I wanted to look upstairs.

There was nothing much of the original cottage in any of the bedrooms: a very long and wide one ran the length of the extension. Then there was a big bathroom and two other guest rooms that were all white walls and interior-design-magazine minimalist. I made some cooing noises but kept them short so we could go downstairs and join the men with their manly drinking.

When we got there Florian had already cracked open the beers and they were both tucking in.

The rear garden was full of sunshine. Carmen offered round a tube of sun cream. I put some on my nose and sat back to take in the view. Very pleasant it was too – Sam was sitting there framed by a proper country garden full of flower borders and well-maintained lawn. There was even a wishing well down one side and a pond that Carmen wasn't sure whether to keep or not. At the bottom she said, there used to be an orchard. Now there were only apple trees. Just beyond them she'd had a studio built for her art projects. She wafted on about the fantastic light and pointed out some lumps of unidentifiable stone in the garden that she said were works in progress and again volunteered to help with the memorial stones, which was nice of her.

I was going to prod her about whatever it was that she wanted to show me when she asked if I'd like a prosecco and cassis, to which Sam responded with 'Oh Rosie likes a Buttery Nipple,' and then winked rather caddishly, I thought.

'Don't we all?' said Carmen and winked back at him.

'It's a cocktail,' I said. 'Baileys and butterscotch schnapps or liqueur.'

'Yes, I know that,' snapped Carmen with blushing haste.

'We should all try it.' Florian licked his lips and glanced at his girlfriend, then me, with a bit too much of a leer for my liking.

'No butterscotch schnapps I'm afraid,' Carmen busied herself pouring the dark syrupy cassis into the glasses then topping them up with bubbles. 'Can I entice you with one of these instead, Rosie?'

I readily agreed and then readily necked it. Then another. Then another. Carmen rolled several handmade ciggies for her and Sam. At some point Florian had one. More prosecco corks whizzed into the air and fell beside the daisies on the lawn.

As the sun arced across the garden and dipped behind the apple trees to the south-west, Florian wheeled the stereo out so Sam could listen to some of his favourite tunes.

It was just as he put the second track on that Carmen said to me, 'Now where is it? I mustn't forget. It's what you came for.'

I looked at her expectantly while she hicced.

'Oh yeah? What's that?'

'Yes, the tin,' she said and tapped the arm of her chair. 'Now where did I put it?'

'What tick?' I said with a misplaced hic of my own. 'I mean tin?'

'Hang on. I'll get it now.' She climbed to her feet and steadied herself on the back of the chair. 'Before I forget or get too drunk.'

'Good thinking,' I told her.

I watched Carmen point through the French windows. 'One of the builders found it under the floorboards you see. When we knocked through.'

I didn't know what she was going on about, but I nodded and she disappeared into the back of the house.

She was a funny sod, Carmen, but I was warming to her. In fact, I was warming to a lot of folk down here in Adder's

Fork. I had kind of thought that they'd all be UKIP and/
or posho jolly hockey sticks. And of course, some of them
were but not all. There were a few village idiots (the local
MP) and some sly snooty types that had the attitude of
benefit fraudsters, but not the accent. But on the whole, the
population tended to be fairly civic-minded. Dog mess, as it
was politely referred to down here, was kept to a minimum
and you never saw any poo bags tied to the trees. Horse
'dung' however was splatted everywhere, which seemed a bit
of a contradiction. But anyway, there appeared to be mutual
respect for the environment and the village. At least there
had been till Friday night. Despite that, I had to admit the
country air was a nice change from the pollution and grime
in Leytonstone. I wasn't keen on the fact that there was only
one retail outlet in Adder's Fork, but Chelmsford wasn't too
far and it had a boutique shoe place called Bunions, which
the owners thought was a hilariously ironic name, though
which I'd discovered through bitter experience wasn't. They
did however do a good line in sexy flats and medium-heel
sandals, which was quite some consolation. Though the
last time I'd been there the charming sales assistant had
convinced me to shell out a ton on a pair of scarlet trainers,
Dolus Speeds, which were apparently about to be *the* 'must-
have' item in Essex and exclusive to Bunions. I wasn't really
a trainer girl but the deal was sealed when I saw the tread,
which had a gorgeous big star smack bang in the middle. The
men's version had the same but set into a circle.

'Everywhere you go,' the assistant had said with a wink,
'you'll create your very own Walk of Fame, leaving behind

a little bit of star-shaped glamour.' Now that idea appealed. And, to be honest, it was just what Adder's Fork needed.

And what the village needed I most certainly was going to supply. In spades.

So, I was feeling rather comfy, and stretched into the sunshine, putting my feet up on the chair Sam had vacated. I'd give the cowboys a rest tomorrow, I thought. It was time to introduce the village to my new Dolus Speeds. A touch of class and flash of glamour, brought to you by Ms Rosie Strange. As ever. And out of nowhere, a feeling of optimism descended upon me. I recollect that I was thinking that I really should savour the moment, which kind of demonstrated some weird prescience. Though obviously I didn't know it at the time.

It was only when Carmen came back with a long rectangular tin and put it on the table that I remembered we were here because of something to do with my family. With all the sunny bubbles, my mind had gone slightly swampy.

As she laid it in the centre of the table top I noted the scratched picture of a very young Queen Elizabeth on the front of the tin box. Underneath it a date commemorated her coronation – 2nd of June, 1953.

'Go on, open it then,' Carmen urged.

The tin weighed heavily in my hands. It was cool to the touch despite the heat of the day.

'Very curious, I thought,' she added.

I ran a fingernail under the rim of the lid and felt tinglings of energy, probably excited anticipation, pass into my fingertips as I prised it open. With a squeak the top popped back and I carefully looked inside. Nothing particularly fascinating there. Just a loosely gathered ball of newspaper, which I lifted out. But it was heavy. I guessed the paper was wrapped around something else to protect it.

'It's 20th August, 1953,' said Carmen, watching me. 'The date of the newspaper. I've already checked. England won back the Ashes,' she added. 'At least they did the day before.'

I scratched my head, momentarily unsure what she was referring to. Were there ashes in here?

'Cricket,' she hastily added, clocking my apprehension.

'Oh right.' I suddenly got it. My dad was always going on about that. Phew. I wasn't particularly okay with running my fingers through the cremated remains of relatives. As I continued to unwrap the newspaper a single folded sheet of paper dropped out onto the table. Another little item fell on top of it with a light thud. I stopped and picked it up in my fingers. It was tiny, no more than an inch and a half long and fashioned from china or porcelain. Some kind of talisman that depicted an open right hand. Blue circular patterns filled the interior. It didn't take me long, however, to work out that within the swirls, two stars of David had been painted either side of a crudely drawn eye.

Carmen stirred beside me and held out her hand. 'I think it's called a Hamsa. I researched it.'

I nodded as I dropped it into her palm. 'It's something I've also seen before,' I told her. She turned it over in her fingers and made a weak 'ooh' noise.

'This kind of amulet,' I said. 'It's meant to bring luck and ward off the evil eye.' That sounded good. Authoritative.

Like I knew what the hell I was talking about. In actuality I'd heard it referred to as such by an old boyfriend who was half Turkish. His dad had put one in his car when he passed his driving test.

I carried on: Carmen was proving a rapt audience. 'It's been used as a sign of protection.' That was true. 'Throughout history,' I added, though this was just a guess. An educated one though. I'd seen enough in the Witch Museum to know that people employed such charms from the present day back to the ancients. And they didn't stick them on to ward off good stuff.

Carmen finished inspecting the Hamsa and put it in the middle of the table whilst I peeled back the last flimsy covering to reveal a small glass bottle, the size of a travel shampoo. It was stoppered at one end with a clay-like substance. I shook it gently. It rattled.

Peering closer I thought I could see something inside it. But the smeared glass meant the contents weren't completely visible.

'Goodness! What have you got there, Rosie?' said a voice over my shoulder.

The blokes had finally noticed Carmen and I weren't paying them any attention.

Sam leaned down, using my shoulder to stabilise himself, and fixed his eyes on the bottle.

'Builders found it under the floorboards,' Carmen explained. 'I thought you two might be interested.'

I'd seen this sort of thing in cabinets at the Witch Museum. I knew Sam would be fascinated. 'It's a witch bottle, isn't it?'

'Let me see.' He had completely lost interest in Florian who was still swaying by the CD player pint glass in hand, a forlorn expression on his face, though apparently determined not to submit to curiosity and join us.

Sam pulled back one of the chairs absently and sat down. I handed it over.

He lifted it to the fading light. 'You're right, Rosie,' he said at last. 'It is indeed a witch bottle.'

'What is that?' asked Carmen.

The curator put it back on the table and picked up the tiny Hamsa. 'From the seventeenth century onwards, the standard way to undo a curse in Britain was to make a witch bottle.'

'Was it really? You seem to know so much about it. Of course, you would I suppose,' she said to herself. 'So how did they undo a curse?'

'Or "neutralise" is perhaps a better way of thinking about it,' said Sam.

'Yes,' said Carmen bopping her head up and down with vigour. 'Neutralise, neutralise,' she repeated as if she'd never heard the word before. 'What was the reasoning behind it?' This addressed to Sam, which was fair enough. Although I'd seen witch bottles in the museum cabinets, or vitrines as Sam called them, I had never stopped to read the labels.

I sat back with Carmen and waited to be educated.

Sam held the bottle up higher and inspected it from underneath. 'Traditionally you got hold of some urine from the bewitched person and heated it until it was scalding hot.

82

Then you poured into a heat-proof bottle. Could be earth-enware, could be glass.' He brought it down to eye-height and tapped the side of it with the nail on his index finger. It made a hollow ting ting sound. 'Often some salt or earth and pins or nails were added.'

'Nails?' I said and screwed up my face. 'As in iron?' We had come across this with Ursula Cadence. Her remains had been pinned to the ground with iron stakes through her thighs and wrists. Poor woman.

'That's right, yes.'

Carmen cleared her throat and left her mouth open. A little twist of worry pulled her lips to the right.

I explained: 'Iron was thought to repel witches.' I wouldn't have had a clue about that six months ago. It was funny how things changed.

Sam smiled at my tiny morsel of erudition. I took it and enjoyed it but said no more.

'So,' he continued, 'the bottle was stoppered and sealed with wax or clay. And buried under your floorboards in this case.'

'Pooh,' said Carmen and pinched her nose. 'You mean I've had someone's wee-wee under my floorboards all this time. Ew. I don't like the sound of that.' She suddenly shivered. 'But why? What does it mean?'

'Originally, like I said it was put together to reverse a specific curse. But by the eighteenth century it was, more or less, used as a protection charm, to prevent any enemy from harming you. A very common practice in all parts of Britain, actually.'

'That's interesting,' said Carmen and looked at me. 'That means someone here felt like they needed a bit of psychic defence and used common folk magic?'

'But not only the kind practiced in the British Isles,' I added. 'What about that Hamsa thing? It was in the bundle too.' I indicated the porcelain hand.

Sam replaced the witch bottle in the tin and picked up the dainty porcelain object, squinting through his right eye at it. 'Hmmm,' he said. 'This is more Jewish or Middle Eastern symbolism. I'd like to have a proper look at it though.'

'Is it for the Evil Eye?' Carmen asked. She dabbed the corner of her mouth with her finger, which gave the impression of nerves.

'Sometimes,' he said. We watched as he turned it upside down, his tongue poking out as he ran another finger over its contours. He'd spend hours looking at it if we let him.

I slid the newspaper over and used his name to get his attention, 'Sam, they were wrapped in this paper in the tin.'

Carmen nodded at both of us, and said, with a tone of triumph, '1953'.

'That would make sense then,' Sam said. 'I think your Great-Aunt Rozalie, in fact all of the Romanovs, had lived in Prague before coming to the East End. This may well have travelled with her.'

Carmen put her empty glass on the table and didn't refill it. 'According to my own research, on that date – 20th August, 1953 – Rozalie was living here with Septimus and his two children.' She glanced at me and bit her lip. 'Your dad I suppose,' she added and looked away.

'And Celeste,' Sam leant back heavily into his chair. 'Now, the Hamsa can also be used to ward off evil spirits.'

He began detailing what kind. Carmen was clearly in thrall. Florian, over by the stereo was putting a new CD on.

I was starting to feel a bit weird. I looked at the back of the cottage and tried to picture my dad living here. It was hard though. My father always appeared to me suburban through and through.

Unlike Rozalie. I had seen a picture of her on the wall in Septimus's lounge. It must have been taken in the fifties because she was quite old, maybe seventy and was sitting in a deck chair in a garden with my dad by her side, sulking as usual. Rozalie seemed a classic, sweet, wrinkled old lady with fuzzy white hair and thick round glasses that had a black rim. There was something ladylike and gentle in her posture and she had been wearing a summer print dress and cardigan. Though her frame was petite and she looked like she was being swallowed by the deck chair.

I suddenly wondered if the photograph had been taken here? In it I had noticed lots of dark trees in the background – maybe the old orchard Carmen had mentioned. The light down that end of the garden was dimming, but one glance told me it could be a possibility.

Rozalie must have been the one to put the bottle together. I couldn't see Septimus doing it at all. He was more about debunking. Or was he, I wondered now? I had thought that originally when I had first seen the museum, but lately I wasn't so sure. There was something schizophrenic about the Essex Witch Museum Septimus Strange had established. There were garish displays, true, sensationalised contents, collections of folk magic paraphernalia and a clear commitment to exposing the witchcraft accusations. At the same time, the building itself seemed to be at odds with the scepticism. Certainly, that was the case with its architecture – the secret passageways and cryptic stained-glass windows and very present character, as if it were a living thing. I still couldn't make it out.

Sam said something in my direction about a Phoenician goddess called Tanit who controlled lunar cycles, and I realised I had detached from the conversation and floated off.

I shook myself and tried to refocus on the contents of the tin. The folded square of paper that had fallen from the bundle first was by Carmen's hand. I'd nearly forgotten all about it. Quietly I moved my fingers across the table and snaffled it back. Then I spread it out on the table before me.

It was well weird.

Not what I had been expecting at all. For I was faced with a collage of different words and letters cut from magazines and newsprint. All pasted onto the page to form a message. The look of it was really quite disturbing for it felt laden with threat. I felt my stomach begin to knot.

My eyes roamed over the words and I started to read, not conscious of the fact I was repeating them out loud: 'Ring a ring of Roses, A pocket full of Poses, She fell down.' I looked up at Carmen and said a little bit angrily, 'What the hell does that mean?'

She and Sam stopped talking and swung their faces to me. Their expressions suggested they were slightly baffled by my explosion.

'What's that Rosie?' Sam asked.

'Ring a ring of Roses?' I held the letter up and waved it.

Carmen shrugged, 'Yes, curious isn't it? I don't really know. It's a nursery rhyme but beyond that . . .' Of course she didn't. I don't know why I'd asked her. I didn't know why I'd sounded angry either. Wasn't her fault.

I screwed up my eyes and glanced back at the paper. It reminded me of the ransom notes you used to see in old films. Except this one had part of a kids' rhyme on it. Hadn't I been taught about this particular song at school though?

'This nursery rhyme was about the plague, wasn't it?' I asked. A faint and rather vague memory visited me – playing in the school playground, lots of small kids doing sneezing actions and tumbling laughingly to the ground at the end. I was sure the teacher had told us it was something to do with the Black Death.

Sam beckoned for the page. His eyes passed over it and widened. So, he was quite shocked too. That was interesting. 'Ring a ring of Roses,' he said after a long pause, 'may well have been pagan in origin, but yes you're right – twentieth-century theorists did associate it with the Great Plague, whether rightly or wrongly.' He shook out the page then smoothed it over the table. 'We can assume it was assembled in 1953. The newsprint and magazine text would suggest that period. But again, whoever has put this together has omitted "A-tishoo! A-tishoo! We all fall down." Look,' he said and turned it round so we could see it. 'The author has inserted "she" instead of "we".'

The three of us reread the page in silence. There was something very clumsy about it – the sender hadn't bothered to be neat. Whoever that was. Indeed would we ever know? Or discover why they had made and sent it?

'I wonder what it means?' I murmured out loud.

'Don't know,' Sam replied. 'But whoever received it certainly seemed to think they had to put together a counter-spell. Presumably against the letter and the sender. The witch bottle and Hamsa indicate an urgency to protect those living in the household.' He ran his right hand over his chin and rubbed it. 'Possibly what we have here is both trigger and response. Though that's a guess, of course,' he said and looked at me with a meaning I couldn't discern. 'Danger represented in this document, I think, was countered with the protection spell and the amulet.'

'And your guess is?' I asked.

'About what?'

'About who did it? Made the witch bottle?'

He thought for a moment then said, 'If the dates are right it was either Septimus, though I doubt it, or Rozalie. More likely to be the latter.'

Good, so we had more or less come to the same conclusion.

I nodded and Sam went on, 'There was a big Jewish quarter in Prague and the Hamsa has a place in that tradition.'

We all transferred our attention to the odd little thing on the table, now gleaming in the last of the sun's rays.

'I wonder what the letter was about,' said Carmen, at length. 'Do you think Rozalie knew? Understood what it meant?'

I shrugged my shoulders then folded my arms and said icily, 'What was the point of it? Was it a threat or a warning?'

One by one, our eyes returned once more to the collaged letter. It was very odd.

Where did it fit in? Was it meant for Rozalie? Or Septimus? I had a handle on the kind of work that my grandfather had done before he opened the museum – investigating alleged paranormal phenomenon as a freelance operative for the shady X-Files department. His investigations might have provoked the sender. On the other hand, maybe it was for my great-aunt. My knowledge on that side was sketchy.

'What do you know about Rozalie?' I asked Sam.

He took a swig from his drink and set it down on the table. 'Septimus told me that she moved here from London.' He smiled at some recollection.

'I mentioned that to Rosie earlier. In the kitchen,' said Carmen, which annoyed me a bit.

Sam continued, oblivious to my tension. 'Apparently she wasn't very good about the house, with domestic chores, but she loved George and Ethel-Rose and played with them a lot. Though I don't think Anne particularly approved.'

'Why's that?' I said, feeling he'd said something he shouldn't have. Not in front of Carmen. Family secrets and all that.

'Rozalie was passionate about her esoteric roots. She introduced Ethel-Rose to the tarot, when she was quite young. Told her stories with them. Made up fairy tales. Frederick didn't mind at all. Thought it was all quite innocent.'

'Ooh,' purred Carmen. 'How exotic, how exciting.'

I didn't want to agree with her but I did. That must have been a lot more fun than *Milly Molly Mandy*.

'But Rozalie also regaled her niece with tales of golems from her native Prague, silverfish and astronomy.'

'Even better,' trilled Carmen.

'She had a gentleman friend David, who lived in London. She used to take Ethel-Rose up with her when she visited him and the rest of the family. I think though, she really fell out of favour when she and David took Ethel-Rose to a meeting of spiritualist mediums uptown. The performing psychic medium, Madam Bouvet, allegedly declared the child to be a great sensitive. Madam Bouvet went on to teach the young girl to listen for voices of the dead and tune into frequencies of the soul. And this was when Anne put her foot firmly down. Such behaviour was not decorous. In fact she felt that her daughter was becoming distinctly unladylike. So when Fred's elder brother . . .'

'Mischa,' added Carmen.

'Yes, Mischa,' Sam agreed, to my increased annoyance. 'When he sold the cigar factory and bought a tea business, both Rozalie and Frederick received a generous payment. Fred and Anne used the money to purchase a larger property up the road and a commercial plant nursery in the grounds. Frederick gave up bookbinding and, with the help of his son George, launched the business. George moved up to the house along with his parents. Rozalie bought the cottage off Fred and Anne. But Ethel-Rose, fourteen and inflexible, refused to accompany her parents up to the big house, declaring her intention to stay on with her aunt. In response, she was packed off to a young ladies' finishing academy in Switzerland. Rozalie stayed here till she died.'

How fascinating. 'And Ethel-Rose returned here eventually did she?'

Sam nodded. 'Yes. She lived here too. In this house.'

'Until she disappeared?'

'What's that?' Carmen's ears sharpened.

'In 1953,' I said. 'Same date as the newspaper.'

'Yes,' said Sam in such a way, I knew it had already popped up in his mind. We were both wondering if this box of tricks had anything to do with it.

Carmen said, 'What's that?' again.

I said I'd tell her later and looked at the letter.

Sam picked up the Hamsa.

A cloud passed over the sinking sun, throwing the garden and our table into brief darkness. Carmen wrapped her cardigan around herself. Despite the heat of the afternoon I shivered.

'Can we keep this?' Sam asked. 'I'd like to have a closer look if that's all right?'

'Of course,' said Carmen. 'Rosie, I was going to suggest you took it. It belonged to your family after all.'

I wasn't sure how I felt about having that in my house. It was starting to feel dark and sinister. But I nodded and thanked her – Sam wanted it after all.

I watched him hand everything back to Carmen who reconstructed the bundle, slipped it back in the tin and closed the lid, pushing it over the table to me.

A slurry voice announced. 'Hey guys.' Then added, 'Arre you going to lishen to this nez track Sam?' It was Florian whining from his sentry position by the stereo.

But Sam shook his head. 'Another time, Florian. I think we better get off now.'

When the sun popped back out, the atmosphere refused to warm up again.

Florian waved a bottle of prosecco at the table but Carmen and I shook our heads.

The three of us appeared to have suddenly sobered.

CHAPTER FIVE

I was roused by a creaking above my head. It was dark. Though a sliver of the waning crescent moon shone through the open window colouring my grandfather's bedroom silver and black. I had no idea what time it was, but I wasn't happy about being awake.

'Damn and blast. Old houses,' I muttered. Then I rolled over, changed sides, wrapped myself up in the bed sheet and began to drift off.

The noise came again.

However this time, it was more of a rustling, like an animal with tiny claws scampering across the attic floor. Although we were in the country I had never really got used to the idea that the local wildlife was likely to cohabit the museum. The thought now made me shudder and pull my head back, tortoise-like, into my cotton shroud. I wasn't up for investigating it. Any new inhabitants in the loft could wait until tomorrow when the sun was up, the sky was blue, and Bronson and Sam were there to back me.

I congratulated myself on a reasonable strategy and started to sink back into dreams once more.

But the patters, I couldn't ignore.

Little thuds or drops seemed to be falling rhythmically in a circular pattern over my door, which would be the centre of the attic-room floor.

Buggeration: it could well be a burst pipe or a leaky window.

Damn it.

I would have to go up and check. Might need to sort out a bucket or three.

Why didn't these things happen during the day? I thought, as I swung my feet over the bed and wedged them into flip-flops.

Maybe I should wake up Sam. He was the curator, after all. The keeper of the museum, custodian, manager, guardian. Someone who in the absence of Bronson went and inspected things that went bump, or patter, in the night. And usually put buckets underneath them.

Although, if I went into his room and started poking him it might be misconstrued.

Or construed perfectly accurately.

On the other hand, he might assume I was waking him up because I was a chicken and wanted him to go into the attic with me.

Of course, this was true. But that gave an impression of weakness.

I wasn't weak.

I was strong. I was capable. I was used to single-handed investigation.

Pitter, patter, pitter, clunk, went the thing upstairs.

Blimmin' heck.

Unhooking my dressing gown from the back of the door, I threw it over my shoulders and stepped into the living room. Briefly I glanced at Sam's half-open door. There may have been a second of hesitation in my step but then I thought sod it, summoned my energy and boldly marched over to the hallway where the attic stairs were hidden behind a concealed door.

I pressed the lever, a device half-hidden by the skirting board. There was the whirring sound of mechanics springing into life then, with a click, the door that was camouflaged by wooden panelling sprang open.

Dust wafted down from above. We didn't go up here very often. It had become a bit sinister.

I tried the light switch then remembered the bulb had blown on a previous visit. Gingerly I ascended the flight of steep stairs till I reached the top.

Lordy – the smell up here was dreadful. A mixture of compost and decay: rotting plants, sulphur. How? I wondered and held the back of my hand against my nose. Was there a leak in the roof? Was water coming in and rotting the carpet and floorboards?

I picked up a torch that I'd remembered leaving on the top stair and flicked it on. The circle of light moved over the roof, but no, there was no discernible break in the ceiling plaster and nothing coming in round the dormer window frames. I let the torch drop down as, pitter patter pitter patter, the sound came again.

It frightened me this time because it was both clear and near.

I swallowed and heard the noise my throat made. It sounded loud.

Then I raised the torch and pointed it at the centre of the room where the noises were coming from.

The beam settled on a large box-like shape as tall as a man, that was covered ominously by a whitish dust sheet.

I knew what was underneath – an old fortune-teller machine, the kind you see on piers and in amusement arcades. A wooden case painted like a horse-pulled caravan. Through the glass window, when it was uncovered, you could see the freaky automaton it housed – Madam Zelda dressed like an old-fashioned gypsy.

But it was faulty. We should have fixed it ages ago. The battery, or part of its wiring or something had gone a bit screwy. The last time we'd both been up here it had gone off and started spewing out ridiculous fortunes. It hadn't been plugged in.

And it was as I was thinking about that strange interlude that the scratching sounds started up again.

This time I was sure: it was coming from the fortune-teller machine.

Ew.

I shone the torch on it and, at the same time, a light came on under the dust sheet, illuminating the shape so that now it looked like a comic-book ghost.

It was rather startling, and I found myself stepping back, away from it.

Something within clanged noisily.

Though I didn't want to, good sense told me I really should see what was going on there.

I sucked down a deep breath and took several tentative steps towards the box. Then in one quick movement I stepped up to it and pulled the dust sheet off.

Madam Zelda's cabinet flashed green as it whirred into life.

The automaton was bent forward, hunched over the crystal ball, which had also eerily lit up. The hands juddered, the chest inflated as if the thing was breathing. Little fingers with painted nails twitched against the glass of the cabinet, scraping grating, as if they were trying to claw their way out. A tinny voice rang out of the speakers. 'A dangerous coupling,' it trilled. 'A dangerous coupling.' Then the head jerked upright.

And I, and I, and I . . . lost my breath.

For the vision was implausible. Utterly repellent.

Oh my God.

The shock was like a physical tremor starting in my heart, like an unexpected explosion, pushing all the air out of me, sending shudders rippling down through my abdomen, my thighs, weakening the joints, unsteadying my knees.

I staggered forwards, reeling, clutching the dust sheet to my chest. When I realised I was about to collide with the hideous thing, I shrank back violently. As far away as I could.

Bile rose into my throat.

I threw down the sheet.

'Jesus, no,' I said, shaking my head back and forth in denial.

For there before me, I saw not the plasticky face of the old automaton, but the still breathing features of Ethel-Rose.

The top of her body had been severed and sewn in to replace the manikin. Terrible black stitches ran across her neck. The wound, scarlet and seeping, purpled round the edges, an ugly gaping seam.

Eyes, both terrified and terrifying, showed only the whites. I watched in paralysed silence as they rolled in their sockets, pained, tortured, animated not by nature but something demonic and perverse.

My lungs contracted as the sense of what was happening began to become clear. I gasped in as quick as I could, sucking down the foul odour that was warping the room, the smell of decay and degradation. Death.

Then in an instant the irises rolled down, black as hell, and fastened on to mine. The lips, purpled and black, drew back and contorted wide. Out of that trembling quivering hole, came the most unholy sound . . .

'Oooooohhhh, help me, ooohhhh,' like a creature caught in a snare.

'Oooooohhhh, ooooohhhh, oooohhhh,' I howled back.

And it was that scream that woke me up.

Thank God.

Drenched in sweat.

But safe in my bed.

In darkness.

The night black.

No moon.

Just a dream.

Nothing more. Nothing less.

But, I think at that point, some part of me sensed what was to come.

I just wasn't connecting things yet.

CHAPTER SIX

If I had been a better chick, a wiser chick for sure, I might have taken stock of the vicious terrors of that Sunday night. Maybe spent time considering the other strange events that were piling up around me: the discovery of the protection spell in Carmen/Rozalie's old house, the tension in the village, the rolling of the stone, the movement in the force and such. You know – reflected. Like normal people do.

As it turns out, however, I was not one of the sensible categories of human species and so on Monday morning when I woke up again, although the residue of nightmare was still bitter on my lips, I decided to shift it by focusing on the imagined torso of the curator: specifically, his six-pack, which I was yet to see for myself but had glimpsed through tight T-shirts. That was much much nicer than thinking about stuff that spun you out.

So, once I had visualised enough detail, my mood pepped up sufficiently for me to jump in the shower and blast the creepy vibes of the automaton dream completely out of my head.

I did concede one thing however, and told Sam about the noises. I wasn't sure if I had dreamt them or not but I thought it best to take a belt and braces approach – the last thing I wanted was the attic-room floor falling in on my bed.

To my surprise he agreed to go up and check it out.

'Well?' I said, when he came back downstairs.

'A few droppings up there. Mice, or maybe bats. I'll ask Bronson to check it out.'

'And the Madam Zelda machine?'

'What about it?' he said. He hadn't combed his hair and the front locks were falling over his eyes.

'Was it covered up? Did it look okay?'

'Of course,' he said and pushed back his fringe so that I could see he was sending me one of his inquisitive looks. 'Why wouldn't it?'

'Oh nothing,' I told him and shut up.

I knew it was in his nature to press me, so muttered some excuses about doing chores in Adder's Fork. Then I gathered myself together and did just that.

I was at the village shop when the next thing happened. I'd powered up there in my new Dolus Speeds, to cheer myself up. And they were working too. The trail of stars I had left in the dust looked rather magical, like a tiny cartoon Milky Way.

'Woah those trainers are blinding,' said Steve as I came in. 'Where's me sunnies?'

'They're great aren't they? Girl can't go wrong with a pair of scarlet trainers,' I said as I handed over my launch-party dress. 'Can I book this in for dry cleaning?'

Steve, the proprietor, dragged his eyes away from my trainers and held the dress up to the light, as he had recently taken to doing with some of my finer pieces. I watched him shake his head and tut, 'Mmmm, not sure about this one. Your last gown was too tight across the hips. No give in it. Quite uncomfortable to sit in. Got anything bigger?'

I rolled my eyes, as I had also taken to doing, and told him to 'give over', when Nicky appeared in the doorway to the upstairs flat and started joking about the colour not suiting Steve.

Which I thought quite rich really, as Nicky himself was often to be seen out and about sporting terrible waistcoats the like of which you only ever saw on children's TV presenters of the seventies. In fact, the analogy tickled me so much I told him that.

He didn't seem to find the comparison funny, but Steve was chuckling as he wrote me out a docket.

Then the bell over the door tinkled.

The shopkeeper raised his eyes and did a micro-scowl in the direction of the woman who came in. Nicky followed suit then speedily about-turned and retreated upstairs to the safety of the flat. I recognised the new customer as Neighbour Val of kimono fame, the impassioned protestor who had thrown herself on the Blackly Be boulder Friday night.

Obviously a woman who meant business, she was trying hard to catch her breath, but continued her march to the counter. Conventional pleasantries were dispensed with rapidly and she launched straight in. 'Steve, start the tweet-athon.' Her voice was compelling (scary). Under the artificial light I saw her skin was glistening. 'Looks like the builders are back. Plus some environmental hippies have shown up by the Blackly Be, talking about some protected species in Silva Wood. Hate to say it but they might be on to something. We need to rally whoever we can.'

Steve scratched his chin and crossed his arms and said, 'I don't know why we weren't consulted, Val. Nicky was saying that you'd have thought the council would have had to work their way through reams of red tape to sell off that land . . .'

Val sucked her teeth. 'Corruption, Steve, corruption. It's always the way. Rich people get to do what they like. They've got enough money to grease palms and lick the council's arse.'

An unexpected and unpleasant mental image popped up on my mental screen – a local Leytonstone councillor with a very large behind.

'You wait,' said Val, noticing me. 'They'll have your Witch Museum next. Once they get the Blackly Be, nothing'll be sacred.'

'It's not for sale yet,' I said wondering if they'd notice the last word, which had popped out of my mouth before my brain had engaged.

They didn't.

Steve was holding his phone close to his eyes, peering over the top of his glasses and jabbing at the screen.

Val spluttered. 'What? You think your intentions have any relevance. They don't matter.' She crossed her arms and did a head wobble. 'These people, they want something – they get it. It's a disgrace. Happening up and down the country. No one gives a toss about what the community want. It's all about filthy lucre.'

Yep, I thought, and that's what I'd be concentrating on when I put the museum up for sale. But not yet. I didn't want to right now. I had fish to fry and eggs to lay. Not that I was a takeaway food vendor or a chicken. Other than wanting Sam to accompany me up into the attic at night. But that was a dream, I reminded myself and tutted out loud.

'Exactly,' said Neighbour Val, regarding my expression. 'She got it,' she said to Steve. 'The penny's dropped with this one.'

'Right,' said the shopkeeper after a moment. 'I got "Karen Vicar", "Duncan Rotary" "Marion Scouts". I'll text them first.'

'You,' Val said waving a finger at me. 'Should get Samuel up there pronto. He might be able to talk sense into them.'

I backed over to the doorway and did some co-operative nodding.

Steve let out a grunt and leant on the counter. 'Val, love, what shall I say?'

Neighbour Val's face blushed and took on a hyena-fierce expression. 'We need to stop a crisis in the making,' she said and thumped her fist on the counter for emphasis. 'Tell them to get to the Blackly Be on the double. It's do or die.'

We couldn't have known how prophetic those words were to be.

I phoned Sam on the way up to the boulder site and told him what was going on.

'I'll be as fast as I can,' he said. I could hear him running down the stairs as he cut the call.

There was a good crowd already there when I arrived. I saw Florian down the front with a couple of crusty-looking dudes I didn't recognise. The backs of their T-shirts bore slogans that started with 'No to . . .' something indecipherable. I thought about joining them but was intersected and then cut off by the Scout mistress and a mixed group of post-retirement-age adults wearing shorts and backpacks and toggles.

When Sam turned up it was hot on the heels of several members of the rotary club and a substantial representation from the parish God squad. There was evidently a graphene-level strength of feeling about this matter locally.

So many had come out. Did none of them work?

Maybe it was all too exciting to resist. I couldn't imagine the sleepy little village had seen this high a security presence in recent times. The developers must have reckoned on trouble and had evidently been in contact with the local constabulary.

Four coppers were positioned around the fast-swelling crowd. Interspersed between them were employees of a private hire security firm: bouncer-like and tough in black uniforms with possibly padded vests or ginormous pecs.

On seeing them, Karen, the rev, guided her flock to the back. I could hear her urging the parishioners 'to protest with peace in your hearts'. There was some low-key grumbling, but they seemed largely to toe the line. Though a couple of their posse, conceivably Morris dancers, got their hankies out and waved them at a young officer in what I thought was rather a provocative manner.

Over on the pub side however things were less sedate.

Partly because the Granddad bloke had appeared and started poking his crutch at one of the bobby's behinds. This was causing much hilarity and encouraging gestures from the onlookers that had spilled out of the Seven Stars.

Beyond the police, builders were carrying out their orders with brisk efficiency, clearing the space round the boulder, sporadically punctuating the work with 'I'm just following orders' and other platitudes along the lines of having to make a living. It didn't cut it with the villagers who were responding with one- and two-fingered salutes and a variety of original and quite amusing jeers. One of the workmen might have been local as he went as red as a Rouge Dior lippy. Up the Morris dancers' end shedloads of Judas jokes were flying about.

A couple of suits with hard hats and clipboards hovered in the background. I wondered briefly if they were the developers. This, however, was dirty work. It was far more likely that the real culprits behind the impending destruction of the local landmark would be paying other people to supervise it for them. No doubt the new owners were on a golf course or a beach in Marbella or maybe watching with glee from a blacked-out Mercedes nearby.

Perhaps it was a lapse of perspective, after all it was just a rock, but I *did* kind of feel that there was Bond-villain-style treachery afoot.

Everything, like EVERYTHING – the tension, noise and hanky waving – ramped up a notch when the builders withdrew, leaving the Blackly Be boulder standing like a lonely lamb waiting for its slaughter.

When the digger trundled down the road and turned left into the cordoned-off arena you could have cut the air with a knife.

The line of people in front of Sam and me booed.

Florian's mates started chanting about greed and 'developer scums'.

In amidst all this came a loud smashing sound. We rotated to view the near side of the pub where someone had chucked a silver tankard through the window of a sleek BMW.

One of the policemen, a sergeant, started making flapping movements with his arms and directed his unit to drive back the gathered crowd.

Taking this as a cue, the digger moved forwards. A couple of the security guys broke off from the front and went to walk beside it. Drawing up alongside the Blackly Be the digger paused ominously. Then, to gasps and some spontaneous moaning, it slowly raised its giant claw.

'They're so short-sighted,' Sam shouted over the increasingly tumultuous uproar. 'Has anyone else spoken to the developers about what it means to the village? There must be a compromise to be had.'

I took a square look at the digger. 'You want to negotiate with that?'

Sam shook his head and pointed out the two men with clipboards. 'Let's start with them.'

I thought we were probably shutting the stable door after the horse had bolted and won the Grand National but said okay.

As we were pushing and shoving our way through the collection of bodies, the digger revved up. Very, very loudly. A chorus of hissing rang out over the road.

'There's no need to make it so theatrical,' I heard Sam murmur. He cast a quick glance over his shoulder at me. 'It'll make them worse.'

But most of the workmen seemed to be enjoying the drama.

With a screech of gears and a muffled thud, the claw dropped into the earth around the Blackly Be.

A number of protestors paused in their moans, temporarily stunned.

Around us there was a collective intake of air that sounded like whistling. For a moment, the jostling down the front stopped.

A rush of shocked awe passed among the villagers.

Disregarding, or perhaps, inspired by this reaction, in his booth the driver of the excavator pushed a lever forward. The huge metallic jaw began to rip through the grass and earth around the boulder.

A Mexican wave of twitches rippled through the dumbfounded onlookers.

Over near the pub people were moving. A strangled cry went up from Granddad who then fell to the ground. I wasn't sure if it was more play-acting, nobody was. Two of the watching drinkers rushed over to him. A bunch of angry shouts went off close by. The shoving started again. The nearest policeman lost his hat.

Things were getting heated.

After swinging its bursting jaw over to the side, the digger spat earth onto the floor, creating a pile of debris. Once fully emptied, it wasted no time in returning, revving up and pounding the ground again.

The sharp jagged side of the claw made easy work of the grass and topsoil. As it continued down deeper, the earth started lifting in dark sheets that cracked and crumbled into the bucket so easily they might have been made of chocolate sugared icing. The strength and power of the thing made me shiver, a contemporary metal dragon plaguing the village.

Good job I wasn't a virgin.

'Quick,' said Sam and grabbed my hand, scooting through the dense pack of Forkers. I followed him as closely as I could, but it wasn't easy: the energy of the crowd was turning, bodies were growing tense and hard-muscled. As I nudged forward, some of my neighbours gave me uncharacteristic little pushes back. All their voices had taken on a pinched quality.

One of them, that could have been Neighbour Val, hollered out with fury: 'I am not having this.'

In response the driver grinned, blew his horn and revved the digger up again.

We all looked on with increasing discomfort as the claw crashed down, ploughing back into the earth beside the Blackly Be, closer and so much faster now, sacrificing accuracy.

Coming back too quick, the corner of the jaw bashed into the boulder's side.

Though it was just a knock, a dislodged splinter of stone flew up at an odd angle and hit one of the nearby security enforcers. Crying out in pain, blood started pumping from the cut it had made on his forearm.

To repetitious gasps of 'Oh no!' 'It's happening!' and one random 'How's your father', the bodies before us seemed to compact and I was sucked into their collective form.

As the digger ploughed on regardless, further and further into the earth, something in the crowd shifted from reaction to action. I couldn't put my finger on what it was that lit the paper which catalysed the energy of the crowd into motion. But somewhere between 'How's your father' and a scream of rage that popped out of one of the scoutmasters, I found myself carried forwards by a storm surge of Adder's Forkers.

Flowing through the police line, they charged at the digger.

Jostled in the stampede, my leg caught on something or someone and before I realised what was happening I had lost my footing and was propelled forwards into bodies and darkness, unable to get my hands up or gain purchase on anything or anyone.

For a brief moment I felt myself sail through the air, then with an 'oof' I landed on someone's back. Possibly one of the adult scouts. Someone else fell over us. I wriggled out of the scrum to discover I was only metres away from the metal dragon.

In the booth the driver chuckled at the chaos beneath and swung the claw to empty its load onto the growing mound of debris.

But this time it didn't fall as easy as icing sugar. This time there were clots and sticks and clumps in it.

And something shiny and metallic that caught the sun as it tumbled onto the pile.

I realised someone next to me was on his knees shouting. Sam.

I couldn't make out what he was saying at first. Well, that's not true. I could make it out quite clearly in fact. I was just having a job of processing it. Because what he was saying seemed wrong and surreal and completely out of place.

But his words had an immediate effect on the nearby police sergeant who checked over the bucket and immediately started waving his arms back and forth at the driver: cease, desist.

'Halt now,' he ordered.

The security team complied.

This time even the digger obeyed him.

When the engine ceased, for a moment, there was a speck of calm. But it was the eye of the storm.

Sam's voice was still frantic but had taken on a weary breathlessness.

'Stop, stop,' he was shouting. 'That's a pelvis. You're disturbing human bones.'

CHAPTER SEVEN

Everything happened rather quickly after that.

Probably because the words were so unexpected and shocking, they punched a hole in the fury of the crowd and, as the collected onlookers sought to get a visual hook on what Sam was describing, the energy that had just been so stormy collapsed in on itself and fell away.

Taking advantage of this fleeting disorientation, the security guards waded in and began to unpick the jumble of limbs that had landed beside the boulder. I wouldn't say they did it with gusto as such, but there was a certain clinical robustness that characterised their movements and very quickly indeed we were propped up onto our feet and propelled firmly away from the hole.

A couple of police helped move the remaining crowd 'back, back, back' to the outer limits of the car park. However, most people had managed to cop a long nosy look at what appeared to be an open grave with yellow bits in it.

'Hang on,' I said to the guard currently manhandling me. 'What's that shiny thing down there?'

But he grunted and said gruffly, 'That's none of your business, that's what it is.' And continued to push me off the land.

I eventually located Sam on the other side of the car-park wall near a large bush, talking to Florian and his mates, who turned out to be two Green campaigners. One, a bloke called Elvin, was in his early thirties. He was slightly swarthy with huge eyes, as dark and deep as pools of water and framed by masses of curly black lashes, and a whip of chestnut hair. He had a red handkerchief tied round his neck, which put me in mind of old-fashioned rogue gypsies. And Dexys Midnight Runners. Beside him, the other, a young woman, was introduced as Ella. She didn't smile and seemed serious, quiet, though I mainly assumed that as she wore no make-up. Choppy reddish hair was cut into a bob. A wide forehead narrowed into a pointy chin, and mossy eyes that were, like the Elvin bloke's, also noticeably massive. There was something similar about the pair of them, which made me wonder if they were siblings. Though where Elvin's skin was olive, Ella's was pale as moonlight. They were both ethical-looking but not unattractive and smelled of rooty earth.

'Got in contact with these guys yesterday,' Florian explained. I was astounded that anyone had taken him seriously given the state he was in at Carmen's.

Elvin and Ella nodded simultaneously at me, then the man, Elvin, said, 'We're part of an activist Facebook group.' His voice was lilting and there was a soft accent there. Irish probably. 'Once we get more details we'll post this up.' He turned back to Florian and winked. 'I think you can be sure of some support here. Have you found out anything about wetlands in Silva Wood?'

Florian sniffed and said to Sam and me, 'Well? You're the locals.'

I shrugged. Though I'd driven past it a fair few times on my way back to London I'd never actually set foot inside the wood. Hadn't had time.

But Sam nodded. 'There's a small pond, the Sitting Pool. But it's not that big.'

The darkness in Elvin's eyes lightened fractionally. 'The Sitting Pool? Sounds promising.' Then he glanced at Ella.

She nodded and whispered into Florian's ear.

Florian slapped his forehead and said, 'Of course.'

Then they all grinned at each other until he spoke again. 'I'll try and get in there ASAP. See if it's compatible.'

This seemed to cheer the three of them very much.

Then Ella stroked Elvin's arm and pointed at her phone.

She had a liquid manner to her movements and a languid gait, which was probably enhanced by the diaphanous clothes she had on – a lacy T-shirt top, classic tasselled hippy skirt. Then I looked at her feet – bloody hell – no way! For, scuffed and a bit baggy on the seams, Ella's tootsies were encased in a pair of 'exclusive' Dolus Speed trainers. And clearly she'd had them for a while – spatters of mud covered the heel, wear had rubbed smooth the suede at the sides, and there were green stains and tears at the toe. And what's more, they weren't even really scarlet. The colour had faded so much they were more of a pink.

Ella caught me staring and shuffled her feet.

'Sorry,' I said. 'Did you get yours from Bunions too?'

'What?' she said. Her teeth crept out and bit her bottom lip.

'Your Dolus Speeds,' I said and raised a foot and waggled it. 'Got mine from Bunions.'

'Oh these,' she said and shrugged. 'Market. In Basildon. A few months ago.'

'What?' I spluttered before I could shut my mouth. 'The market! In Basildon?'

'Yeah,' she said and smiled. 'Dead cheap. But I don't think they've got them any more.' Then she tugged Elvin's hand.

I watched the crusty dude ask Florian to keep him up to date then, whilst I silently cursed the rip-off merchants at Bunions, the pair withdrew in the direction of the village centre. As they rounded the corner of the pub, Ella slipped her arm round Elvin's waist. Not siblings then. You'd hope.

I looked with dismay at the little trail of 'exclusive' stars that Ella's feet had left behind. It wasn't shouting Hollywood Walk of Fame to me.

'They can mobilise a good team,' Florian piped up. He had his hands on his hips and his chin was jutting out, like he was everybody's favourite superhero.

Tosser.

Though maybe that was unfair. I was just a bit prickly from the whole business with the trainers. Maybe Ella had bought a knock-off . . .

'What for?' I asked, a pipsqueak of irritation betrayed by my volume and high pitch. 'A good team for what? To stop the developers moving the stone?'

'Don't know about that,' he said and scratched his stubble. 'But we might be able to halt the development into Silva Wood. Particular habitats can be very useful in that regard. A development like this should never have gone ahead without certain inspections so I'm sure we can find loopholes to put together a case.'

Despite my continued annoyance regarding the exclusivity of my footwear, just then I felt a bit grateful to him, and was going to say so, when I noticed Sam out of the corner of my eye. Someone was arguing with him.

His back was to us, blocking my view. I took a step closer and looked over his shoulder. Neighbour Val was going at him full throttle.

'Surely it can be a heritage site or somethink?' she was saying. Though her hands were stuck on her hips, she was leaning towards him dangerously, boobs threatening to spill over the top of her low-cut blouse. Her tone, I thought, was rather on the accusatory side.

Yet Sam wasn't reacting the way I'd have expected. He was just taking it. Folding his arms and looking down at the floor, shaking his head but keeping schtum, not saying anything.

Val wasn't happy about this either. She had a pronounced stitch in her forehead which she kept rubbing. 'Right,' she said when he didn't speak. 'You can at least tell them about what happens when you disturb witch graves. Can't you?' Then she gave him a push. It wasn't a hard one, but it unsteadied him and forced him to step back and drop his arms for balance.

I didn't like the look of where this was going, having worked for Benefit Fraud for years and borne the brunt of more than my share of misplaced anger. I ducked round and inserted myself in the small space between Neighbour Val and Sam, which had the positive side-effect of my rear brushing against his front.

'Look,' I said to her. 'Back off.' Then I put my hands in front of my chest like a surrender gesture and said firmly, 'No'. I spread them out at the sides and at the same time began to walk forwards. We called it the 'shepherding manoeuvre' back in Benefit Fraud. You make yourself big and start moving towards people, they tend to back off pretty quickly without any physical contact becoming necessary.

'It's okay,' I said to her as soothingly as possible. 'It's okay to be upset. But you need to calm down now.'

Thank God Val did. And continued to retreat a few more metres. I maintained eye contact with her but, once she'd put a safe distance between us, she sniffed and looked me up and down in a kind of 'Who the hell do you think you are?' kind of style. Her nose wrinkled. I don't think she liked the trainers. I was coming round to her way of thinking, to be honest. But anyway – I'd had worse reactions.

'Sam and I run a museum,' I said, pasting a smile on my face. 'We're not obliged to get involved with anything if we don't want to.' I allowed my voice to go up a notch from 'calming'. 'However, if *you* want to go and fill the developers in about the Blackly Be, no one's going to stop you. Apart from them.' I pointed to the several law enforcement officers who were unfolding a strip of police 'Do not Cross' tape a little way in front of the boulder. There was a lot of activity going on over there, though none of it mechanical.

Val took a while to work the scene out but when she realised the implications she sighed and squeezed the bridge of her nose. I thought she was going to concede defeat, but she didn't. She squared her shoulders and said, 'Right. But I'll send them your way, if they need more detail.'

'You do that,' I said and took Sam's arm. 'Good luck.' The chances of her getting to the police or developers had to be close to zero right now. 'We'll be open for enquiries,' I said.

Then I started leading him away. 'Let's get back home. Best not to get involved I reckon.'

Sam remained mute.

We walked down the High Road, passing Steve's shop. A group of people were already massing there, exhibiting a range of emotions from perplexed to sad, excited, angry and frightened. A young male voice was shouting 'It's true! It's true,' as if he were trying to convince someone down the other end of the phone. I thought the voice sounded familiar, but I didn't want to look over because I knew we'd get drawn into the conversation. And there was something about Sam that was odd, out of kilter. It wasn't like him to go so quiet. Not given the circumstances. Though I had seen moments like this pass over him before – sudden silent introspections that triggered a seismic shift in mood. I wondered what had caused this one. It was often hard to tell, they seemed to take him over at different times for different reasons. Possibly now, it was the revelation of the human bones in the pit beside the boulder. It was of course unsettling. Although, at the same time, we had been in grimmer situations – the aftermath of a particularly bloody murder for instance – and Sam had not been bothered by it at all. It was odd.

Out of the corner of my eye I was aware of someone waving at us, but I pretended I hadn't seen them and continued on our way.

A dark and anxious feeling was uncurling in my stomach.

CHAPTER EIGHT

When we got back to the museum, Sam retired to his room, complaining of a headache.

I didn't believe him, but I didn't challenge it either. He obviously wanted to be on his own. I suspected he was going to sit and be morose or maybe investigate the legend of Black Anne. My instinct was to the latter but there was never any telling with him.

I decided to try and lift the feelings of unease that had knotted my abdomen by spending a little time on my own private investigation: that of my grandmother and her peculiar disappearance.

I felt sure that the troubling nightmare vision last night had been a product of not only Carmen's tin and its contents but also the enigmatic loose ends that Ethel-Rose's vanishing presented and which had never ever been tied up. If I could maybe dig down and find some clues then I might bring about some closure for my dad, myself and my subconscious dream-weaving mind.

A free couple of hours stretched in front of me, so why not?

I went upstairs and lay on my bed and texted Monty, our contact in MI5 or MI6 or whatever it was called, maybe the Occult Bureau, to ask if I could buy him lunch uptown tomorrow and quiz him on what he knew about the case. He'd told me a while ago that there was a file. He'd also said that I could not access it, but that he could give me an overview, which was fair enough. So, I was delighted when I received a text back within minutes saying he was more than happy to make himself available. I had promised to foot the bill as payback for several favours he had done us in the past, but there was a restaurant in London, La Fleur, that owed me one. I gave them a ring and booked a table for two at 1 p.m. Monty said he'd meet me there.

Having sorted my plans for the following day, my feeling was one of achievement and progression. Certainly, my mood had improved and as such I later descended to the office-cum-dining-room-cum-kitchen with a vague sense of optimism.

Tonight, I fancied a good curry to blow away some of the cobwebs lingering from yesterday's bender with Florian and Carmen. And it would reset Sam's mood, for sure. I found it impossible to maintain a cold miserable front when faced with a plateful of steaming fish Madras.

I needn't have fretted over the curator however, for a couple of hours later he came charging down for dinner announcing, 'Poltergeist Over England!'

It was a testimony to how much my life had deviated from the straightforward path of Leytonstone Benefit Fraud, that the curator's entrance failed to elicit any stronger a reaction than a gently fluttered eyebrow. And that was only because he was so preoccupied with his studies that he'd failed to do up all the buttons on his shirt correctly. I was consequently also distracted by a smattering of chest hairs, but managed to control myself and come back with an eloquent, 'Eh?'

He threw himself onto the chair at the head of the table. It was set for three, as it perpetually was. Not by myself, but by the unknown hand who regularly and delicately laid it for breakfast, afternoon tea and supper. That's what we had here. Rarely lunch, never dinner unless we had guests. Though whatever the occasion you could guarantee the table would be set perfectly with pretty vintage plates that never matched, and dainty silver cutlery. I reckoned the phantom plate-layer was Bronson, though he fervently denied it. Masculinity issues perhaps.

Sam was waving a slim paperback in his hand and had a sweaty smile on his face. He'd scooped his legs over the arm of the chair and looked like someone ridiculously decadent from *Brideshead Revisited* – all floppy hair, and schoolboy charm. 'Harry Price,' he said with glee.

'Oh yes,' I said, and nodded in acknowledgement of the book. 'You found the Adder's Fork episode in there, did you?'

His grin widened. He rubbed his face. 'Indeed. All his books are up in the study area. I need to alphabetise them, and, oh, Rosie, it must get dusted soon.' He wriggled his nose. 'Very sneezy up there.'

I wondered fleetingly who he was expecting to sweep the study? Not me, that's for sure. I hadn't given up a good solid 9–5-er to turn cleaner of the Witch Museum. Once he'd calmed down I'd suggest he thought about giving the duster a go himself.

'It's all in here,' he said and sent the book spinning across the table. 'Did you know there was a BBC broadcast from the Seven Stars in 1939? Part of a "haunted house" series. I had no idea! Really. Shame that there's not much about the witch between the pages. She's mentioned of course – allegedly a seventeenth-century woman, buried at the crossroads. Though it also stated she'd had "a stake put through her chest".'

I tutted. 'Gawd – what's the matter with these people? They were always sticking things in witches, weren't they? I wonder what Dr Freud would have made of it. Ursula had those iron bolts hammered into her thighs and wrists too.' I was referring here to the woman whose story was now told in our updated relaunched Cadence wing. 'It's a desecration, isn't it? A payback of sorts, I suppose. A post-mortem penetration.' I stopped where I was going on this one and shifted gear: no symbolic necrophiliac rape before supper please, we're British. 'But what's the deal with the stake through the heart? That's vampiric, isn't it?'

Sam put his hands behind his head, adding to the general atmosphere of foppishness. His shirt lifted and clung to the sides of his firm body. 'Smells good in here, I'm hungry,' he said as if he had just become aware of stomach pangs. 'I think it was more about keeping them in their graves so they didn't rise up after death and go aroaming, terrorising the neigh-bourhood, wreaking vengeance. That sort of thing.'

I put a plateful of chapatis on the table. 'Still weird.'

He made a snorty noise but when his face came up he was beaming. 'I thought you might have stopped saying that by now.'

'Never,' I said, and went back into the kitchenette to fetch the mango chutney.

'Where's Bronson?' Sam called after me. 'Is he coming for supper? I want to grill him on what he knows. We should find out all the info that Septimus had on the Blackly Be too. I'm sure Bronson can help in that regard.'

'Yep,' I said. 'He's coming. He'll be here any minute.'

But Sam was too impatient. 'I'll text him,' he said. 'Is it ready?'

'Always,' I said and sent him a winning smile. 'Whenever you are.' But he blushed and gave me a funny look.

Bronson's pocket was beeping when he sauntered into the office minutes later. As was his custom, he relieved himself of his bucket and then made for his place at the table. Even before he'd pulled back the chair Sam had already started on the interrogation.

'Bronson, dear man. Excellent. Tell us everything that you know about Black Anne. It's taken on more importance now, you see.' His manner had completely circled back to brisk efficiency. 'I take it you know about what's happened at the Blackly Be?'

The caretaker's bones creaked as he redistributed his weight across the padded seat. He wiped his moustache and removed the sou'wester from his head, then said, 'Happen, Steve at shop told me. Not good.' He shook his head. 'Not at all.'

Once he had settled I brought out two bowls of curry and rice and offered them over to the big guy first. Then I went back to fetch out the raita and extra chilli sauce, should anyone fancy livening it up a bit. I was a bit of a 'more the merrier' chef when it came to condiments.

I heard Sam pressing him. 'So, you see, anything you can tell us about the old legend would be helpful.'

'That's right,' Bronson replied but he sounded distracted. Other slopping noises indicated he was ladling out several helpings.

When I came back with the sauces I caught Sam rolling his eyes at the caretaker's evident lack of interest. He quickly pretended to inspect the light fitting hanging down over the table.

'Relax and have some dinner,' I told him and passed the raita over. 'This is a meal not a meeting.'

While Sam was sorting himself out with the rice, Bronson, who had already started on my exquisite culinary offering, sat back and interlaced his fingers. I thought he was going to pronounce on the Blackly Be affair, but he merely asked, 'Salt and pepper?'

I stopped myself from pointing at the kitchenette and grunting, and politely went back again, reminding myself it was an age thing not a gender expectation.

When he had seasoned his meal, the caretaker scooped in a heaped mouthful, chomped for about a minute then finally dropped his pearls of wisdom. 'Black Anne,' he said, in a dark low voice. 'Yes, well, she was a witch you see'.

My teeth clenched on a cardamom pod, half of which pinged out of my mouth and over the table, narrowly missing the caretaker's shoulder. Blimey BRONSON, well that was worth the wait, I thought, but I said, 'Great! Can you remember anything else?'

Then I slid more condiments to Sam, so we could exchange a look and a shrug. The curator let go a quick exasperated smile and fixed back on the old guy.

'Remember anything else?' Sam repeated the question through a mouthful of Madras.

'Not much, no.'

I stuffed some rice in my gob for comfort. Come on, Bronson. There was definitely more knocking around inside that old brain of his. It briefly crossed my mind that he might be amusing himself playing with us like this. He enjoyed giving the impression he was vague and waffly but the Witch Museum's caretaker was as sharp as an Inquisitional torture device.

Perhaps some nudging was required. 'Sam thought there was something about Black Anne in the Witch Museum,' I said to him, 'at one point?'

'That's right.' The caretaker replaced his spoon, so he could stroke his chin. 'Panel up near where the Talks Area was. Before it was for talks. Not been like that long. Not in the grand scheme of things. Was one of your ideas wasn't it, Samuel?'

'Indeed,' he replied, his voice a tad strained. 'Do you recall what information was displayed on the panel?'

Bronson gave his moustache a big stroke. 'Don't know what Septimus did with it.'

I bit down too hard on my fork and nearly cracked a tooth. 'But you do remember it, that's good. Any idea what it said?'

Bronson stopped stroking himself. 'Oh, now let me see.' He leant forwards and put his elbows on the table. 'She was very beautiful in that. Long dark black hair down to her waist. Probably where she got her name from.' He blinked and paused. 'Lovely figure of a woman. Full, you know.' One hand came off the table and moved carelessly over the front of his jacket. 'Curvy. In a bodice. And green skirt, I think,' then his voice went squeaky. 'Bit like your grandma in resemblance.'

I raised my eyebrows but said nothing.

'Edward de Vere did the panel painting, if I do recall,' he went on. 'Modelled Black Anne on Ethel-Rose. Always had a soft spot for your grandmother, did he.'

Did he now? I had kind of got that from the family portrait that hung in the upstairs living room. Tempted as I was to deviate and learn more about that relationship, experience had taught me, if I went down that route Bronson would drop his current thread and we might lose a good chunk of time getting him back on point. Anyway, Edward de Vere had invited me up for a cuppa and I was going to take him up on that. So I abandoned my grandmother with a mental note to pay a visit to Howlet Manor very soon. 'Do you remember what was written on the panel?'

'Oh no,' he shook his head. The hair at the sides jiggled about a bit, released from the weight of his customary sou'wester.

Sam moved his chair out abruptly. It squeaked on the floor. 'She was executed wasn't she, old chap?'

'That's what it said,' Bronson mumbled.

Ooh, that was something. 'What for?'

'For witchcraft.'

I opened my mouth and then, when Sam shook his head minutely at me, promptly shut it again. He knew Bronson better than I did so I sat still and waited. In the past he'd shown very good instincts about when to lead and when to follow.

Fixing his gaze somewhere in the middle distance, the caretaker muttered, 'Bewitching cattle and foul, I think what was wrote. Murdered neighbours, a travelling man and charmed her husband to death. Burned at the gallows, in the lane outside the pub, then buried there with a boulder rolled over to stop her coming back.'

I smiled. It had all been there in his head. He just needed time to pull it out and reassemble it again.

'Burned?' Sam's interest was evident in his face. His eyes flicked and whirred sparking amber flints within them. I took a bite of the Madras with extra chilli sauce and started to sweat.

'Seems odd, don't it?' Bronson agreed. 'They was mostly hanged down 'ere, for sure.'

'Although,' said Sam, 'could have some truth in it. Killing your husband was considered an almighty crime against the social order. Treason in fact. And the penalty for treason was burning.'

'You're joking,' I spluttered.

Sam shrugged and turned to Bronson. 'When was this, do you remember?'

I was wondering if that was a step too far. Would Bronson be able to recall the date? His memory seemed fuzzy, although, at the same time he'd done a spectacularly good job of remembering the curves on Black Anne's painted figure.

The caretaker made a grumbling sound then said, 'I have in my head the number 1621 but I don't know if it's right.'

But Sam was delighted. 'That sounds right to me, Bronson. I thought it might be pre-Hopkins. You are a wonder. Do have another helping,' and he pushed the serving bowls over again.

Bronson ignored the rice and went straight for the Madras. 'It's a good one this,' he said and gave me a wink. 'You use your dad's scotch bonnets?'

'Every time,' I said and beckoned the bowl over for another serve myself.

But I was not to be satisfied. For it was just at that moment the doorbell rang.

Which was unusual. We were shut on Mondays but anyway most people didn't like to venture into the museum grounds in the evenings. Though, I remembered, I had stupidly told Neighbour Val we'd be open for enquiries. I hadn't anticipated she'd take us up on that. Hadn't thought she'd manage to speak with anyone of importance, if truth be told.

Bronson started heaving himself to his feet, but I said, 'No, you stay. I'll get it.'

'Thanks Rosie,' said Sam. As I passed him, his fingers brushed against my hand.

Was he getting more touchy feely? I wondered, as I rounded the wall into the ticket office.

The doorbell buzzed again. Whoever was out there was rather impatient. Annoying. I mean we weren't publicly funded. We didn't have to be at everyone's beck and call. It clearly said on the sign in the car park that we were closed today.

But again it went off. Three short jabs.

'Keep your knickers on,' I shouted as I entered the lobby.

When I threw the door back, instead of my regular 'What can I do for you?' the woman standing on the steps outside was greeted with a 'What?'

It didn't faze her. In fact, she simply stepped inside the porch. And I hadn't even invited her in.

There was something supremely confident in her strident pose that made me hesitate for a second before I said, 'Hang on? I'm sorry but we're closed now.'

But she simply flapped ID in my face and said, 'Not to me, you're not.'

Sergeant Sue Scrub was in her fifties, with layered salt and pepper hair and eyes which were deceptively soft and gentle. There was a Northern twang to her voice and a no-nonsense manner about her that suggested a Yorkshire background. West probably. She'd been away a while though, I was guessing, as there was more than a smattering of Estuary consonant fall-out.

'Ah right,' she said, when she entered the office. 'Sorry to disturb you.' This to Bronson and Sam, though cursory.

The boys looked up. Sam frowned, Bronson remained impassive.

'It's the Fuzz,' I said, obviously in the grips of a seventies' flashback.

Scrub didn't appear to care, she'd probably had worse, and introduced herself again. She was wearing a lightweight mac, which looked very police and didn't really go with the season. They say CID don't wear uniform, but to my mind, you can spot them a mile off. If the clothes don't give them away then there's always something in the alert posture that screams 'constantly aware of villains'.

'Which one of you is Samuel?' The sergeant asked, looking at both of them, like she hadn't already worked it out.

Sam cleared his throat, stood up and came over to shake her hand.

'Nice to meet you,' she said and sat down (uninvited) at the head of the table, thereby positioning herself in the power seat. 'I've heard you might be of help to us at the boulder site, Mr Stone. If you can spare an hour, I've got a car outside. Would you mind?'

There was a moment of shocked pause as we all processed what Ms Scrub had said, then Sam jumped up. 'Of course,' he said.

I was thinking about giving out a bit of a fine-don't-include-me-then harrumph, but he added, 'Rosie and I work together. She'll have to come too.'

You could have knocked me down with a feather. This was a first. The curator of the museum giving me some credit.

Scrub switched her shrewd little eyes to me, did a little once-over, then said, 'Fine'.

I made my face neutral like I didn't care and shrugged.

Scrub said, 'Just as long as we hurry. Fetch your coats. It's getting chilly.'

It had quietened down a lot at the Blackly Be since we'd left that afternoon. Mainly because the police line had been widened and now blocked off most of the car park, leaving only a thin strip of walkway through the trestle tables for people to get in and out of the pub.

A few drinkers were standing near the High Road conversing at 'drunk/loud' level and smoking. I spotted Florian among them but didn't wave. I wasn't sure what he'd make of us sitting in the back of a police car, though I think the windows might have been tinted because there was no flash of recognition as we drove past.

Clearly the coming and going of police cars was no longer eyebrow-raising. Only a couple of the older blokes looked on with mild curiosity as we drove up to the cordon, where one of the bobbies lifted the tape and ushered us silently through.

We bounced over the uneven ground past the boulder and into the furthest section of the car park, where there were railings indicating the border to Silva Wood.

I thought we'd be trundled over to the stone, but Scrub got out and led us to a makeshift gazebo affair illuminated by lights on tripods which were, I guessed from the hum, powered by a generator.

She alerted those within to our approach before we entered. When we were allowed in we were met with the sight of several long trestle tables covered with plastic. Around the furthest were gathered two men and a woman. They were done up in disposable forensic suits and examining a series of damp clods of earth.

'Sam Stone,' announced Scrub. 'And Rosie Strange. Essex Witch Museum.'

There was a moment of blankness and a cessation of all mumbling, then one of the three, a man, with sandy strands of hair poking out of his hood, and thick goggles, came forward with his hand extended.

'Good to meet you,' he said to Sam, but I was ahead and shook first. 'Dan Oldham,' he explained but didn't detail his official capacity.

I released his hand and stepped away so Sam could do the same. The other man came forwards and introduced himself as Colin Seaton, a 'SOCO', which later googling revealed meant Scenes of Crime Officer. He in turn gestured to the woman, a Chloe Brown, who he explained had something to do with forensic archaeology and the University of Litchenfield. Some of her hair was poking out too. It was long and shiny and black. Probably dyed. She had lots of black eyeliner on.

'So,' said Scrub, once all the hand-shaking had been completed. 'As you're very aware, human remains have been turned up by the recent digging round here. Point is, they've been buried with some of these.' She gestured to the clods. 'And we wondered, with your expertise regarding local history and er, other specialities, you might have some insight into what they might be.'

I nodded and tried to look knowledgeable by screwing my eyes up and pointing at the clods. 'Yes, yes, I see. Well, I take it you're aware of the legend of Black Anne?' It was a good obfuscation: I had no expertise when it came to mud clods. Or witchcraft artefacts, to be absolutely honest.

Sam glanced at the objects on the table and said, 'Well. Indeed,' and added some more cheesy flannel about being delighted to be called upon. But I could tell from his voice there were no sparks going off in his head either.

There was however an energy in his voice when he stepped forward to the table and asked, 'And the bones? Do they match the story?'

But no one answered. The two other forensic officers, Colin and Chloe, pretended to confer with each other, though the latter's eyes kept pulling towards us.

Scrub sniffed. 'As I said, if you could look these . . .?'

I let my hand trail a line over the top of the items. 'All of them?'

'Actually,' said the woman, 'we're particularly intrigued by this.' And she put on a pair of plastic gloves and carefully moved one of the smaller items along the table to us.

Both Sam and I bent closer and squinted at it.

It was a small roughly hewn sphere of mud that had something metallic poking through the top. Something that was semi-circular and brownish but patchily so.

'What is it?' Sam asked and bent even closer.

'Well,' said the woman. 'We thought you might be able to tell us that.'

And as I ogled the thing I began to see more detail and gradually the outline of a disc emerged from the earth. It was discoloured but there was definitely a glimmer there. Could be gold.

'See here,' said the woman, introduced as Chloe. 'It's engraved.' Her gloved finger directed us to marks at the top. 'There are symbols on it. They . . .' she hesitated. 'They look archaic. Possibly encrypted. Do you have any idea?'

The disc wasn't big, maybe two and a half inches in diameter as far as I could tell. It was still covered in the clay-like mud. But the curve that rose out of it, which appeared to have been partly cleaned, bore a picture of something that resembled a brick tower. There was a name written over the top of it, and then lower down a domed building. Either side had been engraved with tiny looping handwriting that I couldn't decipher from this distance. The beginning of another larger symbol was emerging beneath it, but the rest of it was obscured by the claylike soil.

'May I?' said Sam and reached for it. Scrub hastily stilled his arm and said, 'You'll need gloves,' and pulled out a couple from her pocket.

Duly protected Sam picked the object up.

We all watched him turn it over in his hands. Then he brought it up close to his eyes and had a good long inspection.

While he was doing that I pointed to another object.

Another clod with something protruding from the side: three metal arms that narrowed to a hinged point. 'That looks more familiar,' I said to Scrub.

But the Dan guy answered. 'We're thinking it might be a course plotter. You know, a map divider.' He made a twisting circular movement with his hand.

'Really?' I said, unable to conceal the surprise in my voice. 'That's not particularly witchy.'

The female forensic, Chloe, faced up to me. 'Why's that?' Her voice was high. I reckoned she was fairly young for an academic, maybe late-twenties.

I shrugged. 'They tended to be poor. And thus uneducated. I don't believe map reading was generally a skill they were known for. But then that's the stereotype. I could be wrong. Witches came in all shapes, ages and sizes.'

She raised her eyebrows and said, 'Yes I see.' Then she smiled.

I smiled back too because I realised I'd said something that sounded expert and that curiously made me happy. The Witch Museum was seeping into my bones. Who'd have thought. My smile however soon dropped as I remembered the other set that were lying in an open grave just metres away. The memory of the pelvic bone falling through the air prompted an involuntary shiver.

'Cold?' said Chloe.

'No,' I replied honestly. 'Just thinking about the remains. Have you been told what happened the last time anyone tried to move the Blackly Be?'

Scrub failed to mute a tut.

I ignored her because Chloe was looking like she was interested. That is, her eyes had widened a bit. It was hard to read her properly given the small patch of face that was on show amidst the plastic suit.

I considered giving out some of the details, I'd heard from Bob Acton, but thought that might sound a bit nutty so just said, 'The newspapers at the time reported upon it as "poltergeist activity".'

'Oh,' said Chloe. 'When was this?'

'1944. The Americans needed to widen the road in to gain access to the car park for some of the larger vehicles. They tried to move the stone, but all hell broke loose.' I paused and then strengthened my credibility with an added, 'Allegedly a reaction from the disturbed spirits.'

'I see,' she said, but she sounded bemused.

'Well, not really,' I returned. 'My point is that this is one of the reasons why the villagers are so upset about what the developers are doing now. This lack of consultation. The literal bull-dozing of their land and landmarks. Whether you believe in these superstitions or not, doesn't really matter. It's about lack of dialogue, imposition and consequential feelings of powerlessness. It's not a very sensitive approach. And it will prompt reactions. Responses. Whether they manifest from the spirit world or just look like they do, if you know what I mean?' Bloody hell, I sounded good!

Chloe Brown didn't say anything, however her head moved up and down.

At that moment Sam bobbed his own head up and said, 'Fascinating,' very slowly.

We all turned and waited for the master to pronounce. The tent around us billowed out. A breeze was passing over.

'I've seen something similar of course,' he said finally. I felt like clapping. When it came to weird shit, you could always rely on Sam.

Even Scrub started a smile. You could see she was relieved. I was guessing she had taken a gamble with her credibility bringing us in. Some of the less open-minded coppers probably had us on the same level as clairvoyants, psychics and mediums. I almost let go a little scoff at the notion till I remembered I was descended from one. Allegedly.

How weird.

'You've got something like this at your witch museum, have you?' the sergeant went on.

Sam snorted. 'I wish.' Then realised that we were looking at him and explained less emotionally. 'If this is what I think it is, then it's more valuable than anything we've got at our place.'

'Really?' I said, wondering if we might be able to accommodate the object after the police had finished with it. It was a local artefact after all. Found within an alleged witch grave. We were the obvious end-repository. 'So what is it?'

'This, dear Rosie, may well have a cousin residing in the British Museum.'

Even Colin Smith looked impressed by that.

Oh yeah baby, I thought. We're no bumpkins – take that erudition and stuff it up your paper jumpsuit.

'It bears some similarities,' he went on, 'to an artefact on display there. In the Enlightenment gallery.'

I'd heard him talk about that section before. But in a different context. 'Not the shrivelled merman?'

Scrub tutted again then heaved a big sigh.

I cursed myself for mentioning it. Now she'd put us back in the nut-nut brigade.

'No. Further on,' Sam said. 'A disc belonging to a certain Dr John Dee.'

'Oohh?' I said and whistled. I'd definitely heard that name before.

The rest of the tent looked at me expectantly.

'He was . . .' I scrambled around mentally to remember where I'd heard his name before. '. . . a man,' I paused for drama, and continued searching through my internal filing cabinets. 'Who did stuff.' I shot a quick 'help-me' glance at Sam. 'That was connected to . . .' No help forthcoming from the curator, I went in for the kill. 'Witchcraft!'

'No shit,' said Scrub.

'Well, not exactly,' Sam broke in at last. 'True, he was associated with sorcery. I think he was arrested for conjuring and witchcraft, but acquitted. Though he was also prominently allied with astrology, mathematics and alchemy—'

'Alchemy?' said Chloe. 'Conversion of base metals into gold?'

'Wasn't just about that,' I interrupted, determined to salvage my integrity. 'The alchemists were early chemists. But the idea also concerned the pursuit of a spiritual ideal.' Sam had told me that.

He looked on with approval. 'Indeed,' he said. 'Dee was around at a time when magic and science were interconnected.

He was so highly thought of, at points, he became a consultant to the reigning monarch, Queen Elizabeth I. Advised her on ceremonial dates. Even her coronation. Some people believe he was the inspiration for Shakespeare's Prospero, in *The Tempest*.'

Scrub motioned to the disc. 'So what's his gold coin doing in the arse-end of nowhere?' She sniffed again. 'In the grave of a local witch?'

Everyone looked at the object in Sam's hand and then up at his face. 'No idea,' he said.

Chloe took a step forward and motioned for it. 'And what does it mean? The writings on here? The symbols?'

'Well,' said Sam and handed it over with great reluctance. 'The towers I have seen depicted on the similar disc at the British Museum. They're meant to have described, or commemorated, a vision by Edward Kelly. He was Dee's co-worker, if you like. And this was a vision he experienced. The Four Towers represented the four castles of Kraków where they were living at the time. But on here it looks like they resemble something like an "X" or a cross. Which is unusual.'

'But what did it refer to? Is it relevant here?' Chloe pressed. Behind the massive goggles her eyes widened. She was getting well into this.

Sam, however, was plainly stumped. 'I'll have to do some further research.' He turned to Scrub and took out his phone. 'Do you mind if I take some photos?'

This seemed to upset Sergeant Scrub who then made us come closer and spent the next five minutes delivering what

I assumed was a standard police-issue warning along the lines of 'if this gets out your arse is grass'. She did a good job of sprinkling in legal threats about perverting the course of justice and 'prosecuting the tits off' of us if we mentioned anything, so we'd 'go down for a very long time, dearie'. To finish, she ended with a prison trope about Sam's 'sweet arse' getting 'more attention in the nick than a lifetime at the Witch Museum'.

Clearly she didn't know me.

When she finally drew breath, I gave a nod of agreement. Unfortunately, my curator's attention had drifted off halfway through and he was now bent over the table with a small magnifying glass, evidently unmoved by Scrub's rant and bum threats.

'Okay, okay. We do,' I said, realising I would have to step up and take upon myself the mantle of arse-guarder, a prospect which inspired both pleasure and concern. I really didn't fancy anyone else interfering with Sam's private parts.

I coughed to try and bring Sam back. When that didn't register I poked him in the ribs, which made him flinch but stand up and pay attention. 'What?' he said.

'Agree to Sergeant Scrub's conditions please, Sam. I'll recap what they are later.'

He switched onto the policewoman. 'Yes, I have no intention of divulging any information. These photographs will be purely to assist identification and interpretation. Although I suppose I could do a pencil sketch if necessary.'

Above us rain began to break against the canvas.

'Photos will be fine,' said Scrub and Sam whipped out his phone.

I was sensing a dismissal.

Before we were turfed out, however, I wanted to know what one larger mass was at the other end of the table. While Sam was snapping away I sauntered over to give it a closer look.

'What's that?' I motioned to Chloe, who had followed me over.

'Where's your museum?' she asked. 'Sounds fascinating. Might pop in sometime.'

I gave her directions and told her she was welcome. The muddy cluster before me contained an earthenware container. There was a large cracked ceramic lid on its top. 'Can I get some gloves on and have a look at it?' I asked.

For a moment Chloe looked doubtful so I added. 'Free admission to the Witch Museum?' She laughed and said, 'Go on then,' and fetched me a pair of the plastic latex variety. No one else seemed to be paying any attention to us, for a couple of policemen had come in now and were in conversation with Scrub and the Colin guy. The taller uniform was saying something to Scrub about 'the chief turning up'.

She did not look best pleased.

I came back to the pot thing, put the gloves on then picked it up. 'Wow,' I said to Chloe. 'It's heavy!'

'We know.' She frowned at my fingers creeping towards the lid.

'Do you know what's in here?' I asked feeling the knob on the top.

'Can you not . . .?' Her arms made an involuntary jumping movement, as if she was going to take it off me. 'It ought to be opened under laboratory conditions . . .'

But I was already working it. 'No need for that,' I told her. 'Look I can do it now. I'm quite strong.' And with a squeak and a puff of foul air I wrenched the top off.

'Shit!' I said, as Chloe made for it.

'You really shouldn't have done that.' She reached out her hands.

I was far too hypnotised by what was within the jar to give it up so easily and ducked away from her and back to Sam.

'Oooh look,' I said. 'Sam. It's ancient coins. Loads of them.'

He was beside me in an instant. 'Are they? Gosh. Is that Anglo-Saxon? My God, that one looks Roman.'

But Chloe had motioned to the bobbies on the door who quickly approached us. Within a couple of seconds and in some astonishingly deft moves they wrested the jar from my hands and returned it to Chloe Brown.

'Careful,' she said as she got her baby back. Then as she considered the jar. 'Oh my. You could be right.'

'Wow! That's pretty cool, isn't it?' I said and waited for Sam's reaction. He was staring into the mid-distance, waving his finger in front of him at no one.

'What's the matter?' I asked, for he was starting to pale.

'Oh my goodness,' he said. 'I'm just realising something.'

At which point, Scrub moved in and told him to cough it up.

'It was a legend I thought.' He shook his head. His hair

flopped and swung. 'No, can't be,' he said and pushed his fringe back. 'I thought it was just a story?'

'About what, Mr Stone?' Scrub asked with blistering impatience.

For once I was with her on this.

Sam's eyes glinted as he spoke. 'They said it was buried, by the monks, in the abbey grounds. The abbey, the cloisters, they're now the Manor, you see. Happened some time during the dissolution of the monasteries.' Then he glanced back at the disc on the long trestle table. 'Good Christ. Could it be that golden X marks the spot?'

'What does it mean Sam?' I asked with urgency. Monks, course plotters, golden discs and 'X marks the spot'? This was all starting to get quite exciting.

'I think that there may be a possibility they might have been looking for part of the Howlet Hoard. Treasure.'

In the corner of the tent Scrub made a shrieking noise. 'This is all we need,' she said. 'A bleedin' gold rush.'

CHAPTER NINE

Scrub's words immediately effected a flurry of activity. Police officers marched in and crowded round the table.

We were told to wait and give our mobile numbers to a young constable who took down our details then ushered us towards the tent door. Another period of waiting around was followed by a swift ejection from the tent with no ifs, no buts and no offers of a panda car to drive us back to the museum. Which was a bit rich really considering we'd given up our Monday evening to help them out. At the same time, I could see how uncovering a treasure horde might dramatically complicate the investigation of human remains inadvertently uncovered during a, possibly illegal, property development.

Neighbour Val would be beside herself.

Outside the rain had lightened, but the going underfoot was getting muddy.

I headed towards the High Road. Sam, however, tugged my elbow and said, 'Don't know about you but I could do with a drink.'

As he rarely said anything remotely like that, I concurred.

The pub was packed with people sheltering from the inclement weather and having a good gossip about what was going on in the tents that had sprung up like mushrooms around the Blackly Be. The atmosphere was one of strained excitement which seemed to get a little more schizophrenic when we walked across the floor to the bar.

There was definitely a bit of a celebration going on, which may seem odd given the nature of the gruesome discovery, but I guessed people were counting their blessings that the remains had at least stopped the bulldozer and therefore the proposed housing development.

Anyway, we didn't linger at the bar and once we'd got our drinks, found a free table at the side of the pub, near the inglenook and tucked ourselves in.

After we'd sunk enough to start feeling the relaxing effects, Sam said, 'Well, blow me. This, dear Rosie, has been quite a day.'

I couldn't agree with him more, to be honest. And we clinked glasses.

'These sort of days have been getting more frequent since I inherited the Witch Museum.' I thought he'd protest but he didn't. Just bowed his head, raised his glass to me again and took a little sip of his drink. I went on. 'It's all rather odd, I must confess. I mean, there's been the moving of the boulder, that tin from Carmen with the witch bottle and the note, this afternoon's discovery of human bones and now the golden disc with X marks the spot.'

'Indeed,' he said and stared at his glass. 'We do seem to be at the centre of quite a few mysteries.'

'But that's hardly unusual, is it?' I slid down in my comfy chair and sighed.

'Becoming an occupational hazard since you came along.' Sam grinned.

He wasn't wrong.

'This Howlet Hoard,' I said and pointed vaguely towards the car park. 'Can you please tell me what that's all about?' I don't remember you talking about it before. How does it relate to the Manor?'

'Indeed,' he said and put the glass on the table.

A table nearby let out a collective guffaw, so Sam hunkered down and in a voice just above a whisper said, 'All right. Howlet Manor was originally an abbey, like I said. Founded around the twelfth century, if I remember rightly, by the Premonstratensians. Though they were called the White Canons on account of the colour of their habits.'

'Which were?' I asked, eager for all the details.

He looked at me, head bent to one side. 'White.'

'Oh yes,' I said. 'Just checking. Go on.'

'So, the church and cloister buildings developed on that site.' He gestured out of the pub window behind us, beyond the Blackly Be and over the other side of the road, towards Edward de Vere's Manor. 'On the banks of Piskey Brook. They very quickly became established. The monks were lucky enough to have some powerful patrons. At that point, there were quite a few wealthy landowners in Essex, all of whom thought they could pay the monks to say masses for them when they died. Thus, the abbey soon generated a handsome yearly income, which enabled them to buy expensive decorations and the like. That may have been what made them so attractive to Henry VIII. For come 1536 and the Act of Dissolution, the commissioners descended on Howlet Abbey like a plague of avaricious locusts. Everything of any value was stripped out and sold. Parts of the abbey, like the church and cloisters, were wantonly destroyed. That's why only the main house stands now. I think it was the refectory, dormitory, great hall, brewery, kitchens so on.'

I uncrossed my arms and smiled with encouragement though I couldn't see where this was going really. 'And the treasure?'

'Yes,' he said. 'Well, the legend is that before the commissioners arrived, the monks were tipped off. Prior to fleeing abroad, allegedly through underground tunnels too . . .'

'Really?' That piqued my interest. 'Underground tunnels? Cool. Where were they meant to go?'

Sam leant his head to the fireplace. 'Probably the church and the graveyard, if my memory serves me well. Maybe here. I think I remember hearing something about this once being the gatehouse.'

'Oh. So why did they have tunnels?' I said looking at the inglenook and wondering if there was a secret passage behind it or something. I was judging from the low ceilings that this part of the pub hadn't been altered architecturally for centuries. In fact, on either side of the fireplace the walls were uneven, suggesting that the construction materials had probably come from a long time before building regulations were imposed.

'All the religious uncertainty,' said Sam, following my gaze. 'They were an unobtrusive way to escape. Especially if ambushed in the dead of night. From all sides.'

'Oh right,' I said and felt a flush of exhilaration as I inspected the pub. It was a quirky little place full of coves and nooks. It wouldn't be a stretch of the imagination to discover one led here.

'So anyway,' Sam started up again. 'Before the commissioners came galloping in to confiscate or destroy their abbey, like I said, the White Canons swept up the most sacred and valuable items and buried them somewhere in the grounds so that one day, when Henry was dethroned and order was restored, they would be able to come home and find them and continue their work.' He paused. 'But of course, that never happened. The country stayed protestant. The monks never returned.'

The penny dropped. 'And so that means that the treasure is still there? Hidden somewhere nearby? Unless it's been discovered already?'

'Not to anyone's knowledge,' he said. 'That's the story anyway.'

It was a good one.

Even a teensy bit feasible.

And if it was, then – treasure, wow! Here in Adder's Fork. Who'd have thought? Seriously. 'So how much are we talking about here?' I asked. 'What kind of things were they meant to have buried?'

'Ancient coins, lots of them. Which is what made me think of it when you showed me that jar.'

I nodded, beginning to see how he had put the jigsaw together.

'And gold coins, religious carvings, gilt drinking vessels, cups. There's meant to be a chess set of eleventh-century pieces containing precious jewels, a gold shrine from the high altar, rings, jewellery, statues. Gold, gold, gold.' He paused and took a draught of his beer. 'At least that's what it said the last time I googled it. Which, in truth, was quite a while back. E-book, I think,' he said. 'Hang on.' He got his phone out and started prodding away. After a few minutes, he passed it over and indicated to the screen. 'This is a similar picture to the one that illustrated the treasure in the book I read. It's an artist's interpretation of course.'

'Wowzer,' I said. An old chest was split open. Piles of gold coins spilled out. Golden grails, jewel-encrusted crowns and altar crosses were all visible in the sparkling stream of riches. 'It looks like something out of a fairy tale.'

'Yes, I agree. It's too romantic. I think that's why it's never really registered with me as true. And although rumours abounded over the years, the consensus was, I think, that the story was made up. Just a bit of fun. After all, the abbey was sold off in portions and none of the local farmers have ever turned anything up.'

'Until now,' I said and sent him a meaningful stare.

'Until now,' he repeated, but didn't look up.

'So, you think that earthenware pot is part of it?'

'Those coins looked ancient to me.'

I contemplated the jar and the fact it had been dug up only metres away from where we were sitting. 'And this section of the village would have been part of the abbey back then?'

'In the twelfth century, I think most of Adder's Fork would have been.'

I took a slug of my own drink and reflected. 'I suppose it makes a certain sense, what with that map thing they found there.'

He wrinkled his nose. 'Uh huh.'

'The map divider.' I took a good gulp of wine. 'The thing that you measure maps with.'

He leant back and crossed his arms. 'Oh yes?'

'If Black Anne was looking for gold. She might have had a map. Maybe she was divining or dowsing for treasure?'

He nodded in silent agreement.

'So,' I went on. 'What about the golden disc? The one with the carvings on it? Is that part of the Howlet treasure too?'

'No,' he said with unexpected firmness and he picked up his phone again. I forgot sometimes just how much of an expert he was. 'Not if it's got anything to do with John Dee. It would have been made later. After the Dissolution. 1584-ish,' he added. 'Probably.'

'But that's like at least fifty years later,' I murmured more to myself. 'What's it doing buried with a pot of gold?'

Sam rubbed his chin and met my gaze. 'And, more importantly, what's a part of the Howlet treasure pile doing in Black Anne's grave?'

'Hello?' said a voice from above. We had both been far too caught up in our subject matter to notice anyone lingering by our table.

As we jumped to attention I recognised the willowy form of Carmen's boyfriend, Florian. God knows how long he'd been there.

'What's all this about treasure?' he said with a very pronounced gleam in his eye. Honestly, the cat who got the cream wouldn't have looked much smugger.

'Nothing,' Sam and I said at once.

'Come on,' he said, and pulled out a spare chair, which made me sigh. I really wanted him to bugger off and leave us alone. 'I just overheard you. What's this all about?'

I tried hard to stifle a sneer, unconvinced he'd been there that long. Probably he'd just come in on the tail end of our tête-à-tête and was trying his luck, like journalists do.

Sam and I hesitated. I sent him a look, full of narrowed eyes and tense cheeks, which I imagined suggested, 'No don't tell him, make it up.'

Sam, however, appeared to read it differently.

'Okay,' he said, and held up his hands in mock surrender. 'You've got us – they've uncovered a gold disc in the Blackly Be grave.'

Oh crap, I thought, and intervened. 'Something associated with witchcraft. It's not uncommon to see that sort of thing round here. Witch Museum and that. Ha ha ha.' I nudged Sam's elbow.

Sam shook his head. 'No, Rosie, I told you . . .' What was the matter with him?

We needed to get Florian off the trail asap. Quick action was needed.

'Argh!' I said and flapped my hand about. 'A wasp! I'm

allergic. Get rid of it.' And I waved my hand towards Florian's pint, hitting the rim and upsetting it over the table.

Florian jumped to his feet to avoid the overspill, which was heading straight for his groin. 'I didn't see one,' he said and spun round. 'Where? Where?'

'Oh, it's gone now. I'm so sorry,' I said, and took his arm. 'Let me buy you another.' Then I led him off to the bar.

While I was ordering Florian's pint, a bald bloke at the bar, with an eyebrow piercing, asked me what I was working on.

'What do you mean?' I said carefully. He was wearing a leather jacket and looked neither detectorist nor local history fan.

'You're from the Witch Museum aren't you?' he said and winked. His voice was attractive, surprisingly deep and full of meaty texture. 'Have you been involved with the boulder or are you concentrating on other stuff?'

It was a strange enquiry, I thought. Though perhaps he had visited the museum in the past. It was possible that I had spoken to him there. Though I had a good head for faces and I couldn't remember his.

When I hesitated to respond, he smiled and reached for his glass. His arms were well-toned. Maybe karate or martial arts. He had that look to him. Then a farmer from down the road who kept pigs came over and started having a go at Florian. I muttered my excuses to the bald bloke, took the fresh pint and transported it to the journalist, where I explained that because of the museum being neutral I was unable to express an opinion either way on pig farming, and left them to it.

Sam wasn't looking very happy when I got back to the table. I felt the same. The bald bloke had unsettled me slightly. I didn't know why.

'Oh hell,' he said. 'Just remembered. Florian's a reporter, isn't he?'

At last.

'Sure is,' I said. 'And a vegetarian.'

'What do you mean?' Sam said, and folded his arms.

'I don't think he's trustworthy.'

He gave me what he thought was a long hard stare. Again. 'Well, about twenty per cent of the world population is vegetarian, Rosie. It's not considered woo-woo any more. In fact, it's very healthy. It's good for the planet. And it stands against animal cruelty. I know lots of vegetarians with a great deal of integrity. More than carnivores, it has to be said.'

'Well they start that way, then the next thing they're all glucose intolerant and wheat-free and wearing plastic sandals and doing mandalas, telling you all about how superior they are and that you should do it too. I've seen it happen time and time again, Sam. It's a cult.'

'Have you?' Sam frowned and crossed his arms. 'Have you really?'

I considered his question. 'Okay, well at least once. This guy that I went out with – Martin. All right at first, then he goes vegetarian and wham – straight onto the last train to Nuttsville. And he ain't ever come back.'

The curator sighed and continued his stare. 'Sometimes, I forget what you're like.'

I fluttered my lovely new eyelashes and waited for the compliment, 'And what's that then, Samuel?'

'To quote you, "weird".' Though there was a kink of a smile in the left-hand corner of his lips.

'Huh!' I said. 'Mr Pot meet Mrs Kettle. You're the curator of the Essex Witch Museum!'

His eyes narrowed wickedly. 'And this from the owner. Touché.'

Bugger. Yes, well I walked into that one. I sat there and tried to think of a comeback, but failed so did a bit of fuming and finished my drink instead. 'At least I distracted Florian long enough to stop you spilling the beans about the treasure horde. Hopefully he'll be thinking it's a one-off that's been found.'

'Sorry,' said Sam and licked his lips. 'The Howlet treasure, no less,' he mumbled dreamily. 'That would get some attention. Imagine if it got out. There would be a deluge of people flooding the site. Just think of the trouble they'd have excavating the grave. All those precious artefacts out there waiting to be found by experts, churned up and tossed around by amateurs.' He shivered. 'Doesn't bear thinking about.'

'Hmmm,' I said and chanced a glance at his body. 'I'm not concerned about the trampling of precious artefacts.'

'No?' he said, and looked at me. 'Then what?'

'I'm worried about your bum.'

CHAPTER TEN

I never got to fully explain the bum issue and Sergeant Scrub's explicit instructions, as the landlord called time and we were ejected very quickly from the pub, then cleared from the site by the police, who were securing it for the night.

Florian told us he wasn't over the limit and offered us a lift, which was the least he could do.

On the way back I tried to convince him the whole treasure thing was a non-starter, which made him smile and giggle and then finally guffaw as he admitted he'd already had the news confirmed.

Both Sam and I were gobsmacked. But apparently it had gone round the pub before we'd even got there. Florian tried to pass it off with some bluster about 'sources'. When I pressed him on it, he finally admitted, 'There are local cops working on this too. They might have their own reasons for being, let's call it, indiscreet,' and left Sam and me to munch that one over.

The rain clouds had cleared by the time we got home. In the pale moonlight the Witch Museum was glowing. A breeze rippled the pines that ran along the boundary of the Actons' farmland and wafted the scent of their needles to us. There was something infinitely calming about the cool verdant smell of real pine and I took a moment to breathe it in.

As I passed the memorial garden the roses dipped and nodded their heads at me, like they were encouraging me on. 'Yes, keep doing what you're doing.' The whole place looked quietly alive.

When we got in we both went straight to bed. Separately. I think we were exhausted.

The next morning, I woke up and got myself ready for my lunch date with Monty.

As I was crossing the lobby Sam appeared with a rucksack and asked for a lift up to town. He had decided to go up to the British Library to do some rooting around to find out more about the disc. I told him fine. Although, as he wasn't going to be staffing the museum, that meant we had to brief Bronson and call Vanessa to come in and sit on the till.

We were trying to make up time and pretty much tearing up the High Road, when we hit upon a huge crowd outside Steve's shop. Not literally hit, thank goodness, but almost. I had to break. Because there were a couple of people sauntering across the road. From the playground that edged onto the common land of Mab and Silva Wood up to the old police station at least a dozen people were gathered in clusters, looking at maps, pointing at the sky or consulting phone screens. The largest group, a cluster of men, were gathered on the pavement outside Steve's windows.

'Recognise any of them?' I asked Sam who had already wound the window down.

'Nope,' he said. 'But I can see an awful lot of metal detectors.'

'Oh crap,' I said. 'Florian. He's let the cat out of the bag. Blimey that was quick.'

'Must have caught the first editions,' said Sam.

'Websites,' I said to him. 'He would have gone back to Carmen's last night and written it up.'

'Of course he did,' said Sam and shook his head.

'God. I hope Scrub doesn't think it was us?' I said, shifting uncomfortably in the driving seat.

'Perverting the course of justice.' Sam's lips pursed. 'That's what she said we could be got for, didn't she?'

'Uhuh,' I nodded and gripped the steering wheel.

'Well,' said Sam. 'Florian is going to have to own up and take the flak.'

He absolutely was. I didn't want Scrub to start thinking about Sam's private parts again. It wasn't our fault that she had a leak in the squad.

We rumbled on. It was slow progress. There were a hell of a lot of people roaming around the village. The pavements were narrow so a lot of them were walking in the road which necessitated a lot of horn honking on my part.

As we reached the pub, the numbers of traipsing tourists increased significantly. In fact, right outside the Seven Stars there was something of a crowd of them.

'There he is!' said Sam. 'Pull over.'

Before I could answer 'Yes master', he had jumped out of the car and was hotfooting it towards the thin strip of trestle tables now allocated to the pub as a reduced beer garden.

It hadn't passed me by that all roads seemed to be leading here these days. I felt like I was dividing my time between the museum and the pub. Not that that was usually such a bad combination.

I parked up by the side of the road. It was on a double yellow but that didn't appear to have deterred anyone else. When in Rome . . .

In fact, there were heaps of cars around the place. The only time I'd seen more vehicles here was when a rumour went round that Rod Stewart was having a pint.

It turned out to be David Van Day. The traffic soon cleared.

As I got out I noted an outside broadcast vehicle with BBC Essex branding parked up by the road close to the Manor House. Bloody hell. Sue Scrub was going to do her nut.

The groups of people gathered in various positions about the police tape appeared to fall roughly into three camps: very excited detectorists, locals whispering to each other and another collection of people with placards – environmental protestors I presumed.

Sam was in the middle of the latter. I could see him in highly animated conversation with Florian and two others who might have been Elvin and Ella.

He was still in full flow when I got there. Honestly he is so articulate he can really give it out when he wants to.

Florian, to give him his due, was looking sheepish. Eventually, seizing the moment when Sam paused for breath, he put his hands up and said, 'But I didn't hear it from you, did I?'

I almost felt sorry for the guy and, actually, he was correct in that assertion.

'Sam,' I said and ran a finger along his sleeve. 'To be fair, Florian did say he'd got it from one of the local plods. But Florian.' I turned to him and became emphatic. 'You've got to do us a favour and let Sergeant Scrub know that. It's not right that we should have to take the full force of the constabulary's anger, if you know what I mean.'

He conceded. 'All right, I'll let it be known. But this is going to work for you in the grand scheme of things anyway. You should be celebrating. Look at all this fuss being made about the site, questions are going to be asked. The development will have to be reviewed.'

'But not stopped altogether?' I said.

'Not yet,' said someone at my elbow. It was Elvin. His eyes were twinkling. I guess this was exactly what they were hoping for. 'But we'll manage it,' he said.

I told him that I was pleased to hear that and his smile began to widen. But as his massive eyes drifted from my face and over my shoulder, he froze. The warm expression melted off his chops. 'Oh God,' he said to Florian, 'Incoming at four o'clock.'

Florian followed Elvin's gaze. 'Brilliant.' His tone suggested it really wasn't.

Even the silent Ella let go a groan. Her mossy eyes sagged and she said, 'Vex', like it was a swear word.

Sam and I looked into the road, where we saw a short man with a fat gut and fat groin, wearing an army camouflage jumper and bursting jeans. He was barrelling over towards us with the same sneering look of dogged determination that the bulldozer driver had worn yesterday.

'Vex?' I said. 'That's a funny name.' Then I remembered my company and said, 'No offence,' to Elvin and Florian.

They didn't respond.

Florian, I saw, was arranging his features into something that was almost a smile. But it was false, you could tell. 'It's rhyming slang,' he said out the side of it. 'This is the delightful Reg Rainer, or as we like to call him when he's not around – Vexatious Complainer. Vex for short.'

'Oh,' said Sam. 'I thought he looked like one of your team.'

'He is,' bleated Elvin. 'It doesn't stop him complaining to us and about us. Misery and bad spirits fuel him.'

'He'll fit in around here then,' I said grimly at which Sam raised an eyebrow. 'Bad spirits,' I said and pointed at the pit where the boulder had been. He shrugged and gave me a 'what-are-you-on-about' look, which made me feel a bit stupid.

But Florian got it. 'Ah yes.' He nodded sagely. 'The poltergeist activity. Anything happened yet?'

I shook my head. 'Not that we're aware.'

'What's that?' Elvin asked. But the squat little man had bundled into our circle knocking Sam out of the way and coming to a halt about three inches in front of me, blocking my view of Florian and Elvin and Ella and the pub and, well, everything. Rude git.

He put his hands on the chubby love handles that were sticking out above his belt like two green woolly hillocks.

'Glad to see you've taken the initiative for once, boys,' he said, as if starting a well-rehearsed speech. The fact that he didn't acknowledge Ella also irked. 'About time too,' he went on. 'A full protest is what we need. I've wasted no time, unlike some,' he said and looked at Florian. 'Been on to the rest of the committee since I got here. We've agreed unanimously.'

'How?' said Florian, a deep line creating shadows across his forehead.

'On the phone.' His hand flew past me, brushing some of my hair, and pointed towards the road. A whiff of his body odour snuck up my nostrils and made me cough. It contained a concentration of mouldy home environment, unwashed fleshy crevices and alcohol. I shuffled back a metre. 'Over there. I passed a motion.'

'That's disgusting,' I hissed at Sam. Putting my hand over my nose I stepped well back from the vexatious man. 'I thought they only did that sort of thing in prison.' I darted fearful glances around the place, to ensure I didn't step in it.

Sam rolled his eyes. 'He means a proposal. A proposition to collectively agree on something. To take action.'

Well, he might say that but I wouldn't put it past this guy. There was something about him that made my flesh crawl. A feeling of intense aggro was coming off him, though he was trying to mute it. The way he positioned himself, dead centre, suggested this man was a narcissist who pretended otherwise, but urgently craved attention.

'Reg, this is Sam Stone from the local museum and . . .' Elvin presumably gestured to us because Reg Rainer spun round and glared.

I didn't catch the rest of what Elvin was saying as I was rather bowled over by Reg's face, which was very florid. His skin was rough and bubbly with pockmarks and there were a lot of lines around his mouth. The type you get from scowling a lot. They say people's personalities begin to show in their faces and for sure, this bloke had the look of a troll. Not that I have ever encountered a troll, but there was definitely something Lord of the Rings about him. A bit orc-ish. I wouldn't put social media bullying past him either.

His eyes appraised us. It wasn't a warming sight. More like being sized up by a crocodile. Then he flicked and squinted till his mouth produced an absolute masterclass sneer of disapproval. I'd never seen the like of it. Obviously this expression had been very well used: the lines of his face creased into it with ease.

'Museum, eh?' Vex said. 'Get grants, I suppose, do you?' Then without waiting for us to respond he tightened his arms across his chest and practically spat out, 'Waste of tax payers' money. Hope your accounts are transparent. I will be demanding to see them at the end of the next financial year.' He had bits of white spittle in the corners of his mouth. 'You people should be making sure you get value for money, not just spend the funding on pointless projects for the bourgeoisie.'

Goodness. It was like being blasted by a bionic bullfrog.

Sam took a moment to duck the rancid stream issuing from Rainer's mouth then inhaled a breath of clean air and said, 'We are funded privately.'

If he'd hoped that little dart of information would deflate the balloon of bile that was currently being puffed up somewhere within Rainer's chest, he was to come a cropper. For, as quick as a flash, the Vex came back with, 'Ah, a capitalist framework!' This was followed with a shot of pure contempt all squeezed into the word: 'Scumful.'

I'd never heard that before and hoped I would not be on the receiving end of it in future.

Well, you could certainly see how Vex came by his nickname.

Florian made like he was going to intervene, but I was more than able to fight my own battles. I'd come across plenty of clowns like this before.

'How delightful to meet you Mr Rainer. I'm Rosie Strange. Are you going to acknowledge Ella here, or being a woman, does that make her less qualified for a greeting?'

'So?' he said and stepped towards me. 'Where have you come from?'

'Benefit Fraud.' I waved my ID under his nose, hoping that might put him on the back foot. The presentation of department ID usually had that effect.

A sly smile spread across Mr Complainer's stubble, then he said, 'Oh yeah? That right? And you work at this museum too, do you? Your superior officers know you've got two jobs?'

Damn him. Best to go on the offensive. 'What's yours, then?' I said. 'Apart from being a right little charmer?'

He cleared his throat and straightened his back. 'Currently I'm resting. Between jobs.'

I'd heard that one before. 'Well I hope you won't be spending time protesting here when you should be seeking work opportunities?'

He stopped and pretended to take off an invisible hat which he doffed in my direction. Then he smirked and waved his hands at me in a very patronising gesture of dismissal. 'Do shoo,' he said, then returned to the men. Of course. 'Elvin, Florian. You need to talk your plan over with me.'

I was surprised steam wasn't coming out of my ears. Enraged, I took a step towards him – I certainly hadn't finished with this spanner yet.

However, Sam very deftly curled his arm through mine, which took me rather off guard.

'Come on Rosie,' he whispered. 'We'll be late.' I could tell he was using a distraction technique. Though we hadn't known each other for a very long time, he had enough of a measure of my character to know that my interaction with Mr Rainer was likely to go downhill from here. He began to march me off.

Though I let myself be led away I disliked the fact Vex had had the last word.

In a moment of childish pique I wrenched my arm free, circled round and right up to the stupid Vexatious Complainer.

'You, Vex person,' I said, jabbing my finger in his chest. 'You are blimmin' lucky I'm not pre-menstrual.'

Partially satisfied I'd regained some dignity, I returned to Sam.

'What a hideous man,' I fumed.

'We are in agreement on that count,' he sighed.

'Wonder why Florian and Elvin and Ella hang out with someone like that. I mean they come across as quite passive. But he . . . he . . .' I stammered.

'He doesn't,' Sam filled in.

'No,' I said. 'Give me five minutes with him in a dark alley and, oh,' I stopped mid-sentence. 'Hello.'

Not the most welcome sight in the world, Sue Scrub was blocking our way with an expression that suggested she was suffering from intense indigestion.

'Yes,' she said. 'I was thinking the same thing about you two.'

'I wasn't talking about you,' I said. 'That bloke over there, Reg Rainer. Very unpleasant. And by the way, before you start making unfounded accusations, this,' I gestured to the crowds, 'wasn't anything to do with us.'

She looked like a slab of stone and just as yielding.

I explained: 'You have a leak in your privates. I mean constables.' But that didn't seem to help matters either.

'My colleague is correct.' Sam continued to press the point home. 'If you want to know where the information came from I suggest you go over there and ask a guy called Florian,' and he pointed him out amongst the crowd of protestors.

The sergeant gave a bullish snort, screwed her eyes up so tightly I'd be surprised if she could see anything, then pawed the ground with her foot and, head down, advanced towards her new target.

'Would not want to be in Florian's shoes, right now,' said Sam.

'He's a journalist,' I told him. 'He'll be used to it.'

We began to weave amongst the bodies between the cordon and the road. Just before we mounted the kerb I heard a voice calling my name. For a moment I was puzzled, but then, over on the far pavement, I spotted the unmistakable form of Edward de Vere, resplendent in his familiar white linens. Or almost white linens.

I made my way over to where he stood. The Lord of the Manor was leaning on a walking stick. I hadn't seen him with it before. It made him look a bit doddery, which I was certain he wasn't very much. The lashes might be grey but the eyes underneath them were shiny and hard and blue like glass marbles. And de Vere, for sure, was in full possession of all of his.

When I got to him, he pushed his Panama back and said crossly, 'What's all this commotion? Do you know?' and lifted his stick at the two tents, which confirmed to me that he wasn't as feeble as he liked to make out: the stick was heavy, ergo there was muscle tone there.

I wasn't clear what aspect of the scene he was referring to. But as I shifted to view it from Edward's perspective, I suddenly realised how bizarre and chaotic it looked: all these people, drinking and jostling, pointing and screaming, in different outfits, scattered around a big hole in the ground. In fact, with the pub in the background if someone had painted a picture of it, right then, they might have got away with titling it *Alcoholics Hieronymus*. No wonder the poor guy was confused. It occurred to me that located, as he was, in his ivory tower he might not be totally up to date on all the developments down here. Indeed, he might not even know about the boulder at all, given he and Araminta left the museum launch party long before Bob Acton raised the alarm.

So, I thought: first things first. Start at the beginning. 'Okay, so do you know that developers have bought up the land around the Seven Stars and Silva Wood?'

De Vere grunted which I took as an affirmative. 'They want to move the Blackly Be so they can get their wide lorries in and stuff.'

Edward's facial features tautened. He rubbed his chin. 'Yes, I heard something about that. No good will come of disturbing the dead. Never does. You shouldn't disturb them, you know. Not in this place.' He swallowed and formed his free hand into a fist. 'Is that why the beatniks are waving those slogans about?'

'Oh,' I said, realising he meant Florian's crew. 'No, they're protesting about the development because it's spreading onto the publicly owned land in Silva Wood. I'm not sure it's completely legal. But then people tend to get away with things like that these days, don't they?'

He sent me a look that seemed like he was outraged, 'So, the police have come for that?' Then he put his stick behind his back and leant back on it. 'Will they be locking up the trouble makers?'

'I don't think so. They're not here for that, specifically. Something was dug up when the builders were working around the boulder.' And as the cat was already more than halfway out of the bag I told him about the human remains and then about the treasure in the tent.

'Well, well, well,' he said. 'That's nothing to do with us, is it? Not us.' I wasn't sure what group his use of collective noun referred to. But if he meant the villagers, as a matter of fact, it probably did have a lot to do with them at some point but I didn't say anything.

'And these other fools are here to look for our so-called Howlet Hoard, are they? Poor chumps. That will go nowhere. I'm sure if there was any to be found it would have turned up by now.'

'That's what Sam said,' I told him.

Then he shook his head long and slow and had a good suck of his (probably false) teeth. 'They should stop it, you know. At once. I can't have all this turfing up of the ground.' Again he gestured the stick around. A bit too roughly for my liking. I took a step away.

'It unsettles everything, you understand. You do, don't you?'

I nodded. Unsettled, I would say, was a bit of an under-statement right now.

'There are things that need to be left alone,' he went on, his cheeks becoming rather rosy. 'This land is one of them. I won't allow it, Rosie.'

Mm, I thought. Someone needed to tell him we'd moved on from feudal rule.

Best to put him straight. 'I'm afraid you can't do much about that, Edward.'

Though I didn't think he was in the mood for reason.

He'd started to shake. 'It can't happen you see. It simply can't. Or else there'll be more. Heads will roll,' he blustered, pointing the stick. 'You get off my land,' he shouted finally at a passing group of detectorists, who glanced at him then carried on up the High Road out of the village.

Oh dear. 'Edward, it's not your land is it though?'

'Was once,' he said and cracked the stick on the pavement.

'Well, I'm sure you can definitely keep them off Howlet Manor and its land. The police can advise you. The sergeant is a very nice woman called Sue Scrub. I'm sure she'd gladly come and talk to you.' I was amazed that I was able to trip that whopper off my tongue without so much as a blush or cough. Though in my experience little white lies were acceptable if they achieved the end means. In this case, calming Edward down. Which, actually, it wasn't.

He looked like he was about to start some shouting, and I was wondering about fading away into the background, when thankfully his daughter Araminta showed up.

'Come on now, Padre,' she said and immediately began to usher him away from the chaos towards the little road, which I'd been told led up to his Manor.

To be honest, I was grateful for the intervention, and was about to express my heartfelt thanks, when the thick-trunked woman whipped round and poked a finger in my direction. Her eyes were blazing and full of anger, which I assumed she was going to direct onto the police or the detectorists or maybe the protestors. But she wasn't.

Her eyes bore steadily into me, then she said, in a voice just above a whisper. 'You did this, didn't you? You'll live to regret it, you know.'

Before I could even find the words to answer she had twirled round. I watched her bundle her father up the road, wondering if she'd mistaken me for someone else. Or was possibly a little bit demented. Briefly I considered following them up to the house and telling Araminta that I had nothing to do with the pandemonium outside the pub. Then I noticed in the dust she'd left a track of stars. As I looked up and caught the pair of them rounding the corner into their drive, I noticed the middle-aged frump had a pair of Dolus Speeds on.

Bloody hell. That did it. I was getting out of here right now.

Stupid Essex with its stupid shoe shops and stupid people and stupid lies. I got in the car and hit the accelerator hard, intent on going full steam ahead till I reached civilisation once more.

CHAPTER ELEVEN

Man, it was good to get back in the city. I navigated past a bag lady pushing two trolleys along the pavement, one of which had a giant cuddly panda in the child's seat, and smiled fondly as a flushed taxi driver flicked two fingers at an overtaking cyclist. Some city bloke in a suit talked loudly into his mobile phone while shoving me out his way. A party of tourists stopped en masse outside a sandwich shop. One of them started taking selfies whilst standing on my toe. Ah, London, my sweet metropolis, remained wonderfully unchanged.

Montgomery Walker was seated at the table when I got to the restaurant, looking for all the world like an off-duty city gent, and thus completely indistinguishable from the other clientele.

I apologised for my lateness and began to explain about what was going on in Adder's Fork, but it appeared the agent already had the low-down.

'Came over on the tom toms this morning,' he said. I'd heard him use that term before and figured it referred to some internal secret data collection departmental memo thingy. Whatever it was, it seemed damn up to date.

'Yes,' he said and added enigmatically. 'There's more to come out of there, I'm sure.'

But he wouldn't be drawn further.

I watched him deflect all my questions with a charming smile on his face. The bloke was attractive in a posh competent way. His hair was slightly receding around the sides and temples, black and neatly trimmed. Despite a vaguely military sort of bearing there was something a little raffish about the bloke. He dressed completely nuts though: today he was wearing a sports blazer and a polo shirt and chinos. I imagined if I peered under the table I'd spot brogues.

Monty went on to apologise for his absence at the launch and asked me if it was successful. I told him about how it was disrupted, and he nodded sagely. It was my intention next to go into the real reason for lunch but the waitress came over. I knew Mary-Jane from a previous case or incident or occurrence or whatever you wanted to call it – oddness, perhaps. I enquired after her and the rest of the staff and was pleased to hear that order had been restored to the restaurant. Though, apparently a few of the staff had left. I couldn't really blame them – some of that stuff that we'd gone through had been very upsetting indeed.

The place had been redecorated since I'd last been here and I commented on it. MJ said Ray Boundersby had insisted on it. He was the owner and a friend (somehow) of my Auntie Babs. Apparently, he'd felt he needed to 'reposition and refresh' the restaurant and blow out all the associations with the past. Before, it had been full of blacks, purples and gold. Now, however, it was much brighter – white and chrome with so many glass finishings you'd be forgiven for keeping your shades on.

I could see what Boundersby was trying to do and told MJ to pass on my compliments. She said that the boss already knew I was coming and, although he couldn't be there in person to greet me, he insisted I should accept the meal with compliments of the house. Which was just the result I'd been hoping for, so ordered the sesame tiger prawns for starters and a steak for main, medium rare. Monty was more restrained and went for one course only – roasted hake. I suspected eating in places like this came with Mr Walker's salary.

'So,' said Monty, once MJ had taken our orders. 'I suppose we should talk about your grandmother. I realise it's why I'm here.'

I was quite taken aback by the bald acknowledgement of my motives, but then again Monty, as polite as he was, had never been one to prevaricate. And I was mostly glad for it, truth be told. One had to take the rough with the smooth. And I was pretty much prepared to take Monty most ways as, being a government agent (though in which department I still wasn't sure), he was a good friend to call on if ever things got very sticky. Indeed, he had access to people with guns and black outfits and helicopters and things. In fact he'd saved my bacon (and some of Sam's too) on more than one occasion with his proactive and very direct approach. Oh yeah. Who doesn't want friends like that, right?

And so I didn't contradict him. I did, however, send over a beguiling smile: eyes wide open, chin down, nostrils slightly flared. I had practised it a few times on Sam. With patchy results, I'm sad to say. On a couple of occasions, the curator had responded positively. But like I said, they were few and far between. Mostly he'd gone all eyebrows and enquired after my health.

Monty barely registered my fulsome beam and just carried on talking. 'I must warn you. I do think that some stones are better left unturned. Your family have had a tragic history. Is it wise to stir it up again?'

That was strikingly similar to what Edward de Vere had said this morning. 'How do you mean?' I asked him.

'Well, your grandmother wasn't the only person to come to a sticky end. Your aunt, Celeste, she drowned you know.'

I considered this. That wasn't what I'd heard. 'I thought it was a car crash,' I said.

'Yes. But the car ended up in the Piskey Brook. It was the water that killed her in the end.'

That was a nasty way to go, I thought and said so. Though I was wondering if the agent was trying to divert me away from what I wanted. 'But we're here to talk about Ethel-Rose,' I said firmly, keeping things on track.

'Yes, we are. This time,' Monty intoned, like he was bracing himself.

I sent him a glance full of question marks, but he ignored me.

Though he did let out a little sigh, in an 'it's-your-funeral' kind of way. 'Okay. It's all right, Rosie. I'll give you what you want. I promised I would, didn't I?'

'Yes.' I grinned. 'I know you're a man of your word.'

He inclined his head. 'Your grandmother's case did cause something of a stir at the department,' he said and reached down by his side. 'I understand that, now that you've inherited the Witch Museum, you may want to look into it. But, can I say this?' he paused as though he was considering his words carefully and softened his tone, 'Not that you will heed it.' Then he made eye contact. 'Sometimes, Rosie, it really is better to let sleeping dogs lie.' He sat back and waited for a response.

I couldn't see the logic of that remark unless . . . 'Do you know something I don't know, Monty?'

He crossed his legs and took a sip of his orange juice. 'Dear girl, you know where I work – of course I know things that you don't. Occupational hazard, you see. But I am always keen to remind those intent on digging up the past that sometimes things are forgotten for a reason. Some secrets are better left buried. From your experience I'm sure you'd agree.'

I thought about this and what had happened in some of our other cases. Then in my mind I saw the open grave by the Blackly Be.

Leaving a considerable gap to show I had ruminated upon it I said, 'No I don't. I think it's better to face the strange, however painful or exhausting that might be.' I was thinking now about what had happened here in this restaurant. And next door to it. 'It brings closure and resolution. Mostly. And in some cases it also brings justice to bear. Shines a light on events that only *some* people want to conceal. And, I'd say that my experience has meant I've listened to silenced voices that would otherwise have remained unheard.'

I imagined he might be inclined to agree with me on my latter point but he puffed out his cheeks and said, 'okay' and fumbled in something down by his side. 'On your head etc.,' he said, and produced a briefcase.

As he righted himself he sent me another one of his classic charm-school smiles. 'Now, you're aware I can't allow you access to the files.'

'Come on Monty. I know you're not a red tape kind of guy.'

He withdrew something and slipped it behind the case onto his lap. 'There are some rules that are made to be broken and a quantity thereof to preserve the domain of the rule makers. There are also in addition to that some which seek to serve and defend the realm. A portion of this dossier falls into the latter category.'

'Don't you trust me, Monty?' Might as well continue to try my luck. Persistence, though tiring, could also be a friend.

Monty steepled his elegant hands under his chin for a moment. Steely eyes sparkled. 'You're tough and resilient and loyal. But you're effervescent too and, I'm aware, taken off guard, you might drop a pearl or two. You see, what I'm saying?'

'Wow,' I said, flattered. 'What a great let-down. You can continue to hang around.'

He smiled and bowed his head. 'Thank you.'

But something in my stomach had dropped and bottomed out. I was sorely disappointed, to be honest.

'To avoid any such compromise, I've had one of the clerical staff do a precis. Included extracts from reports I think you might find useful. No more, no less.' He passed over a light-brown-coloured file full of loose pages. 'There was a lot of needless repetition in the file. You could just say I've edited it.'

'Print,' I said peeking at the pages within. 'How quaint.'

'Ironically it leaves less of a paper trail.' As I opened the folder wide, he hushed me. 'Not here. Put it in your bag. Read it at home when you're on your own.'

'Can I show it to Sam?'

'Of course. But no one else, please. Not your father. Anything that helps clarify his situation or what happened back then I must urge you to communicate only verbally.'

'Why not Dad? All of this is most relevant to him? Ethel-Rose was his mother.'

Monty's eyes did a quick sweep of the room. 'We don't know how he'll react. We're very aware of how he feels about . . .' he paused, '. . . our department and affairs. Please Rosie, I'm already going out on a limb sharing this much with you.'

'Okay,' I said and despite the almost unbearable impulse to rip the file open and devour it whole, I opened my bag and slipped it in.

But I could feel it.

Pulsing neon like a sea anemone, beckoning from the darkness below.

'Monty,' I said tentatively chewing over a thought that had plagued me before. 'Is there any way she could still be alive?'

Monty looked sideways at me, 'Ethel-Rose? Yes, there's a possibility. When endings aren't finite there always is.

Multiple possibilities. She would be in her nineties now if she lived.' He cleared his throat. 'Or lives.'

I took that onboard. That was very old. Where would she have gone? Dad and Septimus must have been through this too. Did they go looking for her? I wondered.

My starter arrived and succeeded in completely distracting me. The buttery garlicky smell was wonderful. I pushed the prawns into the middle of the table and Monty shared them.

Placing the remnants of a fried crustacean on the side of the plate, he asked 'What exactly do you know about your grandmother?'

While I licked my fingers I dipped into my own mental file and retrieved a three-dimensional picture. 'She was pretty. And she was a clairvoyant. Allegedly. Heard ghosts.'

'That's clairaudient,' he said with a light smile.

'Oh right, yeah,' I mumbled and scrunched my napkin next to my plate. 'Was the London branch of the Romanov family ever approached to see if she had gone there, when she walked off the stage?'

He frowned. 'Not by us, but I believe Septimus did contact them. They hadn't seen her.'

Another dead end. 'What about her mother's side? This Anne? The mother. Who were her relatives? Where were they from?'

'Mmm,' he said. 'Maiden name Anne Milligan. And yes, her side were also quite colourful characters, certainly. There's quite an extensive file.'

'Which you can't show me?' I ventured.

He bowed his head. 'Which I can't show you,' he said, as if there was any doubt. 'You could ask your father.'

Hah! I thought. The chances of getting any family history out of him was like blood and stones. But I said, 'It would upset him to talk about it. He never mentions the family or the past.'

'Understandable. Some people are like that.'

'So then *you* tell me.'

Monty raised his eyebrows right up into his square forehead.

'Go on,' I said. 'You're not going anywhere for the next hour. Communicate verbally.'

He took a sip of wine, leant back into his comfortable chair and said, 'Are you sitting comfortably?'

I grinned. 'Oh yeah.'

'Then I'll begin. Mrs Anne Romanov was a bit of a snob. Her mother, Emily, had been the daughter of a well-to-do family, landed gentry, who had made good with canny invest-ments during the industrial revolution. Emily Newsom and her sisters were endlessly cosseted and chaperoned. When young Emily first laid eyes on the steaming brawn of the navvies building the new railway across the bottom of the estate, she was utterly lost.'

How Monty knew all of this was interesting. I would have liked to ask, but thought it wiser not to spoil his flow.

'Liaisons were arranged, meetings held, but as soon as the inevitable fertilisation was discovered, Emily was promptly disinherited and ejected from the family seat with only a few donated pounds from her nanny and sisters to help her on her way. She and Rory secured two rooms in Hoxton and filled them with several offspring. Anne was the fifth child of the seven that survived into double figures.'

Some poor waiter dropped a tray. The noise made everyone turn towards the kitchens.

A solitary pair of hands began to clap. A few others laughed.

I tuned back in to Monty. 'There were brothers and sisters then? That would mean aunts and uncles in Ethel-Rose's case. Cousins possibly.'

Monty bent his head. 'As soon as she could, Anne distanced herself from them. Once in Adder's Fork she was able to reinvent herself. She was forced to put up with her grandmother, Roisin, because of family duty but she didn't like it.'

I considered the name and said, 'Do you mean Rozalie? Fred's sister?'

'Oh you know about her then?' Monty said. 'No, Roisin was Rory's mother, Anne's grandmother. Rory and Emily once appeared at the cottage on Hollypot Lane for a surprise visit, with Roisin in tow. The old woman enjoyed herself so much she decided to honour them by extending her stay. Anne cried lack of space, but her daughter little Ethel-Rose, who had been sharing the room with her announced she would be happy to continue the arrangement.'

'Ha ha,' I said. 'She sounds like a tinker.'

'Indeed,' said Monty. 'A toothless Irish grandmother didn't quite help Anne's new persona. But Roisin stayed. For three years. Anne always thought that she was responsible for her daughter's occult interests.'

I scrunched my face up. 'I thought that was Rozalie.'

'They both influenced Ethel-Rose in different ways. Roisin would put her to bed with tales from her ancestors, reputedly travelling people, and stories of the Fey. Roisin had spent a good deal of time in Kilkenny, near to where Brigit Cleary was allegedly snatched by fairies. Have you heard of that?'

I shook my head. 'Was she a witch?'

'No. But it was a famous case in 1895. I'm sure Sam could tell you more. A brief summary: Bridget was snatched by fairies and a changeling left in her place. It looked like Bridget, it sounded like Bridget but it was sickly, unlike Bridget. Her husband, however, wasn't fooled and burnt her to death over the hearth. The court found him guilty of murder, but many folk, like Roisin, thought that rightly unfair.'

'Blimey,' I said. 'Fairies? Really?'

'Indeed. Well, your grandmother was interested in them. She also picked up skills such as palm-reading and the tea leaves from Roisin. She died when Ethel-Rose was ten.'

I remembered what Sam had told me in Carmen's garden. 'It's no wonder Anne packed her off to Switzerland to try and make her normal. I'm sure the last thing she wanted for her daughter was to become clairvoyant. Or audient,' I added quickly.

'Yes,' agreed Monty. 'Ironically it was Anne who pressed Ethel-Rose to perform at that last séance.'

'Oh, I assumed it had been Rozalie.'

'Certainly, she'd been involved in the first round of "meetings", as they called them then. But George, Ethel-Rose's brother was called up in the war and went missing in action. Anne put pressure on Ethel-Rose to try and find him. Rozalie felt the meetings should be open to the public, to offer hope to others grieving so they could find comfort too.'

Rozalie sounded a bit crazy, but compassionate.

'Then later she was arrested. After that she met your grandfather. It's made mention of in the file, if you want more details. One of the witnesses was there.'

I nodded. 'Oh that's interesting. I'm looking forward to reading it. And it was later in the fifties that the next public meeting/séance was held? The one where she disappeared?'

'Indeed. Anne had wanted her to do that, to try and reach out to her father, Fred, who died earlier in 1953.'

I processed this. Some of this Bronson had told me months back.

Monty lapsed into silence as our plates were cleared away. During the conversation we had made our way through our mains, desserts and coffee and now he was making signs about leaving. I needed to wrap things up with just a few more prods.

'Correct me if I'm wrong,' I said, trying to get it all in. 'There were three theories. The first that the government had arrested Ethel-Rose and taken her into detention?'

'Yes,' he said. 'Untrue as far as I can ascertain.'

I cocked my head at him. 'Are you sure?'

'One can never be 100 per cent sure. But I am perhaps 99 per cent.'

'Okay. The next idea was that she had simply run off. That she was having an affair and went away with her lover.' I said. 'Is that possible?'

Monty shrugged. 'It's not impossible. She was a popular lady, your grandmother. Attractive. Glamorous. Quite fun.'

'But that meant she would have deserted her children and left all her clothes and money?'

'It was a hypothesis that Septimus, Anne and Rozalie discouraged.'

'Then what – kidnap? Abduction? Murder?'

'There was never a body found and there were searches conducted at the time.'

'So the police concluded that Ethel-Rose had simply had enough of everything and buggered off somewhere else to find a new life and a new husband. I suppose it's plausible. What do you think?'

Monty shrugged. 'As I said, there are accounts in the file. Have a look at them. Now I really must go Rosie. It has been delightful. Let me know how you get on.'

I stood up to kiss him goodbye.

'And,' he said, as we pulled apart. 'I might have something I'd like you and Sam to look at. To return the favour. Quid pro quo. Something has triggered a hair alarm in Damebury. That's not far from you, is it?'

'Oh, er no. It's not,' I said, rather taken aback. I hadn't considered my request for information might be part of an exchange of sorts. But it was fair enough, I supposed.

'May come to nothing, but if it does "kick off" as you might say, I'll drop you a line.'

'All right,' I said and shrugged. 'Let us know.'

As he turned to leave, I tapped him on the shoulder and said, 'One moment Monty. You didn't answer my question.

Did the police or your department check out the aunties and uncles on Anne's side? Did they find anything?'

'Yes they did, and no they didn't.'

'So she just vanished?'

'Off the face of the earth, you might say. Yes curious.'

'Not curious,' I said as he waved goodbye. 'Impossible.'

CHAPTER TWELVE

'It was absolutely fascinating,' said Sam, as we careered along the A12. 'Diversion ahead. Oh hang on, not for us.'

He had asked me about my afternoon and I'd given him a very very slimmed-down account. Not that he noticed. He was too full of excitement about his own findings.

'It seems there were several more discs made of other visions and given to close associates whom Dee respected and considered to be loyal.' Sam's face had lit up wonderfully. 'It was difficult to trace who received them. However, I started a list of close associates and then cross-referenced them to people with Essex connections.'

'Many female close associates?' I asked, wondering if one of them had strayed down here to become immortalised as Black Anne.

'Dee's first wife, Catherine, died in 1574,' he reeled off. 'That would have been before the Prague disc was made. His second wife whose name we don't know died two years later. Jane Fremond married him in 1578. They had three daughters, Catherine, Mary and Medinia, but it is probable that they all died with their mother of the bubonic plague epidemic in Manchester, 1604.'

'And no connections with Essex?'

'Not with them, but there are articles I need to comb and sections of John Dee's diary that I must read. I did note that in 1591 a William Aspland and Thomas Collinge of Essex visited Dee. Now, the interesting thing about that is that an Edmund Hunt had previously consulted with Thomas Collinge, who was strangely both the local constable *and* a cunning man.'

'A male witch?'

'More respected.'

'Of course.' Bloody sexist ancient Britain. Got on my nerves it did.

'Unusual though eh – policeman and witch?'

I was going to say something about Monty being an agent interested in our witch business, but he was off again before I could open my mouth.

'Guess what Hunt wanted?'

'Just tell me?'

'He had been approached by a good friend of his whose mind had been troubled by dreams which, he believed, were leading him to treasure.'

That caught my attention. 'Really?'

'Uh huh,' said Sam. 'And guess what his name was?'

'Go on, go on.'

Sam took a breath. 'Samuel Howlet.' He registered my gasp then went on. 'The second Lord of the Manor.'

'Well,' I said and tapped the steering wheel. 'I'll be blown over sideways by a coincidental gale.'

'Personally,' said Sam, 'I'm of the opinion that one of John Dee's associates may have been tasked with the mission. I'm not sure Dee would have done it himself even if he had been interested. This was only a few years after the St Osyth witch hunt and we both know what became of Ursula Cadence and Elizabeth Bennett. No, it would have been too risky. He had already been tainted by a prosecution against him for "conjuring".

It was illegal to find money or treasure through sorcery or witchcraft. After one brush with the law he surely would have preferred not to be seen to be publicly involved with treasure hunting and cunning men again.'

'But someone was,' I said. 'And more to the point – why did they give their equipment to Black Anne?'

'It's a fantastic puzzle.'

One of our phones started to vibrate. It was on silent. Probably not mine then. Sam reached into his bag and announced, 'Bronson'.

I told him to plug it into the speaker and he put it on.

'Samuel.' Bronson's deep throaty boom entered the car.

'And Rosie's here too,' I said.

'Right, well good. See, the thing is we've been over-run down here, me and Vanessa. There's all sorts coming into the village. Reckon it's the treasure what's got them so excitable, but we've had other types here, all come to see about the witch. You know, Black Anne.'

'That's great!' Sam said. 'What are the takings like?'

'Well, you see. The thing is they ain't been too happy we got nothing here about her.' I heard him swallow noisily.

Someone in the background, a woman, said, 'Tell them they'll need something up by tomorrow.'

'Vanessa,' Bronson went on, 'says we oughta have something in place by the end of the week. Or as soon as we can.' More mumbling away from the phone then, 'They bin complaining, see. "A witch museum," they says, "without the local witch in it."'

In the background Vanessa made a farty sound with her lips, I hoped it was her lips, then said something loud but inaudible which Bronson interpreted for us. 'One of them were a proper little madam and wanted a refund. Looked around the whole place first, mind.'

Sam was nodding silently. 'Yes. We see. We'll get onto it as soon as we can. On our way back now. Have you closed yet?'

I glanced at my watch. 5.30 p.m.

'Few buggers are dragging their heels in the Cadence wing, but once they've gone we'll shut up shop.'

'Good work Bronson,' I said. 'To both you and Vanessa. And don't worry too much, love – people complain about everything.'

I imagined him nodding. 'Vanessa is saying there's negative feedback on Facebook or something. Nasty stuff written about us.'

Sam sighed. 'Okay. I'll get on it when we get back.'

'I can deal with it, if you like,' I offered but he shook his head.

'Might be obnoxious. Has been recently.'

'No need to protect me. Serious. You want to try doing social media for Benefit Fraud.' I managed it for about three days before Twitter broke under the weight of bile. Then the main Comms team took over. Thank God. Michael, the current social media survivor in post, told me he could announce the second coming of Christ and he'd get swamped with demands for refunds on council tax.

'We'll see,' said Sam. 'But Bronson, re Black Anne, I'm planning to go to the archives tomorrow to see what I can find.'

'Oh right, well there's another thing too,' Bronson crackled. 'Nearly forgot.'

'What?' I said.

'There's trouble over at Bridgewaters'.'

I snorted. 'Isn't that a song by Simon and Garfunkel?'

Bronson and Sam ignored me.

'Young Terry Bridgewater,' the caretaker went on, 'has come in again. Says his dad has started getting his funny turns back. Can you go over and take a look Friday lunchtime? Vanessa says she can cover the till.'

'Funny turns?' I peeped at Sam, then switched my eyes back to the road.

'Oh yes,' he replied. 'He was having them a while back. Seeing things. I wondered if it might not be Charles Bonnet Syndrome.'

'Really?' I was surprised. We had come across this condition before. In fact it had reared its oddly wired head at La Fleur where I'd just dined with Monty. 'Go on.'

'But then it stopped so we all assumed it had resolved itself, and before I got to talk to them about Charles Bonnet, the old man had recovered. But obviously he was only in remission. We must go and see the Bridgewaters. You should come too. You know more about that condition than I do.'

I'd only had a fifteen-minute consultation with an ophthalmic consultant but I was flattered to be asked so agreed.

'Yes, Bronson,' Sam relayed. 'Tell them we'll come over and see them Friday morning.' He broke the connection and swivelled in his seat. 'I have to say this whole Blackly Be incident is becoming superlatively interesting.' Then as if apologising, 'As soon as we get back to the museum I'm going to go into deep research mode.'

'It's okay,' I said, feeling the burn of the folder. 'I intend to do some of my own.'

CHAPTER THIRTEEN

Witness accounts re disappearance of subject Ethel-Rose
Strange, née Romanov

Marital status: Married

Location: Village Hall, Adder's Fork, Essex.

Date: Thursday, 29th May, 1953

Extract One:

Eyewitness account 1*

Ernie Arburton, farm worker

* Arburton encountered subject in 1943 so is of interest re
Walker request outlined here.

'The first time I saw her, the Romanov girl, was back
in 1943. Some of her meetings had been put in the
paper. I wanted to know what all the fuss about. If she
was the real McCoy. Suppose I hoped she might be able
to get hold of Arthur [subject's son, missing in action].
It was in the *Standard* that she was doing an audience in
Litchenfield.

{irrelevant detail}

'When we [Arburton and his wife, Betty] got there we
could not believe our eyes: the place was packed to the

rafters. Word had got around, see, and there was a lot of folk grieving. All (of) us wanting hope. Wanting answers.

'She didn't look like no gypsy [sic] which the wife thought she might. (The) Girl, as she was then, was quite respectable. Polished you might say. Went straight to it when she come on stage. Made us all shut up and go quiet just by being there. She had quite a presence. Charisma you might call it. Then she says something about finding the dead, hearing them, tuning her wireless what is in her head to enter their frequency. And then she stills and quiet [sic]. Eyes open and she's off. Some bloke down the front wants his mother's will. She got the mother on the other end telling her where it is and she tells him and he says "Of course". So that all looks good, don't it? Tells another woman, there was more women than men of course, her husband loved her. Betty [subject's wife] puts her hand up to see if we can't find someone who knows where Arthur is, but this lady comes forward and pushes herself down to the front. Most tearful she was and dressed in black. Betty says something about us all losing people. It don't matter – the Romanov girl says she's tired and needs to rest but the woman says no. She needs to hear about her son, she says. Don't we all says some other Mrs near us. But Ethel-Rose sighs and says all right but this will be the last one, and she closes her eyes. And it's for a long time now and Betty goes, "She ain't dropped off has she, Ern?" And I do chuckle, but then its eyes open again and this time her eyes, they're as large as saucers. And she don't look good. White as a sheet and she swears she can hear a boy speak to her. No more than eighteen and lost in something she calls "the wild vortex". But he thinks he's bobbing over the sea. She says he is reporting for duty giving his name and squadron. And she says it and the mother screams and says, "Yes, yes, that's it." And that starts a bit of a racket in the crowd. And the Romanov girl says that there are others with him too, and they is pleading for help. And in whispers she tells us what they are saying. "We," she says, "are on Burnstow". Then all hell breaks loose. The woman in black screams loud and faints. A few of the audience go to her to help. The Romanov woman, she is still up there, whispering to people we can't see. And then we sees two men, in suits, looking Ministry and they get up on the stage and right there in front of us all they arrest Ethel-Rose and take her off.'

{irrelevant detail}

'Course, later we heard she was done for witchcraft. But Betty reckons she was a spy.'

{irrelevant detail}

'. . . which is why we came back to Adder's Fork. She's not a girl no more. Older now and I know I shouldn't speak unkind, but she looked it. Though my wife Betty was impressed by the way she was turned out. And I remember her dress, because it was so clean and bright. Not really what you'd think a medium might wear: white with pink roses. Betty said it was cut on the bias, so it hung well too.

'Started with some of the regular requests and was going good, until about half hour in, she screams and runs off stage. No, I don't know why. Maybe she saw something? A ghost probly . . .'

Extract Two:
Eyewitness account 2
Name withheld

'I first heard about the HMS Burnstow scandal. I know some people thought she had got the details from over the telephone because of her job at the telephone exchange but I don't. I believe that she had heard those poor souls. How else could she have known the ship had been torpedoed by a German U-boat? She can't. It was all tip-top. The government had hushed it up. I know it was for morale for the country. But there were over 500 lives lost and the families, well they should have been told. I thought what she did was right. Not everyone did, I know, but I did. I was glad they released her.

'I was there at Adder's Fork, the night she ran off. Me and my niece came down from Jaywick. They'd been caught up in the flood you see and June's neighbour had drowned in her bed. It'd upset June. We thought we might try and see if she'd left valuables. Hidden them somewhere. She was old like that [sic].

'There was a lot of people there. Outside the hall, they had agitators. {Question inserted by operative for clarity} Yes, from the church and such. They didn't like what Mrs Strange was up to. Could have done it quieter, if you ask me. But what do I know? {Interruption from operative} Inside? Yes lots. The hall was full. The older woman comes on stage, the foreigner. The aunt. With the accent. Something funny going on with her. I reckon she knew more than she let on. Stayed quiet when they were looking for Mrs Strange. {Interruption} All right, so she introduces her niece. And there's another woman sitting at the back. The mother I think. She don't say nothing though. Just sits. Stony-faced. Then Ethel-Rose gets going.

'She went to a woman with red hair first. Says her name is Sheila. Seemed to know about her. Someone was there with a message. There's a key in the best teapot. It opens the chest in the loft. A lot of detail. There was an old man down the front, dressed shabby. And she tells him "John, I forgive you". And I remember that one because he sits there and he starts bawling and the man next to him, who was a stranger, he patted him and offered him a handkerchief. She did some others, two women I think. She sang a song, I recall. Or part of it. And I think it was when she was singing that, that all them folks that had been shouting outside, I think it was then, some of them got in, burst into the room. They was hollering and clamouring and making a racket. Ethel-Rose, she breaks off. Starts with the stuttering. We thought she was going to go on, but with all the malarkey she goes white. Her eyes go wide. Someone from the outside crowd comes out with the idea she'd lost her wits. More joins in and starts to heckle. Don't know if they were from outside. Now she has gone as pale as a ghost, if you pardon the language. Then she looks at the crowd. Some bloke shouts out "Charlatan". Ethel-Rose comes over all queer. Then she screams and the aunt and the mother go to her. Then the next thing I know she's gone.

'People got up and started giving it the screaming ab-dabs. Some of the audience are having a go at the interrupters, is what I'll call them. There's a scuffle halfway up the hall. Then out of the blue, the police comes in. I don't know where they come from. Hadn't seen them before. There's others too, in suits, councillors I thought or officials. They start wading in. On the stage the mum and the aunt are trying to calm people down. Someone shouted "fire" and that's when it turns into bedlam. Me and June, we'd been to the hall before, for a ruby wedding, so we knew there was doors either side of the stage. We went for them.

'Outside it was just as much of a madhouse. We made a quick exit up to the pub. Then we waited for my husband to come. It was an odd sort of night. Didn't know no one would ever see her again.'

Extract Three:
Operative 1
Name withheld
'Myself and (Operative Two) arrived at the Adder's Fork Hall at approximately 1800 hours on the date in question. The proceedings started promptly at 18.30 and the audience was orderly. Intelligence sources suggested that many had come from the local area and further parts of the county though a large contingent were from the village itself.

'There was flux during the meeting with people coming and going. A few audience members, with whom the subject had spoken, became distressed and were escorted outside. At which point others, who had been waiting, entered. Throughout the meeting most seats were filled, with a dozen or so people standing at the back of the hall, myself and (Operative Two) included.

'The subject gave approximately six readings to:

Mrs Sheila Danton relating the location of a lost key. [Confirmed]

John Eldridge. Message: "I forgive you." [Confirmed]

Unknown audience member. Subject stated: "I have always loved you, oh Danny boy." Gave voice to an extract from the popular song 'Oh Danny Boy'. [Unable to ascertain accuracy]

Norah Shillingford. Message: "Mother, take heart." [Unconfirmed]

A message that was unclaimed: "Mr Graves never got me that raise. He didn't, no he didn't." [Unconfirmed]

No claimant: Message: "So cold here, Stanley, so cold." [Unconfirmed]

'It was during the last "reading" that a number of protestors from the local church forced their way into the hall. The local constabulary had been alerted to the numbers in attendance and had sent three of their officers to manage the event and keep the peace. However, at this point, as mentioned previously, there was some movement amongst audience members which enabled the protestors to overwhelm the officers and enter the hall.

'Altercations took place between members of the audience and the newcomers and a fight broke out. Myself and (Operative Two) felt that it was our duty to assist in keeping the peace and we entered the affray with this intention.

'The local officers were able to enter the building approximately five minutes later. Disorder had broken out. An unidentified member of the public alerted us to a fire in progress [later established to be a false alarm]. At this point it became imperative to switch objectives and evacuate the hall as quickly and speedily as possible.

'I cannot state with any accuracy the time at which the subject left the stage. I would approximate it to be 19.15 hours. Though we were able to ascertain the presence of Anne Romanov and Rozalie Romanov, located in some distress outside the front entrance of the Village Hall, the subject was not present. We concluded that she had returned to her home in Hollypot Lane.

'The following day we were made aware of her absence.

'As a result of enquiries made, in the days after the event, our primary conclusions were that the subject had fled the family. Although there was some speculation that the husband of the subject may have caused the subject's death by foul play, he was found to have a watertight alibi in Hertfordshire for the night in question and the following day.

'After preliminary instructions to investigate, no further action was taken.'

Extract Four:
Anne Romanov
Mother of target

'It seemed to be going well. My daughter had given several readings. All successful, it appeared. It was when those parishioners wormed their way in that everything fell apart. Yes. They were like worms. Snakes in the grass.'

{Question from Operative Two}

'No. I was not aware of what Ethel-Rose was doing. My daughter was facing the audience. She had her back to me.'

{Question from Operative Two}

'Yes. When the fight broke out I saw her falter. That's when I went to her. Rozalie was beside me. She had seen that my daughter was upset.

'Ethel-Rose's face was aghast. I put my hands on her shoulders and I asked her what was wrong. She did not speak at first so I shook her.

'Then she began to move her lips. Oh yes. Her words will stay with me forever because they were exactly what I had come for, the reason why I had made her do this. She stared at me and said, "Father". Then she gasped and shuddered, like she could see something terrible, and then Rozalie took her in her arms.

'I asked her what Fred, her father, my late husband, had said but I could not hear her response. Ethel-Rose brought herself under control and then suddenly she left the stage.'

{Question from Operative Two}

'No, I didn't. I thought I should try and calm people down. I felt a responsibility for the disruption. Though God knows why.

'We expected to find my daughter at the home she shares with her husband and my sister-in-law, but when we arrived later she was nowhere to be found. Mrs Overall, who was minding the children, said she hadn't come back. We thought she might have gone for a walk. But she never came back. The next day we alerted the police. Ethel-Rose has never been without the children for a night. That is how we knew something had gone wrong.'

Extract Five:
Rozalie Romanov
Aunt of target

'. . . the poor love was all aquiver. She had heard many things. She had heard the voices from those poor souls, the lost ones over other side of the veil. However, my niece has reached out to the like many times. She was accustomed to the cries, the cold, the fear. But her face – this time it was as pale as a shell. I knew there was something else that distressed her so.'

{Question from Operative One}

'Yes. On the stage. When she turned from Anne. I thought she had heard something that had shocked her. The eyes, they were like glass. And she could hardly breathe. Fear had frozen her.'

{Question from Operative One}

'Yes, of course I did. When she was able to find her words she said, "Yorinda is here". But I don't think she understood what she was saying. Something passed over her eyes and she cried out, "Maenda, Maenda!" And that's when she went rigid in my arms. Then a moment later she had run off.'

{Question from Operative One}

'As clearly as I can hear you now.

'That was it. We never saw her again. Some harm has come to the child. Great harm. You should not be here pestering us. You should look for her. Out there. In the darkness.'

Extract Six:
Roger Winsome
Parish vicar, Adder's Fork

'Because it is said "There shall not be found among you anyone who uses divination, one who practices witchcraft, or one who interprets omens, or a sorcerer, or one who casts a spell, or a medium, or a spiritist, or one who calls up the dead. For whoever does these things is detestable to the LORD; and because of these detestable things the LORD your God will drive them out before you." There was no choice. Human souls were in peril.

'We had the right to peaceful assembly to give voice to our own expression.'

{Question from Operative Two}

'It was at first. Very. Only when one of my parishioners entered the hall, something I had not advised, the peace was disrupted. Nor, I might add, did he throw the first punch. He is not a man of fire. I can vouch for him. Look to the spiritists for that – they invoke demonic forces. Who knows what depravation coils and uncoils in their bellies? That's why she's gone, you must understand. He's taken her. Oh yes, the Lord will not let her live: "And with the breath of his lips he will smite the wicked." Isaiah, chapter eleven, verse four.'

{Question from Operative Two}

'No. We remained outside all evening. By the front of the hall. I did not see Mrs Strange, the occultist, leave the hall. None of us did. By my reckoning she was taken somewhere low, for the Devil was in her league and the Devil was there that night.'

{Question from Operative Two}

'Because my daughter, Audrey, saw him. She came to us once order had been restored shrieking and declaring she had seen him. "Devil, the devil was over there," she said. She saw him, lurking in the shadows of Mab Wood in amongst the trees. For sure the Strange woman has been taken down low. She has provoked the Lord to anger and he has smited her so.'

CHAPTER FOURTEEN

There are ghosts around us everywhere. In the twinkling sky, the light of long-dead stars still form our constellations and guide us over oceans. In the photographs and images that adorn our sideboards and walls. In the music we hear on the radio, the celluloid figures that haunt the silver screen, the smaller one in the corner of our living rooms, and the ones that we trail our fingers across daily. Ghosts of the departed live in the memories we have and the memories that we create.

Life in fact is shared with the dead. It is a natural state of being.

Or so I was thinking as I surfaced into consciousness the following day. Immersion in the world of the report had been almost instant and intense, as if I had willingly entered an altered state in which I had experienced direct contact with the past.

I certainly felt, in some way, that I had *seen* it.

For now, I could effortlessly picture Ethel-Rose on stage: the details of her summer dress – white with pink roses swishing diagonally across the weave, the way she moved, almost sashayed, across the stage, a hangover from her finishing-school days. She was compelling, magnetic, full of allure. A rose, a swan, a rare exotic beauty born of diverse cultures, carried aloft, celebrated and then magicked from this tiny English village.

No wonder so many came to see her. Their voices in the hall would have been excited, the atmosphere alive with electricity and tension, and then of course cries of dismay. The image of the pale woman stock still, clutching her throat, eyes wide open, was vivid, alive inside my mind. Had she seen someone? What else had she heard?

I almost thought that if I held that image there, and sent my mind over the heads of the audience, across the parquet floor, up onto the wooden stage, buried myself in the glossy black head, then I might find out what was going on there. But I could get no further than the look of complete and total shock on her face, her staggering movements, now ungraceful and clunky, her lips murmuring to Anne Romanov – 'Father' – then clutching her Aunt Rozalie, before she fled stage left, melting out of view.

What had happened?

I wanted to know.

I would find out.

It was in my nature to do so.

I was very grateful to Monty for the file. The witness statements gave me an interesting perspective. Even if they were abridged. I felt like now I could at least grasp the chronology of events that occurred in Adder's Fork on the evening of 29th May, 1953.

My head was still thrumming with questions.

Primarily, who were Yorinda and Maenda?

Because of the alien character of the names, initially I wondered if they might be relations of Rozalie. But she surely would have mentioned it in her witness statement?

So then had Ethel-Rose seen these people? And if so, why had they shocked her so much?

Had they threatened her?

Or were they red herrings with no relevance?

Words dropped by gabbling 'spirits'? And had she truly heard them or was this some form of schizophrenia? Was mental illness an issue here? I didn't want to consider that at the moment though.

It looked to me like the names had also caught the attention of the investigators. I suspected that the police might have made further inquiries though there was nothing in the report to evidence that. Did that mean the names were irrelevant? Or had the investigation been shut down?

So many questions.

What I really needed to do was try and find people who were in the village in 1953. Maybe they could help fill in some of the blanks. I knew some of them were still around.

Before I got out of bed I flicked through the report again. One name I had assumed would be there but wasn't was that of Edward de Vere. He had said he'd known Ethel-Rose back in the day. Maybe he might shed some light on who Yorinda and Maenda were? And possibly also on my grandmother's mental state.

I decided to see if Sam could run the museum so I could pay a visit to Howlet Manor, but when I went downstairs to the office Bronson told me he had already left for the Chelmsford archives. I was slightly miffed that he hadn't bothered to let me know. Though I wasn't, and didn't desire to be, his keeper. At the same time, I had too much restless energy to sit on the till myself so I called Vanessa to see if she could come into work for a few days.

When she rocked up for work Vanessa was animated, bursting with gossip and news to unload.

'Oh Rosie,' she said as she perched her bum on the high seat behind the till. 'It's all kicking off.'

I was so preoccupied that for a moment I thought she was talking about the séance/meeting with Ethel-Rose.

'Blimey,' I said. 'How do you know? Are you a mind reader or something?'

She grinned, exposing her gappy teeth. 'Everyone's talking about it.'

I knew word travelled fast in these parts but I was startled to hear that my research into my grandmother had grabbed the attention of the Adder's Fork tweetathon.

'Bob Acton's chickens got out last night.'

'Oh, right,' I sighed, relieved that the focus wasn't on Ethel-Rose and yet simultaneously rather shocked that this kind of event drew such attention. But then again it was t'country, and all that. Not much happened round here.

Correction: not much happened round here until now.

'And Philip Monk's and Cherry Seaton's,' Vanessa went on, tossing her ponytail about and making her eyes big 'All of them. Probably at the same time, they reckon. They were all locked up proper. But you know what this means, don'tcha?'

'No midweek roast?'

She tutted and rolled her eyes. 'No, silly. It's happening again. Just like it did in '44.'

It took a moment for me to remember the relevance of the year, then all the stuff about the Blackly Be came tumbling back. I'd almost forgotten about it for the last 24 hours what with everything else.

'Well, I'm sure there's a good explanation for it,' I said. 'Probably it's a coincidence. Possibly kids up to mischief?' and I creased up my brow and gave her one of my 'sceptical' looks.

She shook her head and pulled a blue scrunchy out of her hair, unloosing her long blonde locks. 'Some of the kids are saying they've seen a woman. A ghost. White and flowing. Or black and still. In the churchyard, outside The Stars and down the High Road. One of the paper boys said they saw a ghost walking around in the Cannibal House. And that's derelict. Freaked him out. Now they're all refusing to go to school.'

'Hah!' I said, grinning. 'I've heard worse.' And I had. 'Don't reckon Ofsted will accept those excuses to authorise their absence.'

'Yeah, but it's true.' Vanessa seemed like she was trying to persuade me. 'Honest. Granddad's seen it too.'

I sought clarification on this one. 'What, that old bloke from the pub?'

'Yes, said he was out last night. Fell asleep on one of the benches outside The Stars and he sees this figure gliding down the road, like she was rolling. But no feet. Everything was freezing and there was this wailing and a moaning.'

'Mmmm.' I doubted Granddad could see past his pint glass, let alone an ethereal being drifting diaphanously many metres away. Especially after a night at the pub.

'It's the witch,' Vanessa said. 'She's back. Everyone reckons it's so. Now her stone's been moved and her grave's been deconsecrated. She's back like she was in '44.'

'Her grave,' I said firmly, 'was never consecrated in the first place was it?'

Vanessa gave me her confused face. 'Eh?'

'She wasn't buried on sacred ground.'

'Whatever. Yeah right.' Then she sniffed. 'But all this stuff is good for the museum though ain't it?'

On that I had to agree. But I didn't say anything, just went and propped open the front door with a brick. Yep, it was all high tech at the Witch Museum.

'So make sure you get that panel on Black Anne done fast,' she called after me.

'We're on it,' I called back. 'Sam's in Chelmsford looking at the archives. Should have something by tomorrow.'

'Great,' she said. 'Cos they ain't 'alf got it in for you on Facebook.'

I did think about going back and taking a good look at what the virtual idiots were saying but to be honest, I'd already decided to see de Vere and I knew myself well enough to understand if I opened that particular can of worms I might get sucked in and then go off, in all likelihood, in a rather explosive manner. Facebook and Twitter could wait.

'And folks are asking too,' Vanessa called after me. 'About you.'

I stopped before the door and turned back. 'What about me?'

'You and Sam,' she said.

I waited. A blush crept into my cheeks.

'Well, you're the experts, aren't you? They're wanting to know what you're going to do about all this?'

'Vanessa,' I said, relieved they weren't asking about other things. 'It's not our problem. We just run a museum.'

'They'll be coming for you,' she said with a cheeky grin. 'Mark my words.'

I rolled my eyes and said, 'Blimey you sound as mental as Bob Acton, you blimmin' yokels,' then ducked as a carefully aimed pen hit the door just above my head. 'That could almost be classified as assault. I'm sure it's a sackable offence.'

Outside I had a good look for Audrey Winsome. Her father's comments about her seeing the Devil were quite nut-nut, which was really no surprise, but I thought she was definitely worth talking to. However, it was Wednesday, which meant she'd be at her flower-arranging class. Which wasn't a problem. Audrey Winsome would undoubtedly be back on duty tomorrow.

The sky that day was white-grey. Low grey blankets of clouds hung over the horizon. Some of them looked like they might contain rain. However, this hadn't put off the tourists, who were out and about all over the place. As I crossed Snakehouse Rise and Hollypot Lane into the High Road I spied a few by the bus stop. They had obviously just arrived on one of the three daily buses that passed through the village, as they had an old paper map out, which they were (oddly) illuminating with a phone torch.

Over on the playing fields, there were a couple of treasure hunters getting in the way of the local mum and toddler group who were trying to organise some nursery games.

A few older pre-school kids were playing on the swings and roundabouts in the playground, sandwiched between the bus stop and the playing fields that led into Mab Wood. I was watching one kid spinning another a bit too fast when – whack – something fell straight on the ground right in front of me.

It was fairly heavy, and I was confused when I looked down to find a mess of feathers, claws and a beak. It took me more time than usual to work out what it was. Primarily because it moved jerkily then just stopped. And it wasn't the kind of thing you expected to drop out of the sky. Usually they were flying about in it. For as I bent over it I saw it was some kind of bird. Or had been at some point. Now it was really just a muddle of black, grey and pinky reds. It had hit the floor with such impact its skin had split and now grey, glistening guts spilled out from the underside of its body.

I wasn't really sure what to do – whether to leave it there or move it to the side of the road – and I was looking around for someone who might know about these things when I heard a cry go up from the playground.

The roundabout was still spinning, but it was empty, creaking on its own rusty hinges. A couple of the mums were picking up one of the boys who had been holding on to it. He was crying now. The other kid kicked something away. I saw a bunch of little leaf-type things fly up into the air then realised they were feathers.

Bang!

A few metres up the road, where the tarmac met the kerb, another bird splatted on the ground.

Up above me I heard wild, startled trilling. High-pitched avian cries. The flurry of flapping wings.

Bosh. A big one fell onto the bus-stop roof. The detectorists inside jumped. There were expletives.

Seeing this from the playing field, the mum and toddler group, who had been running towards the bus shelter, paused, made a quick recalculation, decided it was their best option and ran for it anyway.

We were all pretty exposed out here. I was beginning to feel my vulnerability too and abandoned the dead bird in favour of joining the squeeze in the bus shelter when – smack – another one landed just feet away from me.

'Shit!' I said, then heard the noise of a car pulling up alongside me.

'Quick, get in,' shouted a voice from within.

It was Florian in a classic MG, which I thought seemed a little at odds with his eco-credentials. But right then was perhaps not the time to raise the issue. As I legged it towards the open door on the passenger side, the speed at which the birds were dropping went into warp-drive.

I swung into the car, as one hit the roof. 'Florian! Dear God! What the hell's going on?'

He gestured for me to put the seatbelt on. 'Fucked if I know.' Then we began pulling out very very slowly. 'Never seen anything like this before. Have you?'

I shook my head.

'It's biblical. Like the end of times,' he said and grinned.

'Oh God, don't you cross over to the dark side,' I said. 'There's got to be a logical explanation. Poison gas or something?'

'I don't know,' he said. 'Why would it only affect the birds? I've been running today, taking down big lungfuls of air. I think I'm okay. You've been out there. How you feeling?'

I stared at the feathery splodges on the road ahead. 'Like I'm hallucinating,' I told him. We were passing the bus shelter which was crammed with concerned adults and crying children. I had an urge to get out and try to help, but there was really nothing I could do.

'Fuck!' said Florian and a split second later a large bird careered into the windscreen, cracking it, but luckily not shattering it through.

He slammed his feet on the brakes and we shuddered to a halt. Thank God, we hadn't been going that fast.

My companion began to open his door.

'What are you doing?' I asked in horror.

'Look,' he said and pointed up ahead.

I stared past the seeping mess of blood and feathers on the windscreen and saw, in the middle of the road, the man called Granddad. He was standing there with his crutch raised to the sky screaming something I couldn't hear.

'He's going to get pummelled,' Florian was saying and jumped out.

I hadn't expected him to be so gallant and watched from the safety of the passenger seat as the eco-writer scooped his arm around Granddad, then with some effort lifted him up, over his shoulder and carried him back to the car.

I reached over and unlocked the door and Florian laid Granddad on the tiny back seat.

'Shit! Granddad, you're bleeding.' I pointed at his head then said to Florian. 'He needs medical attention, right away.'

He pulled the seat down and flew in, 'Doctors?'

I pointed up Snakehouse Rise. 'Dr Patel's surgery is halfway up on the left.'

Another two thuds landed on the roof of the car.

Granddad whinnied like a horse, then opened wide the toothless hole of his mouth. 'The Bridgewaters said summat was up,' he wailed. 'Then they tried to roll away the stone. I don't know, I don't know. What's it all coming to? This, that's what.'

I reached round and tried to reassure him. 'It's probably something meteorological.'

'You,' he said at a lower pitch. His eyes were rheumy and red. 'You're to do it,' and then he uncurled a thin gnarly finger and pointed it at me.

'Me?' I thumbed myself. 'I haven't done anything.'

'No,' he said, and started to speak, but another black thing hit the back windscreen. And this time the glass began to crack.

'We're out of here,' said Florian and pushed his foot down on the accelerator. With a lurch the car sped forwards. Florian twisted the wheel. The tyres screeched. 'Let's hope it's localised.' Then we powered towards Snakehouse Rise.

CHAPTER FIFTEEN

There was a lot of commotion at the GPs. Many faces at the waiting-room window.

When we walked in with Granddad there were no protests. Everyone stepped aside so we could speak to the receptionist and almost immediately the old boy was ushered through to the doctor. His name, we learnt, was not in fact Granddad, but Reed Williams, which was quite distinctive really. I wondered when he developed the wrinkly nickname. Maybe he had always had it.

Florian and I went and sat on the plastic seats and did a few minutes of sighing and head shaking.

'I don't know what to make of it,' said Florian after a while.

An older woman, in a pastel-pink anorak who was sitting in the row of chairs behind us, piped up, 'It's the Blackly Be. They shouldn't have moved it. Now we're going to get the same chaos as what happened last time. The place is going to hell in a handcart.'

Heaving myself round I got hold of her gaze and said very measuredly, 'Things like this often have a logical explanation. How can it be anything to do with a stone?'

'And a skeleton,' she said stiffly and crossed her arms. 'Don't forget the witch.'

'I won't,' I said and swallowed hard. 'Thank you.'

She pinched her mouth in tight then said stonily. 'That's right. You should know – we're all looking to you.' Her nostrils began to flare as she spoke, becoming increasingly more aerated. 'That's your lot innit? What you going to do about it? You, up at the Witch Museum?'

I scrunched my face up and shrugged to diffuse the tension and went, 'Meh?' like I didn't know what she meant, but I was starting to feel like people were pointing at us. Metaphorically. No one in the waiting room had their fingers out, to be fair, but the collective focus was beginning to burn a hole in my back. Or front.

'You're there for a reason,' Pink Anorak went on with barely concealed anger. 'Now it's time for you to step up. Like your grandfather has done in times gone by.'

I was keen to ask what exactly she meant by that, but at the same time I thought that if I engaged her, she might pull me in and club me to death or something.

'These birds,' she went on. 'Well, they're an omen of ill portent. That's what your grandfather and the ghost hunter worked out back then when it first happened. He weren't living here then although he visited the village while he was courting your grandmother. Septimus Strange saw what happened with the Blackly Be and he and Mr Price they got it left alone.'

I wasn't sure what to do or say to that.

It didn't matter because Pink Anorak was going full steam ahead anyway. 'The birds are just a warning. There's worse on its way. Much worse. She'll be wanting a life for a life. You watch.'

Before I could catch my breath Florian joined in. 'They were different species, did you notice? That should certainly be taken into account. The one that hit the windscreen was brown like a starling. Though the one that came through the back was heavier like a wood pigeon.'

I nodded at him, eager to move away from the conversation with mad anorak lady. 'Yeah, I think it was a blackbird that came down in front of me. What would cause them all to drop at once?'

Florian stroked his chin. 'A loud noise? Maybe they hit power lines?'

'Witchcraft,' said the woman behind us and pouted accusingly. 'You have to sort it out. It's your duty.'

A man in his sixties with a broken arm was standing sentry over by the window. 'At least it seems to be stopping now,' he said. 'But for the love of God, will you look at them?'

It sounded like a request, so Florian and I went and stood next to him. I was pleased to get away from Anorak's piercing glare.

The three of us stared out over the Rise. It was eerily deserted. No cars or people. Just lots of little feathered bodies all over the tarmac.

'It looked like they were flying into the ground,' said the man with the cast on his arm.

There were fewer bodies up here than there were in the High Road but nevertheless the view of all those bird corpses littering the street was unsettling to say the least. But he was right, it had stopped. For now. Thank God.

'What are you going to do?' I asked Florian and nodded at the doctor's door. 'About Granddad?'

'I'll wait here and make sure Mr Williams is okay. If he's not, I'll take him to hospital or home. Whichever is preferred.'

Maybe Florian wasn't such a bad guy after all, I thought, and offered to keep him company. He declined and asked me where I had been going.

'I want to see Edward de Vere at the Manor.'

'Oh,' said the woman in the anorak, ear-wigging our conversation. 'Best take the shortcut through Mab Wood. There'll be less birds and it's quicker.'

'Okay, thanks,' I tendered, not convinced. 'Where's the shortcut start?'

'Take a right out of here. Go to the Village Hall. Don't go in, but walk round the side and you'll see the path leading into the trees.'

It certainly sounded better than going back through the High Road, complete with bird cadavers and all.

'Thanks,' I said. 'I will.'

Florian gave me his number. I programmed it in to my phone then called it so he had mine and said, 'Give me a ring and let me know how you get on.'

As the door behind me was just about to shut, I heard the anorak woman call, 'And don't stray off the path. People can get lost in that wood. Have done here for a very long time.'

There was a woman with an apron on outside the Village Hall. She stopped sweeping up the birds when I approached and leant on her broom. We had a chat, like you do with a total stranger after something dreadful has happened like a terrorist attack or serial murder, or a bunch of birds freakily dropping dead at the same time. Our voices were high and over-animated: we were both nervous. I asked her if I could have a look round the hall on the pretext of booking it for a party and she told me to go right in.

I was glad for the change of scene.

This was where my grandmother had last been. And it was so old-fashioned I thought it probably hadn't changed since she'd melted into the night. Apart from a small extension towards the front of the hall which housed a kitchen. This was quite modern and came with a host of white goods. I had a nose around and found cupboards full of floral cups and saucers and lots of glasses and cheap white plates. Everything was well used – the village hall was a popular place then. But the main hall, looked pretty ancient. At the end was a stage which was built into the structure. Quite high, with blue velvet curtains on either side.

Making sure no one else was around I nipped behind one of the curtains stage right and hung about in the wings. There was a door at the side. I tried it but it was locked. I followed round the edge of the stage, wondering if there was a 'backstage' area or green room, but there wasn't. Over on stage left however there was another door just like the first one. Also locked. These were probably where the props and sound equipment came through. If there was no backstage then this was also likely to be where the actors came on for theatrical productions. And clairaudients for theirs.

I climbed onto the raised platform and tried to visualise what Ethel-Rose might have seen the night she died. It wasn't a big room really so she would have had a good view of everyone in the hall.

Who I wondered again were Yorinda and Maenda? Had they been in here that night? What made her mention them? Why had they scared her so?

I was thinking about this when the woman with the broom appeared in the entrance. At first I thought she might tell me off so gave her a super bright smile and jumped from the stage. Then I asked her if she could direct me to the path for Mab Wood. She pursed her lips, told me to be careful, then instructed me to go back to the High Road and avoid the woodlands. 'The birds,' she said, by way of explanation.

But when I left I ignored her instructions for I had noticed a well-worn desire line that led down the side of the hall towards the wood. Probably the one that Pink Anorak suggested. Desire lines are, so my dad tells me, footpaths created by human or animal footfall. Usually they are the shortest way to get from A to B although sometimes they can meander around pretty sights. There were loads all over Dad's allotment.

As I passed the new kitchen extension I clocked the stage door a little further back. Another desire path wriggled out of it and curved into the thicket up ahead. I slanted across the flat grassy common. There were a couple more bird corpses here but nowhere near as many as had been on the High

Road and up at Snakehouse Rise. Which didn't really make sense if you considered how few trees and, therefore, roosts there were back there and how many more would be in the opaque woodland up ahead. But then again, the whole thing was, I think we would all agree, extremely irregular.

Soon I crossed into the shadows of the trees. This was no coppice, but a forest of mass and darkness, an unkempt riot of nature, something more wolfish than domestic and tame.

Around me were mounds of bracken, nettles, tawny rocks, ferns sprouting from twisting tree roots. Some of the trunks had fallen and been co-opted into homes for birds or badgers or other unknown beasts. I could smell an earthy dampness in the place and hear the rustling of unseen creatures in the foliage around me.

I followed the track, which led me deeper into the glimmering darkness hanging thickly about the tree trunks. It seemed that although the light was dimming, the rooty colours – the palette of the woods itself – were intensifying. A strange trick of the light no doubt, for it was summer and the trees were in full leaf, stretching their arms to each other, forming a tight green canopy, blocking out the rest of the real world. And actually, I think because of the difference, the contrast in the mossy spectrum of this ancient woodland spot which was not an everyday place, my mind began to stretch and range and I found myself recalling stories from childhood of woodmen and woods, Hansel and Gretel, their weakling dad, evil stepmother and the gingerbread house where the nasty witch lived. I wondered what poor old woman, cast out of society and forced to live on her own in the wild forest, had formed the basis for that particular fairy-tale baddie.

The path curved north-east and I was going to take out my notebook and record a memo to ask Sam about it, when a noise from the bush on my left stopped me. Well, it didn't stop me, but it did make me turn and look.

It had been high-pitched and wiggly. Like something, halfway between human and animal, had giggled. There was however not *a* bush, but lots of bushes, spreading backwards. It could have come from half a dozen shrubs: none of them were still.

But animals didn't laugh, did they? No they didn't. I told myself off for anthropomorphising. That means human-ising animals to you and me. Attributing human traits and emotions to them. We do it all the time. Sam told me about it when we were discussing recent Yeti phenomena. I know – my life, right?

It must have been a furry woodland thing that had been disturbed by my approach. After all, although I wasn't being noisy, neither was I treading a silent path.

Nevertheless as I continued onwards I kept alert and presently thought I saw, out of the corner of my eye, tiny black shadows, flitting between the trunks, keeping pace with me. But when I looked of course there was nothing there.

I marched on.

Up ahead to the north of the path, I could see a patch in the trees where it was brighter. It appeared that there had been a break in the leaden sky: sun was shining down into a lush ferny glade. It looked like an unlikely oasis of calm and light here in the dark wood, and as I got closer my curiosity got the better of me. For there was something infinitesimally alluring about the succulent and verdant golds, spring onion greens and dazzling light bouncing around the little glen. Shiny sunbeams flashed over the trunks and a large dreamy willow cascaded into what I could see now was a smallish pool of water. A luminescence coming off it lit the undersides of the surrounding branches and leaves so they looked strangely silver. Somewhere to the east I could hear the tinkling waterfall of a stream freshening the pond.

It was quite quite idyllic and against my better instincts I stopped for a moment to take in the beauty of the scene. As I did however I was overcome with a penetrating desire that hurt, almost like a physical ache, to visit the sparkling dell.

I absolutely *had* to see what was there.

But I shouldn't. I was going to the Manor and I'd been warned to stay on the path.

That was the right thing to do I supposed. I continued on my way.

Although within seconds I was consumed by a feeling of unjust deprivation: why should I have to stick to the path? Did the receptionist who instructed me to do so just want to keep that little oasis a secret for herself? Wasn't fair was it? I had just as much right to see it as anyone else.

I peeled off, hungry for a glimpse of the pool. In fact the only thing that would be able to sate this sudden craving was first-hand experience of the glade itself.

Climbing over the bracken, I stumbled across tree roots, ignoring the scrapes and knocks. As I finally reached the glen

I saw instantly what a joy it was – wide rays of sunshine were bearing down between a gap in the leafy canopy onto the calm surface of a pool.

Embraced by a necklace of vines and mossy boulders, a light covering of lime-coloured algae gave half of it an incandescent sheen. Pink foxgloves grew close to the water's edge, sprouting from within twisting roots. Little clusters of mushrooms danced across grassy ledges that were also fringed with purple pyramid-shaped flowers that might have been orchids. I spied a large grey rock jutting out over the pool and made my way to it.

The sun had warmed the stone surface and as I climbed onto the ledge I caught myself wondering if I had ever seen such a beautiful place before?

The seduction of the sun, the glittering of the water, the gentle trickle of the little waterfall combined to relax me and a sense of peace pervaded my whole being.

How lovely indeed.

It was in this rather delicious state that a little internal voice told me I was feeling very sleepy, and suddenly lying down on the ledge seemed like the best idea in the world.

'A five-minute nap won't make any difference,' I thought to myself and stretched my spine along the fluffy carpet of moss on the rock. 'Imagine if I could lie here forever, away from the noise and the stress of life,' I reflected. 'Here in this sylvan grove. Forever.' And my eyes closed. The darkness beyond them was warm and honeyish, coaxing me into a long and soft—

Someone coughed.

I dragged my eyelids open and up, reluctant to come back to the world.

The spluttering came again. It was male.

Now I sprang up like a Jack In a Box.

Who the hell else was here?

Quickly I surveyed the pool, forcing off the snug blanket of sleep. There were bubbles on the surface of the pool. Were they from the waterfall or had they always been there? As I watched, a pearl of moisture licked up from the mist that shimmered on the pond's surface and began to float into the air until it got to head height and popped.

How odd, I thought, then realised that beyond the space where the bubble had been, across the pond, there was someone else, sitting a little way back, on another cluster of rocks. It was hard to see that far with clarity, but as I squinted I thought the figure was likely to be that of the coughing man. Although madly, it looked like he had a pair of horns growing from his forehead. Or were they massive ears? Like a rabbit's? Maybe it was a centaur, I thought randomly. Then shook my head at my silly self. That Witch Museum was permeating my thought patterns again. Enlivening me to myth and fancy.

Get a grip, Strange.

I rubbed my eyes and peered over again.

All that I could make out, for sure, was that the bloke didn't have a shirt on. And, if my olfactory senses were correct, he was smoking weed.

I blinked.

The figure was waving at me.

What was I meant to do now?

I wondered if I should call out, say hello? Maybe ask them who they were?

In the end I simply waved back.

He looked like he was happily minding his own business, which suited me. So, I tried to lie back down, to re-enter the beautiful reverie I had been enjoying. I had so liked it there.

But it was no good.

I kept looking up and over and checking on the bloke, aware that situations like this had the potential to turn nasty. Not all, of course, but a lone woman, without pepper spray, in the middle of the wood was pretty much dependant on the male company to behave themselves.

It was always a risk.

In the end I sighed and rolled off my lovely ledge.

There was no relaxing to be had now I knew Coughing Man was there.

So instead of lounging on my stone lily pad, I set about tramping my way round to the other side of the pond. Probably best to say hello and determine whether aforesaid bloke was a potential attacker. Mind you most of them didn't have 'rapist' tattooed on their foreheads.

As I got within a couple of metres of the man I recognised from his build it was Elvin. He was sitting there half naked, his feet dangling in the pool. And he was definitely smoking a joint. At this proximity, I could see he had a very hairy chest and arms. But no horns. Though his curly mop had been roughly pushed back from his eyes and was held in place by a plastic Alice band. Some of the tufts had remained erect and, viewed from my position over the other side of the pool, may well have accounted for my impression of bunny ears or horns.

'You shouldn't sit there alone,' said Elvin and offered me the cigarette.

I declined, 'Why not?'

'You might doze off, roll in and drown.'

I sniffed and laughed, forgetting that I had recently been snoozing. 'Hardly.'

'Ah, Ms Strange,' he said, with a smile in his voice. 'But this isn't just any old pond is it? This is the Sitting Pool. You must have heard the stories?'

I couldn't tell if he was joking. 'No?' Then I sat down on a nearby boulder. It was in the shade and not as warm on the bottom as my last lovely perch. But it was pleasant enough and would do.

'Site of legend, the Sitting Pool is allegedly the meeting place of witches and fairies,' said Elvin and blew out a plume of pungent vegetably-smelling smoke. 'They say a fiddler once came here to entertain. He sang and played and sat with them all night. In the morning when he went back home he found a hundred years had passed.'

I looked at Elvin uncertainly. I wasn't really sure how I was meant to react to this. So I didn't at all. I just continued to sit there looking gormless.

'And they said the headless corpse was found floating in this pool.'

'Here?' I said, thinking about skeleton recently unearthed not very far from here. 'When was that?'

'Oh.' he took a deep drag on his rollie. 'A long long time ago. Thought to be the body of Thomas Larcher who'd vanished twenty years before, leaving nothing behind but a trail of footprints in the snow.'

'Where did they lead to?' I said. 'Maybe he was there all the time?'

'Why, Rosie, they led here of course. To the Sitting Pool.'

I glanced around and wondered very very briefly if the place had anything to do with Ethel-Rose? 'Here?'

'Here, indeed. In the vale of the fairy. Lots of people have disappeared.' He snapped his fingers. 'Just like that.'

'Well, isn't this a regular Bermuda Triangle?' I laughed.

He nodded. 'Masquerading as a duck pond.'

'Uh huh.' I pointed my head at the pool. 'Without the ducks.'

Elvin grinned. 'And where things disappear, others can appear. Nature fills a space. So they say.' Then he stubbed the cigarette out on the rock and put what was left into the lid of a tin on the stone surface beside him.

'It's a void,' I told him. Then, when he looked confused, I said, 'Nature fills a void.'

He shrugged. 'No void here,' he said completely contradicting what he'd muttered only a moment ago. 'It's full of mischief. I must say, I feel quite at home, I do.'

He fumbled around in the main body of the tin and removed a pack of Rizlas. 'You know I've heard some say witches still meet for sabbats here.' He delivered this line with a gaze of uncertain intent, regarding me with an eyebrow hoisted high.

'Oh,' I said. 'Is it Sunday, then?'

'No,' said Elvin and beamed. 'Then we're lucky, right?'

'Or unlucky, depending on where you stand with all that.'

'So, Ms Strange, and where do you stand with all that?'

I shrugged. 'I don't stand, I fly. Round and round in circles usually. One day, when I've got the lie of the land, I'll find a good spot to settle on.'

'Very wise,' he said and smiled, dipping his head at the water. 'Well, this is a pretty place for a pit stop, isn't it?' His eyes ranged over the pool, the trees, the little waterfall. 'It's rich. Teeming with life. I'm quite amazed by the biodiversity, you know.'

'Oh,' I said, and looked at the trees and caught sight of the flat rock I had been enjoying. 'Have you been here long?' Had he been watching me the whole time I'd been there? I wasn't sure if I was comfortable with that.

'A while,' he said and turned back to me and grinned.

'So it's okay for you to sit here alone? You immune to fairy glamour, then?' I said.

'Ah well, you of all people should know there are some gifted individuals who can see through glamour. Who can every so often glimpse the true nature of things.'

I snagged on a line. 'Me of all people?'

'With your museum and all that.'

'Oh right,' I sniggered. 'And what about you, you're gifted are you?'

'Many a damsel has remarked so,' he said and winked and then chortled to himself and stretched his arms back on the rock so that his chest moved up a bit. He really was quite muscular for a lean man. His skin was tanned and tight, his stomach concave and unwrinkled. Not unattractive at all.

As if aware of my gaze, he coughed and kicked his feet out of the water, swinging them up onto his rock, where I noticed for the first time a range of scientific-looking test tubes and unscientific-looking jam jars.

'What are you doing with them?' I pointed at his equipment. The glass variety.

'Oh that. Collecting samples,' he said. 'Bringing, er, my, er, knowledge amongst other things, to the protest. It all helps.'

Something stronger than a gust blustered through the leaves above us. I felt something settle gently on my hair and ran my fingers through it and brought out what, for a moment, appeared to be the finest metal filigree I had ever seen. As I held it up to the light I saw this truly was the work of a masterful silversmith – an exquisite oval tracery of delicate shiny lace. And then I blinked and saw that it was a leaf skeleton I held between my forefinger and thumb. Not something man-made but indeed a perfect specimen, like a baby's silver lung.

Nature was quite remarkable.

A clink of the jars brought me back to the moment. Something slopped and I saw Elvin pick up one of the larger glass vessels and tip it out into the pond. I glimpsed a dark squidgy thing and for a second thought it was alive and scrambling about as he set it into the water.

'What was that?' I said. 'Did you put something in the pond?'

'Might have,' he said. 'Or I might have merely put something back.' Then he grinned again. This time it was more than a little wolfish and made me wonder about his relationship with Ella and whether it was platonic or not.

I was going to ask him if she was his girlfriend when we heard a splash nearby and a gentle 'whooshing' exhalation of air.

Both Elvin and I gawped at the pool and saw the glistening red mop of a woman's hair breaking the surface of the water.

Talk of the devil, I thought, and she'll surely appear, for Ella was rising out of the water like a river nymph. Her eyes again seemed unnaturally huge, her face tapering, narrowing like a fawn's.

As Ella's mouth, neck and shoulders emerged I saw she was grinning impishly, as if she had heard the fancy that had just crossed my mind.

I swallowed and smiled in an attempt to conceal my guilt. Though why, I didn't know? After all, she couldn't hear my thoughts, could she?

The sun caught the water streaming over her body, so she looked as if she were shining. But not whitely though – her pale skin had picked up some of the algae. At that particular moment she appeared to be glowing greenly.

And yet the uncanny tone didn't make her look sickly or weird. Quite the opposite. The girl looked bloody amazing; clear-skinned, fresh-faced, strong. Mesmerising, like a viridescent Honey Ryder. I had heard Sam use that word before to describe a jade pendant. It worked perfectly to describe Ella right now. Green totally worked for her. She was in her element clearly.

'Hello Rosie,' she said, making ripples on the surface. Sunlight flashed over her body as she rose up. Were those scales across her shoulders, I thought briefly? No, it was probably just the shadow of the leaves above dancing in the soft breeze.

'The water's lovely, Ms Strange,' she said. 'You should come on in.' It was more than I had ever heard come out of her mouth before and I realised that she too, like Elvin, had a bit of a Celtic burr. The flow of her words held a rhythm like a song or an old Irish ballad. I also detected a slight inflection that suggested she might be mocking me, though I had no clue as to why.

'Ella,' said Elvin warningly. 'Don't.'

When she laughed it was like the ring of a silver bell.

'I haven't got togs anyway,' I said.

And as she rose fully out of the water I saw that neither had she.

Nothing but a necklace – a strap of leather from which dangled a silver pentagram.

I'm not a prude but I thought I should probably avert my eyes for fear of appearing prurient, though it was hard: it took quite an effort to tear my eyes away from her green, shining form. As I finally did, her jingling laugh echoed across the pond.

'I don't mind if you look,' she said. 'We've both got boobs and pubes, similar parts, you know. Roughly, we're the same.'

I told her I'd been put off by Elvin's tale of the headless bodies.

'You shouldn't believe everything he says,' she said and sat down next to him. Grabbing a towel off his outstretched arm, she began to rub her hair, still unbothered by her nakedness. 'Anyway, you know as well as we do, those stories are there to scare the local children away. Parents tell them to keep their offspring out of the woods and make sure the kids stay away from the pond so they don't drown.'

'Yeah that's how a lot of witch myths start,' I said. 'Usually after some poor old woman has been picked on.'

Ella smiled. 'I hear you, sister,' she said. Then she turned her gaze on Elvin, 'How you going? Anything?'

'Yes,' he said. 'But I'll tell you later.' Then he hunched his shoulders and nodded to me. 'I think it's time for Rosie to get on her way, isn't it?'

'Oh yes,' I said, though for the life of me I couldn't remember where I was meant to be going.

'Get back on to the path.' Elvin got to his feet and pulled me up in a kind of languid half-gentlemanly manner. Then he took my shoulders and pointed them at the track I had left. 'Go there. When you find it, turn left and keep going till the stile.'

And strangely I complied without a single word of dissent.

Within a few moments I had duly located the track and started plodding east, though my legs were leaden and disinclined to be commanded.

After a few minutes more I remembered my destination: Howlet Manor. And the dozy fog that had clothed my brain began to dissipate.

They were odd those two, I thought. But not bad odd. Just different to people I usually met. Charming though. They had charisma, I supposed. Even if they were weird.

Still, if whatever they were doing helped to save the woods and the Blackly Be I'm sure that they would be welcomed into the bosom of the Adder's Fork community. Not that that was necessarily a bastion of conventionality either.

With its falling birds, gliding spectres and cross-species body count, this particular village was becoming more than a little bit Midsomer.

CHAPTER SIXTEEN

Eventually I emerged from Silva Wood at the back of the yard behind the Seven Stars. There were half a dozen trestle tables scattered around that suggested it might be used as an occasional beer garden, but it wasn't terribly well maintained and you could hear the sounds of the kitchen coming over the fence.

This section though had not been cordoned off by the detectives, so I was able to squeeze round the side of the pub.

The white forensics or archaeology tents around the Blackly Be were still up. There were no bird corpses anywhere, but I could see a preponderance of people of indeterminate gender wearing protective coveralls and facemasks that looked worryingly similar to gas masks. Further back someone was burning debris. I couldn't tell where, but I could smell it – the odour was rank.

Near Hangman's Rise I passed an unmarked parked lorry. Inside, orange toxic hazard tubs were piled high. That meant, I concluded, that the bird cadavers were probably going to be investigated. To be honest, I was glad that it was being taken care of. Whichever way you looked at it – natural causes or even, I struggled to find the correct words, unnatural causes – the whole bird thing was damn freaky.

But, I reminded myself as I glanced at the taped-off boulder – centuries-old dead people didn't kill flocks of birds. Poison did. Or planes. Or, I was sure, lots of other phenomena that the investigators would know about, determine and decide upon. We just had to wait and hear their results. I was certain they would inform us as soon as they knew. You could tell from the looks on the faces around me and the rise of their shoulders, that villagers, treasure hunters and tourists alike were in rather a high state of anxiety. But, I thought determinedly, contrary to whatever Pink Anorak thought, this was nothing to do with me. With the exception of the academic identification of the deceased, which Sam seemed to be handling perfectly well.

I was grateful not to bump into Sergeant Scrub or anyone else who knew me from the village and found the drive that led up to Howlet Manor without any further distraction or impediment.

The grounds were shielded from prying peasant eyes by a line of trees and shrubs that made up a thick reinforced hedge. I walked up the pavement beside it until I came to a break in the border and turned into what appeared to be the main drive.

It was another curling track which, when it opened up, gave a magnificent view of the old house. It was no Downton Abbey. Clearly in need of a bit of TLC it did however have an impressive Tudor frontage. Extensions to the main body had been added onto over the centuries. Some of these rooms were evidently disused and shut up.

The surrounding grounds, home to a number of trees and flower beds, must require the attention of at least one gardener though.

When I got to the grand entrance, I couldn't find the bell, so banged on the door using the heavy lion-shaped knocker.

After a few minutes I was still standing there like a lemon.

Faced with the galling prospect of returning home empty-handed, so to speak, I decided that, as it was a big place, there was probably staff at the back of the house. I recalled Edward mentioning a housekeeper and a cleaner. An agency gardener too. It was clear that there was one at the front of the house. Time to pay a visit round the back and find out where Mr de Vere might be. In my job back in Benefit Fraud, I was used to cold calling and turning up unannounced. I had a good stock of excuses fit for use if someone challenged me.

The walls were ivy-encrusted and high. On my way round I peeked through the lead windows at a very stately living area that looked completely Agatha Christie: all chesterfield sofas, dark wood and expensive but tatty rugs. Although it seemed clean and tidy I reckoned it hadn't been decorated for years. The place had the look of a dowager down on her luck – all patched and mended.

The grounds though were stunning and seriously well kept. Apart from the odd bird corpse still littered about the place. There was a lot of lawn, but it was all neatly clipped. To the north side of the estate a lot of trees formed a boundary. Most of these country places seemed to define themselves like that or with hedges. In front of them was a clutch of greenhouses in various stages of dilapidation. I noted a wheelbarrow parked outside one of them and a bit further down an old rambling shed with a couple of iron chairs placed not far from it round a cute wrought iron table that had been rather weathered. Must be the gardener's base.

I followed the walls and came out at the back into a kitchen garden full of herbs, lettuce and what could have been spring onions and chives. There were some lovely ripe tomatoes too. I didn't think they'd miss one. As I was nicking it off the vine I saw up ahead in the distance there was a summerhouse. The doors were open and there looked like signs of life within. So instead of using the back door I walked up the brick path onto the lawn.

In front of the summerhouse, and slightly to the side of it, was a lovely rose garden. Four beds and a chalked path formed a rectangle. Within that, flower beds full of floribunda and dazzling blooms created concentric circles, culminating in a knoll of exploding colour in the centre which provided the focal point. The smell was adorable even from here. A couple of benches were dotted around the place so the de Veres could sit in the sunshine and admire their wondrous realm.

I approached it, rather hypnotised by the sumptuous little garden, and as I drew closer clocked that the central display was formed of lovely Ethel Roses. How nice that the de Veres had chosen to honour her in this way. Though as it was indeed a very splendid flower one could see why. Bronson had once informed me that when my great-grandfather's flower beds had to be turned over to provide food for the war effort, the rose was handed out all over the village. It was quite likely to be in a number of local gardens. Still, it made me feel a little bit proud, and I stopped to breathe in the glorious scent. Then, as my eyes withdrew, I spied something that looked like a heap of light-coloured clothes on the chalk floor beside the flower beds. As I got nearer I thought I heard a groan.

The clothes twitched.

That definitely was a groan!

A pinky mound was peeking out from the pile of garments. It quivered and at once, I realised it was a belly, for above it ran a seam of buttons on a shirt that had fallen open.

Good God, it was Edward de Vere. They weren't creamy rags, but his customary linen suit.

I sped up and ducked between the plants till I reached him and squatted down.

The old man was lying on his back. His eyes were red-veined and unfocused, his mouth open, slack. If he hadn't started blinking I might have feared the worst.

For several seconds I stared down at him before I whispered. 'Edward? Edward? Are you okay?'

His face registered not a thing. The shoulders twitched and jerked. His mouth twisted into an expression of panic.

'No, no. Don't hurt me,' he said, and threw out one hand. 'You've come up? I'm sorry. Go back.'

With the other hand, which was shaking violently, he covered his face.

I reached out and touched the back of his hand. 'Edward it's Rosie. Rosie Strange from the Witch Museum. Are you okay?'

He stopped and widened his fingers. Then as the shake subsided into a tremble, he peeked through them.

For a moment we stared at each other, then his shoulders slumped. He pulled his hands back and eventually he said, 'Why have you got leaves in your hair?'

I moved my hands over my bonce and felt the curling fronds, which I removed immediately. 'Sorry.'

He narrowed his eyes and then pointed a finger at me. 'They said there have been sightings. A dark woman wandering around. Have you heard?'

'Yes,' I said. 'But the children are saying it. Children make up all sorts of stuff, don't they?'

He let his head loll back and looked up into the clouds. 'Do you think it's true?'

He was very shaken indeed and in his position, lying flat out on the ground, I felt the best thing to do was to reassure him. 'Oh Edward. Of course it's not true.'

The rictus mouth relaxed a little. 'You would know, wouldn't you?' He held my eyes and for a moment I thought he was pleading with me.

So I gave him what he wanted. 'Yes, I would know. That's right. Now let's get you up. What are you doing down there anyway?'

I helped him into a sitting position. 'Fell asleep, I think.'

Which I thought was a bit of a stretch but he was obviously a proud man, so I let him have that.

'There's a lot of it about,' I told him, trying to sound reassuring, and patted his arm. 'Do you want a hand up?'

'Please,' he said, and I gripped under his shoulders and pulled.

'Are you okay, Mr de Vere?' I managed to bend his knees and then push him into a more upright position.

'Yes, yes, that's enough,' he said, once he was up, shifting from frail to fussy in a moment. 'Give me a hand over to the summerhouse will you, dear gal?'

With some effort, we managed to get him upright. I pulled his linen jacket down at the back and offered him my arm, which he accepted.

'Was just having a rest, you see,' he said as we walked with care towards the summerhouse. There was a little patio outside it with a round table and a couple of chairs. 'All this talk and the disturbance at the Seven Stars. It's unsettled everyone, you know. We had an awful incident with the birds earlier.'

'I know,' I told him. 'It happened all over the village. Maybe some poison gas. Maybe it came out of the grave.'

He came to an abrupt halt and looked at me, his face aghast.

'You know,' I said. 'The Blackly Be.'

He took some time to recover. 'Collins got the gardeners to take them down to the tip, if they'll have them.'

'Do you have a lot of them? Gardeners?' I asked, making conversation. 'It's a lot of land to tend.'

'Agency,' he said. 'Haven't had a regular chap since the eighties.' Then he nodded to show he was ready to go again and we moved on, inching our way to the chairs. When we reached them I tipped him into one with a thick cushion tied on to the seat.

'There's some brandy on the dresser inside.' He motioned into the house. 'Be a dear and fix us a couple of glasses.'

I thought that sensible: his hands were still shaking. Probably old age.

Inside, the summerhouse was done up like an artist's studio. Across the walls there were hundreds of pictures, mostly landscapes but some portraits too. Not elegantly arranged but plonked on top of each other. They were displayed only for the artist to view. Presumably works in progress. Most of them were unframed. Half a dozen easels were propped against the far wall, at their feet canvases, some half-finished, some bare. I saw a door behind one of them but there were pots around it and a large chest full of tubes of acrylics and possibly watercolours. It wouldn't be easy to access.

'Don't go in there. Not in the back, please,' shouted Edward with more force and fire than I had thought him presently capable of. 'Not into the house. It's private. Just fetch the brandy, damn it.' Then he paused and added, 'like a dear.'

Rich people had so few inhibitions about bossing others around. I mean, I was no stranger to direct address but even I might add a 'please' or a 'thank you' to avoid aggravation. Still, I did as commanded by the Lord of the Manor, gritted my teeth, reminded myself he was a doddery old codger I'd just found on the floor, located the brandy and brought it out to pour us two large ones.

'You're very prolific,' I said and nodded back to the paintings in the studio. He accepted the statement as a compliment and grunted with pleasure. I handed him a glass. But as he stretched his hand out to mine I gasped.

'Hang on.' I set the glasses on the table and grabbed his palm. 'Look, what's this?'

On the fleshy part of his right hand, just below the thumb, there was a crescent of tiny puncture marks. They had pierced the skin and little trickles of blood, now brown and flaky, had trickled down to his wrist 'Edward!' I exclaimed. 'That's a bite mark. How on earth did you get that?'

Mr de Vere pulled his hand away and looked at it as if he had never seen it before.

'Well, really. I don't know,' he said. 'Must have got it from the flowers.' Then he placed it under the table out of sight. 'All roses have thorns, don't they? Let's have that brandy.'

I gave him one of my 'concerned' looks as I placed the glass in his left hand. He smiled and sipped at the same time. Really, he seemed to have recovered quite well. I knew that for some old people, having a fall was a serious thing. But Edward seemed to be okay. His colour was returning. Maybe he had just fallen asleep.

'That looked like a human bite mark to me, Edward,' I said, wondering about his relationship with his freaky daughter. She seemed very controlling. Dominating. 'Is there anything you'd like to tell me?'

'No, no,' he said, and looked away at the rose garden. 'Nothing at all. Why would I? Never again.'

I watched him glance away and wondered if he was getting moody with me for intruding. But I didn't really care about that – if he was being abused by someone then that ought to be stopped. I'd heard all about elder abuse. We did a course on it at work. Shocking what some people got up to with the frail and elderly.

'It was the roses, was it?' I said sceptically. 'Edward?'

He nodded. 'You of all people should know about that.'

I didn't understand the non-sequitur. Then thought, oh dear. Although he seemed physically not too fragile there was clearly some confusion going on there. Dementia maybe? I'd mention it to Bronson. He knew the family. Edward was old. They probably had an idea already. But best to make them fully aware.

'So why are *you* here?' he said and turned back inches at a time so he could face me. Now he seemed perfectly sane and coherent. His mind was once again working lucidly. Maybe that's how it happened – in interludes.

'You invited me up for a cup of tea,' I reminded him.

'That's right,' he said and smiled but there was not much strength in his lips and I saw them quiver. 'Well, I hope the brandy will suffice.'

The sun was still out and I could see his eyes were watery. There was sleep in one of them.

A kind of tension was creeping across us. I wasn't sure whether to ask him about my grandmother or just make small talk for the time being. But I couldn't think of any, so after I had another few sips of brandy (which was very nice), I said, 'Edward, Carmen told me you were friendly with Ethel-Rose.'

He coughed and jerked his shoulders, then when he had got his breath back he narrowed his eyes and placed his glass on the table but remained silent.

'My grandmother,' I added for clarity, in case he couldn't remember who she was. 'That you knew the family. Back in the day,' I added. 'What was she like?'

He took his eyes off me and swivelled them to the rose garden. 'You've seen the Ethel Rose there,' he said and gestured to it with his good hand.

I nodded. 'Yes. On my way in. I came around the side.'

'Well, there you go.'

I scowled at the flower. 'You mean she was beautiful?'

'And spirited,' he added and shot me an arch look. I wasn't sure what sentiment he had loaded into it. Perhaps he was hinting at the clairvoyance/clairaudience.

I continued with the rose analogy as that was evidently quite comfortable for him. 'And majestic?' Bronson had told me once that the colours had been bred for symbolism: yellow for joy, pink tips for love and gentleness, and mauve for majesty and splendour.

Unexpectedly, Edward laughed. 'Majestic? Hurr, hurr. That's a thought. Well, no. Not at first she wasn't.'

I slapped an 'enquiring' look on my face – all big eyes, hand cupping chin. 'Do tell.' Why did I start to sound posh whenever I talked to de Vere? Was it contagious or something?

'Gave her poor mother the run-around like anything.' He chuckled into his glass. 'When we were younger she was quite the tomboy.'

That was surprising, I thought. She always appeared poised and well presented in the myriad pictures around the museum.

Edward made a clucking sound. 'Summers we all used to go scrumping together over at the Actons. They knew. Didn't mind. Not like my pater. Oh no, father dear did not like his heir apparent messing around with the village scamps. So we kept it quiet.'

I didn't know what scrumping was but thought it probably had something to do with apples and Scrumpy Jack cider. Both of which sounded pretty harmless to me. Unlike Edward's snobby dad. However, I didn't ask him about any of that because really I wanted to know about who formed the 'we' he was talking about.

'Was that just you and Ethel-Rose?'

'What?' His forehead had gone all frowny as if I had dragged him away from some more exciting recollection. 'What?' Then his face softened. 'Me and old Ethel-Rosie? Lord no. There was a whole gang of us used to get up to mischief in the hols.'

'Oh yes?'

'Yes. Half a dozen or so. All around the same age. More or less.'

'Who were they?' I said leaning forwards and clasping my knees.

'Oh, let me see there was Jim Beam – yes like the drink. Winnie Bailey. Now she was fun. Robert White, the doctor's son, and a young rapscallion named Red Hatton. I always thought he'd been christened "Red". Didn't find out till he died in the war that it was a nickname because of his hair.' He laughed sadly. As if feeling his small rise of sadness, the breeze ruffled the leaves in the trees and bushes around us. 'Sh,' it said softly, 'There there.'

I tried to make a mental note to remember the names. Somehow, I felt that writing it down in my notepad might concern him somewhat or stop the flow. 'And did you all hang out together when you were older too?' I went on. Really what I wanted, was a steer on who was around when Ethel-Rose disappeared. 'You know,' I added. 'In your teens and that?'

Edward's eyes crinkled. 'Certainly when she came back from finishing school we were able to pick up again.'

'Ha!, I said, I couldn't help myself. 'So odd that someone from our family went to somewhere like that.'

Edward's eyes glowed with amusement. 'That's right. Her parents came into some money when the family concern was sold. Bought the place up on Snakehouse Rise. Quite grand it was too. Shame. I liked it.'

'Where is it?' I asked him, wondering if I could get in and see it too; after all, Carmen's cottage had reaped a strange reward.

'Oh no. It's not there any longer. Some captain of industry, I believe, knocked it down and built that new estate. Briar's Close. Back in the 1970s. You seen it? Horrid.'

I concealed my disappointment and told him I hadn't and tried to get him back on track. 'So where did they send Ethel-Rose to finishing school?'

He glanced at the floor as if the answer was there then raised his head. 'Switzerland. I believe. She was becoming quite wayward you see. I think they wanted to beat all that mind-reading nonsense out of her. The mother had plans for her you see. Not that it did much good. Not with her Aunt Rozalie still around when she got back.'

'Yes,' I said. 'I heard about her.'

A solitary bird flew over our heads. It flew to a tree by the kitchen and started making sharp frantic noises. I wondered if it too was looking for someone it couldn't find.

Edward sniffed and looked at his brandy. Then he tilted back his head, held the glass for a moment and drank it. 'Always wondered if Ethel-Rose hadn't run away to take up with some of her finishing-school pals when she, you know, went orf.' He wiped the moisture from his mouth with the back of his free hand.

A cloud passed over the sun. Edward shivered.

'Went where?' I said.

'You know – disappeared.' He put the glass on the table. 'Let's have another.'

I was thinking that this new information was worth investigating. That, and maybe tracking down the other friends my grandmother had spent time with in the village. If any of them were still alive. 'Could you remember what the finishing school was, do you think, Edward? I'd be really grateful.'

'Let me see,' he said and stroked his chin. 'Might have a diary I suppose . . .'

We both jumped as my phone started to buzz loudly.

It was the museum.

'Sorry,' I said to Edward. 'Do you mind if I take this?'

'No, no,' he said. 'Then turn the blasted thing off please. It hurts my ears.'

I apologised and silenced it.

As I sat back into the garden chair and held the phone to my ear I caught a glimpse of the most alarming sight.

There, coming up the path that led from the kitchen to the summerhouse was Araminta. Over the house the clouds were darkening and a wind had got up that was blowing out her hair, picking up the ends and kinking them out so she looked more than a little mental. She had a butcher's cleaver in her bloodied hand and a pale blue apron that was spattered with the scarlet splashes. If that wasn't disturbing enough the look on her face suggested she wasn't best pleased to see who was keeping her father company. Not at all.

Bugger. The phone must have alerted her.

'Hello?' I said quickly into the earpiece.

It was Bronson. 'Hello Rosie, you all right. Well the thing is – can you come back to the museum please?'

'Yes,' I said, as Araminta reached us. Immediately she began to berate her father. Though she was trying to keep her voice down, her fury was overtaking her vocal chords and a string of expletives began to flow out of her mouth loud and shrill, as she stabbed the cleaver worryingly in my direction.

The word 'trouble' was bandied about.

'Can you hear me, Rosie?' said Bronson down the line. 'I need you now.'

'Sorry,' I said. 'I'm a bit distracted. Just up at Howlet Manor with Edward and Araminta.'

Edward had taken on a kind of crumpled look. I heard him say, 'No not this time,' and then he coughed and shrugged and said, 'Minty. Please. I'm old. Let it be.'

But Minty was not having it. 'You shouldn't be out here unsupervised. Not with her.'

I giggled. Edward was sprightly, but I really could most certainly repel any of his unwanted advances that might come my way.

Bronson said, 'Very upset. You'll have to see to it. It's only right.'

But my attention was fixed on the Lord of the Manor.

Right then, he was remonstrating with his daughter, asking her to calm down, though I couldn't catch it all '. . . been fine,' I think he said, whilst Bronson was banging on about some bloke at the door.

Edward sighed and extended his hands to his daughter. 'She says there's no walking ladies, no ghost you see,' he said, by way of a pacifier.

Araminta ground her teeth and crossed her arms so that the cleaver was pointing straight up like a bloody metal flag across her breast. 'Huh,' she said.

'But she'd know, see,' Edward griped. 'She's a damned witch from the museum, isn't she?'

I covered the mouthpiece on my phone and said quickly, 'Actually, I'm not a witch. I don't self-identify as one although I'm aware many people do and there is nothing wrong with that . . .'

At this point, Bronson did the closest thing to raising his voice that I ever experienced. 'Rosie!' he thundered down the line. 'For the love of God, will you listen to me? Come back now, d'you hear?. You've got a visitor.' Then he hung up on me. Which was exceedingly unusual.

Oh dear.

'I'm sorry. I have to go,' I said to Edward and began to

back away from his scary daughter. She was doing a good job of blocking the path to the kitchen so I made as if to go back round the side between the roses and the gardeners' sheds. 'And I'm not a witch,' I shouted back. I didn't want rumours starting.

Araminta's face was turning from pink to a colour that matched the splashes on her apron. 'You can try and duck the label but we all know, you see. All of us in this village. You, Strange, are from a long line of witches and sluts and,' she reared herself up and held the chopper up high, 'and, and, and feminists!' she spat as if it was the worst insult she could think of. 'Go away. You're not wanted here.'

I spent most of the journey back to the museum contemplating, in a fairly amused fashion, how Araminta had, in effect, made quite an insightful comment. I was sure that she hadn't intended to enlighten me so. It was quite true, I saw now, that if you formed a Venn diagram of the three labels she'd fired over me – witch, slut and feminist – there would be some that overlapped and probably a set of women fitted in to all three. Or rather there would be a set of women who were *perceived* as fitting in to all three. But that was, of course, the problem with stereotypes and labels – they were so reductive (Sam-speak), and lacking in nuance (my new favourite word) that usually, but not always, they were projected onto their subjects without their consent. I, for instance, had laboured long under the Essex Girl label, which I never consented to. Ever. And they were often portrayed as evil vixens, glamouring sluts out to snare men, with their conjuration of perfection, via fake lashes and fake tans and fake boobs. That aligned them with 'witch' and 'slut'. But feminist? I wondered. And then thought, actually there was something a bit punk about some of them. Like they don't actually care about what people thought. And that was kind of what feminism was all about wasn't it? Wearing what you wanted? Doing what you wanted? Not bowing down to old gender-bound conventions.

I was walking up the gravel drive to the front door, congratulating myself on the idea of the Essex Girl as a nexus for all three of Minty's insults, a bold new icon for the twenty-first century, when Bronson came charging out of the museum shouting, 'Rosie! Get into that kitchen now. There's a man waiting for you. Sam isn't happy either.'

'Bloody hell, Bronson,' I snapped. 'You and me really need to have a talk about gender politics.'

He pressed his lips together and furrowed his brow then said very plainly, 'I'm a Labour man born and bred. No point trying with me.' Then he pointed into the porch. 'I'll hold the fort while you sort yourself out, young lady.'

You couldn't make it up.

I huffed into the museum.

Sitting at the dining table in the office/kitchen was a very very cross-looking Sam and a very very oily-looking bloke in a shiny grey suit.

'What's going on, then?' I asked. 'What's the big emergency?'

'Oh hi,' said the man in grey, rising to his feet.

'This,' hissed Sam through his tightly clenched jaws, 'is Gary Gibbon. From Steadman and Ripper Estates. Apparently you contacted him for a valuation?'

I hadn't done anything of the sort.

'What?' I said, utterly perplexed.

'Yes,' said Gary Gibbon and extended his hand. 'I'd like to get started right away if you don't mind.'

'What?' I said again and then increased my volume as I pleaded with Sam, 'I did not do this.'

He grunted loudly and crossed his arms over his chest, just like Araminta had done an hour ago. What was it with everyone today? Was Saturn in a rare conjunction with Mars that turned people into arseholes?

Not that I put faith in any of that.

'Honestly,' I said to Gibbon. 'There's been a mistake.'

But he shook his head. 'We received an email on Monday requesting a valuation on this property from a Ms Strange.'

Sam let out another long extensive sigh.

'Let me see,' I said.

Gibbon ran his finger over his phone. 'Yes,' he said. 'Right. Here you go.' He handed it over. 'Agreed and arranged for today by Ms Strange.'

I took the phone off him and read the email. It took me a while to get there, but when I saw the sign-off I got it. 'That's M.S. Strange,' I said and turned to Sam. 'That's Maureen Stella Strange. Mum. Not me!'

'If you say so,' said Gary sounding unconvinced. 'I don't mind who arranged it for you – I'm here now, and I have to say you are sitting on a little goldmine, Ms Strange. Or may I call you Rosie? The instruction was to contact a Rosie Strange. That is you, isn't it?' He sent me a wide but fake smile through lips that were shiny and a bit greasy, presenting a yellowish row of teeth that should probably have been sorted in his teens. It wasn't a sight that endeared.

I tried to speak, to suggest that he called it a day, but he continued over the top of me. 'You know developers up at the local pub are having a terrible time there. They'd be keen to make on offer on this. It's more or less centrally located to the village. Lots of land. Could solve a heap of problems for them and I hear you were intending to clear some of your London mortgage?'

At this point Sam could take no more. With one continuous movement he pushed his chair back, got up and stormed out of the office.

I began to go after him, but then thought *Sod it. No point. He won't listen to me now anyway. I'll have to give him a bit of space.* So I returned to Gibbon, who wasn't even looking embarrassed. The guy was used to this and clearly prepared to brazen it out for what he predicted might be a stonking commission, maybe a holiday with the family, or girlfriend, or judging from the suit and vibes he was giving off, a bit of sex tourism in the East.

'Look, I'm sorry,' I began. 'There's been a mistake.'

I gingerly took his arm. Personally I didn't want any contact with this guy, there was something sapping about him. But needs must. 'This is not a good time, Gary,' I said, leading him out past the till, through the lobby, practically shoving him off the steps as we reached the porch. 'You better run – it looks like rain.' And outside, the wind *had* got up a fair bit. Now it was creaking the trees and sending loose leaves scurrying across the gravel drive. In the memorial garden the roses were shaking their heads frantically.

'Well, can I make an appointment to return at a more convenient time?' Gibbon was nothing if not persistent.

'Not now, no,' I said, feeling the museum tensing. It was almost as if it knew what was going on.

'I'll email you and your mother.'

'No!' I shouted rather more loudly than I had anticipated.

Gibbon was so shocked by the volume that he stepped back.

And thank God he did.

For, with another great creak and a very loud splintering sound, The Essex Witch Museum sign, fashioned into the shape of a flying sorceress, freed itself from its remaining hinge and plunged straight into the spot he had just vacated, broomstick first.

'Jesus Christ!' Gibbon yelled, understandably.

'Oh crap,' I said. 'I'm afraid the Witch Museum doesn't want you here.' Even as I said it I knew how crazy it sounded.

'No, no,' he stammered and spun on his heel.

I have never seen a Skoda reverse so quickly.

CHAPTER SEVENTEEN

Once Bronson and I had closed the museum I went into the kitchen and made myself a cup of tea. I could have gone for a wine, but it was a bit too early. And I didn't really want to start drinking alone. Slippery slope and all that.

Sam was still nowhere to be seen but I was trusting my gut on this one and thought I should probably leave him to come round in his own time then explain. Again. I thought he might also find the sign incident amusing. Or at least interesting.

I did.

So as not to be diverted by the whole episode I filed it under my 'Bizarre things to discuss with Sam' list. Really, there wasn't time to go into all of that now. I had other things on my mind: my own investigation.

I settled down at the end of the table where one of Sam's laptops was still on and open. It was my intention to create a document to record the names that I'd gleaned from Edward before I forgot them. Then I could take a methodical approach to finding out where they were, if they were still around and make appointments to interview them. And there was that other little matter of the finishing-school friends. Blimey – this family! And until this year I had thought us so ordinary.

However, as the screen on the laptop flickered and came to life I saw it was open on the museum's Facebook page.

I could not believe my eyes when I began to read some of the comments there. Really, I should have stopped looking at it after the first couple of bitchy remarks and put my energy to better use getting on with the task I'd set myself. But it was painfully mesmeric:

'A bunch of old waxworks, rude staff, no café. In the middle of nowhere. Avoid at all costs.'

'Relaunch! What was it like before?!!!!'

'Vending machine broken.'

'Complained about the toilets. Was told by a fat bird in cowboy boots to "sling my hook".'

'Burn the museum. Not worth the entry price. Burn the witches.'

Another simply said 'Shit'.

For a moment I thought about posting something on my own Facebook, calling up my best disco soldiers to write on reviews that might counter the negatives, but my phone was out of battery and I didn't want to log in on Sam's computer.

It would have to wait.

I went and plugged my mobile into a socket near one of the bookshelves and stupidly returned to the laptop, wondering who the 'fat bird in cowboy boots' was? Perhaps Vanessa's mum. Even so, that was out of order. So absorbed in lathering up a good fury was I that I didn't even notice Sam come in and set his other MacBook down on the table.

'You'll be wanting to hear about my findings I expect,' I heard him say, and jumped.

I muttered, 'Mmm,' and finished reading a particularly foul comment that called the place a 'grubby shambles'.

'Good,' he said. 'Well, it started in the way you'd expect. The odd accusation here and there.'

'Bloody hell!' I moved the cursor over the 'thumbs up' icon. A long list of people popped up including, to my dismay, several names that I recognised including Tone Bridgewater, Neighbour Val and Steve from the shop! 'Even the neighbours!' I squealed.

'Always is,' Sam lamented and shook his head. He was taking the disloyalty well.

'But in a small village like this,' I said, voice still rankling with indignation, 'you have to rub along. What's the point of that?'

He nodded and tapped a pen on the edge of his MacBook. 'People tend to fold in with the dominant voice, sometimes for fear of being singled out themselves.'

'Singled out?' I said. 'How do you mean?'

'Temperatures run high. People want blood.'

'I can see that,' I said and folded my arms. Where was that wine?

'Pack mentality is a powerful thing,' he concluded. His eyes followed me into the kitchenette.

'Clearly,' I called back and opened the fridge. 'I suppose,' I yelled, 'online, people think they're more anonymous.'

'Eh?' he said, accepting a glass. 'What are you talking about?'

'The Witch Museum.' I began to pour us two glasses. 'Facebook page. What are you talking about?'

'The witch hunt,' he said and took a sip. 'Black Anne's.'

'Oh,' I raised my glass to his. 'Well, there you go: same shit, different century. Nothing bloody changes, does it?'

'I told you not to look at social media,' Sam said and put the glass on the table. 'Leave it to me.'

'I think I will.' I sat down heavily in the chair opposite him. Bloody Forkers. 'So it was the neighbours back then that started it too was it?'

'Uh huh,' he said and opened his laptop. 'Anne Hughes, or Hewghes as it's recorded, was tried at the 1621 Lent Sessions in Chelmsford. There were a few other people who'd also been accused of bewitching. An Elizabeth Parnsbye of Ricklynge. She had an accusation of bewitching a doctor, John Tuer. "Billa Vera".'

'Who?'

'Means that they found the evidence to be true. Same for Anne Hewghes. She was also brought before the assizes, accused, as I said, by her neighbours.'

I snorted.

'Poor Anne was meant to have bewitched a John Archer who languished and died; a Thomas Meade and a Margaret Bright, who were still ill during the trial. Then there were the usual cows, goods and chattels of a Richard Edwards that she was alleged to have spoiled with an evil glance. Remember, Ursula Cadence has similar charges filed against her.'

'They all did, didn't they? What happened to flying and cavorting with the Devil? It's all so tame.'

I heard a meow from underneath the table and ducked down to see Hecate rubbing herself against Sam's ankles. I made a sucking noise with my teeth to coax her over but it was Sam she wanted, not me. And who could blame her?

'Continental witch hunts, Rosie,' he said, when I popped back up. 'Don't get me started on them.'

'No.' I took down a long draft of wine. It was well deserved. A black tail appeared above the table: Hecate had made it onto Sam's lap. I sighed. 'It's like, "Have you had an accident at work? Fallen in a bramble? Spoiled your milk or had an old woman look at you funny? Then call Lawyers R Us on 999666."'

'Yes,' said Sam. 'Very good.' He absently stroked the purring creature on his lap.

'That's 999666,' I said again, aping a generic advertising voiceover.

'Quite,' said Sam, clearly not wanting to go down this line of discussion.

'That's a joke,' I told him.

'Heard it before,' he said.

I supposed he probably had. He'd been in this business much longer than me.

I deflated and went back to feeling grumpy. Comments on the socials were still doing rounds in my head.

'Anyway,' Sam went on. 'The thing is – Anne was cleared. They both were. There was a Q there in the margin. Stands for "quietas" or "quieta". Means discharged or acquitted.'

'Oh,' I said. 'But I thought she was meant to be burnt at the crossroads and buried there?'

'I know.' Sam pointed his pen at me. 'Just wondering if, over the years, it's been muddled up with another witch burning.'

'Was there one?'

'Yes, in Ipswich, Matthew Hopkins burned Mary Lakeland. She was accused of charming her husband to death. That was, as we know, treason. Ergo – death by fire.'

'And Ipswich is, what? Thirty miles from here?'

'About that.'

'I suppose it's a possibility. But that skeleton under the Blackly Be – was it burned?'

'No, it wasn't,' said an alien voice from the corner of the office.

We both started in our seats and then turned to see a young woman loitering in the door from the ticket office. She had dyed black hair and strong make-up, a pale foundation and dark purple lipstick.

'One of your employees let me in,' she said.

When we both continued to stare, she added, 'Looks like a fisherman.'

'Bronson,' said Sam and nodded.

'And you are?' I asked, a little on the rude side, but we weren't used to strangers intruding on our sanctuary. Especially after we'd closed.

'Chloe Brown,' she said and came over. 'Forensic Archaeology. We met Monday night up at the crime scene.'

'Oh yes,' I said, remembering her now. Though she'd been clad in a white suit, which had obfuscated any visible clues to her personality. Without it I could see she was well into her twenties, as I had predicted, and wearing clothes with a tendency towards goth. 'Would you like a glass of wine?'

'Love to, but I'm driving,' she said and waggled her car keys. But she did come and sit beside Sam.

'This place looks amazing,' she said. 'Would be great to come back and have a look round?'

I guessed she was angling for a freebie, so I said, 'Any time.'

'I've always been interested in this aspect of our history,' she continued nosing around the office. 'I mean, who isn't?'

I thought about saying, 'Me', but realised that, certainly after Mr Gibbon's appearance, that could open a whole can of worms that Sam and I regularly argued about. So I stayed quiet and let Sam agree with her and tell her yes it was all very fascinating.

'You said something about the remains by the boulder, didn't you?' I interrupted their mutual interest love-in.

'Yes.' Her attention came back to me. She had lots of black eyeliner on again. Black shadow there too. 'We dug up the whole section Monday night and took it back to the lab,' she said. 'Thought it might be easier to process.' Then she smirked at some private joke. 'As if.'

'What? You dug up the boulder?' I asked. Great – the locals were going to love that.

'Lord no,' she said. 'It goes too deep. The section above land is only a third of its total. It's way too heavy. No, we excavated the gravesite only. It's London Clay around here, which is easier to work with.'

Sam's eyebrows were squeezed together. 'But Anne's skeleton wasn't burnt you say?' he asked.

She paused for a moment then said, 'No, it wasn't.'

He opened his hands and sat back into his chair and said, 'Well there you go – she was acquitted and never burnt. It was made up.'

'But,' Chloe leant forwards and pushed her hair back from her face. 'The bones that you saw, well,' she looked at me then back to Sam. 'They're male.'

It took a second for us to let this sink in.

Then Sam gasped audibly.

I said 'Really?' and shot my colleague a significant glance. He was mouthing something like, 'Well I'm blowed.'

'Yes,' Chloe continued. 'And, we think, middle-aged.'

'Not a young witch then?' Sam regarded Chloe with a puzzled frown. 'Do you know cause of death?'

'Incision marks,' Chloe said, 'on the ribs would indicate stabbing. Probably by a long thin metal object.'

'A sword?' I said, genius-like.

'That's what we're thinking,' the forensics lecturer confirmed. 'But not just one. We've identified two different types of weapon. The other was probably a short wider blade. Maybe a dagger. There were at least two assailants.'

'So, it was murder?' said Sam slowly. 'Not an execution.'

Chloe nodded. 'Yes. Not what we were expecting either.' She hesitated, then straightened her back, drew her lips into a line of resolve. 'We've had quite a few surprises, in fact.'

'Go on,' said Sam. 'You sure you don't want a glass of wine?' he asked.

She shook her head. She wanted to carry on, and I thought, get something else out, or off her chest.

'Well, well, well,' Sam said slowly. 'A middle-aged man.' Then he nodded at me as if he thought I'd reached a similar conclusion.

But I wasn't a mind reader. I hadn't a clue what he was thinking.

Chloe was already talking again. 'Yes,' she said and dipped her head. 'But the one we found underneath him.' She took a breath. 'Well, yes, she is female. And younger. Could well be Anne Hewghes. Sorry, I couldn't help overhearing your conversation as I came in.'

Sam and I looked at each other.

I said, 'Wow! There's two bodies there?'

'And there's more.' She bit her lip.

'There's more?' I repeated. 'More bodies?'

'No,' she said. 'Just the two, thank God, but I'm amazed you don't know. In fact that's why I came here – to warn you.'

Sam swivelled round in his chair and eyed her. 'Warn us about what?'

'Well there's obviously a mole in the department,' Chloe replied a little coldly. 'And it's got into the press. Your names have been mentioned. I think Sergeant Scrub might pay you a visit. And she's not in the best of moods.'

It wasn't hard to imagine that.

'What's got into the press?' Sam asked. 'The bodies under the Blackly Be?'

'See for yourselves,' and she threw a paper on the table.

I shuffled round to Sam's side and bent over his shoulder so we could both read the article in the newspaper Chloe was pointing to. 'Came out this afternoon,' she added.

Hecate slipped off Sam's lap and walked over the paper obscuring the small print. But we could still see the bold lettering of the caption: 'Headless bodies found in Witch Museum village.'

'They've got no heads?' I asked. The thought sent a bristle of fear down my spine. Decapitation has to be one of the most revolting means of death. I shivered whenever I heard about it on the news, which was stupidly getting more and more frequent rather than being condemned to the dustbin of barbaric history.

'Correct,' Chloe said. 'There's an assumption that this information has been leaked by your team. To garner publicity for the museum.'

'But we didn't know about any of that,' said Sam.

'So you say,' Chloe responded in a low, thoughtful voice.

'They don't reveal the gender of the skeletons though,' he said, scanning the article. 'I suppose that helps.'

'Why are they headless?' I said. '*Where* are their heads?'

Chloe shrugged. 'We don't know. Hoped you might have a clue.'

'Well, well, well,' said Sam again. Chloe and I looked at him for an explanation. 'Certainly this village has got its fair share of headless apparitions and sightings. I never knew about this though of course – the grave. Anchors them, somewhat.'

'What are they?' Chloe asked, clearly enthralled. 'The sightings?'

Sam leant on the arm of his chair and popped his chin into his hand. 'There have been numerous reports of a headless monk in long flowing robes in the grounds of Howlet Manor, and in the lanes around it. Then there's The Highwayman pub? Just up the High Road. Alleged to be haunted by Jack Goode. His headless ghost is meant to walk the village from down here up to Hangman's Hill where it connects onto the old highway.'

'Where's that?' asked Chloe. 'Hangman's Hill?'

'It's also known as Mentorn Road,' I told her, pleased I also had some local knowledge to expound.

'Oh,' she said, adding it up. 'That's the road that the Seven Stars is on.'

'And the Blackly Be,' Sam added. 'Of course Black Anne is seen periodically over town and in Silva and Mab Woods. But the sightings come and go. Until now with all this attention on the boulder.'

Hecate got up from her curled position at the corner of the table and began a long slinky walk down the centre of the table, acting like it was her own personal catwalk. Which I suppose it was really.

'Fascinating,' said Chloe. 'Well, I'd love to stay and chat more, but really I should be off. You know, in case the sergeant turns up.'

Yes, I could understand that.

'Have you found any more out about that golden disc?' she directed her final question to Sam.

'Definitely connected to an associate of John Dee.'

'The alchemist?' she asked. 'Do you know which associate?'

'Not yet. But Samuel Howlet sent someone to contact John Dee in 1591. It's very possible that Dee responded by sending a trusted friend or colleague down. Someone who found nothing, we presume. Or else we, and history in fact, would certainly know about it. There may have been a trigger event after 1621 which produced another epidemic of treasure hunting. I suspect this may be when Black Anne becomes involved. But the pair of them ended up in the pit'

'And what might that be?' Chloe raised her darkened eyebrows. 'The trigger event?'

'Look, ' Sam drew out the word as if he was thinking it through before completing the rest of the sentence. 'Quite often the sons try to prove themselves by succeeding where their fathers failed, don't they? Maybe Howlet's heir called him back again?'

'Any way of finding out?'

'Mmmm,' said Sam. 'Not sure if it really sheds that much light on the victim. However, the fact your man is middle-aged does narrow it down a little. But we'll have to see.'

Hecate stopped by Sam's laptop and meowed again. This time it sounded something like 'Rhea'.

'Mmm, good thinking,' said Sam to the cat.

Chloe sent me a startled look.

'She's his muse,' I said and added, 'the cat.'

Unaware of this exchange Sam went on. 'There is someone I know who may be able to help. An expert on Essex legend and lore. We should go and see her,' he said to me.

'Sure thing,' I said.

Chloe, possibly now convinced of my colleague's insanity, jangled her keys again and muttered something along the lines of 'is that the time?' and began to retreat.

'I'll see you out,' I told her.

Sam also sprang to his feet.

'It's okay, I've got this,' I dismissed him.

'Thanks,' he said. 'I'll pop upstairs and make us an appointment.'

'No, you will not,' I said firmly. 'We've got to see the Bridgewaters tomorrow. You'll have to fit it in after that. Chloe's right about one thing. This will give us more publicity. We've got to get the museum ready for the weekend. We promised Vanessa. Tonight, we're working on an exhibit about Black Anne.'

CHAPTER EIGHTEEN

After much rather heated debate we decided it was probably best, given the lack of time, to adapt one of our current displays. Eventually we settled on the exhibit that I referred to as the 'What it's all about one' and which Sam called the 'Seventeenth-Century Lynch Mob scene'.

It was a wide display, about four and a half metres in length, which people had to pass on their way to the more conventional areas of the museum. It was in these sections that Sam had spent many long hours labelling and categorising artefacts associated with folk magic.

But this exhibit had more of Septimus's hand. The background was formed of a wooden frame which supported painted plywood which had been cut into the silhouette of a group of Tudor cottages. In front of this a fake tree grew out of the astro turf. It was illuminated at the 'roots' by an eerie green light. From one of its branches hung a young peasant woman in a close bonnet. The girl's hands and feet were bound with rope, her head cricked at an unnatural angle. The eyes were shut and she spun slowly, suspended by a tight noose pulled about her neck.

Around her were gathered angry waxworks with torches and pitchforks, mouths either open mid-rage, snarling and baring teeth, or shut tight and po-faced. On the other side of her, at the front of the display, resting on a stick, stood a thin man in a Puritan get-up. He wore a high, felt hat, from under which flowed long black hair. His 'uniform' was standard 'witchfinder' black although he sported a starched lace collar that had at one point been white, but was now more like yellow. Beside him a masked executioner grinned manically. The sign above read, 'Many an innocent woman perished without trial at the hands of mob justice'.

While Sam got to work typing up what he knew about Black Anne, I entered into the exhibit, literally, via a concealed door at the side and began my renovations.

First I cut down the lynched peasant girl and laid her on the floor. Next I bashed the cheesy backdrop of houses till it fell over, and then lugged it out round the side of the museum where there was a shed and wood stock. I went back in and kicked over the witchfinder (alcohol was involved) then got to work stripping off his hat and clothes.

'Bottoms up,' I said to him, because at that moment it was an anatomically correct description.

I poured myself another glass, then slotted the 'witch' into the place where the witchfinder had been, telling her I'd make her look all right. Then I took his black wig off and put it on her head, removed his collar and wrapped it round her shoulders so it looked a bit like a lacy shawl. After fixing her crooked neck and opening her eyes I thought she could probably pass as Black Anne.

My next move was to turn the 'baying crowd' so they were pointed in Anne's direction. The scene did, in fact, look quite scary – the poor woman was seriously out-numbered, you see. And their faces were monstrous. Even more so up close when you could see the flaking paint and loose teeth. I thought (after three glasses of wine) that you did really get the sense of bloodlust and random, mental bullying.

The only element that didn't totally work, now we had this new information, was the executioner, who I discovered, had a real axe in his hands – don't ask me why. I took it off him and threw it onto the nudist witchfinder. Then I detached the hangman's demonic eye mask, transforming him into your run-of-the-mill lynch mob member, and leant him against the tree because he wouldn't stand up straight anywhere else. As an afterthought I made his eyes go crossed so he looked like he'd had one too many at the Seven Stars and was having a bit of a breather before re-engaging with the unfolding mobbery.

I'd phone Carmen tomorrow to see if she had any stone off-cuts or something we could use to represent the Blackly Be.

Next, I lugged the naked witchfinder and axe out through the museum round to the woodpile.

In retrospect it was not one of my best ideas to start chopping up the wooden backdrop but I thought, as I had discovered a real axe, and had some time on my hands I might as well get on with it. Like I said, alcohol was involved you see.

It was during this cack-handed attempt at 'recycling' that Sam found me. The words 'Good grief' were used several times and the cutting instrument removed from my hands. But after making a case for myself, he sighed and said, 'Okay then, let's get rid of it. But I'll do it properly.' Then he went into the shed and produced what he called a 'proper working axe' and a 'firepit' which was, in point of fact, the old drum of a washing machine. Then he dragged out the wood block and instructed that I went and got the firelighters from the kitchen.

When I came back with them, and another bottle of wine, I was pleasantly surprised to find Sam had taken off his shirt and was chopping the wood on the block. There was something very Mr Darcy about it and, to be honest, I was rather taken. It was all I could do to sit on the woodpile with my glass of wine and try not to look at the muscle definition on his torso. I didn't last long. He was in great shape. Definitely worked out, though I had no idea when that might be. Hadn't been aware of him going to the gym since I'd been here. Though he must, I could see. He had glorious pecs, and biceps – raised and gently curved – and in full use right then. As my eyes slipped down his body I found myself more than intrigued by the downy hair on his chest that narrowed to a trickle, like a seductive arrow pointing my eyes to his groin, before vanishing beneath the waistband of his jeans. I swallowed several times. I could see a small black band of his pants peeking over the top and deduced that they were boxers, which personally I preferred. When he swung the axe back over his shoulders a shudder ripped through me and I actually *heard* myself sigh out loud.

I think he did too because once he'd split that particular length of wood, he rested the axe on the block and said, 'Hey! I didn't mean for you just to sit there and watch me. Get the fire going and give me one of those.'

He meant wine, so I poured him one and put it down nearby so he'd have to come over and get it. 'You don't want splinters in your glass do you?' I explained.

Then I loaded the bits of wood into the washing machine and lit it. When Sam had finished he came over and stood by me and we both watched the flames begin to leap.

'Well, that was an efficient evening,' he said as we sipped the wine. He still didn't have his shirt on. It wasn't cold, but it wasn't warm so I wondered if maybe he was showing me the goods. Maybe this was the moment that our friendship began to turn.

Weirdly the thought made me feel anxious.

Or perhaps it was just breathless.

Whichever, I was becoming hyper-aware of him, of the short distance between us, of the fire spitting and blazing, of the Witch Museum's walls glimmering behind us and the land ahead, the line of dark trees that made up the border of the property.

'Listen,' I said, keen for a moment to defuse the tension. I hadn't managed to talk about Gary Gibbon with him yet and perhaps now was as good a time as any: we'd worked as a team and produced something for the museum. 'You know I didn't have anything to do with that whole estate agent thing?'

He didn't speak, but put one hand on his hip and continued to stare at the fire.

'It was my mum. Maureen Stella Strange. M.S. Strange. Not me.'

Sam picked up another chunk of wood and threw it in the firepit. It spluttered and spat sparks over the rim.

'Honestly, Sam. I wouldn't go behind your back and do that. Surely you know me better by now? Don't you?'

As he leant forwards to poke in a length of wood, an unruly lock fell over his right eye. 'But you have thought about it in the past, haven't you?' he said in a low voice.

'Yes,' I said and took a deep breath. 'But things are different now.' I followed this up with a deep glug of wine. 'I wouldn't do anything without consulting you. You're too important.'

He rotated himself to face me. His lips opened ever so slightly.

I felt mine twitch in response.

'To who?' he said. 'Too important to you or the museum?'

So this was it – push was coming to shove. He had never asked me so directly before. I took a very very very deep breath and then I said it, 'To both.'

If this had been a film and he was the romantic lead, he would have pushed back his shoulders, put his arms around me and got going with a full French kiss.

But of course it wasn't and although I felt my body inch slightly forwards to his, as the movement was processed more consciously by my brain, I was visited again by a crippling self-consciousness and the strange notion that I was being watched.

Not just by Sam, but by other unseen presences. Like the whole place was holding its breath. Waiting.

I broke eye contact and felt a wash of intense heat course over my body. Sweat bobbled on my forehead. Deliberately I hid my face and turned to survey the pines, anxious to recover some self-mastery.

But the scene was perplexing. In the dimness they appeared like a forest of black spires. Was it my imagination or were those dark flitting things that I had seen in Mab Wood, back and dancing in amongst the trees?

I screwed my eyes up but couldn't get a fix on them – they were too far away and altered by the smoke, sparks and warping, heated air. I strained my ears and tried to listen into the trees. The crackling of the fire was too loud.

'What's the matter?' Sam asked and touched my arm.

I felt his energy leap onto me and flush through my veins. It should have been intoxicating, but at that moment, it only wired me more.

Around me, the sense of things alive and unseen intensified. I felt, or thought I felt, a danger in the woods, like a beast that was pushing against its bonds. Then a strange alien phrase visited me: it's going to happen.

Though I had no idea what that 'happening' might be, I perceived it not to be positive, as the phrase brought with it a moment of keen distress, a sharp spasm of discomfort and a mysterious, inexplicable sense of foreboding came down over me.

I tutted. It was bizarre, random, had come out of nowhere. A jumbled physical sensation produced by over-stimulation: the electricity of Sam's touch, the alcohol and the darkening dusk. Yes, that was most likely.

I took a deep breath to calm myself and saw Sam was still waiting for a reply so shook my head as a way of saying 'It doesn't matter', which I hope he got. Although, without being aware of what I was going to say, the words tumbled out, 'Sometimes I think I'm going a bit mad.'

I darted a quick look into his face to see if he'd already thought about that, but he simply smiled with remarkable gentleness and said, 'It's not you – it's everyone. There's something going on in the village.'

'I'd noticed,' I said and began to feel calmer and more dreadful at the same time. Calmer because the tension with Sam had diffused and dreadful because the tension outside of me, I felt, had just increased.

'The coincidences are odd to say the least,' Sam went on and swilled his glass. 'Headless bodies, livestock disturbed and spectres of the dead back and promenading through our streets.'

I resisted the very strong urge to pour another drink as he listed the phenomena.

'And there were dead birds,' I said making a conscious effort to pick up his thread. 'Did you hear about it? They literally fell out of the sky this morning. Hundreds of them. All over the village. I mean I know there's got to be a logical explanation, but it's seriously freaked a lot of people out.'

'As well it would,' he said, his voice soft. 'I heard about it. Wondered if you'd seen it. Yes, you're right – Adder's Fork *seems* to be at the epicentre of a supernatural hurricane.'

'I'm guessing the most important word in that sentence is "seems"?' I said and thought, *Go on Sam knock this silly feeling out of me with your wise words and logic.*

'Well,' he said. 'I did look it up. There have been other instances of a similar kind. Most recently in 2014 on New Year's Eve when over 5,000 blackbirds, starlings and other birds dropped dead over the town of Beebe, in Arkansaw.'

Usually I'd give him a smart-arse retort about him being a walking encyclopaedia or something, but I wanted his explanation more than I needed to be cheeky. 'And what was that down to?'

'Fireworks, they think. It was New Year's Eve. All the loud bangs and explosions disorientated them.'

He let that rest between us for a moment.

'Mmmm,' I said and shifted, thinking over this morning and my walk up the High Road. 'Well, we didn't have any fireworks today.'

'Which makes it unusual,' he said.

'And weird,' I agreed.

'Rosie?' he asked slowly. 'Do you know where that word originally comes from? Weird?'

'Do tell,' I said, trying to change the mood and be a bit flirty and silly but it only ended up sounding pretend-posh and pratty, like when I said it to Edward at the launch.

'Probably from "wyrd".' He spelt it out. 'Which comes from the word "wirt" or "wirp". Germanic.' There was something in his words that was loaded, like he was trying to steer me. I was beginning not to like it.

'And that means what?' I noticed a tremor in my voice.

'To be due, to come to pass, to become. It's also aligned with fate.' He paused and looked at me but his eyes weren't certain. 'You're right – something's in the air. Something or other is this way coming. And it's about to happen in Adder's Fork'

I just stood there and, despite the heat of the fire just feet away, found that I was shivering.

I stepped back and away from the fire and stumbled across the waxwork. The witchfinder was at my heels grinning at me with triumph.

Looking at the smirking dummy, I was suddenly possessed with the overwhelming need to wipe that stupid grin off his face.

Without really thinking about what I was doing I picked him up, dragged him over to where Sam had been chopping and put his neck on the block.

Before he could stop me I had raised the axe. 'Off with his head!' I yelled and then brought the blade down.

It cut through the neck with one stroke. As I straightened up, I was gratified to see the decapitated head bounce off the ground and roll into the darkness.

'Begone with you,' I yelled, then became aware of Sam who was just standing by the fire staring, an unreadable expression on his shadowy face.

But I felt better. Much better. I felt calmer, like I had sorted something out.

'What?' I said to him, breathless and panting.

I suppose it must have looked like an odd thing to do, all things considered, but I didn't want to explain my thought processes right now.

'Can you give me that axe?' Sam put his drink down on the paving stones and took the weapon off me. Then he went and picked up the witchfinder's head from somewhere near the side of the museum.

When he came back, head tucked under his arm, axe in hand, I thought he looked rather wild and sultry. Then he said, 'I think we should go to bed.'

Well, that wasn't what I was expecting. But now my self-consciousness had evaporated and I was beginning to feel a bit more normal again, maybe *this* was what was coming.

Maybe this was the right time for it.

Maybe we were both feeling the same thing.

I knew I was more than a little turned on.

In a flash I consented and went upstairs to my room, where I snuck beneath the covers in anticipation.

Then typically and stupidly the wine netted me and I fell promptly fast asleep.

Sometimes I really am my own worst enemy.

CHAPTER NINETEEN

'It'll do for now,' Vanessa said, as we stood before the new Black Anne exhibition.

Sam's explanation had been blown up and laminated and stuck on the side of the former 'What It's All About' exhibit.

'Well, I think it's quite good really,' I said, a little indignant at such faint praise, after all the effort that I, we, had put into it last night.

'You need to get on the till,' said another voice beside us and Sam appeared by my side. 'It's almost opening time.'

Vanessa sighed and said, 'All right, no need to get your Y-fronts in a twist,' then hurried off, leaving us alone.

Thank God, this part of the museum was dark, I thought, sensing my cheeks heating.

When I had woken up on my own this morning it was with a feeling of embarrassment. Like I'd said too much and made a fool of myself and maybe gone a bit too far with the whole witchfinder/beheading thing.

Though it was probably just the booze talking, or rather me having a bit of a freak-out with an axe, I wasn't yet able to shake the discomfort off.

'Sorry, you know, about last night,' I said, and swallowed and took a step away from him. I could feel his presence now like a rash on my skin. Burning burning burning.

He smiled. 'Oh, that's okay. Someone had to put out the fire.'

I didn't know whether that was a metaphor and would have liked to have looked deeply into his face to work it out, but his gaze was too intense for me in my current slightly hung-over state.

'You realise you've practically got your way now,' he said.

Oh my God, I thought. It *is* happening. I wasn't imagining it. But I said, 'Oh yeah?' and forced myself to catch his eye. Oh wow, they were dark now. The amber in them receding into the big black pupils.

'Indeed. We're almost rid of all the witchfinders in the museum.' He grinned. 'Apart from the Inquisition exhibition. But I don't know – are torturers and witchfinders the same thing? They're both sadistic, both intolerant and dogmatic. I can see several arguments for and against.'

'Oh ha ha,' I said, trying to obfuscate my disappointment. Of course, he was talking about the museum. 'Yes, well it is the Essex *Witch* Museum.' I'd said it before. It was like a private joke. But I didn't feel like laughing.

Then I waited for him to say something else. But he didn't.

So I said, 'I can smell bonfire on you.'

And he said, 'Yes, I need to wash my hair. Should have done it last night but,' he paused. 'I had other things on my mind.'

'What?' I couldn't work him out – the expression on his face was playful. His lips pulling a little to the left. That always made my stomach flutter a bit, I had to admit. Then the lips spread into a grin and he opened his mouth like he was going to say something when, would you blimmin' believe it – in walked Sergeant Scrub. I mean, seriously, that woman had got some issues with timing.

I could have screamed at her. Though it was probably a good thing I didn't. Even so, I might have phrased my next words better, but you can see where I was coming from.

'Oh bloody hell, what do you want?' I said.

She sniffed but other than that was completely unfazed. I expect she got this reaction quite a lot. 'Is there somewhere private we can talk?'

'Indeed,' said Sam and I was gratified to see a little kink on the other side of his cheek that meant he was not particularly happy about it either. 'The office.'

I followed them past several customers who, I overheard, had apparently been queuing to get in.

Things were looking up. And the low mood that had visited me this morning started to incline.

Scrub refused a coffee and sat down at the long table motioning for us to follow.

For a moment I couldn't remember why I knew she would visit us. Then I noticed the copy of the newspaper that Chloe had left, in the middle of the table.

Oh God, we were in for a lecture that we didn't deserve.

I decided to head her off before she started and said, 'Look, that article in the *Essex Chronicle* – we didn't tell them anything.'

Sam nodded. 'We were unaware of what further discoveries had been made. In the grave.'

But Scrub made a flicking movement with her hand. 'Not interested.'

Sam and I exchanged a baffled look.

The sergeant looked from Sam to me. It was a good poker face and revealed nothing. But I got the feeling I was in the presence of a predator sniffing up her next meal. 'What were you doing last night?' she asked outright.

The question caught me off guard, as I imagined it was meant to. In my head I rescreened the events against any laws I knew. As far as I was aware, we hadn't broken any. Unless you needed a license for a bonfire out here or something? And surely, I could do with my dummies as I wanted? They were my property after all.

Sam was already replying. 'We were constructing the new Black Anne exhibit. In the museum. Where you found us.'

Scrub stuck her chin out. 'All night?'

'Till we passed out,' I said and looked at Sam who smiled sort of apologetically.

Scrub unclasped her hands and slapped them on the table. 'And you can vouch for each other I suppose?'

We both nodded. I was feeling increasingly uncomfortable about her line of questioning.

'Well,' she said and upturned her chin. 'I'll have to take your individual statements.' Then her gaze got a bit more fiery, and fixed on me. 'You went alone, did you?' she asked.

Unsure of what she meant, I asked, 'Went where?'

Her tongue clucked in annoyance and she said, 'To bed of course.' Then her eyes narrowed. 'Where else did you think I meant?'

She was becoming, I thought, rather rude, police or not.

Without meeting Sam's eyes, I said, 'Well, um, yes I did.' Although I could feel the heat back in my cheeks.

'And what time was that?'

Gawd, I thought. She's not letting it go, is she? Was she trying to humiliate me?

'I don't know,' I said and glanced at Sam.

Gallantly, he sat up. 'I checked in on Rosie about 10.30 p.m'.

My brain whizzed to attention. A fizz of excitement exploded in my stomach and raced up to my heart. This was great news.

'She was out for the count,' he added.

I was just about getting over the fact that Sam came to my room after I'd gone to bed, when Scrub asked him, 'And did you hear her leave in the night?'

'Why?' I said. Despite my euphoria, this was getting up my nose now.

'Be quiet,' Scrub snapped.

I opened my mouth to say something about that, but Sam came in and cut me off.

'No,' he said. 'I left my door open. I could hear her. She was snoring all night.'

'I don't snore,' I said.

'You do,' said Sam and smiled.

I took his smile and sent it back, then emboldened by the speed at which he had defended me, cocked my head and tried to look cute and said, 'So, is that going to be a problem?'

He raised his eyebrows and sucked in a breath.

At which point Scrub grunted. 'Children, please. When you've quite finished? This is not a joking matter.' With great theatre, she took a phone out of her pocket and showed it to us. Her lips formed a nasty snarl. 'Hopefully this will cool your ardour.'

I mouthed 'oh?' to Sam as Scrub fiddled about with the screen then slid it over the table to us. 'See for yourself. I'm surprised you haven't heard. Went viral before we managed to take it down.'

The mobile was in video mode. Sam pressed the arrow key and the image started to move. I recognised the mustard-coloured walls of the building in frame. It was the front of the Seven Stars.

'Connor Easlea,' said Scrub. 'One of the local paperboys, was delivering to the pub this morning. Got a bit of a nasty shock.'

The screen straightened to reveal the front beer garden with its rows of trestle tables. You could tell from the pinky-blue colouring it was early, not long after dawn.

Scrub continued her narration. 'At approximately 0600 hours this morning he found this.'

There was a giggling off screen, the sound of feet on gravel, the phone wobbled up and down as it got closer to the first table. A high-pitched squeaky voice said, 'The local 5 O protecting the streets.'

The camera kinked up and focused on a man in uniform sitting at one of the benches. He had a polystyrene cup in his hand, and was upright, but his eyes were closed and it was clear from his lack of reaction he was fast asleep. Or possibly dead.

'Constable Reynolds,' Scrub explained with disdain, 'had been on shift all night. His relief, who was due to take up position at that time, had just popped along to the shop to get him refreshments.'

The phone operator tried to zoom into the sleeping officer's face but they tripped over something on the floor so that the camera jerked away and ended up fastening onto the Blackly Be, which had been in the background. There was a bit of swearing then you heard the boy say, 'Eh, what's that?'

Then the phone floated erratically to the boulder.

There was something there.

Something like a grey bag sitting on top of the rock. The screen blurred as the boy got quicker. At three metres or so away, it got a fix and the details started to become clearer. There was the boulder. But it was glistening: brown streaks of viscous liquid were dripping from the bag thing, over the top of the stone and down its sides.

The boy said, 'Oh fuck,' and moved closer and to the side so that the camera fully faced it.

'Oh my God,' I said and flinched as I realised what it was.

'Heavens!' said Sam and did the same.

On the Blackly Be boulder there sat the unmistakable spectacle of a severed human head. The eyes had popped and rolled up into their sockets, but they were open. As was his mouth, which had slacked down at the sides into a silent wail. It was a man. Definitely dead. With short grey hair. The lifeless skin was pockmarked but moving. Bugs were trying to get into the eyes.

I averted my eyes from the veins, flesh and bits of oesophagus which hung in a tangle beneath it, and spread over the stone.

On the audio we heard the boy.

'Oh fuck oh fuck oh fuck' he howled.

Another voice cut in robustly. Older, deeper: 'Oi you!'

The sounds of heavy but speeding footsteps, the quick pants of a child hyperventilating, then the camera juddered and everything went black.

For a moment neither of us could speak.

The sight was so shocking a wave of nausea passed through my stomach and up to my throat. I tasted the bitterness of bile at the back of my mouth.

Sam gripped on to the table top and retched.

'Jesus Christ!' I said in the end.

'Was that . . . Is that real?' Sam stammered.

Scrub gave us no pause but motioned for the camera back. 'Unfortunately.'

I'd seen horror films that were similar, but knowing that scene was real made the skin on my scalp grow tight and tingle.

'The victim,' said Scrub. 'Is a certain Reg Rainer. A known protestor affiliated to one of two groups that have been campaigning about the development.'

'Oh shit,' I said. The name was familiar. We'd met him only a few days before. He hadn't been a pleasant man but no one deserved to end up like that.

'Yes indeed,' said the sergeant. 'May I ask you, Ms Strange, is your period imminent?'

I looked up at her, and opened my mouth, but the question was so dumbfounding, nothing came out.

'That's rather a personal question,' said Sam.

Scrub removed a notebook from her pocket and said, 'I understand on Monday you were heard to threaten Mr Rainer?'

'What?' I said. 'Me? That's ridiculous. Who told you that?'

She flicked through a few pages then put her finger on a line. '"It's a good job I'm not premenstrual", you were overheard to say. So what would you have done if you were?'

'Oh that? For God's sake, he was rude. I was just . . . I was angry . . .'

Scrub's eyes transformed into dark pebbles and fixed on me. 'So, I say again, what would you have done if you were?'

'Look here.' I was aware my voice had notched up a few levels of shrill. 'You can't think I had anything to do with this?' I jabbed the phone in front of her. Another sickly shudder went through me. 'We did the exhibit then we went outside and chopped up the . . .' I stopped as I recalled, I *had* chopped off someone's head last night. But it had been inanimate – a waxwork's. There was no link.

Was there?

I'd just been a bit tipsy and the fire and Sam and the unusual nature of the evening had just made me feel different, odd.

'We chopped up firewood,' said Sam completing my sentence. 'We disposed of the old exhibit.' He sent me a silencing glance.

Scrub screwed up her eyes and looked deep into my face. It was an incredibly excruciating experience and, because of what had happened last night with the witchfinder, I started to feel guilty. Even though I knew I had nothing to do with the sticky end of Mr Vexatious Complainer.

'Well,' said Scrub and snapped her notebook shut. 'We are pursuing *all* lines of enquiry. Two of my officers will be here soon to take statements from you. Separately,' she emphasised the vowel sounds as if she was speaking to people without English as a first language.

I got what she was saying: you better get your story straight before they get here.

Or maybe she was just trying to put the frighteners on us, as I believe they say in the trade.

Slowly, not taking her eyes off me, Scrub rose to her feet.

'Have you found his body?' Sam asked. At some point in the last five minutes the thought had crossed my mind too. Surely there would be clues aplenty on that.

'Not yet,' she said, 'but we have teams searching. Can't be far.'

A memory of something similar I'd been told about recently flashed across my brain: there was a legend about a headless body, wasn't there? And without thinking I said, 'You should try the Sitting Pool.'

'Oh yes?' Scrub regarded me with new interest.

'Someone told me a headless body was found there once. It's in Silva Wood. Maybe it's happened again.'

The sergeant picked up the phone and notebook and put them back in her pocket. 'It's being combed thoroughly. But thank you for the tip-off.'

Oh crap, I thought, I need to develop more impulse control.

'In the meantime,' she said, before she swept out the door, 'do I need to tell you not to leave town?'

She didn't. We'd been caught up in a murder investigation before. Unfortunately we knew the score.

It was starting to become a bit of a bad habit.

CHAPTER TWENTY

By the time we had given our statements to the police, both omitting my own little 'jokey' waxwork decapitation ritual, it had gotten very late.

Sam and I were, not surprisingly, jittery and unnerved. We had Bronson phone the Bridgewaters to see if they wanted to postpone but they were keen to see us despite the late hour so we made our way over after tea. To be honest, it was the last thing I wanted to do. But at the same time I was grateful to get away from the Witch Museum and into the evening air.

I hadn't really had a chance to speak to Sam about what was playing on my mind. In fact it was only when we cut into Church Lane where the Bridgewaters' cottage was situated that I finally managed to bring it up. Their home was white-washed, the end terrace of five cottages that would have been built to house workers from the nearby estate. One had been knocked through to its neighbour to form a larger home.

Not the Bridgewaters' though. It remained in its original condition.

Though a little run down, it was possibly wider than the rest and had an extra bit of garden that ran down the side.

'Sam,' I called, as we began our approach. 'You know last night, when I was mucking about?'

He arched an eye at me, I suppose he was wondering which bit of mucking around I was referring to.

'You know.' I nudged him. 'What I did to the witchfinder waxwork? Well, you don't think that that had anything to do with Reg Rainer, do you?'

'Rosie, good God!' He said and slowed his pace and faced me. The evening was late and the sky darkening around him. Inside one of the nearby houses someone slammed a door. A car, a cream Mini Cooper, pulled up at a bungalow opposite. 'You're usually the sceptical one,' he said. 'Are you suggesting some kind of sympathetic magic was in operation?'

'I don't know,' I said. Then added, 'What's sympathetic magic?'

He stopped at the garden gate. A motion sensor light came on inside the Bridgewaters' porch. Sam lowered his voice. 'It's a kind of ritual that involves mimicry, imitation. When one tries to affect or alter a person, but uses a simulacrum.'

'A what?'

'Something that represents them, like a poppet or a voodoo doll, that kind of thing.'

My mind ranged back over last night's drunken fumblings. 'Oh my God! Like a dummy or a waxwork!'

Sam clicked his tongue with irritation. 'Don't be silly. No, no, no. Usually it needs something that's been in contact with the subject.'

I gripped his arm. 'What if he'd been to the museum and seen it?'

He picked off my fingers one by one and said, 'That hurts. Come on, now. You've just had a fright. We're both a bit shaken. Now, listen to yourself.' Then he opened the gate. 'I wondered if you might think something like that, but then I thought, "Hardly. It's Rosie Strange we're talking about here."'

I considered that and felt better. He was right – I had briefly lost my head.

So to speak.

Usually I was quite down to earth about all of this. It was just that, well, I'd never been a murder suspect before.

'You know,' he went on, holding the gate open for me to follow. 'That's what a lot of the accused witches made the mistake of thinking?'

'What do you mean?' I said, and followed him up the path, smelling the trailing alyssum that flowered around the border. Someone here had loved this patch once.

'It's classic psychology. Don't get fooled by it.'

But I was still none the wiser. 'You'll have to spell it out.'

'Well, back then,' he said, as we reached the cottage porch, 'during the witch hysteria, some of the women accused did start to think they had caused the problems they were accused of. For instance, if they begged for food and were refused, they might have cursed the neighbour. Then if something bad did happen to that neighbour, sometimes they thought they had caused it. Through their curse. That somehow, the Devil had imbued them with power. It's really not such a great jump from "witches are all around us" to "maybe *I* am a witch?" And if you call someone a witch for long enough, a lot of them will think it's true.'

I spoke before I thought it through. 'I'm not at that stage yet, am I?'

He was about to ring the bell, but paused. 'What do you mean? Has someone been calling you a witch, Rosie?'

I thought about Araminta and her parting shot yesterday, but decided to keep it to myself. It would be too long an anecdote to recount on the doorstep and the Bridgewaters might hear me and think I was nuts or dirty or a witch or something.

So I said, 'Oh you know how people are.'

'Don't start believing in things that aren't true,' Sam whispered. 'Not when you don't even believe in things that are.'

I didn't know quite what to make of that but at that point Terry Bridgewater was opening the door.

We were led through the hallway into what, in previous eras, might have been referred to as a parlour. A multi-functional room, with a large fireplace on one side. A sofa and two armchairs looked over the dusky back garden. By the furthest wall stood an old chunky table covered in a lace tablecloth.

I was quite fond of Terry without really knowing much about him. Mainly because, although he was a couple of decades younger, he had the same kind of practical dress-sense as my dad, which might be described as something that hovered between M&S cutting-edge cool to charity shop chic. Tonight, he had got on long shorts and what my dad would call a 'smart' summer top, which looked like a shirt with short sleeves and had a pocket on the front. It was the kind of thing Dad would be proud of finding in a charity shop. Terry, however, probably bought it from the local M&S, as we didn't have any second-hand places in Adder's Fork. Not big enough.

He presently pulled out a chair from the table and motioned for me to sit down. It was a nice old-fashioned gentlemanly gesture and made me like him even more. Once seated, he asked if we wanted anything to drink. It was on the tip of my tongue to request a whisky but Sam declined for both of us and got straight to the task in hand.

'So, Terry,' he said, when the older guy had sat down. 'Rosie and I have had some experience of people seeing things that aren't really there. I thought that might be something to consider in regards to your father, Ash?'

Terry rubbed his hand over his stubble and said, 'As you're aware, he is losing his sight, poor bugger. But the whole malarkey has started up again, that's the thing.'

I interrupted. 'What seems to be the problem?' It sounded more officious than I intended so I modified it. 'Sorry. I haven't been fully briefed on what's happening.'

Terry nodded, unbothered by my crude delivery. 'My old dad, he's been seeing things. Well,' he shifted weight from buttock to buttock and leant back. 'One thing: a man. In the garden. Says he's been communicating with him.'

'Oh yes,' I said and looked at Sam, for confirmation.

'It was happening just prior to the incident at La Fleur,' Sam said. 'Back in Spring.'

'Oh right.' I addressed my next comments to Terry. 'Your father was seeing a man in the garden? Couldn't in fact be a real live man, could it? A gardener perhaps?' It was a stupid thing to say, I realised as soon as I had put it out there. Of course the Bridgewaters must have investigated this possibility, and I was sure many others, before they had been desperate enough to bring in their last resort – me and Sam.

Terry sat forwards now and put his arms on the table. 'No. We checked with everybody we knew. Nobody had been in the garden on the days that Dad had said he'd seen, er, the ghost bloke. Now, my father is an invalid. He can hardly move, but he's as bright as a button. Still got all his marbles. We didn't believe him at first, but he was persistent. That made us think.'

'But it stopped, did it?' I prompted.

Terry nodded. 'We all breathed a sigh of relief I can tell you. But it started up again recently.'

That was unusual, I thought. That he should get better then relapse. 'Where is he when he sees this man?' I asked.

'He likes to sit out here.' He motioned to the tall armchair by the French windows. 'Sits there during the day. You can't see it now in the dark, but we've got a large garden. We all love it. Dad had green fingers and it's passed down to me and my son, Tony, though he don't bother with it now he's got all his music and DJ bits and bobs. But Dad loves looking at it. And when he's had enough, he's quite happy to watch the telly. Me and Tony manage to get back and cook meals and help him if he needs to visit the, er, facilities. He's not unhappy and we want it to stay that way. But now lately he's come troubled again.'

He eyed Sam gravely. 'Same as before. Says he sees the "old timer",' Terry smiled with sadness. 'Them's his words, even though Dad ain't no spring chicken.' Terry chuckled to himself. 'Think it's because of the clothes this bloke wears. "Old clothes" he says they are. Much smarter than what our clothes are. No jeans and the like. Proper trousers.' He winked at us like it was a familiar joke. 'Yes, so he's back again and it's upset Dad. He keeps saying he did what he was told, but it ain't made a difference.' He shook his head. 'Dad's saying he can't rest in peace.'

'Who?' I said. 'Your dad or the "ghost"?'

Terry rubbed his chin, 'Well, both of them.'

'And you think it is a ghost?' I asked him gently. 'For sure?'

'Can't see no other explanation,' he said.

'So you confirmed your dad's suspicions?' I said. 'To him?'

I must have sounded like I was cross, because Sam coughed and sent me a warning glance.

I tried to make my voice softer. 'How has your dad, Ash, described him?' I asked.

There was a moment of hesitation. Terry looked like he was going to say something but thought better of it. Nevertheless, he came up with the goods. 'Button-up green shirt. What dad calls "trews", trousers. Waistcoat. White hair. Jacket.'

'Could be period dress,' I said to Sam.

'Sure,' said Terry. 'That's what Dad says – that he's from another age, a "different era".' He broke off and put a finger over his lips almost as if he was stopping himself from saying something else. But whatever it was, he kept it inside.

'Okay, then. Well that fits,' I confirmed, when I realised Terry wasn't going to add any more detail.

'Go on,' Sam said and motioned for me to tell our host.

I took a breath and treated Terry to the benefit of my vast experience in ophthalmic conditions. 'There's a condition, believe it or not,' I told him. 'Where people with problematic eyesight actually hallucinate figures in period dress.'

'Well, I'm blowed,' said Terry and sat back heavily into his chair. 'It's a proper disease?'

'It's a condition that can sometimes occur when they're losing their sight and have problems with the part of the eye called the macular.' Bolstered by the sound of my own learnedness, I went on. 'The name for it is Charles Bonnet Syndrome. When eyesight is deteriorating, the brain overcompensates for lack of visual detail and tries to improvise with stored memories.' I let that sink in. 'It accounts for a lot of ghost sightings. Could be your dad's. Especially if he's seen the man on blowy days.' I got up and went over to the cottage windows and stroked the pale green velvet curtains that hung there. 'Some movement here, might twitch the fabric. Move it, so that it looks, to your dad, like it might be a person. You mentioned that this "spectre" wears a green shirt? Have you asked your dad if it's the same colour as the curtains?'

Terry seemed genuinely impressed. 'Didn't occur,' he said. 'But I will now.'

I was about to ask for more detail about the 'costume', when we heard the front door slam shut and someone shouted, 'I'm home'.

Before anyone came into the room, a shoe flew in through the door and landed on the rug in front of the hearth. A moment later another one somersaulted on top of it. Scarlet, with suede stripes. One of the trainers had flipped onto its front, revealing a patterned tread: a star within a circle positioned at the centre of the sole. Dolus Speeds.

Of course they were.

The world and his bloody wife, his eco-protestor, frumped-up daughter and teenage son had a pair, didn't they?

I sighed but converted it quickly into a noise that sounded like I was clearing my throat. Bloody Bunions.

The trainers were speedily followed by the entrance of a young man, with short cropped hair, in a T-shirt and jeans, who started as he came through the door. Evidently, he was not anticipating our presence. He took one look at the pair of us and then hung his head at the floor, embarrassed, I supposed, that his shoe-flinging episode had been witnessed by strangers.

'My son, Tony or Tone as he prefers these days,' said Terry and gave us an 'I don't know what these young people are like' eye-roll.

Tony or Tone was not happy about that introduction. He shot a glance at Sam and then me and quickly his cheeks started to colour. But it was okay, I'd been in the company of young men before and knew they could sometimes be flustered by unexpected female company. Especially when that female was me, right? Who could blame them?

Feeling the need to save his blushes I got up and went over and shook his hand. 'Rosie Strange,' I introduced myself. 'From the Witch Museum. It's great to meet you, Tone. Your dad's just been telling us how you look after your granddad. That's so nice,' I said to put him at ease.

It didn't appear to work for as soon as he released my hand he muttered. 'I'll just check in on him,' and then disappeared out the door again.

I turned to Terry and said, 'Bless him. What a commendable young man.' It sounded really middle-aged, but cheered him.

'That's right,' he said fondly. 'He is. Really.'

Sam, however, looked like he was ready to wrap things up and get going. 'So does that help you, Terry? The syndrome that Rosie has described? Perhaps you might want to mention it to your doctor? Is it Dr Patel?'

Terry nodded. 'It is and I will. But there is something else.' He began to shift his elbows onto the tablecloth when we all heard the sound of the doorbell. 'Strange,' said Terry. 'Wasn't expecting no one.' Then he rose. 'One minute.' And disappeared into the hall.

I re-seated myself and said to Sam, 'I think I can get Dr Roberts to email some information over to Terry. He can discuss it with Dr Patel.'

Sam's eyes widened as they clamped onto something over my shoulder.

Two uniformed police had entered the room.

Well, I wasn't expecting that. At the same time, I hadn't anticipated most of the developments that had unfolded this week. Who would?

'Miss Strange?' said the tall thin cop who had a bush of black hair sticking out from under his hat. 'We'd like to talk to you.'

I gawped at him. 'What about?'

The shorter of the two, a sturdier chap, blond, spoke next. 'We've found a body. Where you suggested we should look. We need to talk to you about how you knew it might be there.'

A bolt of adrenaline flew up out of my stomach and hit me direct in the heart. Oh crap. Not good. I touched my chest, aware of the powerful drumming that had commenced within it.

'Eh? What's this?' said Terry running a worried hand through what was left of his hair.

The tall dark constable stepped forwards and pointed out the way they had come. 'We'd like you to accompany us down to the station please, Miss Strange. We have a car waiting for you outside.'

'Station?' I said. A parcel of panic was unfolding in my stomach.

That sounded a lot like 'helping with enquiries' which to my mind was one step away from 'arrest'. 'Why?'

'Like we said,' he went on, bowing his head and smiling. 'Probably best to speak about it there.'

I took hold of the arm of the chair just in case they decided to grab me. 'It was Elvin,' I blurted. 'Elvin told me, when I saw him at the Sitting Pool.'

The officers exchanged a look. 'Elvin who?' said the short blond.

'I don't know,' I said, aware this wasn't very helpful. But I had no memory of a formal introduction to Elvin and his mate, Ella, or being told their surnames. 'He's a friend of Florian's, another protestor. They both know Reg Rainer. Call him "Vexatious Complainer".'

This appeared to throw the cat amongst the pigeons.

The thin dark one leaned back on his heels and poked his cap up. 'Really?'

The fatter one said, 'Hmmm.'

There was something a bit goofy about the thin one, a little keystone cops, that made me think he might be the best one to address my appeal to. 'Elvin said The Sitting Pool was where they had found bodies. Headless ones. Honestly. That's why I said it. Call him. Oh hang on, I haven't got Elvin's number, but I've got Florian's on my phone. He contacted them about the development around the Blackly Be. He's a journalist. He can give you Elvin's contact details.' I thought about trying an eyelash flutter but imagined they'd be trained to withstand that kind of thing.

Thankfully, the pair of them mumbled assents. The short blond was definitely happy with this new information and waited patiently as I brought my handbag up onto my knees.

Sam and Terry also appeared a little more relaxed now that the prospect of an arrest was evidently receding.

As I was shuffling around in the darkness of my bag, I remembered plugging my mobile into a socket in the office. 'Oh, it's at home,' I bleated.

'That's all right.' Mr Short and Stout spoke again. This time he sounded sterner than before. 'We'll give you a lift.'

It wasn't an offer I was going to be able to refuse. I sighed and stood up at the same time as Sam. And it was at that point all the lights went out.

CHAPTER TWENTY-ONE

Holy Shit.

I had thought that my first journey in the back of a police car was going to be the notable event of the evening, but of course I was wrong. Nothing in this bloody (literally) village was predictable.

As we drove through the darkened lanes and streets at a greatly reduced speed, remarking upon the unlit houses and dead streetlamps, the goofy cop got a message about a blackout in Adder's Fork. He muttered something to the other officer about hoping it might 'quieten down the locals'.

But, oh ha ha, how wrong he would be.

For as we turned into the grounds of the Witch Museum, 'notable' got onto a whole different level.

In front of the museum was a torch-wielding mob.

It was quite remarkable.

'Rightyho,' said Sam and rubbed my arm in an effort to reassure me. 'Now there's a sight you don't often see in Leytonstone.'

'No,' I said, a little dazzled. 'You're right. Never.'

Amassing around the entrance of the museum were approximately thirty plus villagers. Some of them had torches, of the battery-operated variety, but I suppose because of the blackout, others must have grabbed the closest thing to hand and had ended up here with more, er, traditional methods of illumination. The smell of kerosene wafted through the car window.

The police were clearly alarmed by this new development, but reacted discreetly by hitting the brakes, swearing and then skidding to an abrupt halt.

When we had come to rest, the blond officer nudged his partner and said, 'Do we need to call this in?'

'Never seen anything like it,' said Goofy and ran a finger under the rim of his cap: sweat was beginning to wet his hair. 'There's a bloke down the front with a bleedin' pitchfork.'

Sam and I nodded at each other and both mouthed 'Bob'.

Which I felt sure signified that we weren't about to be strung up to the nearest tree. At least I hoped we weren't. Like I said, the place was unpredictable.

I spotted Dilpreet Patel marching around near the porch with a loud hailer. The crowd were in good spirits and replying in full voice. Though it took me a couple of minutes to work out what they were saying, eventually I heard her shouting: 'What do we want?"

To which the villagers responded, 'The curse lifted'.

A single voice that may or may not have been Carmen's added, 'or neutralised'.

'When do we want it?' Dilpreet called.

The answer of course was, 'Now'.

Any references to the Blackly Be Boulder clearly didn't scan.

Sam sighed and leant forwards and tapped Goofy on his shoulder. 'Perhaps we should get out and have a chat with them?'

I inched towards the driving seat and pointed out a woman with bleached blonde hair carrying a placard. 'That's Neighbour Val. Hers is the sign that says "Help Us". Might be worse if you turn round now and don't let us go in?'

The two police had a little chat about this and then parked neatly in one of the spaces in the car park.

A couple of the protestors were peeling off, coming towards the vehicle with unclear purpose, possibly. I guess, to remonstrate against what they thought would be police intervention. But they stopped in their tracks when they saw Sam and me emerge from the rear doors.

I saw Molly Acton whizz out from behind one of them and gallop towards us.

'Thank goodness,' she said. As our two escorts darted into formation either side of us, she stopped and asked, 'Why have you got the police here?' Then she shook her head. 'Doesn't matter. Sam, Rosie – everybody's concerned about all the crazy things that have been going on since the boulder was disturbed. This last murder – it's got them all shaken up.' Then she looked over at the police to see if they agreed.

They did. 'Could turn into civil disorder,' our driver said.

'I think you should address them. They need answers. Want something done,' Molly went on. 'They're slightly agitated, you see.'

The shorter blond officer smirked. 'That's got to be the understatement of the century.'

'Come on then,' said Molly and directed the policemen to forge a way through the crowd.

Which they did without any recourse to batons or tasery.

In fact, the villagers parted like the Red Sea and we all made our way safely to the porch where Bronson was standing with his hands in front of him, like he was trying to calm everyone down.

'Ah, thank the lord, you're here. You've got some visitors,' he said, as if we hadn't yet noticed the gathered herd.

There was an empty bucket at his feet (of course there was), which I upturned and stood on, leaning against Sam's shoulder for support.

As the assembled demonstrators clocked me, a hush descended. Well, mostly it descended over those gathered at the front who, I noticed, were mainly formed of primary-aged children carrying wind-up torches in the shapes of penguins, ducks and a Father Christmas, all looking like they were having a whale of a time. There was a real scarcity of babysitters in Adder's Fork.

When their elders had finally realised I was going to say something they also quietened down.

I waited for total silence then shouted, 'So what's the matter? Why are you here?'

There was a collective murmuring, then a raspy voice in the middle of the crowd croaked, 'You got to put an end to the curse of the Blackly Be.'

It was Bob.

'Oh yeah?' I said, and felt Sam disappear from under my hand. Oh no – he wasn't leaving me to it, was he? Although, I thought, that was okay, because I was a proper grown-up girl. And what proper grown-up girl couldn't handle a torch-wielding mob, right? And this was me – Rosie Strange from Benefit Fraud. I'd handled worse.

I think.

I took a deep breath. However, left without my physical anchor, the movement made me wobble a bit on the bucket. Luckily Bronson noticed and came and propped me up with his shoulder.

'It's Black Anne,' yelled Bob. 'They've disturbed her grave and she's not happy. She's come back for her reckoning, she has.'

Oh gawd, here we go, I thought, but I said, for clarity, 'What do you mean – her "reckoning"?'

It was occurring to me this might be the perfect time to regale the villagers with a few home truths.

'It's what's gone before,' Bob continued and I thought he was going to launch into a description of what happened back in 1941. But he didn't. He went on a different tack. 'The old Adder's Fork folk,' he said pronouncing it slowly, presumably for fear of muddling up the Fs. Could be embarrassing. 'They done her wrong. They strung her up and burnt her.'

I saw the pink anorak lady from Dr Patel's surgery push past one of the eight-year-olds down the front. 'And now she's back, starting her murderous spree,' she screamed. There was spittle in the corner of her mouth. 'I warned you, but you wouldn't listen.'

The crowd muttered and swayed. Someone down the back booed. Bob proffered his voice to the mumbling discord, 'First, that bloke last night. Next, the rest of us.'

His neighbour behind him added, 'We don't want that.'

Dilpreet raised her loud hailer and shouted into it. 'What do we want?'

A single lonely confused voice called out, 'The curse lif . . .' then petered out.

Bob raised his pitchfork for silence and when the herd was settled again, said 'Our ancestors killed her. And your museum and that.' He orientated his pitchfork in the direction of the entrance. 'Well it says they, these witches, well they was all probly innocent.'

A little pang of pride thrummed through my heart. We *were* having an effect after all. I would have liked to have tried for a bit more feedback on that particular subject, but it was best, I thought, to focus on crowd dispersal before the police took the task upon themselves.

'Yes,' I said, nodding like I thought someone wise would. 'That's right. They were innocent because there's no such thing as magic, is there?'

A gasp went up from the gathered crowd, followed by a loud tittering at the back and a bit of movement which jogged the flaming torches.

I went on undeterred. 'And if there's no such thing as magic, then she can't have risen from the grave to enact some mental curse, can she?'

But Bob, who had now elbowed his way forward, said, 'Look around you, Rosie Strange. The whole place bin turned upside down by this nastiness. The kids, they *seen* her walking the village.'

One of the girls in the front row whispered at a volume loud enough for us to hear, 'Isabelle said she done a poo in her garden.'

This was followed by giggling and a, 'Be quiet Matilda' from the back.

A blonde head popped out next to Bob's, 'Other people, grown-ups – they witnessed her about the place,' said Val.

'You don't know.' Bob wagged his finger at me. 'You weren't here before. You can't tell us that witch can't rise from the grave – cos I'm telling you, dear, oh yes she can.'

Without realising what I was playing into I *reacted* rather than *responded* to the crowd with a, 'Seriously, Bob, oh no she can't.'

To which everyone aged under ten at the front began giggling and chorused with glee, 'OH YES SHE CAN'.

I made my lips into a tight compressed line and glowered at them.

One of the police behind me muttered something about it being early for a pantomime. Which although was accurate, began to irk me. I put my hands up and started flapping them down, like I was trying to hush them. 'Hang on, now,' I said. 'We need to talk about this rationally . . .'

But to my dismay my words had the absolute opposite effect and elicited excited squeals and cries of 'She's behind you. She's behind you'.

For God's sake!

There was no way I was getting back into an 'Oh no she isn't' situation now so I stayed rigid, staring at them with an expression of what I thought was, 'calm dignity', until something hard prodded me in the back. I wobbled again, regained my balance then turned round. I wish I hadn't.

What gushed forth next from my lungs was a pronounced scream. Then I fell off the bucket.

For there in all her shabby chic glory was Black Anne herself. Kind of terrifying.

Sam had fetched the dummy from the exhibit for some reason I couldn't work out yet.

'This,' he said, raising her up with both hands. 'This is Black Anne. And do you know what?' He didn't wait for a response. 'She's as harmless as this dummy. I have researched her and there is no evidence, no evidence, that your ancestors, that the village as a community, was responsible for her death.'

Which I thought was a bit of a leap. Someone had killed her and cut off her head. At least I hoped it was that way round.

'The documentation,' Sam breathed heavily. 'In the Chelmsford Records Office dictates she was acquitted at court. Released.'

A ripple of surprise passed through the crowd.

Val's mouth fell open so wide she looked for a moment like a ridiculous blow-up doll. She should definitely calm down on the blusher.

There then followed a low collective wittering.

After some consultation with Pink Anorak and Val, Bob said, 'But someone done her in, coz her bones bin found under the Blackly Be.'

Damn. I knew someone would point that out. Everyone was bound to have read the article in the paper.

'And still we've had problems all over town,' Bob pronounced. 'Now someone's lost their head. It's far far worse than it was before.'

That was a reference to the 1944 alleged poltergeist activity I thought, as I pushed myself back up onto my feet and brushed the gravel off my hands and bum.

Sam handed the dummy to Bronson with a sigh. 'This recent murder is something the police are currently using a number of resources to investigate,' he yelled. 'You must co-operate with them.'

Neighbour Val raised her fist and shook it. 'They're not going to go down and arrest the ghost are they? Witch ways call for Witch Museums.'

A couple of 'hear hears' trickled down from the back.

'You've got to sort out this curse,' Bob said and plunged his pitchfork into the gravel for emphasis.

'And find out what they want,' Neighbour Val confirmed.

Dilpreet shouted, 'Now' through her loud hailer.

I presumed the 'they' Val referred to were the bodies in the grave and wondered if I should ask her exactly how she proposed we went about communicating with the dead, for God's sake, but Sam was already talking again.

'All right. We'll sort it out,' he said, to my epic consternation.

'Good,' said Bob supported by approving noises from those around him. 'And get in and do it before something else happens.'

'We're all counting on you,' said Molly, at my side.

No pressure then.

There was a bit more grunting, then Bob reversed and, presumably now satisfied, began to trundle off the property.

Seeing the entertainment was ending, the rest of the crowd gradually followed.

'Wow,' I said to Sam. 'Is this another fine mess you've got us into? I can't believe you just agreed to that. I feel ambushed.'

'We'll talk inside,' he said.

The radio on Goofy went off as we headed into the museum. A tinny voice asked for an update on his progress.

'No, quite the opposite ma'am,' I heard him say. 'They want them here. From what I can make out, sounds like they're trying to hound them *in* to town.'

CHAPTER TWENTY-TWO

Once I'd found my phone and given the policemen Florian's number I thought the pair of them, now introduced as PCs Dennis Bean and Shaun O' Neil, would bugger off and leave us alone.

But they didn't.

Instead Dennis, who was Goofy – the tall thin one – asked us what it was we intended to do about this turn of events.

To which Sam responded by going over to the cupboard where the 'ghost hunting' equipment was kept, though he hated me using that term, and pulling out several items whilst explaining their use to the officers.

'This is it, is it? We're going to do a stake-out, are we?' I asked as he was pointing out the coloured buttons on an EMF meter to Shaun, the short blond cop.

He didn't answer because Shaun frowned and said, 'Hold up – a stake-out? That sounds like police work to me. You can't do it tonight. The crime scene's not been released.'

'Mm,' said Sam and frowned. 'How about tomorrow night?'

And Shaun said, 'Probably. Do you want back-up?'

'No,' I said, getting a bit irritated that I hadn't and still wasn't being consulted about any of this.

'But you heard what they said.' This from Dennis/Goofy. 'That crowd out there. They want you to look into it and you, well,' he poked a long thin finger at Sam, 'he, he said he would. He committed you.'

'Blimey,' I said. 'Am I hearing this right? The police don't mind getting involved with ghost hunting malarkey?'

It was like the whole place and everyone who strayed into it had gone stark raving mad. Or fallen under some strange spell. A glamour, I thought and then told myself off for even allowing the idea to cross my mind. People were nuts, that was all.

'Oh no,' said Shaun and set the EMF meter down on the table. 'Oh no. We won't be involved with it. Absolutely not. No way. We'll be keeping our distance, as is proper. But,' he instructed firmly. 'We'll hear about the results please.'

I opened my mouth to give utterance to sounds of being gobsmacked but found that I was too stunned to even make any. My world was so much more confounding than it had been but five months ago.

'That's fair enough,' Sam agreed. 'Really. And you're right, I think you should stay away. If anything happens we'll phone you. Will you have an officer on site?'

'No,' Shaun shook his head. 'Not once it's released. Just phone the station if you require assistance. There may well be a patrol car in the area.'

Dennis/Goofy cleared his voice and gestured towards me, 'And you're going to investigate who they are, I understand?'

Hmm, I thought, so he was presuming Sam did the stake-outs and I did the paperwork. How bloody typical an assumption. In fact, we shared most of the duties. I communicated displeasure at his unwitting gender bias by scowling.

He put his hands in his pockets and shifted awkwardly. 'There's still some disagreement about the male victim's identity.'

'Indeed,' Sam nodded. 'Rosie and I have an appointment with Professor Thea Crossley of Fortenbras University Saturday morning.'

'Really?' I said. He hadn't told me about that. 'But Saturday? The museum's going to be busy.'

'We'll have to draft in extra help,' said Sam. 'This is important.'

'It is,' said Shaun and nodded with gravity. 'If you can't get cover, I'll ask around at the station. Collaboration with members of the public such as yourselves is not without precedent. And this matter needs your attention as a priority, I think we'd all agree.'

Whatever next? I thought as I went off to phone my friend Cerise. Sergeant Scrub manning the till? Chloe Brown giving lectures in the Talks Area? Goofy touring groups round the Ursula Cadence exhibit?

Then I stopped myself from thinking on – stranger things did not just happen at sea. Since I'd inherited this blimmin' museum stranger things kept happening to me.

CHAPTER TWENTY-THREE

I learnt that my friend Cerise was having her hair extensions done, which normally took about six hours, so couldn't get down till later, if indeed we still wanted her then. Auntie Babs was on the other end of the hair extensions business and had her hands full with several appointments to attach them to various heads so couldn't get over until Sunday. There was no point asking my mum and dad as they'd freak out and I didn't want Dad getting agitated, not when he was being investigated for angina. My brother, John, was simply too lazy and wouldn't turn up even if I begged him or paid him or made threats.

Thus, it was with some trepidation and a large dose of bemusement that we left our little Witch Museum that Saturday in the hands of Bronson, Vanessa, Vanessa's mum Trace, and Chloe Brown from Litchenfield University's Forensic Archaeology department. Just don't ask. Seriously.

Sam and I had our usual fight about who was going to drive, which I won and by midday we were making our way through the county's pretty B-roads to a small village called Pedlar's Green, outside of Litchenfield.

Thea Crossley, Sam informed me, was an expert in local folklore, myths and legends who he consulted with from time to time on matters concerning his thesis. After his description I imagined a little old lady with grey hair in a bun and dusty pink cardigans rambling around a big old ramshackle house.

As it turned out Professor Crossley was quite the opposite and lived in a swish new duplex that looked out over the very picturesque village brook.

She threw her arms around Sam like he was an old friend and greeted me warmly enough. Although her hair was indeed greyish she'd had it cut short in a very blunt but cutting edge asymmetric style that would terrify Auntie Babs. I thought it was more Hoxton than Pedlar's Green, but I liked it. She capped off this rather uncompromising look with a pair of thick black-rimmed glasses, scarlet lipstick, a silk top with a tie at the side and a pair of palazzo pants with a Liberty print that just oozed positive self-assurance.

As soon as we got through into the hall Thea showed us around the place, which she seemed very proud of. It transpired she had recently bought it. We followed her around as she pointed out the great views and roomy interiors with minimalist fittings and chic design classics, before settling us in her 'studio' while her girlfriend, Dawn, went off to make coffee.

It was an amazing space, with floor to ceiling windows, a thick white carpet, modernist desk and a Le Corbusier chaise longue. Two walls were lined with bookshelves, one of which had its own ladder. The third wall was curved. Thea explained that behind it, she'd designed a temperature controlled closet for books and artefacts that required extra special care.

Lucky cow, I thought, as I settled into one of the two Barcelona chairs parked opposite the desk. I was definitely in the wrong business.

Of course I was in the wrong business. Who'd run a blimmin' witch museum?

Muggins, that's who.

I sighed out loud and said, 'It's so nice here.' Though didn't ask about the price tag, which I really wanted to do.

And Thea smiled. Her eyes creased heavily in the corners. She must have heard that a lot. 'Dawn's an investment banker. We've been very lucky.'

Right on cue, Dawn, entered the room and slid a bronze tray onto the shiny desktop and unloaded a matching cafetiere, copper milk jug and three mugs with different pictures of fish on the sides. In her daggy grey jogging bottoms and sports-bra top that showed off several dragon tattoos, she definitely did not fit my idea of an investment banker.

I asked for sweetener, but they didn't have any so said I'd do without. Dawn sent us all a big, fresh and extraordinarily wide smile, that was definitely one of her most lovely assets and then said she'd leave us to it.

'So.' When Dawn had closed the door Thea poured out the coffee. 'After our phone conversation the other night I managed to pull out some books that I thought might be related to the discoveries in Adder's Fork.' She gestured to a pile on a silver trolley at the side of the desk.

After handing our mugs over she lifted a battered green volume off the top. 'Now, you told me that there was an entry in Dee's diary that dated to 1591. Concerning treasure? Well, I couldn't see anything that specifically matched this date but I did find, under "divination", a reference to a Bessie Moor character from Little Baddow, who was known to divine for treasure, amongst other things.'

Sam had bent closer to the desk, eager to hear more. 'Was she indicted at all?'

Thea shook her head. Dangly silver earrings swung about her neck. 'Not that I could see. According to this parish history it seems she was respected in the village, for her exotic healing methodology.' She paused and turned a page. 'Or possibly feared, you know how it is.'

Sam nodded. 'Unusual,' he said. 'Given the political climate. I wonder what protected her from accusations?'

I shrugged. 'Well, in my experience people don't like to play with fire. Usually if that fire is more powerful, wealthy, connected and more violent than them. That sort of thing.'

'Lord of the Manor,' Sam nodded. 'Who was?'

Thea read out a name from the book. 'Samuel Howlet.'

Sam grinned at me. 'Could work. Dee could have sent someone down, who may or may not have linked up with Bess to find the aforementioned treasure?'

'It's a possibility,' I agreed. 'But how does that explain the two bodies in the grave?' I thought it through. 'They have got to have been buried post 1621 as that's when Anne was in court. Could there be a link between Anne Hewghes and Bessie Moor?'

'Two witches working within the same area. They would have known of each other, for sure.' He paused. 'Names were quite fluid back then. Most of the population were illiterate. If Anne had been married her name would have changed.'

'What are you thinking?' I said, but I was getting his drift.

'Given the timing. Is it possible Bessie Moor and Anne Hewghes could have been mother and daughter?'

Thea nodded. 'It's not unlikely,' she said. 'Weren't you more likely to be accused of witchcraft if another family member was thought to be a witch?'

'Sure were,' I said because I wanted to be part of the conversation.

'"The sins of the father shall be visited on the sons",' Thea intoned with a solemnity that I hadn't expected.

'Or the mother,' I said. 'In this case. On the daughter. Sad and unfair. As usual.' Did get on my nerves how much mud tended to stick back then. Although, actually, it was still like that today, really.

'So,' said Thea. 'Moving on. I found this story associated with Adder's Fork.' She replaced the book and picked up a thick blue volume. 'There's no specific date attached but this edition of the book, *Tales of Old Essex,* was printed in 1919. This story is called *The Return of Bartholomew Elkes.* I got a sense, from the contextual introduction, the legend was approximately four centuries old – an enduring cautionary tale so to speak. Shall I read it?'

'Please do,' said Sam.

'Okay.' She pushed her glasses up to the top of her nose. '"*The little village of Adder's Fork is not only renowned for its tinkers and May fayres.'"* She looked over the top of the book and explained 'Previous chapter.' Then got her eyes down again. "'*Many Essex folk were reputed to avoid the village after dark and at points on the yearly calendar. And not only for fear of highwaymen! For it is well known amongst members of that rural community, parts of the ancient village are enchanted, controlled, it seems, by the Fae.'"* Thea looked up at us and said, 'Fairies'.

Sam responded with an 'ah', nodded with eyes closed, then opened them and said to me, 'Pre-Disneyfication they could be quite nasty little buggers.'

'Well,' said Thea. 'Perhaps more flawed and more human than they seem now. Anyway, shall I go on?'

We both nodded.

"'*Although for the most part the two communities rubbed along well taking care not to tread on each other's toes, from time to time a stranger would present themselves in town and, ignorant of the unspoken courtesies that existed between the two realms, would come quickly undone. And that is what happened to poor Bartholomew Elkes. Known to be a wise-man and an astrologer from London, Doctor Elkes had frequented the Elizabethan Courts.'"*

Sam looked at me and whispered. 'Could have met Dr John Dee there? Dee was an advisor to Elizabeth I.'

"'*However, the ways of the court were no protection in Adder's Fork. Elkes returned to the sleepy village to seek the treasure legends tells us he had failed to find years before. This time however he was given a clue, or a vision, by a local lady, one of dark nature often called a witch. It was said that so full of confidence was Bartholomew Elkes he announced in the local tavern that he was about to find the greatest treasure of all. A magical bounty every man could only dream of. That night he slipped off into Silva Wood and was never to be seen again. It is said that the Fae, outraged by the arrogance of the Doctor Elkes and keen to keep their treasure hidden, set a trap and tempted him into fairy land.'"*

'Anything else?' asked Sam.

'It goes on about a fiddler, who came to perform at the Sitting Pool.'

'Played for the Fae and the witches all night?' I said.

'That's right,' said Thea.

'When he got back to the village a hundred years had passed?'

'Correct,' said Thea appreciatively and snapped the book shut.

'How do you know that?' asked Sam.

'Ella and Elvin told me,' I said.

Thea leant forwards. 'Sorry, did you just say an elf told you?'

'No,' I said, 'a bloke called Elvin. Although now you come to mention it . . .'

Sam snorted and punched my arm. 'Rosie, come on. No need for sarcasm.'

I was going to tell him I wasn't being sarcastic but then realised that might make me sound completely off my rocker. And actually, what was I talking about? Elvin and Ella were as real as me and Sam, for gawd's sake.

'Indeed,' said Thea. 'There's glamours in that there village.'

I sighed. She wasn't wrong. 'Don't I just know it,' I said.

Sam tutted. 'Thea's referring to the spell,' he said.

Before I could answer, Thea herself had come back with, 'It's a power, an ability of sorts, to give the illusion that something is more beautiful than it is in reality. A sort of fantastical and magical cloak . . .'

Out of the corner of my eye I saw Sam cringe.

'Yes, thank you,' I snarled at Thea. 'I'm fully up to date on what it is.'

'Oh, right,' she said and glanced at Sam.

He was still wincing.

An awkwardness descended over the three of us sitting round the desk.

I broke it to ask where the toilet was.

Thea directed me with gracious smiles and delicate gestures. As I exited the room I heard her whisper to Sam, 'Sorry. When you said you were bringing your partner I assumed . . .'

Didn't hear the rest as I was now a) fuming because she had assumed I was a thicko who had come along for the ride and b) Sam had said I was his partner, NOT the blimmin' owner of the museum. Could he still not accept my seniority? Was that a bloke thing or was that a Sam thing, I wondered as I washed my hands in the Japanese-style bathroom.

That irritated me too as it took me about five minutes to work out how to put the tap on. It was a stupid tap with no actual tap bit to it, just a motion sensor somewhere on the neck that chucked out water in what the designer, no doubt, thought would be an elegant waterfall but actually, after all the mucking around, had a tsunami element to it which meant the water now bounced off the ceramic sink and onto my jeans so it looked like I had wet myself.

It didn't improve my mood.

Instead of taking a right and going back into Thea's studio I took a left and went into the large open plan living area with its view of the bubbling brook.

I was standing at the window forcing down some deep breaths when a voice said, 'Are you all right?'

It was Dawn. I hadn't noticed her when I had come in because she was sitting in a pod chair that was hanging from the ceiling. Inside she sat cross-legged like a contented, but thin and female buddha, albeit with a sports-bra top and lots of tattoos.

I regarded the investment banker snug in her little pod and said, 'Don't you get fed up with how people make assumptions about you?'

She raised her head and treated me to one of her beautiful smiles. 'Nope. Not any more.'

'How so?'

'Oh, come on Rosie. Only a fool judges a book by its cover.'

'Hmm,' I mumbled. 'But people do. People make judgements about you as soon as you walk into a room, about the way you speak, what you wear . . .'

'Like I said – more fool them. That gives you an advantage, though doesn't it?' She winked at me, like I knew the answer to the question, which I didn't. 'They can't see how sharp you are. It's their first mistake. And sometimes it's in your interest not to correct them. Sometimes it's in your interest to manipulate them, to get what you want, right? Not show your true colours, hide your hand.'

God, she was good, I thought. No wonder the pair of them could afford this pad.

'How do you know I'm sharp?' I said.

She lengthened her spine along the curve of the chair. 'There's no beating around the bush. You came right in, intuited some of the experiences I've been through. Guessing you know my line of business or worked out from our lifestyle, we're not poor. So I'm successful *in spite* of the way I look.'

I thought about denying it but realised there was no point.

'That's a lot of processing and quickly too. You also knew I wouldn't be offended by your question. And I'm not, so there you go.'

'An advantage,' I said. 'I'll have to remember that the next time someone's patronising me or assuming a low knowledge-base.'

'You do that,' she said and grinned serenely. 'But we judge people too. We're not exempt. You can't help it. Just remember no one is ever what they seem? We're all complex people with different modes of address and masks for the outside world. All of us are playing a lifelong poker game.'

I changed position so I could face her properly and saw Sam coming into the room. 'Well, that's an interesting philosophy,' I said.

He stopped short of the pod chair and frowned. 'You talking to yourself again?'

'Use it to your advantage,' said Dawn from the chair, and kicked her legs out and swung the globe round.

'Ah,' said Sam. 'Hello.' Then he searched me to see if I'd got over my strop and said, 'Glad tidings: in 1591 a Bartholomew Elkes visits Dee's house in Mortlake, to see John Dee's wife. It's him. The timing fits. Bartholomew Elkes is the returning man of the tale. The man in the grave.'

'Wow,' I said. 'Good work. Very impressive. How did you do that?'

'Thea has a programme that detects plagiarism which can also work for other purposes.'

'She's good at multi-tasking,' said Dawn as her girlfriend appeared behind Sam.

'Come on, Rosie, let's go and get some lunch.' Sam tried to make me smile. 'This is something to celebrate, surely?'

'There's a nice pub, The Green Man, just outside the village,' Thea said. 'We'd join you, but we've got a big dinner on tonight.'

It was a hint – they needed to get on.

'Come on,' said Sam, sounding a bit whiney. 'This is great news. Part of the puzzle for sure. Should put us in Scrub's good books.'

I thought about smiling and agreeing but then I remembered what Dawn had said about hiding my hand and so looked a bit glum instead.

'It's on me,' he added with a hopeful grin. And that did the trick.

'Excellent,' I said and winked at Dawn. I could see this whole assumption thing starting to work out.

CHAPTER TWENTY-FOUR

The Green Man was one of those pubs that are perfect for a warm summer weekend. We ordered our food, which was of the gastro variety and then went out into the beer garden.

The back of the pub was covered with a yellow rambling rose, which not only made the wall look alive with little round beams of sunshine, but also scented the air with a seasonal sweetness even though, my dad told me, roses were rarely blessed with both beauty and perfume. The Green Man had clearly brought out the best in the plant.

At the end of the garden cherry trees gathered around a little stream. Tubs of flowers provided splashes of colour around chic rattan lounging furniture on the terrace. But these were already fully occupied.

We opted for one of the more conventional trestle tables on the lawn towards the brook, both acknowledging we didn't want our conversation overheard.

Sitting down we tucked into our pints of diet coke as heartily as one can on a hot afternoon, when the sun's high and everyone around you is happily necking ciders and turning a nice shade of rosé.

'Right,' said Sam. 'Let's work out what we know.'

'Collate an information audit.'

'Correct.'

I nodded, and feeling the need to look efficient, brought out the notebook I kept as a habit in my handbag. 'First: we have a disturbed grave.'

Sam shook his head. 'Goes back before that. First we have a boulder said to mark the burial site of a certain Black Anne.'

I agreed and wrote down Black Anne. 'Aforesaid boulder is then disturbed.'

Sam nodded. 'We witness the discovery of human remains: two skeletons. One man, one a woman, presumably Black Anne.' He paused.

I thought about this and said, 'We're looking at circumstantial evidence here and making assumptions. Are there any more witch trials around the same time? With women from the village?'

'No.' He grinned. 'I had the same thoughts. Adder's Fork has a rash of accusations in the 1570s and 80s. There's an accusation against a Thomas Saye in 1600, but that looks more like sheep theft to me, of course it's all dressed up as counter-accusation. We've got Anne Hewghes in 1621 then it all goes quiet until Matthew Hopkins rides into town in 1645, then the place explodes.'

'So no one else either side of her for twenty-odd years?'

'No other woman is in the frame as a witch.'

'Mmm,' I said. 'So it's probable that it's her.'

'And we know the story of the Blackly Be. Parts of it are inaccurate,' he said. 'The burning, for instance. However, the remainder was grounded in truth – she was accused of witchcraft and taken before the courts.'

I nodded. 'But acquitted.'

'Yes,' said Sam. 'So it seems.'

'And not executed by them.'

'Quite true. I wonder how she died?'

We both looked at our drinks and took a long glug of them.

'Before she got her head cut off?'

'That's right,' he said.

A bird in a nearby cherry tree started singing chirpily. A group of drinkers all laughed at the same time. Below the murmur of gentle conversation, you could hear the brook burbling. The scene was on so many levels quite idyllic. And yet here we were discussing another brutal murder. It had happened a lot since I'd inherited the Witch Museum. If I'd learnt anything from my grandfather's gift it was to try to be constantly vigilant. Your life might be going pretty okay but it could change at any moment and quickly send you spinning into the brown stuff.

'And he,' Sam was saying.

'What?'

'Her grave fellow died from stabbing.'

I wasn't following. 'Her grave fellow?'

'The man. I think she probably went the same way. Generally if you find two bodies in a grave in unconsecrated ground, there's a reason for them being buried together. Their mode of death is usually not good, not conventional. It's been covered up. Because, I suspect, they were murdered. By the same people.'

'Who cut their heads off.'

'Poor Bartholomew and Annie,' said Sam.

We lapsed into our own thoughts for a while then I said to him, 'But at least we know what he was doing now, don't we? And why he came to Adder's Fork. He's an associate of Dr John Dee, which we know from the disc.'

'Indeed.' He nodded. Then jutted his chin out proudly. 'And if that didn't date him well enough we also know, because he was middle-aged when he died – around 1621 – and appeared in Dee's house in 1591, we can be pretty sure that like the old tale decreed he is in all probability Bartholomew Elkes.'

It sounded convincing. I nodded.

'I'd put money on it,' said Sam, as if trying to persuade me. 'Presumably though, his efforts to find the treasure came to nothing. There is no evidence anywhere to suggest that it was ever found. So if he failed in 1591, what made him return thirty years later?'

I shrugged. 'I guess it might be for the same reasons that the police re-open old cases – new information? New technology? If the story Thea told us bears any resemblance to the truth, Bartholomew Elkes had come back to find the treasure. At least he did find some of it before he died.'

'Eh?' said Sam and raised an eyebrow.

'He found his treasure,' I repeated.

Sam continued to look blank.

'Part of the Howlet Hoard,' I said.

Sam screwed his eyes up even more thoroughly and looked at me through the slits.

'The pot,' I explained. 'It was full of old coins.'

'Oh no.' Sam's face broke into lines. 'That might be a clue or a token but it wasn't a haul. Remember the Howlet Hoard was fabled – cellars and cellars filled to the brim with ancient treasure and precious gems. More gold than you could dream of.'

'Oh yeah,' I said. 'But he must have found that pot. Before he was "tempted into fairyland".'

'Quite,' said Sam. 'Which, as far as I'm aware, has never been a metaphor for a cold dark grave. Although there's always a first.' He leant back to allow space for the waitress to put our lunch on the table.

Despite the heat the talk was starting to dampen me, so I was happy to shove a sausage in my gob and that was not a euphemism either.

'Still,' said Sam, as he chowed down on a salmon baguette. 'This is all very useful should we actually see something, or even make contact tonight.'

'Tonight?' I asked.

'The stake-out,' he said. 'I've got all the cameras ready.'

Oh, bugger I thought as I tucked into the mash. I'd forgotten. 'Are we really still going to do that? We've kind of fulfilled our commitment to the police now – we've identified the bodies.'

'We've made other commitments though,' said Sam. 'To our community.'

He was really too dutiful for his own good.

And mine.

The museum was shutting up by the time we got back.

Vanessa and Trace were keen to get off as soon as we kicked out the last visitors but Chloe had heard we were doing a stake-out: she came up to us while we were in the lobby sorting out the till and volunteered to help.

To my amazement Sam agreed.

This was without precedent.

What was going on?

And why wasn't I being consulted again?

I considered having a huff then thought about what Dawn had said about showing your hand, so remained nonchalantly quiet until Sam suggested he take Chloe into the office to show her his equipment. I was about to disrupt this unexpected show of friendliness by throwing myself on the floor or pretending to faint, when we heard the front door open.

'Look,' I said. 'It's very nice of you Chloe, but you need a certain amount of expertise to conduct a, er, ghost hunt, so to speak.'

'Rosie,' said Sam, his voice heavy with disapproval. 'We don't call it that do we . . .?' Then his voice petered out.

Beside him Chloe was looking at me, her eyes tapering out at the ends.

'Oh sorry,' I heard Sam say. 'We're closed now.'

I realised then that someone was behind me.

When I turned, it took a moment for me to process the dark silhouette that filled the doorway.

'Did someone mention a ghost hunt?' said my friend Cerise.

CHAPTER TWENTY-FIVE

Once we'd got through the introductions we went into the office to discuss the night's plan.

I was delighted to see my friend and impressed with her multi-layered extensions that were arranged in an exaggerated statement afro at least two feet in diameter. Cerise was totally rocking the look, which she'd enhanced with a fringed T-shirt, tight jeans that might have been jeggings and gold platform trainers. This chick was a serious urban goddess.

I think Chloe and Sam were a bit taken aback at first. But I thought they probably wouldn't know class if it walked up to them and headbutted them in the face. They both, in my opinion, erred a bit on the conventional side when it came to fashion. Even Chloe with her dark eyes and dyed black hair wore plain jeans and T-shirts that suggested a lack of commitment and part-time attitude to Goth.

While Sam went into the kitchen to put the kettle on, the three of us girls took our places at the table.

'Hmm,' said Cerise, drumming her recently glued nails as she surveyed the room. 'It's not as much of a dump as I thought it would be.'

'Shhh,' I glanced at Sam to make sure he hadn't heard. 'We've put some effort into the place with the relaunch and that.'

'Uh huh. But you're still going to sell it, right?' said Cerise, continuing with her 'considerably unimpressed' face.

'Really?' Chloe popped her head up. 'Selling? Why would you sell it? It's fascinating here? Why would anyone sell a museum?'

Cerise sucked her teeth. 'Why would anyone keep it?'

'Look,' I said quickly. 'It's complicated. Can we not talk about this now please?'

And luckily as Sam came back with the tray of cups, they both shut up.

'So what's all this about a ghost hunt?' asked Cerise, nails reaching for the nearest mug.

'Well, we've had a few incidents lately,' said Sam.

I smirked at Cerise and said, 'The peasants are revolting.'

She sent Sam a wink and said, 'Oh they don't look too bad to me, babe.'

Chloe and I both sighed with irritation then Chloe said, 'It's been prompted by developers who were trying to move a local landmark.'

And then Sam told her about the myth and Chloe filled her in on the forensics results.

'So,' Sam told her. 'We thought, to allay the fears of our friends and neighbours, and maybe even get to the bottom of what's been going on, Rosie and I—'

Chloe cleared her throat. 'And me.'

'Yes,' he said and smiled at her. 'Rosie and I and Chloe. We're going to stake out the road by the Seven Stars. Just to see what's going on. Phenomenon have been reported.'

Cerise took this all on board whilst twiddling a curly extension.

'Well,' she said, eventually. 'If you want me sitting in the road all night, I need some fuel in ma belly.' She sat back and patted her mound. 'Fancy an Indian anyone?'

It took a while for us to explain that the nearest take-away was several miles up the road. After a long and circuitous conversation we all agreed that the best thing to do was to go and eat at the Seven Stars and then take up positions in the road outside.

That settled, it was further decided that Cerise and I should go up and get a table in the pub and Sam and Chloe would join us later with the equipment. Which, apart from the fact that it meant Chloe and Sam were going to be spending more time together, quite satisfied me. When Cerise suggested we should pop into the village shop before it closed and buy some prosecco for 'night provisions', I was out of that museum faster than you could say 'Cirrhosis of the liver.'

The Seven Stars was packed. There were lots of non-locals in attendance, who had been down to the village to sightsee what was apparently now being called 'the murder pit' or the 'witch pit'. Judging from the various metal detectors dotted over the pub, I guessed many were going to try their luck with the Howlet Hoard.

Cerise, though not impressed by the range of cocktails on offer at the pub, was happy with the price of the prosecco, and we downed a couple of pints before Sam and Chloe showed up with all the paranormal gadgetry.

As it was busy it took us quite a while for us to order, wait and then consume our meals. So, by the time everything had been cleared away, the landlord was ringing the last orders bell.

Once the remaining drinkers had trundled off and the staff had finished their chores, we set out our equipment on one of the tables in the front beer garden.

There was still police tape cordoning off the Blackly Be, which we assumed meant we should avoid it. Accordingly, after careful consideration, Sam announced he and Chloe would assume positions by one of the bushes that sprouted along the low wall between the pub and road. I was annoyed by this pairing but let it go until Sam spotted our night-time provisions and insisted on confiscating one of the bottles.

'So what? Are *you* going to drink it?' said Cerise, similarly outraged. 'That's not fair.'

'No, I am not,' he huffed. 'Look, there's no point doing this if you're just going to get pissed.'

To my astonishment Cerise conceded the point and picked up our bag and pushed off to erect the cameras.

Over the other side of the road was the border of Howlet Manor formed of a thick nest of hedgerow and trees. At some point in the recent past one of the Seven Stars' merry regulars must have driven out of its car park and straight into the hedge, for there was a section of about a car's width that was flat. It was through here that Cerise and I disappeared, nestling behind the trunk of a thick oak tree.

We mounted a night vision camera with a good view of the road, and programmed the EMF recorder and erected a normal digital camera. Sam had given us a pair of binoculars, apologising that he only owned one set of night vision goggles, which he wanted to use. He had, it turned out, had a discussion with PC Shaun O' Neil about security. Thus we were instructed to put the number for the local station on speed dial on our phones. And we had been loaned two walkie-talkies to communicate with.

After testing them out, agreeing to start our vigil and note anything that was either ordinary or extraordinary, Sam signed off with cautions to be vigilant and alert, leaving Cerise and me to get stuck into the first bottle of our 'provisions'.

Oh, come on, it was Saturday night after all.

We assumed radio silence.

The night became still. The air was humid. I was wearing shorts and a T-shirt and cowboy boots, but still sweating. Only a soft breeze fluttered the tops of the trees around us, sending a sibilant hush over our heads, echoing the faintly persistent pop of the bubbles in our plastic glasses.

There was a distance of about fifteen metres between our spot and Sam and Chloe's. To my right, was Hangman's Hill, which led up to the new road to Chelmsford. To my left the lane ran down towards the churchyard on the High Road, past the Highway Man and round the corner on to the Witch Museum.

After fifteen minutes, as part of a council initiative to save on utility costs, the pair of street lamps that illuminated this stretch of road went off.

The moon was high up in a mostly cloudless sky. Although there were dark patches of navy that were elongating as they drifted eastwards. From time to time they passed over the moon, dulling the light and turning the boulder from silver to black. Yet still it somehow glinted.

In the distance a crow cried three times.

The midnight hour was upon us. A quiver of anticipation ran down my spine. If something preternatural walked the earth round these parts I felt sure it would do so now.

'I didn't know that Sam bloke was so good-looking,' said Cerise and burped delicately. 'You never let on.'

In the darkness I couldn't read the nuance of her expression.

I took a swig of prosecco and said, 'Didn't I?'

'No, you did not,' she said and reached for her glass. 'I might have to come down here more often.'

'Well that might not be possible,' I said, suddenly defensive.

'Why not?'

I paused to come up with an excuse. 'We're so busy with the museum, you see.'

There was a silence where I felt Cerise's eyes swivel over me. 'So you do like him then, do you?'

This one was easy. 'Well of course, I like him. We *work* together.'

'And?' she said and paused. 'Nothing else going on?'

'It's complicated.'

My friend Cerise chuckled under her breath. 'While you work out your complications, can I assume he's mine for the taking?'

Okay, this one I was firm on. 'No.'

'All's fair in love and war,' she said breathily and snickered.

'Cerise! I can't believe you just said that.'

'Just joking.'

'Were not.'

'Of course I am. Solidarity in the sisterhood, right?' she gave me a playful push. 'As if. This is me, babe.'

'Hmmm,' I grunted. The girl was damn attractive.

'But,' she said after a glug of fizz. 'If you want to keep him girl-free, you better move in on him soon. I reckon Chloe's enjoying herself over there.'

'What?' I popped my head up and round the tree trunk, aware something in my neck had clicked painfully. I couldn't see anything other than the bush that the pair were hiding behind.

'Come on,' said Cerise. 'She's well into it. You can tell by the way she looks at him.'

'Shut up,' I said.

'Just saying. So you're aware. Hope they don't get it on.'

'What?' I said again. 'Sam wouldn't. He's too professional.'

'Hah!' said Cerise. 'He's still a man.'

I thought about this then emptied the remains of the prosecco into our glasses and radioed Sam.

'I need our last bottle of provisions,' I said into the walkie-talkie.

There was a blast of static then Sam's voice came on. 'Do it properly. You have to say "Rosie to Sam. Over." Before you start talking.'

Oh for God's sake. He did get anal about some things. 'Why? Why do I have to do that? You know it's me.'

'Sam to Rosie. Over,' he radioed. 'It could be someone else masquerading as you. Just to confuse us. Over.'

I gritted my teeth. 'But if they're masquerading as us then you wouldn't know that it wasn't us, would you?' I said. 'They would probably start with "Rosie to Sam, over," anyway.'

'Sam to Rosie. Over. Maybe.'

I looked at Cerise and said, 'Sod this. You keep watch.' Then I handed her the radio.

The walk across the silver-lit road took me less than a minute.

To my immense relief I found Chloe with a pair of headphones on, holding a microphone that was doing an impression of a badly dressed poodle. Sam was scanning a row of EMF meters that he had set up on an upturned black case.

'Oh God. What's happened?' he asked as my head poked through the bush on their side – in this situation I favoured the element of surprise.

Chloe started, swore and removed her earphones. 'What's going on?' she said.

'Nothing yet,' I said and glared at her. 'I hope.' She met my gaze evenly so I added, 'but we've got our eyes and ears open over there. We can hear *everything*, you know. Everything. The sound travels, you see. It's like some weird acoustic effect.'

This news didn't appear to bother either of them.

Sam just said, 'Good, good. Works well to our purposes. Did you come over to tell us that? You could have radioed?'

'No,' I said. 'I want that prosecco.'

'But, really Rosie,' said Sam. 'What about staying alert?'

'We're fine. Cerise is drinking most of it,' I lied.

He let out one of those sighs that he did when he wanted me to notice him.

'Well?' I said and stuck out my hand.

For a second I thought he was going to be stupid enough to resist. In fact he opened his mouth to start so I said, 'I'll make a scene . . .!' And he crumpled.

Within seconds he'd produced the bottle from his holdall and handed it over. To be honest, I could have done without, I was feeling quite squiffy and more than a little parched. Plus, the bottle was on the warm side. However, I had to take it now after pretending it was my main reason for coming over.

'Thank you, Sam,' I said and decided I really should stake my claim. 'You look pretty fit tonight, you know.'

But he just tutted and said, 'How much have you had?'

I ignored him. Having now ascertained there was no activity of the rumpy pumpy variety occurring, I was happy to return to my position with my friend Cerise.

However, there was no real need to hurry back, so rather than march, as I had done coming over, I decided to saunter, taking in the night air, checking the lanes on either side: only one car had passed by in the last half an hour and now the place seemed to be totally dead, if you'll forgive the figure of speech.

When I was halfway across, indigo clouds began to eclipse the luminous face of the moon throwing everything into semi-darkness. I heard movement down by my feet and squinted at the surface of the road, which was kind of sparkling. It was one of those old types of concrete finish that had sand and stones mixed into it. It was these stones that were now catching the light.

Except there was very little of it around.

Enough however to see a quick darting thing run over the toe of my boot.

'Blimmin' hell,' I yelped and moved back.

What the heck was that? And where had it vanished to?

Too small for a rat, too big for a mouse, I was glad to note.

I blinked and realised it must have crawled under the instep of my boot, which I then raised. And indeed, the thing darted out from beneath it and froze, a mere foot away. I bent over to have as good a look at it as I possibly could.

'How weird,' I muttered, for it revealed itself in the darkening gloom to possess the attributes of a mini dragon: half a foot long with two beady eyes and a crest that looked like a mountain range wavering down its spine. There might well have been spots across its scales. Certainly, it had a lighter streak across its tail that could be silver.

As I watched, it blinked, but aside from the eye movement remained motionless and still, as if guarding or serving as a lookout.

I heard the static blast of Sam's radio from behind. He was probably going to have a go at me again for drinking but, ha ha, he couldn't – Cerise had the walkie-talkie.

Maybe, I thought, he was simply concerned. Which was unnecessary – I was just taking my time, admiring the freaky wildlife that stalked this freaky village.

I turned round to give him a wave, but as I did, I realised that something very strange was distorting the air: the darkness was warping, rippling, thickening.

For a moment I felt dizzy. Perhaps I had moved too soon? For my eyes were playing tricks on me.

It was like I was looking at a liquidy black veil. Except it wasn't constructed of liquid, it was made of air or something else I couldn't work out. I mean, it wasn't opaque. I could see through it – the road, the bushes, the unlit street light, the pub beyond it. They simply looked darker.

I blinked. It was still there.

Strange.

As my eyes adjusted to what they were seeing I realised that this veil thing had an outline, a form.

Oh shit. Was it humanoid?

Certainly, it stood about my height and mirrored my width, though there were no discernible features within. What I did note within were lots of flinty things that were getting denser as they whirred and turned, though still remained translucent. It was a paradox.

I felt my heart step up a notch and said, 'Woah.' And my breath formed fog.

As if responding to the suggestion of icy weather, a chill passed through me. It didn't touch my skin, which was sparking and felt not cold but super-sensitised and alive, but pounded through the blood in my veins from shoulder down to the tips of my toes. The quizzical reaction forced an involuntary shudder and a rash of goosebumps crawled up my bare arms.

What was this that I was seeing? I thought.

My mind flicked through its mental filing cabinet of possibilities: a cloud of gas released from the murder pit? The phenomenon that had caused the avian carnage. Or was it a sudden confluence of breeze-riding dust? An optical illusion brought about by shadows and the strange arrangement of clouds against the moon?

And, as I stood there wondering and not moving, a part of the veil-thing flowed out from the main body, as if it was going to detach. It thinned and stopped short about three feet away where it formed into a point that undulated and coiled, ebbed and flowed in the direction of the flat part of the hedge, where Cerise and I had been stashed away.

I squinted into the shadows and identified the outline of my fellow investigator's massive afro sticking sideways out of the trunk. Her mouth was opening and closing like a hyper-ventilating fish, but I couldn't hear her.

Yet I did hear the gentle tinkling of little silver bells and tried to tune into them but as I directed my senses to the sound my head was blasted with a harsh static.

Blimmin' heck – was this sinusitis? Or tinnitus? Is this how it came on?

And it was getting worse, amplifying, second by second. I clamped my hands over my ears but it made no difference. It was almost as if the sound was coming from inside me.

As it continued it dawned on me I could still hear things outside of myself.

Like a shuffling on the ground.

Looking down, I saw it was the mini dragon. It had moved.

Now, almost as if it had communicated silently with the gaseous form, it seemed to me that it too, just then, had purposefully shaped its body into an arrow – head forward, two stubby limbs shaped into its points, tail the fleshy shaft – which pointed at the gap where Cerise was now crouching and waving with urgency.

Was that a coincidence?

I looked back up to the gas cloud.

It was dissipating, as if the effort of keeping together the veil, made up of all those whirring sparkling flinty things, was too much for it to sustain.

In fact, at that moment, the breeze whipped up and shook the leaves in the trees so that I thought I heard in amongst the rustle and the static, something that sounded like 'rosh hush'. Though it was hard to tell if it was coming from without or within my head.

The staticky blast climaxed and receded in a steep decline.

At my feet the dragony creature darted out again, stopped, sniffed the air, pivoted round, and then scrambled away, tail waving, towards the bush over which Sam and Chloe's heads were bobbing up and down.

'Rosie!'

This time the word definitely came from outside of me. I also noted with relief, it was definitely human. Cerise's in fact.

She had emerged fully from behind the trunk and was looking like she was going to come into the road.

Oh dear. Breaking ranks on an investigation was sure to exasperate Sam.

I took one last glance at the dust thing, which had all but gone, leaving only thin strips of translucent darkness hanging in the air, then I jogged over.

'What are you doing?' Cerise, whispered. Her voice had a husky urgent quality that I couldn't fathom.

'What am *I* doing?' What are *you* doing?' I said. 'You're meant to remain hidden, under cover.'

'Yes, but . . .' she whispered, as the radio screeched into action.

'Sam to Rosie. Over.'

I held up a hand to Cerise and took the walkie-talkie with a roll of my eyes. 'Probably wants to talk about the booze,' I said and gave her the bottle.

I clicked on 'transmit'. 'Rosie to Sam. Over.'

I heard Sam say something like, 'Thank God'. Then bafflingly he asked, 'Who was that with you?'

That was a bit of a curveball.

I frowned and looked at Cerise who nodded.

An unexpected prickle of energy ran down my spine.

'What?' I said to both of them.

'Didn't you see them?' Sam's voice came through the speaker. 'Over.'

'See who?' I replied. 'Over.'

'There was someone out there. Dressed in black. They were following you . . .'

I was aware my eyebrows were rising up high into my hairline producing frown lines that may need chemical attention at a later date.

My friend nodded. 'I thought you were talking to them.

Seemed weird though – they were doing all the talking. Usually, it's you that, well,' she clicked her teeth, 'well, you know what you're like.' She shrugged. 'I couldn't work out where they'd come from either.' Her head swivelled up and over me into the middle of the road. 'Or where they went?' Her neck bent to the left. A scowl crept over her face.

The radio beeped. 'Who was it, Rosie?'

I took a breath before I pressed the transmission button. This was more than odd. 'No one,' I told him. 'There was no one there. Just a dust cloud and a little creature that looked like a dragon.'

There was a pause in which I heard Cerise make a pfft noise with her lips. Then she took the radio off me and spoke, 'Cerise to Sam or whatever, I think we need to call it a day, babe. She don't sound too good. I'm thinking the prosecco is messing with her head.'

'But there was no one there,' I bleated again. 'It was just a kind of dust cloud or flimsy veil caught on something hanging there.' But even as the words were uttered from my lips I knew they didn't make sense. My brain was starting to goggle and disagree with itself and a fog of confusion was beginning to descend.

I sat down and leant against the tree trunk and tried to go over the moment. It hadn't been very long. A minute or so, perhaps.

There was a shape made of darkness, then the dragon creature. Or had it been the creature then the shape? Had the dragon thing maybe emitted a vapour like those weird Cane Toads did in Australia? Maybe that had made me hallucinate.

Or was it just a trick of the unusual light. My eyes seeing things that weren't there.

But Sam had seen it.

And Cerise had too.

I was inclined to make a move like a TV tramp – look at the prosecco, shake my head, chuck the bottle over my shoulder.

Though wasting prosecco? That was a step too far.

However, when Sam agreed to Cerise's suggestion that we pack up and go back to the museum to review the footage, I didn't dissent. To be honest, I was glad to get out of there.

I noticed, when I looked, my hands had begun shaking.

CHAPTER TWENTY-SIX

We were unloading the equipment from Sam's rust bucket when Chloe remarked upon the entrance of the Witch Museum. It was ajar. A rectangle of light was spilling out of it over the porch floor.

'Sam?' I said. 'Didn't you lock the front door?'

'I did,' he said, and put the box of wires he was holding on the roof. 'And I turned out the lights.'

'Take this.' I handed Cerise a tripod. 'Can you and Chloe finish unpacking?' Then I began to run to the museum.

Sam made it to the lobby before me but we both saw the roses at the same time: a thin track of petals trailing in past the 'Abandon Hope' door.

'Oh God,' I said. We'd seen this before. 'Not another flower bomb.'

Sam was ahead of me, pushing against the door, following the petals round the museum, past the witchfinders' torture equipment, the folk magic and artefacts, the Hedgewitch in her chair, alongside the poppets and voodoo dolls, the new Black Anne exhibit until finally the trail arrived in the Talks Area.

Just as it had done in April, the same strange scene met our eyes.

Dozens and dozens of flowers were arranged in concentric circles around a central podium upon which was displayed a dazzling bouquet, at its heart a clutch of Ethel Rose stems.

Sam padded between the buckets and makeshift vases that supported the assorted blooms.

They were more vibrant this time. Dazzling almost. But I guess it was summer. They would be so.

'Bella donna,' said Sam and whistled. 'Wolfsbane.'

I clocked the watering can that he was examining. The purple-headed flowers poking from the spout were pretty and looked so innocent. 'Like the last time,' I affirmed.

'Begonias, marigolds,' he said.

'Beware, pain and grief,' I intoned. We had looked up their meanings the last time this had happened. Despite the beauty of the flora the message wasn't pleasant.

Sam stepped into the next ring. 'Hyacinths.'

'I'm sorry. Please forgive me.' The meaning was so specific I could remember it clearly.

'Lobelia.'

'Malevolence. Such a pretty flower,' I added. 'Shame that the Victorians had it down as that.'

'Chestnut. Black-eyed Susans.'

'Do me justice. Justice.'

'It's emphatic,' said Sam. 'Someone is directing us to something specific. It's not simply a warning. They want us to assist with reparation of some sort.' He stepped over to one of the buckets that was more commonly seen in Bronson's hand. 'Do you remember what orange lilies signified?' he asked. 'Poppies are obviously The Fallen.'

'White lilies are purity and chastity. But I think orange meant hatred, jealousy and also fascination.'

I heard a splutter behind me. 'Are you two sweet talkin'?' It was Cerise.

'Jesus! What's this?' said Chloe beside her and put a cardboard box full of equipment on the floor.

'We call it a "flower bomb",' I told them. 'It's happened before.'

'They should have used Interflora,' said Cerise and tutted. 'Would have been way more neat.'

Sam was bent over, investigating the central bouquet. 'It's not like that,' he said. 'We figured it out – it's a message.'

Cerise sighed. 'And I bet you gonna tell us – it don't just say "I love you".'

I shook my head.

'What's the message?' Chloe asked. Her eyes were darting around the place, a seasoned forensic evaluating the crime scene.

'We're not entirely sure yet,' I said. 'Sam thinks whoever set it wants us to work it out and do something.'

Sam had now stepped up to the central podium. 'There's a few flowers that are all about justice. There's an issue, here. Something that needs to be redressed. Rosie, do you recall the symbolism of wreathed ivy . . .?'

'Marital fidelity,' I translated.

'Again, positioned to encircle the Ethel Rose,' he finished.

'It's got to be about your grandma then?' concluded Cerise.

I nodded. 'Looks like it. But what? And more importantly – who is it from? And why don't they just come and talk to us?'

'Maybe they're afraid?' Chloe stepped forwards to smell the flowers in the nearest bucket. I reached out my arm and knocked her off course.

'Hey!' she said.

'There's wolfsbane there! You have to be careful.'

And immediately she jerked back. 'Fuck.'

'What's wolfsbane when it's at home?' said Cerise. 'Not one of the X-men then?'

I apologised to Chloe, but understood from her reaction that she already had a handle on the damage it could do. 'It's a poison,' I told Cerise. 'Its juice has been used on arrows to fatally wound enemies.'

Chloe backed me up. 'In large doses death is always almost instant. Symptoms can occur within the first sixty minutes of consumption: nausea, vomiting and diarrhoea, tingling, and numbness in the mouth.'

'Jeez,' said Cerise.

'Confusion, sweating and dizziness,' Chloe continued.

'You what?' said Cerise. 'There ain't no way I could have got it just by being here, is there?'

Chloe shook her head. 'You're fine. You have to ingest it in large quantities.'

'I'm putting the kettle on. I think it's time to sober up and have a cup of tea,' Cerise said and then glowered. 'What the fuck is going on?'

I shrugged back. 'Don't know.'

Then, as my friend left the Talks Area, I said to Chloe. 'You seem to know an awful lot about this?' I had tried to keep the insinuation out of my voice, but it had crept in there.

'Had a case a couple of years ago. Bloke killed his wife. Thought it was the perfect murder. They all think that.'

'Why?' I asked. 'Why would it be perfect?'

'Sometimes the only post-mortem signs of this kind of poisoning are similar to those of asphyxia.'

'Strangling?' I said.

'That leaves bruises and can fracture the hyoid bone. U-shaped bone in the neck,' she added and pointed to where her Adam's apple would be. 'If that is not in evidence then other conclusions might be drawn.'

I stood and stared at her for a minute. 'Do you like your job?'

'What do you mean?'

'Sounds a bit ghoulish,' I said and darted a glance at Sam, but he was still poking around the central bouquet.

To give her credit, Chloe actually stopped for a moment, dropped her mouth open exaggeratedly, put her hands on her hips and pouted. 'And, sorry, you're the proprietor of the Essex what Museum?'

Well played, I thought, and was about to respond with some kind of cobbled-together argument that I thought might pull Sam into a defence of me, roughly about lecturers working with the judiciary and victims of miscarriages of justice with some added examples of police brutality that were totally informed by hearsay, when luckily, we were saved by a wail from within the museum.

'Rosie! Sam! The other one! Get your arses into here.'

I measured the lack of volume and deduced Cerise's voice was carrying from somewhere near the new Black Anne exhibit.

Sam was the first to leap into action, closely followed by myself and then Chloe, who I could see was gearing up for a (probably) intelligent discourse on pots calling kettles black.

When we got to the exhibit however, my friend was nowhere to be seen.

'In here,' she yelled from inside the secret entrance. This lay behind the witchfinders' torture equipment wall and concealed a shortcut from the museum into the office. I paused to wonder how she'd found it, then reminded myself Cerise was the embodiment of 'resourceful'.

When we pushed through the door we followed her voice till we reached the kitchenette.

'Look,' she said and pointed at the window.

The frame was jagged and fractured. Shattered glass covered the work tops. My recent efforts at domestic neatening had been upturned. The coffee canister was broken and the contents of the sugar pot and a speckled jar of flour spilled over the countertops and floor. 'This is how they got in,' she said.

Sam spluttered, 'Good God! It doesn't let up.' Then he wiped his mouth. 'Same entry point as before, isn't it Rosie?'

I heard Chloe asking if we'd already called the police. But I couldn't answer. I was too fixated by a mark on the counter.

Within the coffee granules, flour and sugar I had spotted a pattern.

There were blurred marks around it but I could make out the five lines of a pentagram. Or a star.

CHAPTER TWENTY-SEVEN

It took a while to calm everybody down. It had been an eventful night after all. What with hallucinations, trailing shadows and flower bombs the four of us were quite disturbed.

This current state of anxiety was for once justified in my books.

After I'd carefully taken some photos, Cerise helped me clean the surfaces and cover the window with cellophane and tape, which although it wouldn't deter anyone who really wanted to get in, psychologically made us feel less defenceless to the outside world.

The latest turn of events, however, seemed to have upset Chloe, who decided that she was 'pretty fatigued' and needed to get off.

I didn't mind.

Sam also started going on about reviewing the tapes and took the equipment off to the library.

I mentioned to Cerise that we should don gloves and think about clearing up the flower bomb but she said she was too 'freaked out' by this 'mental' village that I'd brought her to.

Instead I showed her to the spare room. But she wasn't impressed and said she wouldn't be able to get to sleep with Sam outside reviewing 'ghost tapes'. In the end she nested down in my four-poster and after a little while I climbed into bed beside her.

But I couldn't sleep.

That star I'm sure had to be left by a Dolus Speed. The 'exclusive' footwear that I'd been duped into paying over the odds for, that was owned by half the village.

As Cerise started snoring I let my mind roam, trying to remember who had a pair but I was fuzzy and couldn't get a fix.

Until early in the morning when it came to me in a dream: I was walking down Adder's Fork High Road and there was a man ahead of me. He was hunched over and stumbling.

I saw him hobble into a familiar lane. Despite my comparative youth I couldn't keep pace with him and only got my chance when he disappeared into a cottage. And in my dream, I ran up to it and marched in. Then I saw it. The thing flew in through a door and landed with a light thud on the wooden hallway floor.

As it hit the boards it bounced and turned over and I recognised, with a distinct clarity I must have evoked from before, the trainer. On its underside I could see the patterned sole – a bold star shape within a circle. The men's version of the Dolus Speed.

'Tone Bridgewater.' I sat up as I said the words out loud.

Cerise murmured in her sleep, 'Shut up,' and rolled over.

Damn! Would you credit it? I knew I had seen it before.

But really?

Tone Bridgewater?

Teenage Tone with his DJ hobbies and adolescent mortification?

Why the hell was *he* breaking into the museum to bring us flowers?

It was crazy. It was confounding.

But I knew right then, there was only one way to find out.

I went downstairs and into the kitchenette. Yes, I could see the star and although it was half smeared and smudged, there was a circle round the outside.

It was early-ish. I hoped that Sam would set his alarm in time to open the museum. Cerise was there and Vanessa was going to turn up, so hopefully in terms of staffing I thought, they'd do fine without me.

I was sure Sam would approve of my initiative anyway. Especially if it reaped rewards.

The sky that morning was a very funny colour. A kind of ashy-orange. The sun, though full, was hazy, dull and weak, lilting through the clouds, looking as if it would have better suited a winter's afternoon. The only clue to the fact it was a mid-summer morning was its position high in sky.

Outside the museum Audrey was erecting her one-woman protest camp. Which meant she had already been to church.

Although I had other things on my mind I decided that she was worth a detour and made time to go back into the museum and brew her a cup of tea. Luckily the tea caddy and mugs had not been touched by the break-in, though our resident protester would have to make do without her regular spoonful of sugar.

'Hi,' I said to her as I tramped over the gravel drive and held out the mug as a peace offering.

Audrey's eyes narrowed. She put one hand on her hips and waved the placard that was in her other hand. It depicted myself, Bronson and Sam as devils with cloven feet and horns. She wasn't a bad artist, and I was pleased to see that she'd made me look thinner than I actually was. The demonic eyes she'd drawn on also hinted at a smoky sexiness.

I could work with that.

The movement of the placard, however, caused Audrey's black trench coat, which she seemed to wear whether it was hot or cold, to fall open. I got a waft of Eau de Cologne and cat wee and tried not to gag.

'Hmm,' she said at last and reared herself up on her lace-up boots. 'Ain't seen no "For Sale" signs go up of late.'

But she pitched the placard into the ground and accepted the mug I held out to her.

'Actually,' I said. 'I had an estate agent around just this week.'

I neglected to inform her he had run away after an Omen-style impaling incident and was unlikely to return.

Such was my life.

'Gary Gibbon from Steadman and Ripper Estates,' I added for good measure.

The detail of his name appeared to cheer Audrey a great deal.

'Well, at last,' she said and took a long draught of tea. Then winced. 'Ugh. No sugar.'

'No,' I said. 'We had a break-in. It got spoilt. Amongst other things.' Then I gave her one of my suspicious glances. 'You didn't have anything to do with that, did you?'

'What, me? How dare you?' she exclaimed and slapped her free hand against her lapel. 'I'm an upstanding Christian citizen! One of the pillars of this community! I wouldn't. It's against my principles.'

'Hum,' I said. 'And also in the small print of the restraining order.'

'A misunderstanding with Septimus,' she said, and busied herself with patting the lapel down. 'You can say what you like about his witches, but that man was a gentleman. We got along perfectly well. Even if we did disagree on some fundamentals.'

I nodded and let it go. To be honest I couldn't imagine her buddying up with Tone Bridgewater for a spot of breaking and entering. Let alone crawling through the kitchen window.

At the same time let me insert the word 'unpredictable' here again.

'That's nice,' I said, steering her into my line of questioning. 'It's good to know my grandfather had a kindly female ear to talk to,' I went on, despite the fact I didn't really see Audrey as kindly. Or particularly female come to think of it. 'You know.' I nodded. 'Seeing as his wife wasn't around any more.'

Audrey sniffed and wiped her nose. It was perpetually red and dewy. 'That's a true thing,' she said, rather tight-lipped nonetheless.

'You were here when Ethel-Rose disappeared, weren't you? At the hall, the night she did the séance. Or meeting as she called it.'

Audrey leant on the camping table and eyed me slowly. 'Can't remember much about it,' she said and wrinkled her nose. ''Cept the devil was there too. Of course.'

I took a moment to process those two comments. 'If you can't remember it how do you know the Devil was there?'

'I told the police.'

I screwed my face up. 'Eh? How does that make you remember?'

'They kept saying it to me. Wanted to know who the Devil was?'

'And? Who was he?'

She paused and gaped at me like I'd just asked her what the sum of two plus two was. 'I mean, what did he look like, the Devil? If you saw him? As you said you did.'

She shook her head slowly from side to side. 'He came out the side door, then vanished.'

'In a puff of smoke I suppose?'

She pursed her lips. 'Don't be flippant, Strange.' Then she aimed her thumb at her feet. 'It's not just God who moves in mysterious ways. Him downstairs does too.' Her gaze sharpened. 'And the others,' she said emphasising the last word. Her eyebrows lifted. Beneath them pale grey orbs bore into my skin.

For a second I regarded her from under my lashes. What 'others' did she mean? Satan's minions? Witches? Ghosts?

Could she have heard about what happened last night? Out by Hangman's Rise, in the shadow of the Seven Stars? Already?

That wasn't fair. I hadn't got my own head round it yet. It was just one thing in a cascade of weirdness that had piled up in recent days and were currently careering into my brain like an avalanche. To be honest, I felt quite overwhelmed. Which was why I was presently only focusing on sorting out the flower bomb, now that I had a lead.

Oh and doing a bit of Ethel-Rose research at the same time. But then again, the two things were connected. I was wondering if the flower bomb was meant to warn me off researching into my grandmother's disappearance? Which clearly was not working.

Audrey chuckled. 'I see you know what I mean.'

For a moment, I forgot what she was talking about, then I snapped back to her face. Her cheeks were pronounced, shaping her mouth into an expression that wasn't quite a sneer but had the semblance of a grin with disapproval sewn in. Her wiry hair quivered.

I was not going to get drawn into Audrey's craziness. It was time to get back to the matter in hand. 'So, how did you know it was the Devil you saw that night? Did he have horns or something?'

'Pah,' she scoffed. 'Don't be ridiculous.'

Well, that told me.

'What then? A black robe? Or maybe a red cloak and a trident?' And then I thought of something else. 'Or perhaps a pitchfork that you thought was a trident?'

Audrey snorted. 'Don't be daft. He's smart. He's the Devil. He was in disguise.'

'Yes,' I said. 'Elvis.' I was going to add something about my dad liking that song but Audrey was trundling on.

'When he comes amongst us he looks like me or you, see.' She made it sound like an instruction. Or a command.

'Look like you or me?' I repeated. Then opened my mouth as I thought I got her meaning. 'Oh wow. You mean a woman?' This was getting a bit *Bedazzled*, circa year 2000 version.

But she stopped that thought. 'No,' she said and raised her chin up high. 'A man, of course. But he don't have those pointy horns or tripod or whatever. That would make it too easy, wouldn't it?'

I did a bit of thinking about exactly what the Devil would look like if he wanted to blend in in Adder's Fork and said, 'Yes, you're right. That would have been inappropriate.' Even in Little Nutsville here. And looking like Elizabeth Hurley might catch some glances too.

'So what did the Devil wear?' I asked, thinking about another film. 'Prada?'

Audrey took a moment to think about this, which surprised me, somewhat. 'No.' She slurped her tea and smacked her lips. 'Savile Row, girl, Savile Row.'

All right, I thought, keep your hairnet on. 'A suit then? A black one no doubt?'

'Oh no,' she said again. 'Remember – the Devil, he was an angel once too.' She picked up another of the placards resting against her table. This depicted Lucifer being kicked out of heaven, his white wings disintegrating as he plummeted hellwards. 'Never wears what you expect him to. Covers himself in camouflage. That night he wore a white suit. Cream. Light.'

I took this on board and ran my mind through what I knew of fifties male fashion, which was mostly Teddy boys or men in tweed. Couldn't imagine it. Couldn't see where this barmy talk might take me either, so I smiled and said, 'Lovely,' then tried a different tack. 'Do you remember anything about a Yorinda or Maenda. Were there foreign nationals living in the village then?'

Audrey tutted then shook her head fiercely. 'No there weren't. We went through all of this back then with the detectives. There were none. If you ask me, the Strange woman, well, she just ran off didn't she? That's what they're like you see. They run off. It's in the genes. You can't blame foreigners for that. Mind you, they did have some of their blood running through them too. On the father's side.'

I shook my head, mainly so I could re-concentrate my attention on the identity of Yorinda and Maenda. Though I was sorely tempted to wade in on behalf of my grandmother and the allegation that disappearing off the face of the earth was in her genes. I didn't even want to get started on the implications about 'foreign blood'.

I supposed there were probably references and jabs at my Aunt Celeste too. But I would pursue that another time. Right now, I wanted to tackle the Ethel-Rose mystery.

Despite the chunk of festering outrage firing up my belly, I plastered an amenable smile on my chops. 'And you're sure there weren't people at the séance, the meeting, that might have been friends of the Aunt, Rozalie Romanov?' I wanted absolute assurance on this point about the exotic names she had referred to in her witness statement. It was, I thought, an important clue. 'She was there that night, wasn't she? On stage too.' But, just as I said it, the thought occurred to me that if Rozalie had recognised the names, she would have said so in her statement. 'Maybe they weren't living in the village. Maybe they were overseas visitors or tourists here that night? Can you remember?'

Audrey's face had taken on a pinched quality. I think she was tiring of my questions. 'No,' she said, then added with unaccustomed weariness. 'We told them all this. There were no foreigners down here. If there was we would have known. They would have stuck out like a pair of sore thumbs.'

I guessed that might well be so. Adder's Fork wasn't particularly cosmopolitan now. In the 1950s I speculated it would have had as much colour as a block of vanilla ice cream.

'You're like one of them.' Audrey wrinkled her red hooter and flapped at the museum. 'Aren't you?'

I looked at her blankly, wondering if the fact I usually resided in London meant that I was considered a 'foreigner' too. Some of the older villagers could get very territorial.

'Outside you look normal,' she went on. 'Act all high and mighty and virtuous like you're the saviour come in on a white horse. But the bloodline is strong in you. You're a witch, ain't ya? Like the rest of 'em.' Then she rolled her eyes and sucked her teeth at the same time.

'Needs to be gone, that hellmouth. You got to put it on the market and be done with it. It's the only way you can save your soul. You do want to save your soul, don't you?'

Oh gawd, I thought. Here we go again. At least I'd had a good five minutes of sane conversation before she started to go down the 'burn the witch' line.

Fine.

I had to be off anyway. 'Well thank you for your time, Audrey. Leave the mug on the pavement and we'll collect it later,' I said and swivelled on my heel.

I heard her give a little bit of a half-hearted protest. 'I will set my face against witches,' she called. 'They're all around us.'

'You say that as if it's a bad thing,' I muttered and marched off into Hobleythick Lane.

Oh well, that was useful. Not.

The whole Ethel-Rose mystery was still eluding me. There were a few lines of enquiry that I needed to pursue, but although I'd got a better idea about the night of her disappearance, I really had no defined theories of what might have happened once she fled the stage. Or why.

That said, I was getting a clearer picture of who was responsible for the flower bomb at least. Though, why the hell a part time DJ was breaking into a Witch Museum and scattering flowers around, was really quite puzzling.

And yet, this was the mystery I was about to crack I thought as I trooped into Church Lane where the Bridgewaters lived. It was ironic really. I would have thought it would have been more difficult. More obscure.

I knocked on the door.

The nearby church bell rang eleven o' clock which made me realise it was quite early for a Sunday morning.

No one came.

There was a possibility that, despite the weird gingery light and low clouds, the family might be relaxing in the garden unable to hear my knock.

I took the initiative and circled round the back.

We hadn't seen the garden when we'd last been here, as it had been dusky. Then we'd had that blackout, so visibility had been low. But now in daylight you could see it was massive.

Closer to the house there was a concrete patio. A short grey stone balustrade that seemed rather grand for a country cottage led down steps to a spotless lawn. There were flower beds laid up the sides, and several weeping willows further back. I caught sight of a movement down by an old shed and saw Terry was pegging out washing on a rotary clothes line.

Now normally I give some privacy to men fiddling with their underwear, but today I was a woman on a mission. Sacrifices had to be made and this meant Terry's smalls.

'Mr Bridgewater! Terry!' I shouted, trotting over the lawn. 'Where's Tony? I need to see him about something.'

Despite the fact that I was not very happy with Mr Bridgewater Junior I had already decided that I wouldn't reveal the reason for my visit. It might become a bargaining chip.

Mr Bridgewater Senior seemed stunned to see me in his garden.

'Sorry,' I said, as I neared the clothes line. 'I did try the bell. Is Tony around?'

Terry finished pegging a pair of boxer shorts and picked up the empty laundry basket. 'Hello Rosie. Well, sorry to tell you, he's not here.' He was heading back to the house.

'He isn't?' I said and fell into step. 'Where is he?'

'He's got a shift at The Stars. Won't be back till 5 this afternoon I'd have thought. Do you want to leave him a message?'

I thought about this for a moment then said, 'No, it's fine. I wanted to talk to him about a DJ set.'

Terry looked relieved. 'Ah right. Well, do you want his mobile number then?' he said as we climbed the steps onto the patio. 'Actually, if you wait here I think I've got one of his business cards in the kitchen.' Then, basket under his arm, he disappeared into the living room.

I stood on the patio and looked back out at the garden while I waited, noticing that beyond the shed, just over the fence, I could see headstones. In fact, I realised as I walked over to get a better view, the Bridgewaters' back garden bordered onto the churchyard.

That put a different perspective on things. Anyone with half an imagination might think they were seeing ghosts walk in their back garden if they knew there were a zillion corpses buried right next door. The notion was enough to give the sternest disbeliever a mild attack of heebie jeebies.

As if on cue, at that very moment a wail went up behind me. It was horrible though. A thin drawn-out shriek of terror that began like a fox's scream but faltered, then petered out into an emphysemic splutter. 'Ooohhhhaaaawwwwaaahhh.' Wheeze, wheeze.

I whipped round and surveyed the living room where it was coming from. The French windows were open and I could see the sofa and the two chairs within. Over to the right in the shadows of the room was the table around which we had sat just nights ago.

'Ooooowwwwwaaaahhh! Tel!' It came again, a weak and reedy voice, aged and thin.

I gently gambolled over to the doors and peeked in.

'Awwwwww. Is that her?' said the voice, which I now realised was coming from one of the high-backed armchairs positioned by the windows.

In it was a little man, with white hair and translucent skin and very wide, peeled back eyes. He clearly wasn't happy.

'Oooowaaahhhh,' he went off again and pointed at me. His hands were shaking. I could see blue veins and liver spots doing noughts and crosses over them. It had to be Terry's dad, Tone's granddad. He was much frailer than I had imagined him.

'Sorry to disturb you, Mr Bridgewater,' I said. 'It's only me, Rosie Strange. From the Witch Museum. I was looking for your grandson.'

But this seemed to frighten the old guy even more. 'Oooohhhhh,' he called out. 'Terry! She's back. Help me.' He lurched deeper into the cushions and brought one of his legs up into the chair as if he was going to crawl into it.

'It's okay.' I said and stretched my hands out and up in a surrender gesture. 'I'm not here to cause any trouble.'

The little button-like eyes did their best to focus. 'I just did what I was told, you see.' Then he coughed and started hocking up phlegm. 'He couldn't,' wheeze, 'let it go.' He paused, then hocked up a golly. 'Even now,' he gasped at last. 'Complicity.'

'I'm sorry,' I said and wondered if I should do something to help. 'I don't understand. Are you all right?' I stepped towards him.

But his head jiggled from side to side – he didn't want me coming any closer. 'Oh don't shoot the messenger,' he said and began to heave again.

And then Terry was there, fussing around his dad, comforting him with low words, bending over with a glass, getting him to take a sip and calm down. Turning to me, he stood up and almost 'shooed' me out with his hands.

'Sorry,' he said, once I'd retreated off the patio. 'Dad's not been himself this past day.' Then he took my arm and, rather roughly I thought, shoved me round the side of the house and up the garden path. 'Most unsettled he is. Please excuse us. I'll tell Tony you called.' Then I was unceremoniously ejected from the property.

It was only as I was brushing myself off and walking past the church I realised that Terry hadn't given me the card.

Never mind, I thought, determined to get my man. The Seven Stars was only a fifteen-minute walk up the road. Now, I felt, really was time to seize the day.

CHAPTER TWENTY-EIGHT

The pub wasn't open to the public yet but that wouldn't be a problem. In Benefit Fraud, we were rarely welcomed in the front door and if we were, that usually meant the back door was expediting a quick getaway. I had a good idea of where it might be in a workplace like this.

I was right. Round the side of the pub which faced onto Silva Wood there was a gate. I found it to be unlocked and went through into a fenced-off yard with a newish white extension that had a condenser letting out a long trail of steam over empty barrels and some red crates piled up in a tower. Near the rear door were a couple of green plastic chairs that had seen better days and a matching table with an old industrial sized Nescafé tin that was currently being used as an ashtray.

They did a lot of smoking here.

I thought about knocking but concluded that once again the element of surprise was probably going to be my friend. After all, if I was Tone and was confronted by the owner of the place I had broken into the night before, I might well be inclined to do a runner as soon as I clapped eyes on their lovely mug.

The head cook, however, intercepted me as I was halfway into the little corridor which led to the main kitchen prep area. It was a testament to his powers of observation really, as when I entered I saw the kitchen was a hive of activity and full of steam. All of the staff were in there getting ready for their busiest lunch-time of the week. I was quite taken aback by how hot it was: the day was already close but in here it was like a sauna.

When I asked if I could see Tone, the chef tutted but said 'Okay, then. Though be quick.' He was a skinny man, with a high squeaky voice and no hair under his hat. I got the impression he was used to Tone's acquaintances disrupting the kitchen.

To be fair, the boy played it very very cool. Though I saw a spasm of panic pass over his face when Baldy announced my name. This was followed by a wobble of his Adam's apple. Presumably he was stocking up on air should any Benny Hill-like chasing routine get going. All we needed was a naughty nursie and along with the chef we could be off round the Blackly Be humming the catchy TV theme tune.

Tone's eyes stayed set, his mouth neutral. He straightened himself up, put down the rolling pin he was holding, adjusted his standard-issue catering staff cap, and clenched his fists.

I tried a friendly smile but he wiped his brow and grimaced.

'Outside?' he said when he reached me. He didn't stop but padded down the corridor in his Dolus Speeds and shambled into the little courtyard through which I'd just come. I followed him over and watched him lean against the wall near the chairs and take out a packet of cigarettes from his checked trousers.

'Want one?' he said.

I declined.

He lit up and blew out a long plume of smoke.

In the distance, over the rise of Silva Wood, we both heard the low grumble of thunder.

Tone crossed his arms and glared at the floor.

'Can I see your shoe please?' I asked him when it looked like he wasn't going to say anything.

'What?' he glared at me. His voice was quite low for a young 'un. Lots of smoky bass notes going on there.

'Your trainers.' I pointed. 'The Dolus Speeds. Can I have a look?'

He pushed himself up from the wall with his butt and had a good go at looking outraged.

'You know why, don't you?' I said, suddenly feeling like I'd wasted enough energy on silly games.

When he pretended to look blank, I got my phone out and showed him the photo of the kitchen window and countertop back at the Witch Museum. Then I enlarged the picture of the footprint in the coffee and sugar grains.

Tone swallowed again. Sweat was bobbling across his forehead.

Mind you, I could feel it on mine too. 'Look, you can deny it but we've had Forensics in.' Chloe Brown's eyes had roamed over it, and she had something to do with a forensics department, so it wasn't completely untrue. 'I remember seeing your trainers when we were round at your house. They're . . .' I was going to say rare and expensive, but checked myself, '. . . distinctive. If there's not a matching star in a circle, just like the one you left in my kitchen, I'll eat my hat. Or yours. It's just a matter of time before the police come knocking.'

I could have a word with PC Dennis Bean aka Goofy I supposed. Though actually right now I didn't want to involve the police. I'd rather squeeze it out of Tony myself. Luckily the lad was starting to look pretty pasty. 'Do yourself a favour, Tone,' I made like a cop I'd seen on telly. 'Give it up. Or we'll press charges,' I said. 'And you'll go down. And you wouldn't want anything to happen to your pretty face in prison, would you?' Oh God, I thought, I sound like Scrub. This was ridiculous.

Tone by now was sucking on his fag hard and repeatedly, like it was the only source of oxygen in a twenty-five-metre radius. His eyes were beginning to pop too. It made me feel sorry for him.

'Look, it's all right,' I said, changing tack. 'I haven't called the cops yet. We probably won't. But I know that you broke in last night. And I do know a forensics person who could match that imprint to your foot, not to mention the lashings and lashings of DNA you've left round the window. So why don't you just tell me what's going on.'

Tone took a final drag of his fag then threw it on the floor and ground it out.

He pulled out one of the plastic chairs and looked at me. I thought he was going to sit in it then realised it was an invitation.

'Thank you,' I said and accepted the gesture. The cordiality surprised me. Though I could see a lot of Terry in his son's manners. It was nice to see the quality pass from father to son. Despite the fact that, thinking about it, the son had the edge on 'courteous' over the father today.

Tone sat down in the other seat and put his packet of cigarettes on the table.

'Were you responsible for the one back in April too?' I said.

He bit his lip and nodded though kept his eyes on the ground. After a minute more of silence, he spoke. 'I'm trying to find a way of explaining so that I don't sound psycho.'

I tutted. 'Oh blimey, don't worry about that. I got "crazy-sounding" covered. Have you seen where I work?'

Tone's shoulders went down a bit. The hint of a grin slivered out.

Then, irritatingly, my phone buzzed.

Auntie Babs.

Bugger. I'd forgotten she said she could come over today.

Too bad. I'd have to get back to her presently.

'Sorry about that.' I turned my phone over and switched it to silent. Her timing was rubbish – just as Tone had started to speak, for gawd's sake.

'S'all right,' he said. 'But it wasn't me.'

My eyebrows began to hoist themselves like a couple of flags. 'Really?' It clearly was.

'I mean,' he said when he read my expression. 'It wasn't my idea.'

'Whose was it then?' I drew closer to him as he had lowered his voice.

Tone darted a glance around the yard then leaned towards me. 'Granddad's,' he whispered and spread his hands on the table. 'Please don't tell the police. He's an old man. I'll pay for the window myself. I didn't mean to break it. It was an accident.'

That was a turn-up. 'It's okay, I won't tell the police. Why did your granddad tell you to break in?'

He paused for a moment. 'It wasn't his idea either.'

'No?'

Would Terry have got his son up for doing this? Didn't sound likely to me.

'It was the ghost's.'

Ah, I thought. That old chestnut – the ghost did it. I sighed. Sam and I had certainly heard that one before.

'No, serious,' said Tone. 'He's been haunting granddad for a while. He didn't mind at first. He's funny granddad is. Said he quite enjoyed the company. 'Course Dad thought it was dementia, but I always believed Granddad. Just something about the way he was telling me. And it weren't too bad at first, like. But then it got a bit too much for him, because the ghost was so unhappy.'

'Why was the ghost unhappy?' I asked, hearing an inner voice titter at myself.

'Granddad figured the old dude couldn't move on. You know, upstairs, to heaven or whatever. Reckons he's in purgatory. He's looked up all that stuff. Says the ghost is haunted too.'

I folded my arms. 'The ghost is haunted?'

'Yes. He's got to atone for his sin.' This seemed like an odd phrase to come out of the mouth of the young DJ.

'How? I mean why? I mean, what sin? I mean, *really*?'

Tone winced. 'You said you were used to crazy . . .'

'Sorry, you're right, you're right.' I bowed my head. 'I just have this high incredulity bar. You wouldn't credit it, would you, considering the Witch Museum and all that. But it's there.' I tapped my head.

Tone reached for his pack and flicked out another fag.

'Look, sorry,' I said, trying to sound gentle. 'How does the flower bomb come into it?'

He frowned, then I supposed realised what I meant. 'Oh, the floral messaging?'

I nodded. Young speak. Very good.

'Granddad took down the instructions. From the ghost. The flowers, the different types, they all have a meaning.'

'Uh huh.' I nodded. 'We found that out.'

Tone tapped a cigarette on the table. 'He said you would. I think half of it's a warning – he was worried. But there's clues in there too apparently.'

'Clues?'

'From the ghost.'

Now it was my time to sit back and chew my lip. 'Do you know what they are? The clues?'

Tone shook his head. 'I just did what Granddad asked. And I think Granddad got all this from him. Sorry about the break-in. Couldn't think of another way round it. Granddad didn't want to upset you. He thought you might be in danger because you're back in Adder's Fork. And he wanted to help Mr Beckinsdale.'

There was a lot to unpick in that info dump. However, I was keen on getting the facts and detail down. 'Mr Beckinsdale?' I asked. This was interesting. We had a name. A solid lead.

'Old Albert,' said Tone. 'He used to live next door.'

I tucked my chin onto my chest as I tried to process everything.

'I don't remember him.' He gave his head a light shake. 'Granddad said he died before I was born.'

I shook my head. 'So why did Old Albert ask your granddad to flower-bomb us?'

He shrugged. 'I think it was because of his trade?'

'His trade?'

Tone nodded. 'You know. He used to be head gardener up at Howlet Manor for the de Veres.' He jerked his head in the direction of the Manor House.

'Did he? Is that relevant?'

Tone shrugged. 'How should I know?'

'Mmm,' I said, more to myself than Tone. 'Might pop over there and check that out. Well, what does it mean? The flower bomb or flower message thing.'

'I don't know,' he said. 'You're meant to get it. Granddad said you'd be the one to work it out.'

'Me?' I said, genuinely taken aback.

'He said you'd work it out because you're the key.' Then he paused. 'No, you're not the key. But you can unlock it or something. You'll *see* it.' Then he started.

The chef had appeared in the doorway. 'Time gentlemen please,' he intoned with a half grin and prodded his watch.

As Tone scrambled to his feet I said, 'How? How do I unlock it and *see?*'

He shrugged. Then before he disappeared through the door, he said, 'It's your family.'

CHAPTER TWENTY-NINE

There was a lot going round and round my head as I walked towards Howlet Manor.

I mean how was *I* meant to solve the riddle of the flowers? Wasn't there anyone else who was better equipped? And what did Tone mean when he said, it was my 'family'? I didn't know that much about my non-immediate clan until I'd inherited the Witch Museum.

It was a conundrum.

However, I was very close to the residence of someone I thought might be able to shed light on the matter. And also, I had never got round to asking Edward de Vere about Yorinda and Maenda. As I was seizing the day anyway, I decided to grab the bull by the horns and lots of other clichés that suggested you do something without really thinking it through properly and trooped across the car park of the Seven Stars, past the boulder, where I remembered the weirdness of last night and felt a quick shudder run down my sweaty back.

The black shape had been freaky. What with one thing and another I hadn't been able to give it much thought since last night. Everything was happening all at once. And here I was, back again at the Blackly Be, the centre of the storm, where the strange curling mist thing had pointed. I paused and looked through the flat part of the hedge where we had sat and watched last night. Beyond it, above the hedge, in this light I could see chimney tops. The cloudy spectre I realised now, had pointed me in the direction of Howlet Manor.

As had the peculiar spotty dragon thing.

Which was a bit nuts.

And probably a coincidence.

Not worth dwelling on.

Though fate had brought me back to it.

I understood that the more conventional thing to do was to sit down, maybe adjourn to the Witch Museum, talk all of this new information through with Sam and maybe Cerise, and then make an appointment with Edward for a chat. Possibly with my Scooby crew as reinforcements should Minty turn up with her bloody chopper.

But I was not most people, and to be honest, I was getting quite addicted to this 'element of surprise' tactic as it was yielding quite a lot of results. Plus I could smell a result. I was getting closer to cracking part of the mystery, I was sure.

And Edward, well he was a posh polite person. I doubted he would send me away for fear of offending me. Especially as the clouds around the village were darkening from dull amber to brown, and it looked as though a storm might break at any moment.

I retraced my steps from my previous visit and took the left-hand route round the side of the house, past the trees, the greenhouses, then the dilapidated gardeners' shed, where I paused again. Was that where Old Albert, if he actually existed, had sat and pondered his work? I was already thinking about how that particular apparition was more likely to have been a projection of Ash Bridgewater's guilty conscience, but I was here now. I ought to check it out.

As I rounded the corner of the Manor I saw Edward by his summerhouse, standing on the decking, with a canvas on an easel and, I conjectured, as I couldn't see it, a paintbrush in his hand.

Keen to avoid a confrontation with Edward's lunatic daughter I decided to give the kitchen garden a miss and took the longer, circular route between the shed and the rose garden. As I was coming up on the north side of the flower patch Edward finally noticed me and started. The paintbrush fell from his hand.

I was, I supposed, the last person he expected to see on a Sunday afternoon.

'Hi!' I said. 'Edward! It's me, Rosie!'

He took a moment, then his face cracked into a smile.

'Ah,' he said. 'You've come back. I thought you might. I said to Minty, "You mark my words – that one will turn up again."'

'Always,' I said and when I reached the patio, stooped to pick up his paintbrush. 'Like a bad penny.'

His left eye twitched. 'Thank you,' he said, taking the brush. 'Care for a brandy? I could do with one and I think we are approaching the acceptable pre-luncheon hour.'

Never one to look a gift horse in the mouth, I agreed, and Edward motioned me towards the table and chairs we'd sat at before. There was a shake to the Lord of the Manor's hands so I offered to get the drinks in, as I had the last time I'd been here.

Edward readily agreed.

I loped into the summerhouse, wiping the sweat from my face, and poured us two large ones. I was still a bit icky from last night's pile-up of units and I thought a bit of hair of the dog might work to sort me out.

'So, to what do I owe the pleasure of this visit, Rosie dear?' Edward trilled as I emerged with the glasses.

'Well,' I said and put his brandy in front of him. 'I was just wondering . . . did you have a gardener here called, er . . .' What was his proper name? 'A Mr Beckinsdale?'

Edward was reaching for his glass but stopped and looked up at me. 'Old Albert?' he said unsteadily.

'Yes, that's the one.'

He folded his hands on his lap. 'We did. How odd. Why do you ask about him?'

'Oh, his name has popped up recently. Alleged haunting,' I said and scoffed.

But Edward didn't. This time he did take his drink. And necked half of it. 'History,' he said. 'It all comes round again. Doesn't it? Loops and whirls and comes back again.'

'What's that?' I said.

He fluttered his hand at me then put a finger on the space between his nose and top lip. 'No matter.'

'Okay,' I said, relieved he didn't want to veer off into a

philosophical discussion. 'So did he work here a while?' I asked. 'This Albert?'

'All his life.' Edward smiled.

I took a sip of my own brandy and savoured the burning sweetness. 'Do you know anything about his personal affairs?'

'Not really. No. Lived down Church Lane. Quite happily, I presumed.'

'You don't know anything that might have weighed on his conscience then?' I pressed on.

Edward straightened his shoulders and took a breath. He seemed about to speak when we both heard a shrill voice and turned to see Araminta charging up the garden path.

'Miss Strange!' she yelled.

I braced myself.

But when she reached us she was doing a grimace intended to be a grin. 'Oh Padre phoned you, did he?' Then she smirked at her dad. 'I thought you said you hadn't?'

Edward looked a bit disconcerted by everything and said. 'You told me not to. Said I should do it in person or it would leave a mark or some such.'

Minty ignored him and beamed at me. 'I wanted to have you over to apologise for my behaviour last time,' she said with a grace that I found astonishing. 'Still, you're here now. Perhaps you'd like to join us for Sunday drinks?'

Edward raised his glass and said, 'Beat you to it, dear.'

'Well.' Minty pouted and snatched his glass off him. 'Brandy's not what the young folks like to drink these days is it, Rosie?'

I grinned. 'Oh, I don't mind.'

'Come on now,' she said. 'We can do better than that for our guest. What's your poison, Miss Strange?'

'Well,' I said, continuing to not look a gift horse in the mouth. 'I won't say no to a glass of prosecco.'

Her beam drooped slightly. 'Oh, I don't think we've got any of that. How about a glass of proper fizz? Champagne? We have a couple of nice vintages in the cellar, don't we Padre?'

Distracted, Edward replied, 'What's that? Oh yes. Indeed.'

'Wonderful!' she said and clapped her hands. Then with that, she sped off like a rocket back into the house.

It was a marked change. But it was still a relief not to have her ox-like bulk monitoring the conversation at the table. It gave me time on my own with Edward, which I preferred.

'So, you might wonder why else I've popped in?' I said.

'Not really,' Edward replied and sent a longing look over to my brandy.

'It's about Ethel-Rose. We were interrupted last time. I wanted to ask you about the meeting she held the night that she vanished. Were you there that night at the Village Hall?'

He narrowed his eyes, then looked back at the kitchen door, presumably to make sure Minty wasn't yet on her way back. 'Yes. For part of it.'

'Really?' I said. 'Your name wasn't down on a . . .' I stopped myself from adding witness report, aware I might be dumping Monty in the faecal matter if this went any further.

'No,' he said. 'I slipped outside when it went pear-shaped.'

I was surprised to hear that he'd been there at all. 'Are you a believer then, Edward?'

He laughed. 'Not really no. At least not then.'

'So why did you go along?'

'Moral support I suppose. We were friends. Good friends. We'd grown closer after the birth of Celeste. She'd become depressed. And your grandfather was away a lot and, well, when the cat's away . . .'

A clatter of shoes came down the concrete path.

'Here we are,' said Minty and presented us with a silver tray. Sliding around on top of it were two glasses and a serving dish full of crisps and a smaller finger bowl of olives, which she set down on the table. 'No fried food for you, Padre. Not with your cholesterol.' And she placed the crisps in front of me and gave him the olives. 'If you'll excuse me, I'll be back in a mo', just got to check on the chicken.' And she was off again.

I picked up a crisp and popped it in. It was easy – my jaw had already dropped open at Edward's insinuation about pussycats.

'Are you saying that you were lovers?' I said, keeping my voice stable. 'When Septimus went on his trips?'

Edward picked up the new glass of champers. 'We'd courted during the war for a while. Everyone commented on it. We were quite the talk of the town. "Such a glamorous coupling," her mother used to say. Of course, Anne was a bit of a social climber. The old gal was desperate for me to make a decent woman of her daughter, but, well I knew my father wouldn't approve. And then Septimus came along.'

I finished my brandy and took a large mouthful of champagne. It was quite bitter, although I wasn't really used to the posh stuff. 'But were you lovers, then?'

'That's the thing,' said Edward, reaching out for his glass once more. He was caning it quite quickly. Good for him. 'I thought it was on the cards. Especially after we went to the film.'

'What film?' I asked, taking another crisp. I shouldn't be filling up on crap really, but the brandy had loosened my inhibitions, not that I had many, and now the bubbles were going straight to my head.

'We went to a film together. She wanted to see it. *Strange Fascination*, it was called.' He paused and looked over my shoulder into the past. 'Wasn't very good really. A Hugo Hass. But Ethel-Rose wanted to see it. Oh, she loved the pictures. Was about a man who becomes enthralled by a glamorous femme fatale.' He swivelled his glass of champagne around. 'I thought she had taken me to see it to, er,' he took another sip and savoured it. 'To suggest something.'

Blimmin' heck. This was not what I was expecting. Maybe a bit of info on Mr Albert Beckinsdale's private scandal. But not this full frontal about the Lord of the Manor and my grandmother. I reached for my champers and took a deep long glug.

Edward went on. 'I was convinced you see. Thought she'd put a spell on me. She had ways,' he said and tapped the side of his nose. 'You must know all about that.'

I wasn't sure if I did or even desired to, but anyway, I nodded him on.

'And she'd wanted it in the past. I knew she was unhappy at home. I suppose that I thought I meant more to her than I really did.'

This was all very interesting, albeit sick-making. It was starting to stir up a bit of an unpleasant rumbling in my stomach. I really really did not want to hear details of how my grandmother 'wanted it' so tried to guide him off the subject and onto the more important stuff. 'So, you went to the meeting that night to support her?'

'That was it. Yes. To support her,' he repeated.

'And did you hear about this Yorinda and Maenda?' I was getting closer than I ever had before.

'I did,' he said and bowed his head. 'She was upset about it. Of course. Hearing a thing like that. Well, you would, wouldn't you?'

That stopped me. According to the witness statements, she had disappeared off stage after uttering these names. Never to be seen again. 'When did she tell you, Edward?' I asked slowly.

'Back here,' he said as a matter of fact.

For a moment I couldn't work it out. It didn't compute. 'Here? At the house? Howlet Manor?'

He took another sip and smacked his lips. 'That's right.'

I watched him, sitting in his chair in the stifling gloom, and wondered if he was making it up. 'But I thought she ran off stage and no one saw her again?'

'That's right,' he repeated. 'But I saw her. I was hanging around at the Sitting Pool.' He turned his gaze back to focus on me. 'Have you found it yet? A beautiful spot. Of course, there's all that claptrap associated with it but I'm not one for superstition. Not if you're in possession of the facts.' He smiled and for a second I thought, with his thin jaw and white hair, he was really rather lupine. But it was the booze I think. I hadn't had any breakfast. It was really hitting the spot. In fact, I was starting to feel very relaxed. And this conversation with Edward, well, it was giving me a buzz – it was going places.

I smiled back at him in a woozy kind of way and said, 'Did you tell that to the police?'

'Oh no,' he said. 'Best not to. Not with what happened after.'

Oh yes. Well I could see how that might look. 'And then what happened?' There was, I noted now, a slur to my words. I should slow down. Brandy and then champagne. Not a great combination on an empty stomach.

A shadow covered our table and I realised Minty was back again. She'd refilled the tray with two more glasses.

'This one's for you,' she said and put a glass in front of me. 'Come on, chin chin.'

Despite my resolution only moments ago, under her gaze, and because she was making such an effort I felt obliged to down the contents of my flute. I held the empty out for her, but it felt suddenly heavy. My hand weakened and crashed onto the table top. She took the empty anyway and, ignoring my clumsiness said, 'Just checking on the spuds.' Then with a wink at her father she twirled off again.

Edward was only halfway down his glass, but he necked the rest of it and sent me a benevolent grin. 'Feels good, you know, to be telling you this. Been a while.'

'Of course,' I said. 'Let it all out.' And couldn't help but give a wee yawn. I wasn't bored, but what with the heat and closeness of the day and everything, I was starting to feel a bit drowsy. The alcohol was definitely getting into my system.

He nodded at the house. 'Minty said not to. But I said, "She should know."' His eyes narrowed, and the brows hunkered down low and I thought of a wolf again.

'Better out than in,' I said and laughed at myself. Because I was very funny sometimes, you know. 'So, moving on,' I said, but so quietly I had to put effort into repeating it and making it louder.

'I mean, what happened next?' I asked anxious now to bring the matter to a close. Though, in truth, I wasn't particularly anxious at all. I was more like floating.

'Well, I got her back here. And she was in a bit of a tizz.' He kept his gaze on me. 'That's when she told me what she'd heard from her father.'

'Go on,' I said, feeling the back of my chair against my spine. Despite the fact it was made of iron it felt slinky and good.

'She said Frederick, her father, told her "Yorinda is here." And I said "Yorinda?" And she said no "Maenda". That's what *he* was saying. "Daddy" she said. Then she translated it so I understood: "My ender is here."'

He let that run over me for a while, then continued. 'And I said, of course, "What do you mean?" And she said, "My killer." And I laughed and laughed. Never heard such rubbish in my life. But, as it happened, it was true, of course.'

'Quite, quite,' I mumbled and nodded my head languidly.

'And then she cried,' he said and took up his new glass. 'Now I'm a gentleman, as you know, dear Rosie.'

'I know, I know,' I slowly intoned.

'And it was of course comfort I had in mind.'

'Of course, of course,' I said and let my head fall onto my chest for a mo'. Just to rest it.

'But I thought, she wanted me. Wanted me to put my arms around her.'

'Of course, of course,' I said, then realised what he was saying and tried to raise my head to see his face. I managed it but with difficulty. Jeez, I might have to cut this short and go. I was getting far more pissed than I intended. Best to drink up and make my apologies.

I stretched my hand out to my glass but found it wouldn't reach that far.

How bizarre, I thought. But then Edward reached it and said, 'Do you want some more?'

And I managed to nod and leant forwards and he poured the liquid into my lips.

'That's it, drink it down.'

I could feel some of it running down my chin and spluttered out an, 'I'm sssssssooorryyyyy . . .' My limbs were becoming strangely useless.

He didn't mind, bless him. And kept on talking. 'See the thing is when some girls say no, they do mean yes.'

Ah, right I thought. 1950s hero here we come.

'And of course, when I tried, she was quite adamant.'

'Of course,' I crooned again and yawned deeply.

'The way she dressed and glamourised, anyone could see what she meant. She had allure and she knew damn well how to use it.'

Oh bloody hell, I thought, it's such a cop out – people figuring women talk with their clothes. I should put Edward right and tell him, like most homo sapiens, women talk with their mouths. But I was way way too slow and Edward was waving his hand around airily.

'Thought she'd bewitched me, you see,' he said. 'Thought I was spellbound. See the way I *wanted* her, was compelled to ravish her, it was urgent. So, it really was no surprise, I think you'd agree.'

I nodded heavily and said, 'What was no suprish . . .?' It was an effort to get the words out so I left them unfinished, hanging in the air.

Edward tutted and shook his head at the memory. 'And then after, well she said she'd tell everyone. I couldn't let that happen. Of course, it was an accident really.'

There were alarm bells going off in my head now. But not digital ones. Slow giant Big Ben hands turning slowly through degrees, donging out their warning chimes across the dull landscape of my mind, as I began to compute his meaning. 'Hang on . . .' My lips were tingling. Felt like they were swelling too. 'Trout pout,' I said out loud and giggled again. 'Go on. What washn't acciden . . .?' I couldn't finish.

'She would have told the world.'

'Sheeeee wouuuuld,' I said. 'It's trooooooooo.'

He shrugged. 'I just wanted to stop her. Running off. That's all I wanted to do.'

I, personally, just wanted to nod my head but found, although my chin sank down on my chest, I was completely unable now to raise it again. At all. This was not right.

'Old Albert had been digging up the rose garden. Readying it for new blooms. There were rocks around. I don't know how one of them got in my hand, but I knew I had to stop her.'

Despite the fog that was descending on my brain, his words were triggering adrenaline. With a gargantuan effort this time I managed to bring my face up and look at him as he said, to my horror, 'I just smashed her with it. On the back. Here.' He pointed to a section above his neck. 'And she went down. Quite dead.'

Fuck.

The bloke was completely deranged.

Dangerous.

I needed to get out of here while I still could.

I tried to get up but found my limbs were like hundred-weights, far too heavy for me to move.

Oh God.

'In the end it was quite poetic,' he said. 'I put her in the hole in the middle and planted the Ethel-Rose rose on top.' He swilled his glass and then sipped it.

No way.

My head was wobbling on the top of my neck, but I knew it was important for me to stay focused and try and keep my wits. Though Fear was curling round me like a python, squeezing my inner organs.

'She's over there,' he said and pointed to the rose garden. 'Always has been. Well, most of her.'

I wanted to move my head to look at where he was pointing but I was fat and stupid and now my vision was starting to dim. Something inside me was working against my body.

'Old Albert knew,' said Edward. 'Of course he did. I never showed any interest in gardening. Then, after she went, tending to the rose garden was all I ever did.'

Oh.

My.

God.

I had got it.

A confession.

It was terrible.

It was awful.

Hideous.

'But,' I said, full of slurs and starting to feel rather lopsided. 'That meansh.' Pause to try and breathe. 'You.' Wait for it, wait for it. I summoned up my strength. 'Killed her.'

He raised his glass to me. 'Yes,' he said. 'I did.'

The table and Edward were starting to slide out of focus.

'But that's,' I stuttered and stalled and couldn't find my words. 'Mudder,' I said.

'Not the first, and not the last either,' I heard Edward say. He was beginning to sound like he was a long way away. 'That other man was impossible though. Greedy. Couldn't be helped. And he was trespassing.'

I wanted to ask who he was talking about but it was taking me too long to form the words and my tongue was so swollen it wouldn't work.

Over in his seat Edward was comfortably spooning it out. 'Thought he'd caught me. Caught me digging up the treasure!

What a hoot!' he said and laughed. This time I heard his true nature in it, for it was a cruel laugh that jangled. 'Walks up to me as bold as brass even though he's on *my* land, which I duly informed him of. But he says something about property being theft and then,' he spluttered. 'And then he says, "I know you parasites have found spot X." But of course, I hadn't. And I'm not a parasite, am I?' Edward reached over and clinked his glass against mine still half full on the table. 'It was after all these sightings of the lady in the lanes, I was just checking Ethel-Rose was still where I put her. Not up and walking around. When I saw you the other day – right above me, hair full of leaves, looking so much like her. Well, it put thoughts into my head.'

I wanted to say, 'hang on'. I wanted to say a lot of things. I wanted to get up and run down the lane screaming 'Help, help! Murder!' But I couldn't. I could only manage a 'Haaaa . . .'

'But he wouldn't have it, would he?' Edward raged on. 'Thought it was all about the money. Picked up another shovel on the floor and started digging himself. So, I hoofed him. Right on the back of the head. Just the same as Ethel but with the spade this time. Went down like she did. Then up comes Minty, old dear, and says 'Oh Daddy. What are we going to do with him now?'

He laughed again. Meanly, with a kind of righteous and proud spite. 'Chopped his head off she did. Said, we should put it on the boulder like the stories go and everyone would think it was something to do with the old myth.' He bent towards me. I could see yeasty balls of spit in the corners of his mouth. 'People are queer like that, aren't they? Prefer to believe in the impossible.'

Another shadow loomed over the table, blacking out all other light. 'Oh you've told her, have you, Padre?'

Minty! Never before had I been so pleased to hear her voice. I tried again to raise my head but found Edward's daughter was already helping me. Thank god. Albeit by grabbing my fringe and jerking my bonce around.

'You should have left it alone. But like daughter, like mother,' she said, pulling my head up to face her own. 'And I'll have you know, before you start cursing me, that I was the one who saved you from the car. Yes! So, you can thank me for,' she surveyed the rest of my body, now lumpen in the chair. 'The thirty odd years of life you've had.'

Her mouth was slip-slopping in and out, getting bigger and smaller, the words coming out of it punctuated by angry horsey snorts.

'Tsk, tsk. That bloody Celeste,' she spat. Then it was as if the next words came out under water. 'Your mother, Celeste bloody Strange, she worked it out, she did. Heard some gossip from one of the staff or some such, didn't she, Padre? Worked out Daddy's accident with her mother. Came up here, confronted him and the bloody old fool confessed. Idiot!' she hissed and I think she must have shifted her face to her dad, because her voice slightly fell away. 'Weren't you, you old duffer? I said, "That'll be the end of us."'

Mother? I remember thinking. Celeste?

'Didn't I say it? Padre? When you were with her in the study?'

I was desperately trying to commit all this to memory, but it was no good. The black mist that was crowding me was getting heavier. Whatever drugs they had fed me were working speedily now. Everything, all senses, my vision and hearing, everything had become fuzzy and blurred.

'You did, you did,' said the white creamy mass that was Edward.

Araminta de Vere jerked my head and brought my numbing attention back. 'But I couldn't leave you there,' she said, and muttered something I couldn't catch. 'Chased her out, I did. Her and her "partner". Never heard such a word before. And it wasn't my fault. They lost control of the car, skidded off the road and hit the tree. But they didn't go in the brook. I don't know how they ended up there. They were still breathing when I left them. Though I thought the car might blow, and you.' She paused and ran a finger over the line of my jaw. If I could have moved I would have shuddered. But I had become distressingly paralysed.

'You,' she went on, 'were crying in the back seat in one of those baby seats. I'd just had Sebastian and it pulled on the heartstrings, you might say. I couldn't leave a baby there. So I took you, seat and all, and left you on the steps of that monstrous museum. Now Audrey does her bit, but she hasn't got you away, has she?'

There was a clap of thunder.

It echoed over the roof then into the fields.

The meaning of Minty's words hit me.

Celeste?

Could it possibly be?

Did it matter anyway? I mean I was beginning to realise that this wasn't going to end well for me. See, I knew I should think about putting up a fight, but right then I really just wanted to go to sleep. Maybe, I thought in my strange drugged state, we could talk about this in the daylight, like reasonable human beings, after we'd all got forty winks and calmed down a bit.

I tried to suggest it, but the words merged into the air before they had left my lips.

A sudden flash of white descended on us. Small drops of rain began to spatter.

'They say they drowned in the river, your mother and father,' Minty went on. 'But,' she said and jolted my head again, this time so hard I thought the roots had probably come out. It woke me up a bit but also made me feel very dizzy and sick, 'I want you to know.' Her mouth was full of saliva. 'I couldn't kill a baby. That's not Araminta de Vere, you know. But perhaps more fool me that I didn't.'

At this point, I can safely say, I was now experiencing the urge to scream the place down. And yet. And yet I was too tired to do anything about it. Darkness had got me in its clutches.

With a final effort I tried to force open my lips so I might be able to yell, but was stilled by something cold and narrow and sharp against my throat.

'What are you doing?' inquired Edward, in a manner that suggested Minty might have moved a chess piece unconventionally.

'Off with her head, hey Padre? It's a bit of a family tradition.'

I felt the cool thing bite into my flesh and a bobble of warmth trickled down onto my collarbone. Oh God help me.

'No no,' said Edward, reasonably. 'It's all right. You've cut her: the spell has been broken. Now I've told her it all. The Strange Fascination, I told her about that. It isn't compelling me any longer. I can feel it, Minty. It's gone. Just let her die. She can go peacefully.'

His daughter grunted. 'It's not poison. It's your sleeping pills. We'll still have to dispose of her.'

I was aware of Edward pausing then he said, 'Why don't we burn the witch, Minty?'

There was a moment's silence, during which Araminta pondered my fate, then I heard her breathe in and declare, 'Excellent idea, Padre.'

Two strong arms dug in under my armpits and I was lifted onto the floor. From there Araminta picked up my hands and began to drag me off the summerhouse decking. I could not even raise my head and get it out of harm's way. Instead it flopped and rolled back, hanging off my neck, periodically hitting the ground as Minty hoisted my body in fits and starts over the bumpy lawn.

Beyond the pain and swelling I was still able to detect a trickle of warm liquid running over my jawbone down along the side of my face and into my hair line. *This is how it ends*, I thought. *I'm going to die.*

And yet another voice within said, 'Oh no you're not.'

This is no time for a pantomime, I told myself.

Though my eyes wanted to close. I tried in desperation to keep them open.

But my senses were leaving me, letting me slide into an almost vegetative state where I was becoming immune to the stones and rocks, the scratches and burns on my back.

When we reached a rusting wheelbarrow, I guessed we were just outside the gardeners' shed. Minty let go of my arms so I fell onto the grass. Unable to steer it, my head lolled sideways towards the house, where I saw to my sluggish amazement a duo of pantomime dames gambolling in the shadow of the eaves.

I was hallucinating. But I didn't mind so much, for I was leaving this body.

'Shush,' they said and put their fingers on their lips.

If I could have muttered 'okay' I would, but Minty had opened something creaky and I was dragged again over a low step and then abandoned on a dusty wooden floor.

The door banged shut.

I heard Minty say. 'She'll be all right here. We've been talking about getting rid of the shed for years. No one will notice if it goes up now. And if we get the temperature high enough, she'll incinerate. We can sprinkle her ashes on the Ethel-Rose. See,' she said and cackled. 'I'm not heartless really, am I?'

Edward was wheezing, but he let out another wolfy laugh.

'I'll get the mower petrol,' said Minty. 'It's just round the side.'

Then the door opened. There was a strong odour of gasoline and a splashing sound. Liquid was poured over me.

'I'll do the honours,' said Edward. 'You go and fetch the stove lighter.'

I heard the tramp of hefty steps retreat across the lawn.

'Sorry, Rosie, that it ended this way,' said Edward.

There was another loud roll of thunder.

Then a different voice, one that I trusted, that I knew, said, 'Oh no you're not,' and 'I'm not having that.'

Briefly, lightning lit up my shack.

Another, shriller voice said, 'Men like you, at your age, think you own the place. That you can do what you like.'

'But it don't work like that,' said my friend. 'Not no more. Time's up. Ain't you heard?'

Edward's voice rose, shaky but clearly affronted. 'Get your hands off me.'

There was another rumble of thunder, an 'argh' was thrown into the din.

And then I think I passed out.

Which was fair enough.

It had been a bit of a day.

CHAPTER THIRTY

The fire in the hearth was roaring when I got up to leave. Full of joy, full of hopefulness I ne'er looked upon hitherto.

I finished my tankard and told the innkeeper. 'I'm off, as I said I would.'

'You found what you wanted?' he asked, a sly smile against his whiskers.

'Greatest joy a man can know,' I told him in earnest.

'You be careful then,' he said, as I strode outside the door. 'There's others that want it too.' And then he said no more.

It was but a short trek into the woods when I felt the crack upon me. And going down, I turned around and saw them gathered here. About me and around me and behind me looking too. And I said, 'I am to meet her,' but they took me for a fool.

The sword it pierced my side in half, the blood it ran full. And in the dying light, I saw her there. 'No more,' she said. 'It's me you want.' And she took off into the gloom.

CHAPTER THIRTY-ONE

I'd never had a hangover like this.

It got much worse when the first person I was able to focus on turned out to be Sergeant Scrub.

I must have done something seriously bad in a previous life.

At least she came into focus gradually. One must be grateful for small mercies. I registered the big slightly coiffed bob, then the standard police issue 'smart' suit jacket, the sensible grey skirt. Her eyes were still large and still slightly doleful, but as I struggled up to consciousness they sharpened fully.

I must have let something slip because Scrub sighed and said, 'If it's any consolation I don't want to be either.'

I squinted and blinked. What was Scrub doing in my flat?

'How you feeling, Sleeping Beauty?' she asked sounding untypically concerned about the answer.

I propped open one eye and looked around the room. It was rather bright and rather white. Not my flat. Not Septimus's bedroom either. Oh no, I thought! I've died. And I never managed to snog Sam.

Another male voice rumbled, 'Has she got brain damage, ma'am?'

There was an ache at the back of my head. I reached round and felt through my hair several bumps, a couple of which were crusty. It smelled a bit and hadn't been washed.

I opened my other eye and asked, 'Am I alive?'

Scrub smiled, but not like she was enjoying herself. 'More than ever,' she said. 'But any more of that champagne and you'd have slept another week or so.'

'*Another* week?' I said, pleased to have my continued existence on the planet confirmed but unsure and a bit screwy on what day or time it was.

'You've got concussion,' Scrub explained. 'Been out for a while.'

I thought about sitting up a bit but became aware that I was in some kind of puritan babydoll outfit that was gaping round my back so pulled the duvet up over me. Except it wasn't a duvet. It was a sheet. With a horrible blanket on it

'Where am I?' I said trying to read the name printed on it.

'Litchenfield General,' said Scrub very very calmly.

She was sitting in an armchair. There was another tall shape lurking at the end of my bed, who I eventually identified as PC Dennis Bean, or 'goofy police guy' as I had politely labelled him.

'Oh my God!' I said, and sat up. The room tilted and swam and I got those weird flashes of light you see in front of your eyes when you do stuff too fast. I sat back against the pillows and waited for the world to stop spinning. 'Edward de Vere and his daughter. You have to arrest them. They were trying to kill me!'

'We know,' said Sergeant Scrub. Again very calm.

'And, oh my God, they killed Reg Rainer. Edward said! I'm sure that's who they were talking about. Did his head in with a shovel and then cut it off. Jesus!' I paused to draw breath as the memories came stumbling back. 'Oh God! And my grandmother Ethel-Rose. Edward said he killed her. And, Minty said she drove Celeste off the road,' I said recalling the next revelation with horror. 'Celeste. Who,' I chewed the moment over, 'who Minty said was my mum.'

My *mum*, I thought. No Celeste was my *aunt*. They'd got it mixed up. Everything was muddled up.

But Scrub said again, 'We know. And we'll get through all of that in due course, but right now . . .'

'Hang on,' I said and held my hand up, then winced at the movement. There was a great deal of aching going on around the shoulder area. 'How do you know?'

Scrub slipped off her suit jacket and rolled up her shirt-sleeves. It was still very muggy. 'Well,' she said and flicked through her notebook.

And it suddenly occurred to me that I didn't know how I got here either. I tried to sit up properly once more but my head was still rather weighty. A big cloud of dopiness was hanging around it.

'We've statemented the de Veres. When my colleagues arrived they both seemed eager to accompany them. Your aunt I believe.' She glanced at her notebook, let out a kink of a smile and then coughed to disperse it. 'A Barbara Cockaday, and a Cerise Tempest . . .'

'My friend,' I filled in.

'Yes. They alerted Control to what was going on. We had a police car in the area anyway, as it's been something of a crime blackspot of late,' she narrowed her eyes and smirked. 'So they were able to reach the scene quickly. When they did they found you unconscious on the floor of the shed, doused in petrol, and Edward de Vere and his daughter Araminta fastened into two garden chairs with what appeared to be human hair extensions and bonding glue.'

I was beginning to see why Edward and Minty might have been so keen to help the police with their enquiries.

'Edward de Vere has confessed to the manslaughter of Reg Rainer,' she said and smiled. 'So, you're off the hook. Not that you were ever really on it. But there was a perceived element of foot-dragging regarding the bodies in the murder pit, amongst some of us. We thought a little pressure might spur you on.'

I nodded, winced at the sharpish pain in my neck and felt a bandage on it. A memory of Minty holding a blade to my throat reared up and had me shuddering into the hospital linen.

'I'm sorry,' said Scrub. 'Procedures weren't followed properly.'

'It doesn't matter,' I answered rather breezily, though I thought that there was a possibility that I might actually not be as happy about it later down the line, when I was less drugged up and foggy. 'You said Edward confessed to manslaughter? Why not murder?'

'He said it was self-defence.'

'I don't think so. Not the way he told me. Sounded like he wanted to stop Reg Rainer digging up the grave. Oh God! The grave,' I said as I remembered who was down there. 'That's where he said the body was buried. Of Ethel-Rose!'

'Yes,' she nodded. 'We have a team excavating the rings of roses.'

'Good, good. Hang on,' I said as the words resonated in my brain. 'What did you say?'

Scrub frowned. 'We're looking at the alleged burial site.'

'Ring a ring of roses . . .' I said, recalling the strange note cobbled together from cut out letters from magazines and newspapers, that Carmen had shown us in her garden just the other week. And then, in my head, saw once more the rings of the flower bomb. Wow. The two were connected. 'She fell down,' the letter had read. Could 'she' have been my grandmother? Could the note, rather than being a threat, have been a clue from the only person that de Vere himself said might have known what had taken place? An employee, gardener to the Lord of the Manor, torn between his loyalty to the family who gave him work, and the grieving bewildered family of his victim?

Had to be.

Scrub was looking at me like I'd lost the plot. 'That's right,' she said. 'It's a couple of rings of rose beds. Yes, a bit like the nursery rhyme.' Then she cleared her throat and made her voice a bit softer. 'But, Rosie, we've already ascertained that his story is true.' She darted a quick look at Goofy who immediately dropped his gaze to his feet and started shuffling them.

'You have? That's great,' I said though murder wasn't really great. But like I said – I wasn't firing on all cylinders.

'Edward seemed to want to make a clean breast of a number of things,' she said in a measured way. 'It seems that the family had quite a few secrets to hide. Although they didn't seem particularly bothered about the nature of them,' she added. 'He directed us to a back room in the summerhouse.' She paused and glanced down at her notepad. 'It was here we found an old chest. When we opened it we discovered' – the gaze came up, direct and firm – 'three mummified heads.'

She waited a moment for the meaning to roll out and sink in.

It didn't so much as sink, rather punch me in the stomach. 'Yes?' I said, disregarding the pain there and my neck as I sat up. Fully this time.

'One of them was your grandmother's.'

'Oh my God!' My hand flew to my mouth. 'What a dreadful thought.' It better have come off post-mortem. 'Why did he do that?'

'Presumably for the same reasons his forefathers did – to try and obscure the identity of the victim should she ever be found.'

'His forefathers?' For a moment I couldn't follow her train of thought.

'Yes,' she said. 'We're at an early stage but we think the other two belong to the bodies in the murder pit.'

'Oh my God!' I said again. 'The de Veres murdered them too? Why?'

'Their ancestors we presume. We were hoping you and your curator might be able to shed some light on that.'

I thought about the strange dream I had had during my coma-like sleep – being in the Seven Stars, then surrounded by men and stabbed in the side by a sword. Had that been connected? Wasn't it just a dream?

'But, they aren't really our priority at the moment. Obviously, Reginald Rainer's homicide is the most pressing issue. His family are incredibly upset as you can imagine. We need to get a statement from you about what de Vere reported?'

I nodded and flinched again.

'I'm afraid, I need to ask you for a DNA sample,' she said and stood up. 'To ascertain the identity of the woman we think may be your grandmother.'

I nodded. 'You're testing her head?' And as the words popped out of my mouth I had a vision of our Madam Zelda fortune teller machine. 'A dangerous coupling,' it had warned. 'But I couldn't have known,' I said, more to myself than anyone else. 'Back then. Couldn't have understood the dream? Could I?'

Scrub motioned for me to open my mouth and dabbed around the inside of my cheek. 'Of course not. There was no way you could have had a clue about what happened all those years ago,' she said soothingly.

But that was not what I meant.

The sergeant motioned for Goofy to take her place. 'Dennis will help you with the statement, if that's all right with you. I'll be back to collect it later. Then when you've finished with that, you've got a few visitors here.'

'Oh good,' I said as she handed a sheaf of paper to her constable. I really needed to talk all of this through with Sam.

'So,' said Goofy and took a recording device out of his pocket. 'Do you want to start at the beginning?'

I wasn't sure where that was really. I thought about the first flower bomb back in April but then remembered I'd promised Tone Bridgewater I wouldn't mention him. So I started with what the young lad had told me about his granddad. I think by the time I'd reached what happened by the shed, I'd lost focus and was falling back to sleep.

When I woke up next, Cerise and Auntie Babs were buzzing around me like two angry wasps. I think there was some competitive caring going on.

'She needs a bit of lippy before she sees him,' Babs was saying.

'But not that shade. She don't do purple.'

'I think I'm well aware which colour lipstick my niece prefers thank you very much Cerise.'

'Well, that's two things you got wrong there then, Barbara . . .'

I heard an audible in-take of breath and then a, 'Sorry. That was out of order.'

My gritty eyes opened.

The room was darker than before. But I was still alive which was good. 'I can hear you both, you know.'

SYD MOORE

Their heads moved apart. Beneath her make-up Babs started to flush. Cerise put her lips into a firm straight line.

My aunt flapped round to my pillow and began stroking my hair. 'Rosie, darling,' she said. 'Oh thank gawd you're all right, love. We've been so worried, you know.'

'I'm okay.'

'Chick,' said Cerise. 'You well don't look okay. That's why we've been trying to fix you up. Before himself gets in here.'

'Himself?' I said and felt my heart chug a smidgen faster. 'Sam?'

'Oh, he's been in a right state, Rose. Really he has.' Babs rolled her eyes. 'Been blaming himself for not paying enough attention to what you've been up to with your nan and that.'

Cerise clicked her tongue. 'Well that's something we agree on.'

'Where is he?' I pushed up onto my elbows, and felt my head throb.

'Outside.' Cerise nodded at the door.

'We thought we better get in first and just give you a freshen-up,' said Babs. 'Seriously, you look better than you did when we found you.'

Cerise nodded. Her previously immaculate hairdo was looking quite uneven. 'I was thinking you was going to be a goner. If that mental chick – you know the one that looks like a trucker with a hair helmet –'

'Araminta de Vere,' Babs nodded. 'Or whatever her name is. She was married once I believe.'

'If she'd got there with that lighter before us, babe, you would have gone up like a nylon nightie.'

'But she didn't, did she,' Babs said soothingly and darted a look at Cerise. 'Your friend here saw to that.' She leant over and patted Cerise on the shoulder. 'Well done, love.'

I tried to smile at my friend. 'How did you do that?'

Cerise shrugged. 'Tripped her over and sat on her.'

The pair of them exchanged a glance which told me that this was their story and they were sticking to it. I'm sure the truth would out eventually. It was doing so with everything else.

'The old bloke,' Cerise tore her gaze away from Babs and continued. 'He got some nail varnish in his eyes. Don't know how that happened.'

Babs started fussing with my hands. 'How are yours? Oh yes. Quite chipped. Need a bit of a polish. I'll sort them out next time. Now, Cerise managed to get some foundation on you before you stirred.'

'Natural Sand Beige,' my friend detailed.

'But you could do with a touch of blush,' Babs went on and produced a small brush. 'Got a nice Russet Rose here . . .'

'I'd go for Apricot Adoration,' said Cerise.

Babs' lips clenched. 'All right then,' she compromised, then got to work on my cheekbones.

While she was applying the orange powder I asked, 'So did you hear what Araminta said about Celeste?'

And Babs stopped mid-circle.

Cerise looked at her then back at me and nodded grimly.

'Well?' I said to Babs and caught her hand. 'Is it true? Do you know?'

She opened her mouth then shut it then put her bum on the bed and said, 'Your parents will be down to see you tomorrow.'

'Oh fuck, it's true,' I said.

Cerise said, 'Don't think about it now, babes.'

'How the hell did this happen?' I bleated. 'Why did no one tell me?'

'You need to speak to your parents about it, love.' Auntie Babs tried out her soothing voice again. 'They had the best intentions.'

I could see she wasn't going to say any more and I was feeling tired and wired all at the same time but without the energy to see it through.

'How did you know I was there anyway?' I said.

Cerise made a sucking noise with her lips. 'I heard you say "Tone Bridgewater" when you woke up. Didn't think nothing of it but when Babs showed up to see you and you weren't answering your phone we went looking.'

Babs shuddered at the memory. 'Those awful people. I was expecting to get maybe a cup of tea and peek at the Manor or something. Not that. Poor Wosie,' she said and flattened my hair.

'And poor Ethel-Rose,' I moaned.

About half an hour later Babs and Cerise left. When Sam came in, I did something very uncharacteristic: I burst into tears.

It was all getting a bit too much and I was tired and emotional and actually really upset about everything.

I know I'm a tough cookie, as they say these days, but I'm human too. And sometimes you have to give in to your softness and let it all wash over you.

And I wanted to tell Sam that I was grateful for him coming and that really, I was feeling crazy because suddenly everything had changed, and that I felt like I was on a ship at sea, cast off its anchor and left to the currents of the ocean to toss and pop like a cork. That, right then, I felt like he was the only constant and truth in my life, my North star, and that I appreciated him. That I needed him and that also I really needed to be weak.

But I didn't manage a word.

I just held my arms out.

And he got onto the bed and wrapped himself around me.

I put my head on his chest and felt his heart beat.

And then I wept for my grandmother, for Septimus, my mum and Ted and Celeste, awful Reg Rainer, the bodies in the pit – everyone involved in this sad and tragic story. But most of all, at the end, I finally wept for me.

CHAPTER THIRTY-TWO

'And so,' said Florian with a flourish. 'There is no way the land can be built on.'

'That's so great,' said Sam and adjusted the large patio umbrella so it shaded all of me. 'Don't want you to burn,' he said, then frowned. 'Oh, you know what I mean.'

I told him it was okay. I got it.

We were sitting out the front of the museum in the memorial garden. Sam had brought out some chairs and a table as the day was sunny and pleasant. It was nicer out here to receive visitors than inside the office.

The decision had been made to shut the museum for a few days whilst we all recovered, which everyone locally understood. And anyway, since I'd been released from hospital we'd pretty much had a constant stream of well-wishers, which was exhausting but I appreciated it.

Cerise and Babs had done most of the tea-making and hosting but my aunt had gone back home this morning and Cerise was about to head off soon. So they'd written up instructions for Sam and Bronson to look after me, refilled the tea, sugar and coffee canisters and stocked up on lots and lots of cakes.

'So, what is this Great Crested Newt?' asked Chloe who had just dropped in to see how I was, and apparently had some interesting news which she'd yet to unload. We were all letting Florian hold the floor right then.

'They're a protected species,' he was saying. 'Which means you can't injure them, kill them or cause damage to their breeding grounds which generally is, in this case, Silva Wood. Specifically, the Sitting Pool. Ergo, the development cannot go ahead. It would split up the sites they've been found in so disconnect their habitats, remove other species from their food chain. Not to mention produce changes to the water supply, pollution, noise, shade, dust, traffic and population – all of which would impact the newts' environment. Ergo – it ain't happening.'

Carmen laughed her tinkling laugh. 'Some of the developers were grumbling that they'd been deliberately introduced to the site to stop or delay the project.'

'As if,' said Florian and shook his head. I couldn't read his expression properly, but I was receiving a 'smug' vibe loud and clear. 'They'll find out soon enough that human beings are part of nature. We don't "own" it. We are it. And why should we assume we have more right to the land than the newts or trees for that matter? Anyway, in strictly commercial terms, the murder pit has not been the best advertisement for any potential buyers. That probably finished the development off. People get creeped out by that kind of thing.'

'Some people get turned on,' said Chloe and we all looked at her.

I was gratified to see Sam recoil. An expression of distaste touched his lips. He tried to distance himself from the involuntary reaction by picking up the plate of biscuits and offering it round. 'Chloe, you said you had some news?'

I smiled at him approvingly. He could turn on the charm when he needed to all right.

'Well, it's about the murder pit remains actually,' she said.

'Murder, murder everywhere,' said Cerise and rolled her eyes. 'This place. It's worse than inner city London.'

Carmen laughed. 'Not what I was expecting when I moved down here.'

'Me neither,' I added and everyone laughed uncomfortably.

'Well, regarding the murder pit,' Sam said, moving the conversation on. 'We're pretty sure the remains are those of Anne Hewghes and Bartholomew Elkes.' He left the biscuits in front of the forensics expert and retook his seat.

'I'm not denying that,' said Chloe. 'The tests we've run – they confirm the ages and the dates you have suggested to us, as far as we can tell.'

Sam smiled with triumph.

'Clever boy,' I said and clapped my hands.

Florian whistled then said, 'Bravo, that man.'

Sam gave a little bow. 'Couldn't have done it without my trusted side-kick,' which I didn't think really was true, but I inclined my head slightly to show that I accepted the acknowledgement.

Then I said, 'Hang on. You're *my* side-kick.'

'Am most certainly not,' he said and pretended to pout.

'Are too,' I insisted.

Cerise tutted and said, 'Get a room.'

Then Chloe went, ''Scuse me,' and put her hand up. 'Actually, what I was going to say is that, the remains, the bones, well they share a lot of the same DNA. We think they're father and daughter.'

I gasped. 'Wow. That's amazing.'

Sam's face became a question mark. 'Oh my God,' he said, sounding very like me. 'So that's interesting.' He raised his eyebrows in my direction. 'This fits the timeline: Bartholomew Elkes comes down in 1591 or '92 at the bequest of Samuel Howlet.'

'Meets Bessie Moor,' I could see where he was going. 'Who is considered a sorceress or witch but under the Lord of the Manor's patronage. Howlet introduces them so they can team up and find the treasure.'

'But they find something else,' said Sam and winked. Wowzer, what a cutie.

'Love,' said Carmen and sent an adoring glance at Florian.

'He goes back empty-handed to London,' Sam continued. 'Thirty-odd years later he returns with some new device or with new information or at someone else's request, to find the treasure. Sees Bessie, who must have told him about his daughter.'

'Oh my God,' I said, recalling the glee of my weirdy dream. 'Everyone thought Bartholomew had found the treasure.'

Sam nodded, tuning into my thoughts. 'But it wasn't the treasure they thought it was.'

'No,' I said. 'It was his daughter, not gold.'

Everyone made surprised cooing noises.

Carmen sighed, 'Children *are* treasure.'

Florian bent over and stroked her arm.

'I had a dream,' I said. 'I saw him, Elkes, in the tavern. He was announcing he was off to find his treasure, and then there were men, but there was a woman there. They attacked them . . . There were knives, swords –' My fingers crept up to the bandage on my neck and played with the fraying cotton edge.

Cerise took my hand, pulled it away and stroked it. 'It's all right babe, you've had a bit of an eventful past few days ain't ya? Need to think pink thoughts right now.'

I looked at her bright eyes and beautiful lips and realised they were twisted into the same fixed rictus grin as everyone else in the company. Apart of course from Sam, who was nodding. And his smile went right up into his cheeks.

'Rosie,' he said. 'That's phenomenal. We have to talk about some of this.'

I kept his gaze with me a second longer than I should have in public. But there was a communality there that I realised was singular and welcoming and totally mine.

'So,' said Chloe at length, and Sam and I broke eye contact. 'There was another thing. She was black. Or mixed race.'

'What?' said Sam. 'Really? Was that possible back then?'

'Oh yeah,' said Cerise. 'Black people been here since the Romans. I just read a book on black Tudors.'

'I never knew that history,' said Carmen.

'How exciting,' said Florian.

'Bessie Moor!' said Sam. 'She must have been a moor.'

'They were Arabs, weren't they?' said Florian. 'North African Berbers, and Muslim Europeans?'

'Thea said she was renowned for exotic healing rituals,' I added to the mix.

'She was foreign,' said Sam. 'Had to be.'

'And, oh my God, she bore Black Anne,' I said. 'Who'd be,' I paused thinking about the name. 'Mixed race.'

'And underneath the Blackly Be,' said Chloe, musing it all over. 'It has credibility.'

'Bloody hell – all this time,' I said and shook my head. 'Never occurred. She wasn't called that because of her hair or being burned like the legend decreed . . .'

'I know,' said Cerise. 'It's called whitewashed. There's an artist down here – Elsa something – who's done a whole project on it.'

'Sounds like a new exhibition to me,' said Sam and cupped his chin.

I thought that was a very good idea. Something to start thinking about once we'd got through other things – the formal identification of my grandmother's remains, discussions about burial, and then what to do with Anne Hewghes and Bartholomew Elkes. I had it in my head that they could come here if nobody else wanted them. I knew from previous experience that some churches still wouldn't accept remains of women they thought were witches. I know, right? In this day and age.

'Wow,' said Carmen. 'It's mad. And to think, it all started off here at the museum launch party when they tried to move the Blackly Be. Seems like weeks ago. Thank God all the hauntings and weird stuff have quietened down now. The village feels like it's returning to normal.'

'Oh, it's never been normal,' said Sam and beamed.

'Certainly has been a crazy couple of weeks,' Carmen went on. 'At least all the mysteries have been solved. Though all these years later.' And she leant forwards to Cerise, presumably to start a conversation, but stopped as we all heard the sound of a car pulling into the drive.

I recognised it. 'At least some of them,' I said.

'Oh God,' said Cerise. 'Rosie, it's your mum and dad.'

A wave of recognition went through the rest of those gathered and our guests began to clear up saucers and mugs and say their goodbyes.

Personally, I would have liked them to stay, but everyone knew something big was on its way and they didn't want to be witness to any explosions that might occur, or become collateral damage.

Cerise bent over me and kissed me on the forehead. 'I love you. Call me if you need me. I'll be around tonight.'

Then she hoisted her overnight bag on her back and headed towards her car. I saw her wave and heard her greet 'Mr and Mrs Strange'. Then she got in and reversed out of there speedily.

I felt a quiver of apprehension go through me, aware I was on the cusp of a change and suddenly fearful of what it might mean – a realignment of relationships? A withdrawal of love? An approaching sequence of shame and blame?

But even as those ideas rolled across my conscious mind, I knew they wouldn't come into being. After all, I had lived with these people all my life, well, nearly all my life, and I understood their natures well enough to trust in them implicitly.

And as soon as Mum and Dad stepped out of their Fiat and into the light of that afternoon, I knew nothing would really change.

As the rest of our company scattered to the winds, Sam greeted my parents and guided them over to my, now solitary, spot, which was quite ironic really – the memorial garden. Or maybe it was the perfect place to rake over the past and talk about truth. We would have to see.

'Oh Rosie, darling.' Mum flew at me, as soon as she reached the table, full of bosomy concern. 'What did you get yourself into, you silly thing. Don't change do you?'

Sam excused himself. 'I'll get Bronson to bring out the teas,' he added. 'I'm up in the study if you need me,' he said and pointed up at the eyes of the museum.

Then he scarpered, leaving the three of us alone.

Dad bit his lip and pulled out a chair opposite me. 'Hello love. How are you feeling?'

He had more colour in his face than I'd seen for months. Despite what must have been a very troubling weekend for him, I thought Dad looked well.

'Bit bruised,' I told him truthfully. 'How are you?'

He clasped his hands together. 'Very shaken to hear about what happened to you, my dear. But in other news, we're a bit relieved,' he said. 'In all honesty.'

I wasn't sure which of the many gigantic revelations he was referring to. 'Your mum? Ethel-Rose?'

He nodded and lifted the creases of his slacks to get more comfortable. 'It never goes away, Rosie, the "not-knowing". I never would have wanted it to end this way, but now we can reunite her with Dad.'

I had never heard him refer to Septimus like that before. It was rather affecting and prompted me to say very quickly, 'I'm so sorry about it all.'

Dad reached forward and patted my knee. 'Just glad you're in one piece, love. John sends his best.'

I couldn't imagine my brother organising his thoughts like that, but I knew he loved me and he would care about what happened. Then I suddenly realised he might not actually be my brother at all. Not if the Celeste stuff was true.

'He's going to try and get down to see you next weekend,' Mum was saying. 'He was worried, love. We all were.' Then she blinked violently as a flash of light passed over her face. 'Ooer, what's that?' she said and pointed to the museum. Sam was opening one of the windows in the library/study area. The pane had caught the sunshine. 'Looks like it's winking, don't it Ted?'

I was watching Dad, waiting to see how he reacted, and was amazed to see a slight smile begin to stretch his lips.

I said, 'That's a good sign. From the museum.'

Then Dad and Mum looked worried.

I took a deep breath and thought if I don't do it now I never will, then I beckoned forward the elephant in the memorial garden. 'So, are you going to tell me what happened with Celeste? Back then? Is it true?' I gestured round the table. 'How we – came about?'

Mum sighed though it wasn't a sad sigh, more like an expression of release. Like things that had been pent up and stoppered for years were now able to free up and float out. 'We knew it were coming,' she said, rubbing my hand. 'Soon as we found out Septimus had left you the place. Thought it was just a matter of time, didn't we love?' she swivelled her eyes to Dad and nodded. 'Once you'd started to come back here.'

Ted Strange's voice was calm when he told me, 'Your granddad wanted us to tell you earlier. When you were much younger. Thought you should know. But we weren't ready, were we Mum?' he said batting the exchange back.

'We weren't,' she said and squeezed my fingers tight. 'You'd just settled into Juniors. Thought there'd be time later but it sort of ran out. And it never seemed to matter really, because really, I am your mum and Dad's your dad. We do love you, you know.'

'I know,' I said and patted the hand held by mine. It was very sweaty. Poor Mum. 'But I'd like to know the facts.'

'It's time, I suppose.' Dad cleared his throat. 'Well, it was a dark and stormy night,' he began.

AUTHORIAL NOTE

Anne Hewghes did exist. That we know. She was a real woman who was taken to trial in the Lent Sessions at Chelmsford in 1621. Her crimes? The usual: causing the death of a pied cow and a neighbour through magic, charming two more so they became wasted and consumed, and bewitching the goods and chattels of another. She did not live in Adder's Fork, but in the village of Great Leighs north of Chelmsford in Essex. I relocated her legend, and the boulder with which she is associated, to my fictional village where the Essex Witch Museum resides for obvious reasons. Anne was alleged to have been burned at the stake and her remains buried under the boulder. The records do state that although she was tried, she was also acquitted. Whether the villagers found her guilty anyway and exacted their own form of justice or if her story became conflated with another witch tale, that we do not know.

It is true that, centuries later, Harry Price visited the site to investigate poltergeist phenomena when the boulder was tampered with. This incident made the national newspapers in an article entitled 'The Witch Walks At Scrapfaggot

Green'. However, when I spoke to the manager of The Castle pub, where you can still observe the boulder in the car park, he told me that the stone had been moved many times since, but not with fanfare and without manifest phenomena.

My reference to John Dee is based in fact – his diary states he was approached by men from Essex seeking his assistance to locate treasure. However, Bartholomew Elkes is a creation solely of my overactive imagination.

ACKNOWLEDGEMENTS

First up – massive thanks goes to Sean and Riley. Geniuses in their own right, who are generous enough to give me the time, space and understanding to write these books. They also listen to my rough drafts and moans and pat me on the head when I'm feeling down.

It's a lesser-known trade 'secret' that Jenny Parrott has the ability to stop time and whizz around accomplishing three times as much as any mere mortal. Sage, sensible and sexy, she's a bit like Wonder Woman but without the tiara, though I only see her at work and anything's possible with that one. Thanmai Bui-Van would win a 'Wicked British Bake Off' contest, hands down. Rumours abound that she has a magic cauldron at home. Works her own special spellcraft on the sales side too, for which I am ever grateful. Lovely Margot Weale clones herself and never sleeps. She also has thirty fingers and six hands which enable her to answer emails from twenty authors at the same time. Best publicist ever. Wild, raven-haired Mark is the Einstein of book publishing: inspired buzzy ideas are made real on his watch. Design wizard James Jones comes up with jacket after jacket which never fail to inspire. Paul Nash produces the goods out of thin air and on time and with care and patience. Thanks also to Francine Brody for sweeping out the prose and sprucing the text. Juliet Mabey is an absolute peach, helping me along not only with sound advice AND publishing my books, but also mirrors for straighteners and lippy when necessary. While Novin Doostdar, along with the rest of their Oneworld coven, has donned Halloween garb in the guise of a freaky friar simply to help *Strange Sight* on its way. Seriously – what more can one ask for from one's publishers? Thank you.

I am extremely grateful to Joyce Froome, Steve Simmonds and the whole team at The Museum of Witchcraft and Magic for their unending tolerance of my very niche questions. They are a fantastic team with such vast knowledge who have helped me on several occasions. On this one they were able to point me in the right direction for Rozalie Romanov's spell. Also, Joyce, thank you for my piskie. It worked!

Thanks to Darryl Webber at the *Essex Chronicle* for his extensive knowledge about all things newspapery and Joss Hawthorn for his insight and advice regarding police procedure.

And to David at BlueBookBalloon.com for implanting the idea of Sam with his top off. I think that worked quite well in the end, don't you?

I must also acknowledge Kristen J. Sollee's book *Witches, Sluts, Feminists: Conjuring the Sex Positive*, which my friend, Jo, bought me for my birthday. This most excellent title of course formed the insult hurled at Rosie by the dastardly Araminta de Vere. It is also recommended reading for all fellow witches, sluts and feminists and any readers interested in herstory.

A special shout out goes to Helen Smith for showing me the ropes and being an amazing criminal mentor. He he. Cathi Unsworth, my wyrd fiction sister, has been a great support and shares some of my obsessions, which luckily means we can talk endlessly about the intricacies of crime, feminism and occult history both in private and public. Thank you Cathi. Chris Simmonds must be thanked for his support, as must Ros Green and Jo Nancarrow from the Essex Book Festival with whom it has been both fun and exciting to plot. Thank you also to Suzi Feay, Kelly Buckley, Steve Neale, Ian White, Amy Freeborn (genius photographer and editor of *Phox Pop* magazine), Curly Dan Newman, Daryl and Jules Easlea, Fiona Cummins and all the Leigh Luminaries. Thank you to Martyn Hockless on Facebook who came up with the name 'Terry'.

I must also express my gratitude to Simon Fowler, my friend and very talented photographer, who stumbled across the legend of Anne Hewghes when he was photographing The Castle pub in Great Leighs. Simon texted me that day and said I had to get over there and see 'this witch stone' for myself. I did and thus a novel was born. Thanks Simon for starting it all.

Other notable mentions have to be Sadie Hasler, Rachel Lichtenstein, Colette Bailey, Steph Stevenson, Heidi Wigmore, Jo Farrugia, the Easleas, Mark Lancaster and other friends who have supported me throughout my endeavours with transport, handouts, jumping in at the last minute to do

Q and As, their own individual brand of cheer and lashings of white wine. Sometimes too much. Steph Roche and Kate Bradley get their own private mention because they have always pushed me on when netted by self-doubt. And they're amazing. My friend Elsa James must be acknowledged for sharing with me her research for her project on Black Essex. Do check it out.

My mum and dad want everyone to know that they aren't anything like Ted and Maureen Strange. My dad does sometimes park on 'double yellas' but that's where the comparison ends. Thanks to both of them for being them and to Pauline and Ernie for being their lovely selves too.

Thanks also to the rowdies at the TEAC, my gorgeous sister Josie and talented bro' Rich. I am lucky to be part of a large and colourful family that gets bigger by the day and who are joyous and thoughtful in equal measure. Joanne, Lee, Ronnie, Harry, Matty, John, Jess, Isla, Rye, Anais, Effie, Kit, Obie, Samuel, Arron, Arthur, William, Tegun – I'm proud of all of you.